T0244146

THE
KING
of
ITALY

Other Books by Kent Heckenlively

Non-Fiction

Plague - Coauthored with Dr. Judy Mikovits

Inoculated

Plague of Corruption - Coauthored with Dr. Judy Mikovits

The Case Against Masks - Coauthored with Dr. Judy Mikovits

The Case Against Vaccine Mandates

Google Leaks - Coauthored with Zach Vorhies

Behind the Mask of Facebook - Coauthored with Ryan Hartwig

The Case for Interferon - Coauthored with Dr. Joseph Cummins

Ending Plague - Coauthored with Dr. Judy Mikovits and Dr. Francis Ruscetti

This Was CNN - Coauthored with Cary Poarch

Presidential Takedown - Coauthored with Dr. Paul Alexander

The Diversity Con - Coauthored with David Johnson

The Great Awakening - Coauthored with Alex Jones

Fiction

A Good Italian Daughter

KENT HECKENLIVELY

THE KING of ITALY

A NOVEL

ARCADE PUBLISHING • New York

All rights reserved. No part of this book may be reproduced in any manner without the express written consent of the publisher, except in the case of brief excerpts in critical reviews or articles. All inquiries should be addressed to Arcade Publishing, 307 West 36th Street, 11th Floor, New York, NY 10018.

Arcade Publishing books may be purchased in bulk at special discounts for sales promotion, corporate gifts, fund-raising, or educational purposes. Special editions can also be created to specifications. For details, contact the Special Sales Department, Arcade Publishing, 307 West 36th Street, 11th Floor, New York, NY 10018 or arcade@skyhorsepublishing.com.

Arcade Publishing® is a registered trademark of Skyhorse Publishing, Inc.®, a Delaware corporation.

Visit our website at www.arcadepub.com
Please follow our publisher Tony Lyons on Instagram @tonylyonsisuncertain

10 9 8 7 6 5 4 3 2 1

Library of Congress Cataloging-in-Publication Data is available on file.

Cover design by Erin Seaward-Hiatt
Cover image from Getty Images

Print ISBN: 978-1-956763-95-9
Ebook ISBN: 978-1-956763-96-6

Printed in the United States of America

For Julian, who always loved this story.

"In our sleep, pain which cannot forget falls drop by drop upon the heart, until in our despair, comes wisdom through the awful grace of God."

— *Aeschylus*

BOOK I

VINCENZO'S STORY

Chapter One

IN THE FALL OF 1907, A boy of six accompanied his mother to the court in Taormina on the eastern coast of Sicily. The courthouse was a gray and forbidding building of stone and Roman columns. Yes, the Romans had left their mark, just like the Phoenicians, Carthaginians, Greeks, Vikings, Vandals, Normans, and even the Muslim invaders from North Africa who had once claimed Sicily as part of their caliphate. As the largest island in the Mediterranean, Sicily was like a ravaged woman, fought over for centuries by east and west, north and south, by those who wanted to stay, and yet never did.

Sicily was officially part of Italy. It had been since 1860 and the arrival of Garibaldi's Thousand, an expeditionary force of Italian "patriots," and his agreement with King Victor Emmanuel II, in what became known as the Italian *Risorgimento*, or "reorganization." Italy was now a unified country, not just a patchwork of tiny kingdoms as it had been ever since the fall of the Holy Roman Empire. After just a few years, the Sicilians had revolted, their cities bombed by the Italian navy, the island placed under martial law for several years, and thousands of people executed. The Italians were no better than any of the other occupiers who had come to this dry, mostly arid land in the middle of the peaceful Mediterranean Sea over the past several thousand years.

As his mother walked through the marble hallways clutching his hand, the boy looked at the men who moved quickly past him, severe in their black robes and sober uniforms. Much of it was confusing to young Vincenzo Nicosia. He knew only that his father had been taken by the police and was in grave danger.

Vincenzo and his mother were dismissively waved to a seat, treated with the disregard shown to all country people. Gloomy furniture and stark walls rose on all sides. Clerks moved about with an air of superiority.

His mother stared at the empty judge's bench and twisted her rosary beads over her pregnant belly as she recited silent prayers. She was only twenty-four, but the arrest of her husband a month earlier had greatly disturbed her, and she appeared much older. Her normally round face, soft and olive-colored, had become sharp, angular, and pale. Every day since his arrest, she'd trudged down to the village church at first light and spent hours kneeling before the statue of the Virgin Mary, as well as a statue of Santa Lucia, a Sicilian saint, and prayed for a miracle to free her husband.

Like most Sicilians, Vincenzo was well-acquainted with the story of Santa Lucia. Lucia was a young Sicilian woman of the fourth century who consecrated her virginity to God and intended to distribute the generous dowry that would have gone to her husband to the poor. At the time, Christianity was a forbidden religion, and the Romans regularly persecuted members of the faith. When it was discovered she was a Christian and refused to marry, soldiers came to take her away and put her in a brothel. Lucia became so filled with the Holy Spirit that the soldiers could not move her. The soldiers tried to burn her, but the fire would not start. She was tortured and her eyes gouged out, but God restored her vision the next day.

"Do you know why God gave Lucia back her eyes?" his mother asked him one morning while they were praying for his father.

"Because of her strong faith?"

His mother shook her head. "No, Vincenzo. It was a sign from God. So people know that God sees all things. Even those attempted to be hidden from Him."

Eventually, the soldiers tortured Lucia to death, and as his mother told him, she was welcomed into heaven by a host of heavenly angels and Jesus Himself, who must have wept at her devotion to Him.

For the sentencing, Vincenzo's mother wore a brown dress of coarse wool, washed the night before with water from the town well. Vincenzo thought she smelled clean and fresh. He was dressed in his best Sunday clothes; gray trousers, a white shirt, thin black tie, gray coat, and a cap that he removed when they entered the courtroom. In all things he looked not like a child, but a small, serious man.

"Are they going to let papa go?" Vincenzo asked.

"Hush now *cara*." She touched his hand. "We want them to think well of us. Let them see papa has good people waiting at home for him. He did a bad thing, but there must be mercy. Perhaps papa will just be away for a few months."

Vincenzo's mother returned to twisting her rosary beads and murmuring quiet prayers. He looked at the large, imposing judge's chair. It was made of dark wood with a high back and appeared to be the type of throne God might decide to seat Himself upon if He came to Earth.

"Silence!" the bailiff called out from the front of the room. He announced the entrance of the judge, who quickly appeared in his long black robe. Trailing behind him was a guard escorting Vincenzo's father in chains.

"Papa!" Vincenzo shouted. He was thinner than two months ago and hung his head in shame. His father did not look up.

The judge took his seat on the bench. Sternly he peered through thick glasses at a slip of paper in front of him. Vincenzo's father was led forward. "Guiseppe Nicosia," the judge began, "the facts in this case are clear. On September 28 you entered the jewelry store of the victim, Fabrizio Bufalino, and asked to buy a small woman's ring, which you would pay for with your labor. Signor Bufalino did not agree. On that same night you broke into his store and stole the ring. Not content with mere thievery, you entered Signor

Bufalino's room located above the store and beat him severely. Do you have anything to say for yourself? Do you have anything to say before I pronounce sentence?"

Vincenzo's father raised his head and narrowed his eyes at the judge. "Bufalino treated me with disrespect."

"That may very well be," replied the judge, "but it's no excuse for the injuries you caused. If you had stolen to feed a starving family, this court would look with sympathy upon you. Or if you'd merely taken something by stealth, I would be inclined to be lenient for the sake of your family, represented here today. But as the esteemed Alessandro de Leone, Duke du Taormina, uncle to our dear King, is so fond of saying, we cannot allow this type of lawlessness to go unpunished." The judge motioned to a well-dressed man sitting in the front row. Next to him sat a less impressive man, thin and pasty faced.

Vincenzo had seen "the Lion of Sicily" enter the courtroom. Alessandro de Leone stood over six feet tall, had a long mane of black hair streaked with grey, and was in his mid-fifties. In effect the governor of this province of Sicily, the Duke had great influence. He nodded at the judge.

"Because of these circumstances," the judge announced, "I'm afraid I can't show you any leniency. I sentence you to the maximum term of twenty years." He brought his gavel down with a noise like a shot.

Vincenzo's father glared defiantly at the judge, raised his shackled hands, and said, "You don't sentence me because of what I did. You sentence me because of who I did it to!" He pointed an accusing finger at the pasty-faced man next to the Duke. "If he'd been a nobody like me, you wouldn't have cared. The mistake I made was to rob the Duke's relative and teach him a lesson!" Vincenzo's father moved his gaze to the Duke, who moved uncomfortably in his chair. "That is why you come down so hard on me. I warn you, someday I will have justice!"

The guards grabbed Vincenzo's father and hustled him away. The judge stood and walked to his chambers as the gallery began to empty. Vincenzo heard a sound like pebbles bouncing on the marble floor. He was startled and looked at his mother. She'd twisted her rosary beads so hard the string had broken. The individual beads were cascading on the floor. Vincenzo dropped to his knees to gather them.

He crawled under the bench to get them all, and then held up the beads to his mother. "It can be fixed, Mama."

She stared vacantly at the empty judge's chair. "No, it can't. It can never be fixed."

"I can do it, Mama," he vowed. "I'll make it the way it used to be." Vincenzo hated the Duke for making his mother break her rosary beads.

One day, Vincenzo would hate the Duke for so much more.

* * *

"Is something wrong, Mama?" Vincenzo asked.

She wavered at the threshold of their mud and stone house. Moonlight silhouetted her slim, still-pretty figure. Vincenzo knew it must be two or three in the morning.

He was eight now, and his father had been in prison for two years. For the first few months they'd survived on the charity of friends and relatives, but among poor people that did not last. His mother tried to work as a washer-woman, but it wasn't enough to feed her two children, especially little Angelina who was always sick and needing medicines. The only job certain to pay the money to keep both children fed was the one good people didn't talk about. His mother was gone most nights. Often she took to her bed for several days after she'd taken a medicine to expel the life so casually deposited in her body by a customer.

"I'm fine," she replied, holding onto the doorknob. She took a small step and staggered.

Vincenzo rushed to her side, slipping an arm around her waist. She winced as if she'd been kicked in the ribs. The right side of her face was bruised. "Just get me to a chair," she told him.

Together they walked across the dirt floor to a rickety wooden chair at the kitchen table. She took a breath after sitting down, then smiled at him and ran a hand down his cheek. "You're a good boy, Vincenzo."

"Did somebody hurt you, Mama?"

She shook her head. "Nobody can hurt me as long as I know my children are all right."

"A man hit you, didn't he?"

His mother smoothed back Vincenzo's hair and nodded. "They usually pay a little more if they rough you up. But it's all right. I can do nicer things for you and your sister."

"That's not right, Mama. Nobody should hurt you. I'm going to find him and pay him back. I'll sneak up behind him with a knife and cut his throat." Vincenzo drew a finger across his neck and made a cutting sound.

His mother shook her head. "No, Vincenzo. It's against God to do cruel things. Even if they are done to you. He sees all things and punishes those who do evil."

Vincenzo had seen enough in his short life to know bad people normally escaped the consequences of their actions. He doubted God would ever punish the nameless man who beat his mother. All of this happened because of the Duke. Vincenzo was older now and understood more. He understood there were those who had power over him, like the judge and the Duke, and that above them were the King and finally God. But his mother didn't have his feelings of anger toward these people. She even occasionally complimented the Duke for his efforts to break the intimidation of the mafia, and the efforts he made to get Rome to pay more attention to Sicily. But Vincenzo couldn't find such forgiveness in his heart.

* * *

TWELVE MORE YEARS dragged by, marked only by a daily struggle for food. Europe was convulsed by four years of war, ending only when the United States entered the conflict, routing the Kaiser from Germany, and the Czar was killed by the communists in Russia, but little changed in Sicily. At the age of fourteen, Vincenzo stopped going to school and alternately found work as a fisherman and a farmhand during harvest. In the springtime, he slaughtered the young lambs and dressed them for market.

By the time he was twenty, he'd been the sole supporter of his family for the past five years and had started to gain a reputation as a capable carpenter. It was his job, but more than that it had started to become a passion. He loved the planning necessary to build, the sweat and labor of creation, and the pride in seeing what had once been simply drawings on a piece of paper exist in the real world.

For a carpenter he had a slight build, but his slender physique concealed an almost catlike dexterity and strength. And yet there was always something fragile about him. His face was long and narrow, and when he was pleased or angry a distinct v shape appeared on his forehead, advancing almost like a set of horns into his curly, black hair. His eyes were large and liquid, almost angelic, and they often seemed to be at war with the more severe features of his face.

On this day, Vincenzo was building a smokehouse for a wealthy client, Signor Claudius Pellegrino, a portly man who gave generously to the church. It was whispered among his workers that his hunger for Jesus was surpassed only by his hunger for food. Pellegrino was known to eat an entire leg of lamb and three chickens at a sitting. But Signor Pellegrino had been good to Vincenzo. If pleased with the smokehouse, he promised to recommend

Vincenzo to several other wealthy men. Vincenzo knew such a patron could be the difference between the meager existence he'd been able to provide for his mother and sister and the better life of which he dreamed.

The smokehouse stood near a vineyard and a grove of olive trees. Vincenzo was attaching the shingles on the roof and did not hear the approach of footsteps.

"You're a fine builder," Marcello Lupo called up to him, "but when will you learn that it's often necessary to destroy before you can create?"

Vincenzo stopped his work and gazed down from the roof of the smokehouse. They'd known each other as children, but Vincenzo had never trusted him. Marcello's father was supposedly a soldier for a mafia don and renowned for his brutality. It was said that Marcello's father had killed a man and put his heart in a clay jar. As a boy, Marcello had pointed the jar out to Vincenzo and dared him to open it. Vincenzo never had.

But Marcello had bigger ambitions than working for a local don. For the past few months he'd been crisscrossing the country-side trying to win converts to Mussolini's fascist party.

"And what exactly do you wish me to destroy, Marcello?"

"Everything," he replied. "The whole government. Can't you see how corrupt it is? Good people are reduced to poverty, and the bandit landowners get everything. We're no more than their playthings, to do with as they want. If it pleases them to imprison your father, they'll do it. If they want to shame your mother. . ." Marcello's voice quickly trailed off, as if he knew he'd stepped over a certain line.

Vincenzo gripped his hammer with anger. He'd always had a fierce pride in his family. Many times he'd started fistfights when another boy spoke about his mother's work, but to Vincenzo those days seemed like another life. It'd been several years since she'd had to sully her honor with those types of men.

He started hammering again at the shingles, and the repeated motion lessened his anger. Vincenzo even felt momentarily amused by Marcello's shameless politicking. "You sound like a communist," Vincenzo teased. "Perhaps you should join comrade Lenin in Russia."

Marcello's face reddened, and he spat into the dry dust. "You know I'm no communist. I follow Mussolini. He's the one to lead us back to glory. He is our new Caesar! A man for all Italians, even Sicilians. I even spoke with him recently. He's a great man. The kind who can bend history to his will. You should join us. I know you have some scores to settle. Some legitimate ones."

"I have no vendettas to settle."

Marcello wagged a finger at Vincenzo. "You think I don't know you. We joined the gangs when we were nine. Two years later you stabbed Lorenzo Debruzzi in the gut because he insulted your mother. Your eyes were cold, like death. You have a devil's heart, Vincenzo. A devil that will not be ruled by anyone. I thought you would've settled things with the Duke a long time ago. What happened to you, Vincenzo? You're not a free man. You're a slave. But once you were a warrior. I saw it in your eyes when you stabbed Debruzzi. You would not bow down before any man."

"I'm a builder." Vincenzo was proud of the work he'd put into the smokehouse. It was his design; he'd hired additional workmen to haul the stones and done the mortar work himself. Even though it was a small project, he took pride in it, knowing that if he did a good job, it might stand for fifty or a hundred years.

"I'm surprised at how little you're happy with," Marcello sneered. "The Jews think pigs are unclean animals. Are you satisfied building an unclean house?"

"I'm happy to keep my family fed," said Vincenzo. "I do honest work for an honest day's pay. Why don't you get Zappatini to follow you? The village fool will follow you anywhere."

Marcello pointed a finger at Vincenzo in anger. "You're not the son of Guiseppe Nicosia! Your father took what he wanted and did not let himself be disrespected. You reach for nothing but the scraps from a rich man's table and thank him like a beggar!"

"My father's still in jail, useless to everyone." Vincenzo thought of all the nights his mother had been gone, the loathing she'd had for her work in the dark streets, and how he'd rescued his family from all that.

"An unfortunate event, but one I could reverse," Marcello hinted slyly.

"Do you think I believe you? Since we were children you've never been honest. You always had some scheme. I don't know what it is this time, but I'm not playing along."

Marcello pounded a fist into his hand. "I offer you a plan! You think you've escaped so many things, but you haven't. You don't know how fragile your life is. The rich men promise you enough to eat for two weeks, and you consider yourself blessed. But what if they tire of you? We're going to change all that. A man will be able to live with dignity under Mussolini. Join with us!"

Vincenzo turned away, thinking Marcello looked anything other than a friend. "I don't need stupid talk about Mussolini. They're all a bunch of bastards. I just stay away from all of them."

* * *

A DAY LATER the smokehouse was nearing completion. Signor Pellegrino approached and asked, "Vincenzo, may I speak with you?"

Vincenzo was on the roof, hammering a white, wooden cross above the door. Every room of Signor Pellegrino's villa had a portrait or statue of the Madonna with child, a crucifix on the wall, and a rosary close at hand in case he was suddenly gripped by the need to say a prayer.

The day was sweltering, and Vincenzo was covered with perspiration, but the work gave him a satisfaction that could withstand any heat. He pulled a small rag from his back pocket and wiped his brow. He smiled at Signor Pelligrino. "I'm just about finished. I figure only a couple more days and you'll be able to start dry- ing some—"

"I don't know if you're going to be here a couple more days," said Signor Pellegrino in a curt voice.

"Why?" Vincenzo asked, confused. Signor Pellegrino couldn't be firing him. He'd been very pleased with the work, and had already given Vincenzo's name to several other wealthy men in the area who wanted additions to their villa.

"You know I'm a religious man, don't you, Vincenzo?"

"Yes, everybody does. But what does that have to do with me?" he asked, coming down from the roof and standing before Signor Pellegrino.

Pellegrino looked Vincenzo squarely in the eye. "You know I believe in judging each man according to his character, not where, or who, he comes from, right?"

Vincenzo nodded.

"I knew your father was a thief when I hired you, but I didn't let that prevent me from judging you on your own merits. In fact, I've given you free reign on all my property to demonstrate my good faith. However, one of my wife's rings is missing. You're the only workman who is allowed into my house. My servants have been with me for years, and I trust every one of them."

"It wasn't me," said Vincenzo, but even as he did he felt a sink- ing feeling. His cheeks burned with the shame of his father's guilt, and he knew he wasn't putting on a very good display of his inno- cence.

"Tell me, Vincenzo," Signor Pellegrino said softly. "Do you have some pretty girl in town to whom you wish to give the ring? I'm not a hard man. If you admit it now, things will go much better. All I ask is that you give it back to my wife. Her father gave her the ring when she was very young. It has great sentimental value."

"I didn't take it," Vincenzo replied in a firmer tone.

Signor Pellegrino's face became red. "I'm trying to make this easy on you. I didn't listen to others when they said I shouldn't hire a man who has stealing in his blood. I'm sorry, Vincenzo, but I have no other choice. I'm letting you go. And I'm telling my friends who I recommended you to that I take back the recommendation."

"Signor Pellegrino, please listen—"

"Enough!" shouted Signor Pellegrino, raising his hand. "I'll not listen to lies. Leave right now, or I'll press charges. My patience has been sorely tested by this. I'll not stand for a thief in my employ, but I won't send a man to the hell of our prisons. Think well of me for giving you this one chance to turn your life around, Vincenzo, but don't ever let me see your face again."

Pellegrino stalked away, and Vincenzo watched him disappear down the path to his villa.

* * *

FOR OVER AN hour Vincenzo walked through the steep fields at the edge of town, kicking rocks to vent his fury. Finally, he went home. The moment his mother saw him, her expression became stiff and frightened. "What's wrong?" she asked.

"I lost my job. I think it'll be a long time until I work again."

Vincenzo sat at the meal table, and she brought him a cup of water. He told her the story. When he finished, he looked at her for a moment and then took a deep drink. The water was so bitter he was tempted to spit it out. Instead, he made a face and swallowed the brackish fluid. Usually he avoided water from the town well, normally having enough money to purchase wine or fresh milk, but he'd been at the end of his funds, expecting to be paid by Pellegrino in a few days. Now, he knew he would get no more money from Pellegrino.

"I can work again, Vincenzo." She sat next to him. "We won't starve."

Sorrowfully he studied her face. The years as a prostitute had aged her greatly. After Vincenzo went to work she'd steadily regained some of her beauty. She was still older, though, with gray hair, and her figure had become plump. Men would not pay to spend time with her, or at least, they would not pay much. Vincenzo couldn't bear the thought. He recalled one day a few months after his father had been taken away to prison. The charity of friends and relatives had begun to wear thin, and there was no food in the house. His mother's stomach had rumbled all night.

Vincenzo snuck out of the house early in the morning. At the market he was able to pass almost unnoticed through the fruit and bread stands. By the time he'd left, he had a full breakfast for him and his mother. When he arrived home, she was still sleeping. Vincenzo put the food on the table and then roused her.

"Where did you get this?" she asked him.

"I took it from the market," he answered proudly.

For the first and only time in his life, Vincenzo's mother slapped him. "I never want you to steal again! Do you understand?" She shook a finger at him.

"But you were hungry," Vincenzo protested, holding his stinging cheek.

That night his mother first took to the darkened streets to begin her life of shame.

Angelina came in from the room she shared with her mother. At thirteen Angelina was a woman in every way. Her round, olive-skinned face had a shy, but ready smile. Vincenzo was aware of the interest her full figure stirred in men. She was about the same age that Santa Lucia had been when the soldiers had tried to take her to a brothel.

"I'll go fetch some water from the well," Angelina said, smiling at the two of them sitting at the table and then going out the door.

"If I can't find a job, she'll have to join you, won't she?" Vincenzo asked.

"How can you say that? Do you think I'd let my children suffer like—"

"Like you have?" Vincenzo cut in. "I know you've suffered, mama. You kept us alive, though. But if nothing comes up for me, Angelina will be our only hope."

Vincenzo hated the calculating part of his mind that could conceive of his sister doing such things. But if he couldn't find a job, they would need to survive, and only a few would pay to be with his mother.

That would mean starvation, and Vincenzo saw little holiness in an intact virtue and a still heart.

"I can't have Angelina doing that." She stood from the table. "I already sold my soul. I don't want my children to do the same." Her eyes were filling with tears.

"Then I'm going to have to find another job, and quickly."

A knock sounded on the door. His mother looked quizzically at him. "Maybe it's Signor Pellegrino, come to give you back your job."

She went to the door and opened it. Her face seemed to fall when she saw it was only Marcello Lupo. He bowed his head to her. Vincenzo could see his mother's mind was immediately on other things. "Vincenzo, I'm going to go to the church and pray. Things will turn around for you."

She quickly gathered her things and left, saying good-bye to Marcello.

"I heard you are no longer working for Signor Pellegrino. Could it be because of this?" Marcello held up a woman's ring with a small diamond.

Vincenzo snatched the ring from him. "How did you get this?"

Marcello shrugged. "It was simple. One of the servants is a fascist supporter. I had him take it. The rich always think their servants love them," he said with a laugh.

"Damn you!" Vincenzo snarled, grabbing Marcello by the lapel. "I got fired because this was missing, my reputation ruined. We're going to Signor Pellegrino to straighten this out!"

Marcello grinned and rested his hands on Vincenzo's arms. "I've done you a favor. What else could you expect from Pellegrino except a temporary reprieve from suffering? What could you have done with that money?" Marcello arched his eyebrows with self-assurance. "Live for another two or three weeks, then what? I come to offer you something to solve all your troubles, so you don't have to work until your back breaks, and everybody thinks they should just slit your throat like an old burro."

"I don't need any favors," Vincenzo replied, releasing Marcello. "I need you to straighten this out with Signor Pellegrino."

"You're the one with the ring in your hand," said Marcello. "You straighten it out."

"Damn you to hell, Marcello."

"We're already there, my friend. I'm just trying to get us out."

"Who are you talking to?" Angelina asked, walking back through the door with a pail of water. Her eyes lit on Marcello, and she smiled shyly. She knew men were starting to look at her, and Vincenzo realized she was starting to look back.

Marcello gave her a thin smile, revealing sharp, wolf-like incisors. "A friend of your brother's and a friend of all," he said, giving a slight bow of his head.

Angelina blushed.

"Go visit Mama," Vincenzo told her. "She's at the church."

Angelina gave him a look of protest, but he responded with a withering expression. She nodded, put down the water, gave a side-glance toward Marcello, and with the slightest hint of a smile, walked out.

"You stay away from my sister," Vincenzo warned after she left.

"She'll be ready to marry soon. Maybe we'll be in-laws," Marcello joked, then his expression became serious. "A girl so lovely must be careful. It would be so sad to think of anything happening to her. But so many are driven to unfortunate ends by the need to keep body and soul together. You would do well to hear what I have to say."

"What do you have to offer? It had better be good."

Marcello went over to the door and motioned to somebody down the street. Vincenzo caught a glimpse of a man in a coat, with his hat pulled down low. The man stood about five-foot-six and wore a black shirt, morning coat, black trousers, and a bowler hat. He was muscular and moved with a predator's grace. As he came close and removed his hat, it was the man's eyes, large, dark, and piercing, which seemed to grab Vincenzo by the heart.

"Il Duce," Marcello said, "Benito Mussolini, the writer, the patriot, the savior of Italy."

Mussolini's work as a journalist and political activist was well-known to Vincenzo, as well as his opposition to much of what had taken place in Italy. Mussolini had opposed the Italian war in Libya in 1911 and earned a five-month jail sentence, but had supported Italy's intervention in the Great War, earning the scorn of his fellow socialists. He'd written a popular, bitterly anti-clerical novel and a biography of a Czech political reformer, and had been editor of a socialist newspaper, increasing its readership from twenty thousand to well over a hundred thousand. In recent years, Mussolini had moved away from socialism, advocating an Italy free of class distinctions, hoping to raise his country to the levels of its great Roman past.

Mussolini had also been a school teacher, and some of his followers referred to him as "the professor." He'd written an account of his service in the Great War, where he'd been promoted to colonel because of his mental calmness, his lack of concern for his own safety, and his aggressive fighting quality. During his military service, he'd contracted paratyphoid fever and been injured by the explosion of a mortar bomb in his trench, leaving him with at least forty pieces of shrapnel in his body. As the war drew to a close, Mussolini was most well-known for his statement that the country needed a man "ruthless and energetic enough to make a clean sweep."

Vincenzo noticed that Mussolini's stocky, bulldog face gave way to a high forehead. As Mussolini extended a hand to Vincenzo, a smile spread across his face, and Vincenzo couldn't help but feel that destiny had just put its hand on him. "I enjoy meeting men of steel," Mussolini said calmly. "Those who will help us build a new Italy, a new Roman empire. An empire in which all the citizens will share in its benefits."

"C-come in," Vincenzo stammered, deeply impressed that someone so well-known would come to see him.

Mussolini nodded, walked in, and took a seat at the meal table. He gestured for Vincenzo to sit down. Mussolini sat erect in his chair, like the ruler of a great and powerful kingdom. Vincenzo suddenly felt the house no longer belonged to his family. It was somehow now the property of this man, Mussolini, whose name was becoming known throughout Italy, even in the smallest villages.

"It was his personal request to see you," Marcello whispered to Vincenzo.

Vincenzo sat down. He hadn't been in the presence of someone so well-known since his father's trial. Mussolini's magnetism was undeniable. It was partly the fine clothes, the way he sat so rigid and proud, but most of all the way his eyes locked onto you, as if there was nobody more important in the entire country.

"I need something very important from you," said Mussolini.

Vincenzo's mind raced, unable to imagine what this powerful man could want from him.

"I have a stone in my path," Mussolini began. "I want you to remove it. I think you'll be happy to accept this task."

"What is it?" Vincenzo asked.

"Alessandro de Leone, the Duke du Taormina. I think you remember him." Mussolini waited, and the faint hint of a smile flickered at the corner of his lips.

Vincenzo tried to remain impassive, but knew the mention of the Duke's name had made his expression turn hard.

Mussolini continued, "He's the one who made certain your father was sent to jail where he languishes still. I hear his health is poor."

"I remember," Vincenzo replied. "But why do you bother with him?"

"Although illegitimate, the Duke was the favored son of our great King Victor Emmanuel II." Vincenzo remembered his mother's stories about King Victor Emmanuel II; how Italy fell from the greatness of the Holy Roman Empire into quarreling little kingdoms, only to be reunited by the joint efforts of the revolutionary, Giuseppe Garibaldi, and the king. Victor Emmanuel II had been a warrior; a sovereign who slept on the same hard ground as his troops during the wars of Italian unification. He'd been awarded the Order of the Garter by Queen Victoria in 1855, a distinction that used the image of St. George slaying a dragon on its badge. After meeting him, the Duchess of Sutherland had quipped that he was the only knight of the Garter she'd ever met who "looked as if he actually would have had the best of the dragon."

But the king's royal lineage had been less distinguished. His son, Umberto I, had taken Italy into ruinous wars, only to be assassinated by an anarchist in 1900. Italy was now ruled by King Victor Emmanuel III, a diminutive and timid man so small in stature that he was often referred to as "the dwarf king."

Mussolini continued, "There was much talk that the Duke should have been made king when his father died, rather than Umberto." Vincenzo knew the stories. King Victor Emmanuel II had so many bastard children that it was often said he truly was "the father of the fatherland" as it read on his tomb at the Pantheon in Rome. The Italians were a lusty people, and many thought it odd that Catholicism had taken root so deeply in the country, as there was an almost schizophrenic divide in them between the earthly pleasures of the flesh and the philosophical asceticism of the divine. The Italians forgave the king his many mistresses and bastard children, and even took some measure of pride that he was a man who took whatever pleased him. And yet at the same time they demanded that only his legitimate progeny sit on the throne. "That was why they sent the Duke to Sicily, but Umberto had no reason to worry. The Duke never aspired to the throne. In many ways he is a patriot, but a misguided one."

"And why does this patriot bother you?" Vincenzo asked.

"He's cultivated a terrible dislike of my party," Mussolini replied. "King Victor Emmanuel III has already met with my emissaries. He's agreed to stay neutral when my people march on Rome and demand that I be made Prime Minister. The army can't be sent into battle without the approval of both the Prime Minister and the King. The Duke means to stop that ascension, possibly even resurrecting his claim to the throne. He means to send the army after me, and I know we would not survive an all-out assault."

Vincenzo thought about Mussolini's words. The country was ripe for revolution. The dwarf king, the Lion of Sicily, and Mussolini: it was simple to figure out who would come out on top in that struggle.

Mussolini smiled. "I see you understand my dilemma."

"Why me? You have a lot of followers who'd be willing to do this."

"I believe in giving the important jobs to a man who is well-motivated. One who is not likely to fail."

"And with no ties to your party," Vincenzo shot back. "If I fail and am captured I'll just be an angry young man avenging an injury suffered long ago. Maybe they'll even think it was mafia. You muddy the waters well by using me."

"Confusion serves my purposes. I will not deny it." Mussolini smiled, a hint of slyness playing at the corners of his mouth, as if he was a merchant about to make a large sale. "I'm certain your blood burns when you think of Alessandro de Leone, the Lion of Sicily, and how your family was caught in his jaws. Your father imprisoned and your mother's honor shamed. I know you've never killed a man, but I also know you wouldn't turn away from protecting your family. This is something good for you and good for me. Why can't you accept that?"

"I can't be your only hope of stopping the Duke," Vincenzo protested.

"No, but it is to you I give the first chance," Mussolini admitted. "I know this would be personal to you and you would not fail me. I'd rather stop him before he ever leaves Sicily than deal with him on the mainland. He has significant support among the generals of the army. It will spare much bloodshed to have him out of the way."

Vincenzo laughed. "I think I understand. The journey is smoother if nobody even knows there was this obstacle in the road."

"Your journey will also be smoother," Mussolini replied. "I'll have your father waiting here for you when you return. I also promise you that when the Duke is dead and I've been made Prime Minister, you will have all the Duke's property. You'll be the richest man in Sicily and your family will never again know deprivation."

* * *

AFTER THE VISITORS left, Vincenzo's mother came back. "I prayed, Vincenzo. I got such a good feeling. That your father and I were to be reunited and we'd be so happy. Like we were in the old days. And we would be free from worry."

"Marcello has a job for me."

Her expression grew dark and crow's feet formed at the corners of her eyes. "I do not like him. He comes from a bad family. I was so happy when you stopped spending time with him and started working."

Vincenzo reached out his hands, and she took them. "Mama, do you remember when I was in the gangs?"

She nodded solemnly. "Yes, Vincenzo. I was very worried. I thought you were going to end up a *ruffiano*."

"The day I decided to get out, I was fourteen years old. We'd just stolen some fruit from the markets and were eating it in an alleyway. Zappatini wandered in looking for stale food in the garbage. He saw me with my stolen food and said, 'A Nicosia. He's just like his father. This one's going to jail, he is.' That scared me so much. A beggar and he strikes fear into my heart, like it was the voice of God speaking to me. I decided I'd rather be powerless and starving, than end up like Papa and make you unhappy."

She smoothed the back of his hair. "You could never make me unhappy, Vincenzo." She smelled clean and fresh again. During the years she'd been working, there was a different smell to her. It was a musky odor of male perspiration, seediness, and fear. In the times she'd taken to her bed after an abortion, there'd been a sickly sweet smell of death.

"But now I don't know what to do," he confessed. "It'll probably be a long time until I work again, and even then I'll still be at the mercy of people like Signor Pellegrino. Marcello and . . ." He paused. "His friend has asked me to do something that will change all that."

His mother moved away from him. "They've asked you to do something criminal, haven't they?"

"Yes, Mama."

"Don't do it, Vincenzo," she warned with a wrathful look. "You were right to worry about ending up like Papa. He's a good man, but he made foolish choices. When he saw how I looked at that ring in the jeweler's window, he decided he had to get it for me. He'd been too poor to give me a nice wedding ring when we were married." Vincenzo had heard the story several times, but she still repeated it whenever they talked about his father. "He thought he could work for the man, but when he treated your papa so badly, he'd just had enough." She looked away and her eyes began to tear up. "He wanted to give it to me for Angelina's birth. But his temper, his terrible temper—"

"They'll let Papa go if I do this," said Vincenzo.

His mother's gaze snapped back at him. "They'll let him go?" she asked in a soft voice.

Vincenzo nodded. "And they'll bring him back here after I do this thing."

"They must be powerful people."

"They are."

"Tell me this, Vincenzo," she said, putting her hand to his cheek. "Is this a good thing? I mean, after it's done, will you be able to face yourself?"

Vincenzo searched his thoughts for any guilt that might attach to this potential action, but nothing came. He had no conscience when it came to his family's welfare and safety. Marcello was right: when he'd stabbed Lorenzo Debruzzi, his eyes had been cold. His family had been wronged and that was the only conscience necessary. He'd been powerless too long.

"I can face myself," said Vincenzo. "If I do nothing, it all gets worse. If I do something bad, then good things will happen. It's the same thing you did, and now we are alive instead of being dead."

His mother kept looking at him, but he could see the shift in her feelings. She would not try to stop him. She was reluctantly reconciled to whatever he had to do.

"I want you to promise me something, Mama."

"What?"

"When I go to do this thing, you'll leave. Visit our cousins in Caltigirone. But tell nobody where you are going. Wait until I send for you."

"But your father," she protested. "He'll come home to an empty house. I want to have a hot meal waiting for him."

"Promise me, Mama."

She nodded. "All right, Vincenzo. I'll go and take Angelina with me."

Vincenzo pulled his mother close and kissed her on the cheek. "Thank you, Mama. I'm going to see Papa now. We need to talk."

* * *

VINCENZO LOOKED THROUGH the iron bars at his father sleeping curled on the narrow wooden bed provided by the prison. His thin blanket was riddled with holes like an old fishing net. The cell stank of urine because the guards wouldn't always bring back their chamber pot. It was one of their petty torments. His father had been here for fourteen years and was supposed to serve six more. The nearly bald crown of his head emerged from his cocooned body, and tufts of white hair attested to how the years behind bars had affected him. Vincenzo doubted his father would last even a few more months.

"Papa," Vincenzo called softly. His father had always gently awakened him as a child. Perhaps Vincenzo could wake him from a different kind of sleep. His father did not stir. "Papa," Vincenzo called again.

His father opened his eyes, blinked for a moment, then looked at Vincenzo and smiled. "My son, it's good to see you." He rose and reached his hands and thin arms through the bars, and the two of them embraced. His father kissed Vincenzo on the cheek. "I was just dreaming about you. You were building a great structure, and we were at the very top. It was not like any building in Sicily. It made me dizzy just to look at you. I think it means you have a bright future and will make your papa very proud."

"No future is bright while my papa is in prison," said Vincenzo.

"Do you know why I'm really in prison?"

Vincenzo shook his head. In the first few years of his imprisonment his father had raged against the Duke, but it had been a long time since they'd talked about the Duke.

"Because I was a coward," he said quietly. "I did not seize those things that were right in front of me. I walked away from fights, stayed with things that were safe, even though it barely fed you and your mother. You should've had a stronger father. When the jeweler treated me with such disrespect, I was angry because I knew it was what I deserved. But it felt good to beat him because for once

I was acting like a man. All my life I was less than a man. Don't run away from a fight, because it always stays here." His father pointed to his chest. "Promise me, Vincenzo, that every day of your life you'll be a man."

Vincenzo had never seen his father so emotional and regarded his father's thin body, his shirt hanging on him like a scarecrow. Vincenzo blinked, trying to hold back the tears because this was always something he'd thought about his father. He'd been a timid man, instead of like stone as Vincenzo thought he should be. But it still pained Vincenzo to hear such words. It was too intimate a thought for a parent to express to a child. Finally, all Vincenzo could say was, "I promise."

"Good," his father replied. "You'll never live in a prison like the one I've created. These bars are nothing compared to what I've done to myself."

"Papa," Vincenzo whispered, drawing new strength from the plan that lay ahead. "Your time in prison is at an end. Your son will be freeing you. You will be going home."

* * *

THE PIERCE SILVER Arrow moved quickly on the Sicilian mountain road. The driver had the windshield up, but still wore goggles to protect his eyes from the dust. His section of the car was open, exposing him to the elements, while the rear of the vehicle was enclosed, giving it the appearance of an elegant horse-drawn carriage mated to a fast roadster. In the back seat sat Alessandro de Leone, Duke du Taormina, the Lion of Sicily, and two burly *carbinieri* bodyguards.

The Duke glanced out the window at the countryside and remembered the enthusiasm with which he'd come to this land forty-five years earlier. Then he'd been part of a great government effort to bring the island into the modern age. There had been many mistakes, he knew that, but there had also been much progress, most of it unfortunately lost in the devastation and neglect which followed the Great War.

The snow-capped peak of Mount Etna lay to the north, the green vineyards encircling her peak like an emerald necklace, and below them lay open plains of golden grass. In the distance, Sicilian towns rested on the summits of hills, the better to defend against the invaders who had marauded across the Mediterranean throughout history.

The Duke had to admit that even in 1922 this land remained close to what it had been in the Middle Ages. Infant mortality was high and beggars stretched bony hands imploring the rich passerby to spare a couple *lire*, while the ever-present specter of the mafia loomed. Sicilians disbelieved the benefits of modern medicine; money destined for local improvements found its way into the pockets of local officials, and those who sought change were often silenced. The Duke had sought change, but because of his status as a member of the royal family he had been largely immune from threat. Instead, the mafia sought to silence those who would talk to him, those who had seen crimes, and even those who had once wielded terrible power. Sicily was a land of fear—fear of poverty, fear of the mafia, fear of the vendetta—and it was a constant from the poorest beggar on the street to the most powerful landowners. The Duke considered his fight against the mafia and for the people of Sicily to be just shy of a complete defeat.

But the mafia did not concern him today. Mussolini and his fascists had declared their intention to take over the government. At the moment the Duke's car was speeding along, Mussolini and his brown shirts were marching on Rome. Mussolini fancied himself a new Caesar, a new Garibaldi, and yet to the Duke he was unlike any of them.

For the Duke, Mussolini was a figure like Lenin in Russia, somebody who promised bread and peace and prosperity to the masses, while he merrily marched them to the graveyard. The Duke knew that his nephew, the King, had been so demoralized by the butchery of the Great War and what had happened to Italy in the four years since the end of that conflict, that he was ready to give into Mussolini's demands, rather than risk civil war.

Coup d'etat, thought the Duke.

The words rolled off the tongue so easily in French. The generals of the army had been alerted to the plan. They were eager to fight Mussolini, believing they could quickly dispatch the upstart, but wanted the pretext of a legal order.

The Duke was central to this plan.

He would go to the King and try to convince him to fight Mussolini. The Duke knew he'd always had a special hold over his nephew. And yet, if he could not convince the King to issue the order, he would have his nephew arrested.

And who will be Caesar then?

The Duke sat back in his seat, thinking of the Prime Minister waiting for him, probably pacing in his Rome office. The generals were waiting, talking quietly with their aides about the plan of attack against the fascists. But even more than the politicians and the generals, the Duke thought of the simple Italian people, like his longtime servant, Salvatore, with whom he'd shared all his thoughts and fears since his children were small.

It was people like Salvatore who had risen up sixty years ago, good, decent, and loyal, who'd supported his father, King Victor Emmanuel II, and Giuseppe Garibaldi to free their country from Austrian domination and a Pope who still believed in the Holy Roman Empire. It was the simple people of Italy who had wanted a country free of both governmental and religious tyranny. They were the ones who had fought and bled to make Italy a republic, and they were the ones who would pay the price if he failed in this effort.

* * *

VINCENZO STOOD WITH one foot on the running board of a black, Ford Model-T and took a last drag from his cigarette. He dropped the butt and crushed it into the dry, brittle dirt blasted by the furnace of the Mediterranean sun. When he exhaled, he felt the pain of hunger in his stomach. He accepted the pain, exulted in it, as a martyr would accept torture from a heathen. The fascists had offered him food, wine, even a woman, but this was a time he needed to be clear-headed.

The Model-T was parked so it blocked a narrow mountain road between Taormina and the port at Messina. To one side was a cliff with a two-hundred-foot drop and on the other, a rocky, scrub-covered hill. The hood of the car was up, as if they'd had engine trouble.

"Bet that damned fool doesn't even know what's coming to him," said Michael Carlucci. He walked nervously in front of Vincenzo, scanning the road for the approaching car. Michael was another man with a grudge against the Duke. His brother was in jail for killing a man during a card game. The Duke refused to listen to his brother's plea for clemency.

Michael's brother swore the dead man had been cheating.

"Maybe none of us knows." Vincenzo took out another cigarette and lit it. He inhaled, letting the sharp, acrid smoke nestle in his lungs. He looked at Michael; the fraying white shirt, black vest, gray, weather-beaten pants, and wondered if he himself looked like such a wild child. Michael's face was burned red from the sun, while his black hair fell long and ragged underneath a Greek fisherman's cap.

On the rocky, scrub-covered hill, the other member of the Duke's welcoming party had concealed himself. Roberto Bonnini was a tall, strapping twenty-year-old with a scar across the right side of his face and a marksman's eye. He could shoot the head off a sparrow at seventy-five yards. From his position, Roberto covered the road before and after the curve.

"I don't like this plan," said Michael, pacing in front of the Model T's open hood. He checked that his pistol was still within easy reach. "We shouldn't be sitting out here in the open. You're putting us at risk. We should be hiding behind some rocks and come out shooting."

"You cut with a dull knife," Vincenzo replied. "My blade is sharp. The Duke has two bodyguards and a driver. There's a wall of human flesh between him and us. With my plan we separate him from his watch dogs."

"And leave him alive," said Michael sharply. "I don't know why you want us to avoid—"

Roberto gave a sharp whistle from the hillside to announce he'd spotted the car. Vincenzo and Michael rushed to appear working on the engine. Vincenzo strained to hear the sound of the car. In the distance the other car's engine was humming quietly, almost indiscernibly, with the precision of a finely made machine. As the large motor car drew closer, he heard the crunch of wheels on gravel, the tires spitting out small pebbles as they sped along.

The Duke's silver Pierce Arrow came into the corner at a fast clip. Vincenzo turned quickly, eyes locking with the driver. The driver rose up in his seat and slammed on the brakes. The car skidded to a stop, throwing up a cloud of dust.

Vincenzo lowered his eyes to let the dust pass over him. The car was stopped about forty feet away. Good, he thought. The distance would give the Duke and his party a feeling of security. Vincenzo studied the car with suppressed disdain.

It looked like the automotive age's answer to the royal coaches of previous centuries.

The driver lowered his goggles and with a scornful wave of his hand said, "Get that out of the way! We're in a hurry!"

"If you would help us," said Michael, walking toward the Duke's car, repeating the words Vincenzo had given him. "We would be most thankful."

The left door of the car swung open and a blue, uniformed *carbinieri* stepped out with a rifle. He took quick aim at Michael.

Michael raised his hands, affecting a surprised look. "We just need some help with our car."

"Check him for weapons," the *carbinieri* ordered the driver.

A middle-aged man in a suit that made him look like an English butler stepped out of the car. He patted Michael's sides and the back of his trousers. Vincenzo's arms were also raised, his expression concerned, but inside he was bursting with excitement. The plan was working.

"No weapons," the driver reported.

"Check him, too," said the *carbinieri*, motioning to Vincenzo.

The driver repeated the same exercise with Vincenzo. "Nothing on him, either," said the driver.

"See what you can do with the car," the *carbinieri* ordered.

The driver shrugged and walked over to the car.

"I don't know what happened to it," said Michael, babbling like he was a dim-witted fool. "My master wanted us to go to his sister's for a case of oranges, and then it just died. The last few miles it was behaving strangely, like a donkey who wants to stop and you must keep striking it. But then it would not go at all."

"You probably didn't have enough petrol," said the driver as he started to peer into the engine.

Michael stepped next to him, pulled out the pistol he'd secreted in the engine, and fired at the driver's chest. The driver flew back and fell on the gravel road, a scarlet circle of blood blooming into his fancy clothes.

Vincenzo saw the first *carbinieri* take aim at Michael, then heard the sharp crack of Roberto's rifle and watched the *carbinieri* fall. Predictably, the second *carbinieri* came rushing out of his side of the car, looking wildly about, and that was the moment Roberto fired another shot.

The second *carbinieri* was down.

Michael checked the driver, nodded to Vincenzo that the man was dead, and then checked the first *carbinieri*. He was dead as well, but the second *carbinieri* was still alive. Michael quickly dispatched him and then hurried back to Vincenzo.

Four shots and three men were dead.

His team had done well.

Vincenzo's eyes bored into the passenger compartment of the Pierce Arrow and the dark eyes of the Duke. Through the glare of the window the outline of a figure was visible, proud and upright, not cowering as Vincenzo had expected. Only the Duke's head moved nervously, as if looking for a possible escape route.

"Why don't you get out of your car, Duke du Taormina?" shouted Vincenzo. "Or is the 'Lion of Sicily' too scared to come out of his gilded cage?"

The door clicked and opened. As the Duke stepped out, his black, polished shoes crunched on the gravel. He wore a crisply starched, white dress shirt, and a three-piece gray suit with a gold watch and chain attached to a button on his vest. The Duke looked older than Vincenzo remembered from the trial, his face furrowed with deep, jagged wrinkles. But there was still a power that radiated from the man, his long dark hair having turned a centurion white. Vincenzo's breath caught for a moment. This was what a king was supposed to look like.

The Duke looked at the dead men on the ground, and his expression turned pale. "You are an efficient killer."

Vincenzo smiled, proud of his work. He did have a mind for the attack. "I am a soldier, just as you are."

"Yes, but in an evil army," said the Duke, locking his gaze with Vincenzo. "The fascists will be the ruin of Italy."

"Sicily has been in ruins for centuries and nobody has cared."

"Are you so certain it is the fault of others that Sicily suffers?"

"What do you mean?"

"I've spent most of my life here, but I have been to other places as well. You fight each other so much; when you hate, it is something that lives in your bones, and yet you do not see the path to the future. And now you look to Mussolini."

"I'm not a fascist," Vincenzo said as he cocked his rifle.

"No?" The Duke gave him an arch, disbelieving look. The color was returning to the Duke's face.

"But when the fascists wanted someone to stop you, they knew who to get."

"Why?"

"Because I've spent years waiting for today," Vincenzo began. "My father is Giuseppe Nicosia. He robbed your cousin, Fabrizio Bufalino. You made sure the judge sent my father away for twenty years. My father suffered, and now you will, as well."

The Duke puffed up his chest. "Yes, I was there in court the day they sentenced your father, but that's because Fabrizio was my cousin. I held no discussions with the judge. The judge gave the sentence he did because of your father's violent ways. It appears the son is no improvement over the father."

"I protect my family," Vincenzo snarled. "The fascists are going to make sure my family is taken care of. I'll take that to your justice anytime." Vincenzo raised his rifle.

"It won't happen."

"Why not?" Vincenzo asked.

"The fascists are only interested in power," the Duke replied in a matter-of-fact voice. "You're a means to that end, and once you've fulfilled your purpose you'll be thrown out with the trash. Mussolini once marched with the communists, and now he makes war on them, as well. Now that the communists have caused enough trouble to the government, they've fulfilled their purpose in Mussolini's eyes."

The Duke's tone had taken on a confidence Vincenzo didn't like. It was true that large-scale battles had taken place in southern Italy between communists and fascists. While Vincenzo had no love for the communists, their treatment at the hands of the fascists was troubling. There were reports of fascists torturing their captives, beating them with horsewhips, and cutting off fingers and toes.

Vincenzo straightened up. "Mussolini himself gave me his word."

The Duke made a dismissive wave with one hand. "You're a fool. He'll wipe out anybody who knows about this plan. It'll be a lot easier to take out your little band than a hundred thousand communists. The great Mussolini relies on assassins like a mafia don. Is that the kind of change you want? He's a coward who hides behind other people. Say what you will about me, but I'm no coward. I risk treason by going against the King. I may wind up in a jail cell, myself."

Vincenzo walked over to the Pierce Silver Arrow and swung the rifle butt into the car's window. The glass shattered. He turned on the Duke and shouted, "Before I came here I went to see my father in jail. I barely recognized him. Most of his hair had fallen out. He's so thin he might blow away. He'll die soon, without even getting to share a meal with his family. What kind of son would I be if I turned away from him?"

"What kind of man would I be if I stood aside and watched my country be ruined?" the Duke asked through clenched teeth.

"And what price are you willing to pay to do that?"

The Duke seemed momentarily taken aback. "What do you mean?"

Vincenzo rested the rifle on his shoulder and spoke easily. "Mussolini's offered to free my father and make me the richest man in Sicily."

"So we are negotiating?" the Duke replied with a sneer. "You want to know how much I'll pay to keep you from killing me?"

Michael stepped in front of Vincenzo. "What do you think you're doing? After what this man has done to our families?"

Vincenzo pointed his rifle so that the barrel was gently touching Michael's ribs. "I'm in charge here. You'll listen to me."

Michael looked down at the muzzle, shrugged, and walked off.

"I don't ask for any money," said Vincenzo. "Keep your land and your properties. Just release my father. Then vow never to come after us. I've always heard you're a man of your word, so if you swear it, I'll know it's true."

The Duke looked at the dead men on the ground. "And what do I tell their families? Do you think they didn't have people who cared about them?"

"Tell them they died in a war," said Vincenzo.

"I cannot do that," said the Duke, locking eyes with Vincenzo. "I have never dishonored my oath to help this land. Justice is the only thing that can save you. We must all surrender to God's justice. We're merely instruments in a far greater plan."

"You're a foolish old man," said Vincenzo.

Vincenzo raised his rifle and fired. The shock of the recoil hit his shoulder like a hammer. He'd never fired at a man before, but he did not hesitate.

The bullet struck the Duke in the chest, rupturing muscle and bone as it threw him backwards like a slap from some great, unseen hand. The Duke lay on the ground, gasping and struggling for life.

Roberto and Michael rushed to look. A great red flower of blood had blossomed in his chest, but the Duke's face was calm, almost serene. His eyes moved slowly from man to man, finally landing on Vincenzo. "You've done a terrible thing."

Vincenzo stared at him pitilessly. The Duke had ruined his family and was now suffering. This wasn't revenge. This was justice. "Another lion is going to come and stop us? I don't think so. You're the last lion in all of Italy."

"Lions are always being born," the Duke whispered, closed his eyes, and all around the car was silence.

Chapter Two

Vincenzo reached the last rise before Licodia Eubea and even though it was night, he imagined the bright future that lay before him.

The Sicilian hill town was located about twenty miles from the Mediterranean, overlooking the valley of the Dirillo river. The name Licodia came from the Arabic term, *Al-kudia*, which meant "rock" or "base" and referred to the rocky outcropping upon which, centuries earlier, a Roman fortification had been built and then a Norman castle, which had stood for centuries before being destroyed by an earthquake in the late seventeenth century. The remains of one of the towers were still visible from much of the town. The name Eubea came from a Greek colony that had been established near the present day town more than two thousand years earlier. The mainland Italians considered the Sicilians a "mongrel" people, and there was a good deal of truth to the belief.

The area was known for olives, almonds, citrus fruits, and grapes, and even though Vincenzo had spent many difficult years in the town and surrounding areas looking for work, Licodia Eubea was his home. Recent rains had washed much of the dust off the dull, stone gray houses and their red tile roofs, making everything look new again.

They'd gotten rid of the Model-T and were now back on foot. To reach Vincenzo's house, they passed in front of the Church of the Rosary. He crossed himself as he passed, as did his two companions. Despite what they'd done, Vincenzo couldn't help but feel an enormous sense of optimism about the future. He thought not only of his family being back together, but of the uses for his new-found wealth. There were ways that people could be helped so much in the town. He imagined himself taking responsibility for the local people in the way the feudal landowners never had. One had to have been poor to know the desperation of it, the hopelessness, and how to find the narrow road out of it.

"It's very quiet," said Michael.

Vincenzo felt himself stir out of his reverie. There was an uncomfortable silence in the narrow streets, but it was late. The sun had set several hours earlier, and it was those last precious moments before the great majority of the town went to sleep. Country people did not stay up late.

Vincenzo rounded the final sharp turn of the alleyway and saw the tiny stone shack his family called home. At times it was a barely adequate shelter against the weather, but now it looked comforting to Vincenzo as if it was a great palace. He shifted the rifle from his shoulder as he pushed to open the door. That was when he heard his sister's muffled scream.

He knew immediately.

His mother and Angelina had not left. Vincenzo burst into the house. It was full of people. His father sat at the head of the table, leaning back as his dead eyes looked toward the ceiling. He'd been shot through the midsection and on the wall behind him was a sunburst of blood. His mother was lying on the floor at the threshold of the kitchen, her long black hair thick with blood from where she'd been shot in the head.

His sister lay on the table, held down like a sacrificial animal in full view of her murdered father. She'd been stripped naked. Marcello was on top of her, thrusting away. Her head was rocking back and forth and her eyes were closed shut. From her mouth came unintelligible moaning sounds. Other fascist soldiers urged him on.

Marcello smiled at Vincenzo with cold betrayal.

The room erupted into gunfire. Roberto and Michael opened fire and the five fascist soldiers grabbed their guns and started shooting.

Marcello quickly scrambled off the table and lit off through the kitchen. Roberto and Michael made quick work of the soldiers. Three were dead and the other two were on the floor, crying out in agony. Michael finished them off with shots to the chest. Within a minute there were no sounds of pain, only the scent of gunpowder mixed with the coppery smell of blood.

The floor was littered with spaghetti, broken dishes, crushed fruit, and pastries for a celebration that would never take place. "Mussolini did this," Vincenzo muttered to himself.

Angelina still lay on the table, her eyes closed, and her head writhing as if in a nightmare. Roberto and Michael averted their gazes from her nakedness while Vincenzo found a blanket to cover her. As he tried to lift her, she cried out, "Don't!"

She opened her eyes, looked at Vincenzo for a moment, then closed them, and rocked from side to side.

"Angelina, please," he begged. "Get up! Come, *cara*. We have to hide."

The sound of his voice brought her out of her stupor. She was suddenly very agitated and grabbed his arm. "Vincenzo, they're doing terrible things to Mama and Papa!"

"Shh, shh," he soothed her. "It's all right. Don't think about that now." Vincenzo stole a quick glance at his dead father, presiding over a fated celebration.

Angelina looked at Vincenzo with what appeared to be recognition. The light of reason appeared to be returning to her eyes. "Mama and Papa are in heaven, aren't they?"

Vincenzo wanted to sob, but the hatred in his soul was too great for that. He nodded. "But we have to go now. I have to save you." He caressed her face with his hand. Vincenzo cursed himself. He'd meant to save her honor, but now he'd be lucky to save her life.

Angelina shook her head. "I'll be joining them soon. Already I can see them on the other side. They have a white light around them." She pointed to a corner of the room. "There, Vincenzo!

Can't you see them? They're so happy! They want me to come to them. Mama! Papa!"

"Nobody's there, *cara*," said Vincenzo.

She smiled with the radiance of a fading flower. "Yes, they are. Oh, they're so beautiful. I never saw mama and papa when they were happy, like you did. They were happy once, weren't they?"

Vincenzo felt tears welling. "As happy as two people could be." He remembered the tenderness they'd shown each other. At the breakfast table they held hands and on the nights Vincenzo was scared and couldn't sleep, he'd go into their room to find them curled in an embrace. Vincenzo once overheard his mother telling some women that even on the warmest nights her husband had to be touching her, skin to skin, to know she was there in the darkness.

"I never saw that," said Angelina. "Mama was always so sad. Papa was a shrunken man. But now they're like two people should always be."

From the doorway, Michael and Roberto gave nervous looks. "We have to go now," Vincenzo told his sister. "Others will be coming for us."

Angelina shook her head. "I'm going with Mama and Papa. Oh, Vincenzo, we're going to be so happy!" She squeezed his arm in excitement.

"No," Vincenzo whispered fiercely. "You can't go. You're all I have left!" Angelina couldn't be dying. She was his little sister. He'd helped her take her first steps, rocked her to sleep on the nights their mother was gone. A world which allowed so short a bloom was too cruel.

Angelina reached up and stroked his face. He took her hand and pressed it to his lips. "I go where our enemies can't harm us," she said. "Where is their victory if the worst they can do is send me to heaven? I feel sad for you. You remain in this world of pain. Run, my brother. I'm beyond their grasp, but you aren't. Forget what happened here today or it will consume you. Remember what was good about us." Her hand fell away from his face.

Vincenzo pulled her lifeless body to him in a fierce embrace. Hot, stinging tears spilled down his cheeks. He had no one. His own life was worth nothing. Carefully he laid his sister on the ground and pulled the blanket over her peaceful face.

He picked up his rifle, looked at his comrades, and said, "Today I have a devil's heart."

* * *

VINCENZO, ROBERTO, AND Michael were hidden at a boarding-house when they met the stranger. He was of tough peasant stock and might have been thirty-five or fifty. At first they spoke cautiously with him of their hatred of the fascists. Mussolini had made his march on Rome, and the King had welcomed him into the government. The stranger seemed to listen intently to their words. Perhaps he was also on the run.

Informers were everywhere now, wanting to be on the right side of power, while Mussolini's men consolidated their hold on the country.

Mussolini was vowing to serve as a democratic prime minister, but Vincenzo knew that wouldn't last long. Mussolini wanted to be Caesar.

It was the stranger's eyes that made Vincenzo trust him. They were wary and quiet, like Vincenzo and his group. Vincenzo sensed an informer would have freely proclaimed his hatred of the fascists, hoping to ensnare any foolish enough to reveal their true thoughts. The stranger reminded Vincenzo of his father, cautious and deferential on the outside, with the hatred buried beneath.

The stranger said little, only that he was no longer welcomed where he once worked. After several hours Vincenzo suggested the stranger share their lodgings, a small room with four cots on the second floor of the *Pensione Verdi*. The stranger offered to pay half the costs. Roberto and Michael quickly accepted him, appearing starved for new companionship. They began to talk excitedly.

Vincenzo was almost asleep when he heard Roberto bragging about the assassination.

"We should be in the Quirinal Palace right now, instead of being hunted!" said Roberto. "If we hadn't done what we did, Mussolini wouldn't be meeting with the King and getting ready to see the Pope! He'd be in some jail waiting for the hangman's noose or the firing squad. The least he could've done is give us a title or something. Count Roberto Bonini. That sounds good!"

"Roberto!" Vincenzo said sharply. "This man is not interested in our situation!"

The stranger looked at Vincenzo, then the others. "You think I am *fascisti?*" he asked. "You think I am one of the men who hunt you?"

Even though the room was only lit by a sliver of the moon, Vincenzo could see the stranger sitting up on his cot, a wry smile on his face. Vincenzo picked up his shotgun and pointed it at him. "Are you *fascisti?*" Vincenzo demanded.

Calmly the man replied, "I swear on the soul of Mary, the Virgin Mother of God, that I am no *fascisti*. I wouldn't follow such a coward. Do you know what he did while his people were marching on Rome? He stayed at his office in Milan so he could flee to Switzerland if things went bad. He's a snake, and I'm glad to say I've always been against him. Pull the trigger if you don't believe me. For unlike Mussolini, I am a man."

Vincenzo stared hard at him. Vincenzo felt an informer would have looked away or made light of the accusation, and Vincenzo would have fired. But he didn't look away. There was a look of near madness in the stranger's eyes that was anything but mercenary. There was a hatred lurking behind the eyes, a passion that went beyond words. Vincenzo knew that feeling.

"You look like somebody's servant to me," Vincenzo told him. "Did you kill your master? Is that why you're on the run?"

"I was responsible for his death, yes," said the stranger.

Roberto grabbed the muzzle of Vincenzo's gun and pointed it away from the man. "This is our friend," said Roberto. "He probably wants to join us. The fascists have made all men of spirit outlaws."

The man looked unmoved by the conversation. "I'd be happy to kill some fascists," he said simply.

Vincenzo trusted the hardness in his eyes, thinking he was a true Sicilian, not a fascist. "If you want to come with us, I must know your story. Then I'll know your heart."

"You do not trust me with your story; why should I trust you with mine?" replied the stranger.

Vincenzo smiled. That's the way his father would've answered. A Sicilian is always cautious. "Fine. Tomorrow you can make your bones with us. We hear there's a local fascist official who's been demanding heavy bribes from people. We plan to settle things with him."

"I look forward to settling with those who've done injustice." Without further discussion they kicked off their shoes and lay back on their cots. In the dim light, Vincenzo drifted off to sleep.

Some hours later a shotgun blast exploded within the room.

Vincenzo sat straight up, the sound ringing in his ear.

Fascists!! he thought. The owner must have turned them in.

He reached for the shotgun he'd leaned against the bed. He felt only air, and then looked around to see the stranger standing over Roberto's body with the gun in hand. As Michael reached for his own rifle, the stranger spun toward him and shot Michael.

In his panic, Vincenzo saw the open window with the white drapes blowing in the night breeze. He sprang through the window, onto the small balcony, and then leapt the two stories to the ground toward a small pile of dirt. Vincenzo hit the ground hard, heard the snap of bone, and then a clump of earth exploded next to him. As fast as he could, Vincenzo, spurred by adrenaline despite his broken leg, tried to put some distance between him and the gunman.

Above him the stranger cursed and ran onto the balcony. Vincenzo saw a dim stand of olive trees several yards ahead of him. He scrambled for them. The stranger fired another round.

Vincenzo wanted to scream at the top of his lungs for the pain in his leg, for the murder of his family, and now his friends, but knew that the stranger's next move would be to stalk him through the olive groves. Vincenzo climbed one of the trees, dragging his broken leg. Each time his leg bumped against the tree it felt like a hundred stilettos were being jabbed into it.

In the crook of a tree, maybe about fifteen feet above the ground, he slipped into unconsciousness, waiting for death.

* * *

VINCENZO WOKE IN a soft bed. His eyes struggled to focus on a black and white figure staring at him. The face was clearly feminine and for a moment he wondered if he had died. Maybe it was his sister, Angelina, waiting for him in the world beyond. His vision came clear, and he saw a middle-aged nun sitting in a chair next to his bed.

"You're at the Sisters of Mercy Hospital," the nun said as she took his hand, "and I'm Sister Constantina." Her skin was leathery and lined with wrinkles, but there was a kindness to her face. Vincenzo thought she looked like the contented grandmother of a healthy brood of children. "The doctor has fixed your leg," she said, "although he says you may always walk with a limp."

Vincenzo pulled back the thin white sheet to look at his leg. His once strong, muscular limb was now distended and blackish in two places where the bone had broken through the skin. Quickly he averted his eyes and pulled the sheet over his leg.

"Perhaps you don't know this," said Sister Constantina, "but your friends are dead. There was nothing we could do for them. I was wondering if there was any family we could contact for them?"

Vincenzo shook his head. "They had nobody." And now, he didn't either. He wondered why the people he loved were always being taken away. First, his father to prison, then his family by

Marcello's brutal betrayal, and now his friends. He felt there was nothing more that could be taken away from him.

"And you?"

"No," he said bitterly. "I don't have anyone."

"Except the fascists who pursue you." Sister Constantine sat back in her chair. "The innkeeper found you and notified us before they found out."

Vincenzo raised himself up in his bed. "What do you know of them?"

Sister Constantina gravely folded her hands in her lap. "I know they were very interested in you and your friends. I made sure you were hidden before they arrived. And we told them that only three men checked into the *pensione*."

"Why did you do that?" Vincenzo asked.

She smiled. "I thought you looked so terribly alone. Your friends dead and you so close to death. But you had an incredible will to live. The bone in your leg had broken through the skin and was bleeding terribly, but still you climbed up into that tree. Its trunk was streaked with blood. There was something magnificent about your determination. You reminded me of Job. Do you remember the story of Job?"

Vincenzo remembered the terrible afflictions God had visited on Job, taking the animals which comprised his wealth, killing his children, and afflicting him with terrible boils. All because of a bet God had with the devil that Job only loved God because of the good things He had done for Job. But Job had continued to love God despite all the pain and sadness visited upon him.

"I'm not like Job," Vincenzo said, almost spitting out the words. He felt a great loathing for the promises of religion. There was a time he'd believed. As a child he'd spent every Sunday at mass in the darkened cathedral. He'd seen the sunlight bursting through the stained glass images of the Virgin Mary and Jesus and the apostles. He'd listened to the Latin incantations of blessings and prayers. He'd watched the procession of the priest down the aisle,

young altar-boys preceding him and waving *cerabuls* from long silver chains with white, sweet-smelling smoke. There was a time
when he'd believed that, as the priest lifted the communion host
and chalice of wine to the heavens and asked for God's blessing,
an actual transformation did take place, making the offerings the
actual body and blood of Our Lord, Jesus Christ.

But when his father was taken away, that had changed. He began
having nightmares of fire and torment. In bed he would writhe as
his skin was seared in Hell's furnace. Behind the flames was the
devil himself, always coming after him and trying to take him away
to everlasting agony. And then around the time his work had been
able to support his family it had all changed. There were no more
nightmares, and he'd come to believe there was no God or devil,
just an indifferent world in which a man must make his own way.

"You are like Job," said Sister Constantina. "Every man who's
afflicted with terrible problems is like Job. That's why we're given
the story. The question is whether to give into despair or fight the
darkness. You seem like one who would never give up fighting."

"I don't believe in Him, anymore," said Vincenzo, lifting his
eyes to heaven.

"It doesn't matter," Sister Constantina replied in a calm voice.
"He believes in you."

"Did they ever find him?" Vincenzo asked.

"Who?"

"The man who killed my friends. He was a fascist, wasn't he?"

Sister Constantina shook her head. "I don't know. When we
arrived we found only you and your friends. The innkeeper remembered him, but he had vanished."

"Then who was he?" Vincenzo questioned, knowing that his
desire for vengeance was clear to Sister Constantina.

"That can't concern you now. You're in danger. The fascist tide
is rising and soon they will find you. But I have a plan." Sister
Constantina unclasped a gold necklace with a cross around her
neck. "This is what my father gave me when I joined the convent.

I can trade it for your passage to America. It will save your life, but you must promise to save your soul, regardless of what happens."

"Save my soul!" Vincenzo exploded. "My family was my soul! Where was God when they were murdered and my sister raped? My soul was taken from me!"

"I have also lost people," said Sister Constantina. "I had five nephews. One of them got on the wrong side of a powerful man and was killed. His brothers took revenge. Now all of them are dead. I buried the last one three weeks ago. I know the darkness you feel. Let me do this. Let me send at least one young man away from this place to one where I know he will be safe."

Vincenzo looked at her stoic face. No tears or even a hint of grief for the five boys she'd lost. But that was the Sicilian way. Life was hard and you accepted it. "My sister wanted me to leave," said Vincenzo. "It was one of the last things she said to me."

"Words from heaven," Sister Constantina said. "She wanted you to live your life, not to avenge hers."

"I fought for her. So she wouldn't have to sell her honor as my mother did. So my papa could see his wife again without iron bars between them. All of it was wrong, but there was no right answer."

He felt the sister's hand running through his hair. "You're young, but you've seen what many people never see in a lifetime. Leave this place of sadness and start again. Make a life better than the one you leave behind. If you want a new life, God will grant it to you."

Vincenzo was pleased that the good sister had fixed his leg, and relieved that they put his pants back on him. He fished in his pocket and handed the sister a small, gold ring, which had been taken from Signor Pelligrino. "I want you to have this ring."

A warm smile came across the sister's face. "I've always liked jewelry. I think that was even more difficult than giving up the idea of having a husband," she said with a slight chuckle.

Sister Constantina slipped the ring onto her finger. She held her hand away like a young bride looking at her wedding ring.

"I hope God will forgive me my vanities, but I do love it. I will always look at it and pray for you."

She kissed him on the forehead and left. He lay still. For another hour thoughts and memories assaulted him. He remembered the gold cross that had grown warm in his hand.

As he looked at it he knew he could leave Sicily, but doubted whether Sicily would ever leave him.

* * *

VINCENZO LAY DOWN on the moist, wooden floor of a pitching ship. Seawater had slipped into the hold during the previous night's storm and was slowly draining. A small pile of straw and a blanket had been provided for him, but no pillow. At times his neck ached even more than his shattered leg. He was jammed in among metal cans of olive oil on a small steamer bound for America. Four months had passed since Marcello had first approached him.

The fascists were now the undisputed rulers of Italy. They'd even made peace with the Vatican, long at odds with the rulers of the Italian Republic who had been too "democratic" for their tastes.

At Palermo, he was smuggled on board the *Naut Violento*, protective of his still-healing right leg. A crude splint had been placed on it. When Vincenzo looked at his leg, he felt repulsed by it. Instead of the smooth muscles he remembered, taut like a free and wild animal, there were protruding mounds of bruised flesh where the bone had come through.

When they'd cast off, the waters off Palermo were calm and the bobbing motion of the waves had acted as a sedative to his overwrought nerves. Past the Strait of Gibraltar the ocean had grown rough, and then they'd run straight into an Atlantic storm. When he'd slept, there were only dreams of fire and damnation, the devil chasing him through a blasted landscape as in a story his mother had once told him of what the lost city of Pompeii had looked like after the eruption of Mt. Vesuvius. But as the devil came close to him, his demonic face changed into that of Mussolini, taunting him as a pawn in his evil power play.

Vincenzo had been given the choice of going to New York, but he preferred to be as far away from Sicily as possible, so he chose San Francisco. He did this even though it meant additional weeks at sea and going through the Panama Canal.

As Sister Constantina had wished, he wanted to put his previous life behind him.

* * *

"You want me to help you?" Augustus Patrio asked Vincenzo in Italian.

Vincenzo was pleased that the older man spoke in his native language. After three months in America, he'd acquired only limited proficiency in English and still felt more comfortable in Italian. He stood in Mr. Patrio's office in North Beach, a converted storefront with a large front window announcing, "The Patrio Building Company."

Vincenzo swallowed, suppressing his need, the hunger that had been gnawing at his belly for more than a week, knowing that he meant nothing to this man. "Yes," he replied, "very much."

The office was sparsely furnished, decorated with paintings of the Old West as it had been before the turn of the century, cowboys driving a herd of cattle through a storm-swollen river, Indian braves hunting buffalo, the gunfight at the O. K. Corral. On his desk was a black and white photo of his wife as a young bride and another of Mr. Patrio in a tuxedo with a prominent inscription that read, "1912 Man of the Year, Knights of Columbus, San Francisco Chapter."

Mr. Patrio rested his elbows on his desk and stroked his white mustache. He was a stocky man and reminded Vincenzo of a feisty old bulldog. "But what is it exactly I can help you with?" Mr. Patrio asked, pausing for just a moment before continuing.

"Do you see what I'm asking? I know you're looking for work, and I can help you, but that's temporary. That just puts food in your belly and a roof over your head for a while." He was near fifty, but still retained the muscular bearing of the young man who'd been the 1898 lightweight boxing champion of the Northwest Territories, having been one of the many who'd headed north for the Yukon Gold Rush. He'd come to California after several years of failure in the gold fields, working construction, and then shortly after starting his own company, the 1906 earthquake and fire struck the great city. Patrio had been one of those who rebuilt San Francisco, allowing him to realize his ambitions on a grand scale.

"A good job, let me buy some food, get a room somewhere," Vincenzo answered at once. "I've been staying at St. Anthony's Church, and Father Cristiani has been good to me. But I don't like to live on charity."

"And I don't like to give it," said Mr. Patrio. "I like to give something that's more enduring, an opportunity." He pulled out a thick, black book. The front was embossed with the initials A. J. P. "Do you know what this is?" he asked.

"An accounting book?"

Mr. Patrio visibly brightened. "No, but a good guess. That's what a typical man like me might have. But I am not typical. I like to think of it as the 'Book of Souls.' Tells me what I really need to know about a person."

He opened the book and handed it to Vincenzo. The white pages contained various names and additional scribbled information about each person. "Jim Stinzani," read one entry. "Wife, Ethel. Children—Tommy, Mary, and Ruth. Met at church picnic. Has a wonderful singing voice. Likes to bet on the ponies, but never more than a quarter. Works as a stone-mason, but can also do amazing sculptures. Self-taught."

"I have more than two thousand," said Mr. Patrio. "People I've known over the years. If I need some legal advice, I've got more than a dozen attorneys I can call. For a health problem, I can call just as many doctors. Or if I want some companions for the symphony or an outing in the country, I just look through here."

Vincenzo immediately understood the value of such a powerful book. "But how do you get people to help you?"

"Just ask," Mr. Patrio replied with disarming casualness. "Doesn't hurt. And it's not like I haven't done things for them over the years. Matter of fact, I won't ask a favor of anybody that I haven't done some little act of kindness. You see," he added with a smile, "all I'm doing is being everybody's friend. So naturally when I need something, I've always got a couple friends I can call on. And they always want the best for me because they know I always want the best for them. So let's now take a look for you. You just want a job that'll put a few dollars in your pocket."

Vincenzo handed back the book. Mr. Patrio flipped through the pages, stopped, then went onto another page and squinted at it like a jeweler looking through a lens. Vincenzo's heart beat faster. Was it really this simple? Where was the catch?

"Here's somebody I helped out recently," said Mr. Patrio. "Mr. and Mrs. Nicolas Falcone. A young couple that wanted to get into the apartment house business." Mr. Patrio looked at Vincenzo and raised an eyebrow. "Or at least, she did," then chuckled at his own joke. "Husband's a hard worker. Mechanic, engineer. Even got a degree from Boyle's Business College. Great mind. Can fix anything. But the wife, she's the one with the vision. First years they were married he worked as a mechanic for the fire department, and she ran a little grocery store. Got a safe, and then since the banks don't really cater to people like us, she kept a lot of people's money for them, learned how to be a bookkeeper. Comes from money back in the old country and said her father was going to send them money for the building, but then something happened. You know how it's going over there, now, right?"

Vincenzo nodded.

"I'm just happy to be in America," said Patrio. "Europe is run by a bunch of bastards, am I right? Every damned country! Anybody with a damn bit of sense gets the hell out of there."

"I did."

Patrio laughed. "And so you did! Smart boy. Okay, back to the Falcones. I helped them out with their loan by making a call to my friend A. P. Giannini over at the Bank of Italy. They got their building, but the basement needs to be cleaned out and she's very pregnant, so needs somebody to do the work. You okay with that?"

"Yes."

Mr. Patrio picked up the phone, asked the operator to patch him through, and then leaned back in his chair. Vincenzo didn't know what to make of Patrio. In Sicily you needed to swear loyalty to the local mafia boss, but this man did not require such oaths. He did good and simply expected that when the time came you would do the same for him. Was this the secret of America?

As he waited for the connection, Mr. Patrio looked at Vincenzo and smiled. His expression had a quality of reassurance and faith. Mr. Patrio's eyes darted away, and his chair came up straight as he started to talk.

He greeted the woman on the other end of the line as if she was a relative. Then he said, "Listen, I remember about your basement. Have you gotten Nick to do it?" He paused for a moment, seemed amused by the response, and then said, "No? Well, I always appreciated his work ethic! Listen, I've got a man here who needs a few dollars in his pocket. He'll jump at the opportunity for some work. Do you think you can use him?" There was another pause, and then a broad smile broke across his face. "Well, good. I'll send him right over. Vincenzo Nicosia, a fine young man." Without pausing for breath Patrio went on. "How's the pregnancy going? Less than a month, huh? Me and the Mrs. to be godparents?" He grinned into the receiver. "Why we'd be honored. Well, I've still got Vincenzo here, and I need to send him on his way. Give my best to Nick." Patrio put down the receiver and neatly closed the book.

Vincenzo could not believe what he'd just heard. "How'd you do that?"

"Do what?"

"Get me a job and become godfather to their child?"

Mr. Patrio smiled amiably, as if secretly pleased that Vincenzo had been so taken by the entire exchange. "I told you. I'm a friend to people, and we do business together. I know there's an old saying that you shouldn't mix business and friendship, but I only want to do business with people I like. Then it's not really work. But I can't really be a friend to somebody if I don't know what's important to them. So, I ask the question again. What is it that you really want?"

Vincenzo knew what he wanted, but he hesitated to tell Mr. Patrio. He never wanted to be poor again. He wanted to never again know the shame he'd felt during his father's long years in prison. He wanted to kill the fascist bastards who had butchered his family. Then he wanted to go home and tend the Nicosia graves. He had only been able to watch the funeral from the hills, boiling with anger and grief.

But these were not things to be said to Augustus Patrio, a man of the civilized world. Vincenzo sensed his own feelings sprang from the darkest side of human nature. He knew he was some deformed creature, bent on vengeance, and kept separate from the rest of humanity by the rage in his soul. His crippled leg was only a superficial manifestation of this truth. He often walked about with clenched fists, ready to strike at anything that got in his way.

In the presence of Mr. Patrio, though, these feelings vanished. There seemed to be no room in Mr. Patrio's world for such angry thoughts. It made Vincenzo feel uncomfortable and brought out a great hostility for the optimistic certainty with which this man viewed life. But the feeling that things could be different gripped

Vincenzo as he started to speak to Mr. Patrio. "At times I've been good, and at others not so good."

Mr. Patrio nodded. "That can be said about most men."

"But I don't think that can be said about you," Vincenzo replied, looking Patrio directly in the eye for the first time. "I think you are a good man always. I have not been. But I want that to be in the past. One day I want to be like you are now."

Chapter Three

Vincenzo stared at the woman who couldn't have been more than five years older than him, but seemed from an entirely different world. Mrs. Falcone wore a voluminous white dress with blue irises to conceal the final stages of her pregnancy. Her thin face with dark eyes seemed to regard him as if he were a slightly disappointing foreign emissary being presented to her court. She lacked the puffiness he'd seen in the faces of most pregnant women.

"Hello," he said in cautious English. "I, Vincenzo Nicosia. Mr. Patrio send me."

Her fine, black hair hung in a slight curl halfway to her shoulders. She looked nearly able to put on a black beaded dress and feathers in her hair like the flapper girls in eastern glamour magazines. "This is all wrong," said Mrs. Falcone, shaking her head. "You're all wrong."

Vincenzo felt as if he'd been punched in the stomach. It had been two days since he'd last eaten, unwilling to keep accepting Father Cristiani's charity. Vincenzo had vowed that the next food he ate would be earned by his own hand. "What, what you mean, I wrong?" he stammered.

"I mean there's a lot of heavy work to be done in the basement," said Mrs. Falcone, easily switching to Italian. "People have left boxes and furniture, and it's dirty as hell. I sneeze just walking in there. So I wanted to get somebody with a little strength to move those things."

Vincenzo's eyes furrowed together and tensed like a predator ready to snap the neck of his quarry. He wanted to strike this woman for her condescending, superior attitude, her affected nobility, just as he'd done with the Duke, but he realized he had to hold his temper. He saw her demeanor become slightly fearful in the face of his determined stare, so he looked away before speaking.

"I do anything you need," he said in stubborn English, "and I do it better than any other man. I no eat in two days. No charity. I work, you pay me, then I eat. You no happy, you no pay me."

"Hunger is not a qualification for this job," replied Mrs. Falcone, still speaking in Italian. "Strength and ability are. Now, if you're hungry I'll give you something to eat, but that's—"

"Hunger should be a qualification for every job," Vincenzo said quickly, reverting to Italian so he could speak more fluently. "I know how many well-fed people do bad work. I'm not one of them. Even when I get fed, I have a hunger more than anybody else."

Mrs. Falcone folded her arms over her full stomach and looked at him. Vincenzo was so hungry that other images began to assault him. For an instant, he saw the Duke standing before him. When he drifted off to sleep at the church he was often plagued by nightmares of what had happened to his family. There would be a rush of images; sometimes he arrived just before the fascists, interrupting his family's celebrations, and he'd try to warn them, but they wouldn't listen to him. At other times, he would arrive months or years later at his family home, only to find his family's shriveled bodies, still lying where they had fallen. Vincenzo blinked quickly. Mrs. Falcone was in front of him. *Those days are gone*, he told himself. He had promised Sister Constantina. He was living a new life.

"There's a lot of heavy things that need to be moved," Mrs. Falcone said finally.

"I can do," he answered her again in English.

"All right," she replied in a dubious tone.

Vincenzo could tell she'd been expecting an ox of a man, the kind who could lift heavy objects with little trouble. He was just a few inches taller than she was, and although he'd always been strong, but slender, he knew that the weeks on the ship had made him even thinner.

She motioned for him to follow, but stopped suddenly, and grimaced at the peeling paint in the entryway. Vincenzo saw another opportunity for a job, even though he did not know how to paint. He might get a week of meals out of such a job. She started walking again and then looked back at him.

"You're limping," said Mrs. Falcone.

"I have accident," Vincenzo replied quietly, "My leg no heal very good."

After his escape from the *pensione*, he knew he had the courage to face any adversary. The death of his family had grieved him deeply, but the physical pain from his shattered leg had made him want to put a bullet through his head. If he'd had a gun, he might actually have done it.

"Does it hurt?"

"It was bad at first, but like most pain, it go away."

"Are you sure you can do this job?" Mrs. Falcone asked.

"I give you promise."

"All right. We won't go through that again."

The storeroom was located in a small open square between her apartment building and the one adjacent to it. The door was nearly blocked by odd pieces of furniture, tables and chairs covered with blankets, and a clutter of wooden boxes.

"This hasn't been cleaned in years," said Mrs. Falcone. "I've asked the tenants if any of this belongs to any of them, but nobody's claimed any of it. I want you to drag it all out so we can take a look at it. After that, clean everything with soap and water." She motioned to a mop and metal bucket that were standing by the door. "Do you understand?"

Once again Vincenzo humbled himself and assured her he was capable of the job.

"I'll be just upstairs in case you need anything," she told him as she left.

Mr. Patrio told him he'd begun by sweeping out a grocery store. That was the way it was done in America. Vincenzo decided he wasn't ashamed to be cleaning out a basement, even though it was a more menial job than those he'd performed in Sicily. Vincenzo started to move boxes out of the basement. Curiosity overtook him, and he opened one. Inside he found several men's suits in good condition. He wondered if Mrs. Falcone would give them to him if he painted the entryway. For a moment he considered taking them, but decided that would be dishonest. He let himself have a private laugh.

He'd killed several men, but was now concerned about his honesty.

As he was putting the suits back, he saw something else. It was a sword. He lifted it out. The brass at the pommel was tarnished and the shark-skin of the handle seemed to be flaking away. The blade was badly in need of cleaning, but he could make out a cornucopia of fruit engraved on it, the United States eagle, and the words *E Pluribus Unum*. The ornate designs made Vincenzo think the sword had to be from the American Civil War, when the North had fought the South over slavery. It made him vaguely sad. There always seemed to be reasons for men to kill each other.

Vincenzo put the sword back in the box and continued his work.

One day he would have even more money than the fascists. One day he would have what they had promised him. He worked for hours and finally knocked excitedly on Mrs. Falcone's door. He had finished the work so quickly, and he was excited to show it to her. He'd always known how to impress those in power. It had come so naturally to him, like a boy who could run so much faster than the others. He knew he had a calculating mind, allowing him to see several steps forward when everybody else seemed to simply plunge blindly ahead.

Hadn't he committed one of the greatest crimes in Italian history?

If it hadn't been for him, Mussolini might have fled the country or ended up in jail like that foolish Austrian corporal who had just tried to stage a coup in Munich with about two thousand men. It had been a fiasco.

Vincenzo knocked on Mrs. Falcone's door and after a few moments she opened it. Her hair was matted to one side and a red line appeared slashed diagonally across her face where she'd been lying on a pillow. She appeared disoriented.

"Are you all right?" Vincenzo asked.

"I think so," she murmured. "I had a bad dream. My father was calling to me, as if he wanted to warn me about something. It was very important, but I couldn't understand it."

"Can you write him letter?"

"No, he's dead. My mother died, too. Shortly after him. Broken heart, probably."

"I'm sorry," Vincenzo made the sign of the cross to honor her parents.

"Thank you. Your parents? Are they back in the old country?"

Vincenzo shook his head. "They are also dead. My sister, as well. I am the only one left."

"I'm sorry, as well. We're just orphans in America, aren't we?"

Vincenzo started to smile when Mrs. Falcone suddenly grabbed his arm with a talon grip. Her long, red fingernails dug into his arm, nearly drawing blood, and then she doubled over, grasping her stomach with her other hand.

"The baby!" she said in a panicked voice.

A pool of water formed at her feet.

* * *

IN THE NEXT few minutes Vincenzo did things he'd never imagined, which were in some ways more frightening than any violence with guns. First, he took Mrs. Falcone to her bed. Finding himself in the bedroom of a married woman, for whatever reason, mocked his Sicilian upbringing. Once she was situated, Mrs. Falcone begged him to call the doctor, and he quickly spoke to the operator, explaining himself in broken English.

Her regular doctor had been called away to Los Angeles on a family matter, and a Dr. Fobitano took the call, but said he didn't handle deliveries. Vincenzo let fly with a string of Sicilian curse words, and Dr. Fobitano must have realized he was making an enormous mistake because he said he would be there shortly. Vincenzo next called Mr. Falcone at his work, but was told he'd gone to San Jose, about an hour away, to work on a machine at another factory.

Dr. Fobitano arrived about fifteen minutes later, clutching his black bag and looking like an adolescent boy trying to look grown up in his ill-fitting Easter suit. He muttered something about never being good at this type of thing in medical school. Vincenzo shook his hand, noticing how soft and fleshy it was in contrast to his own worn and callused fingers.

The doctor entered Mrs. Falcone's bedroom with the hesitation of a chicken fearing the farmer's axe. "H-how often are the contractions coming?" he stammered out.

"About every ten minutes," she replied.

"Good Lord!" Dr. Fobitano dropped his black bag, moved quickly to her side, and pulled the covers off. "This is an unusually fast delivery. They said in medical school it usually takes much longer."

Mrs. Falcone glared at Vincenzo standing behind him and flushed red.

Dr. Fobitano turned to Vincenzo. "Would you care to leave the room, Mr. Nicosia? Maybe boil some water and get some hot towels ready?"

"Yes."

Vincenzo left the room and prepared things in the kitchen. He kept checking in with the doctor every five or ten minutes. Mrs. Falcone soon went into labor, and Dr. Fobitano asked for Vincenzo to assist him. After about an hour of pushing, the doctor whispered, "The head!" Vincenzo looked down to see a small, smooth sphere making its way into the world.

Dr. Fobitano stood to his full height, his eyes fluttered, and he crumpled to the ground.

Vincenzo quickly went over to the doctor and patted his cheek, but he was out. Fobitano was still breathing, so Vincenzo simply returned to Mrs. Falcone.

"Help me!" Mrs. Falcone shouted. Vincenzo saw her face contort in an exquisite grimace of pain. He had participated in the delivery of horses on some of the estates in which he'd worked, so he assumed many of the same principles could be utilized.

Vincenzo reached down and gripped the child's shoulders that were just emerging. The child slipped out quickly, like a stranded cart suddenly freed from the mud. Vincenzo took the small, bloody, and pale form into his arms. He picked up a towel and swaddled the child, a boy.

A groan came from the floor. Vincenzo looked down to see the doctor rubbing his head. Fobitano stood up. "I see the child has already been delivered," he said.

"No thanks to you," Vincenzo replied.

Dr. Fobitano was clearly perturbed. "Yes, well I'm sorry about that, but I told you I was no good at these things. I always fainted when we had to attend births at medical school. The dean almost didn't let me pass, but he was a good friend of my father. Mostly, I try to stay away from them now. I hope we can keep this between us."

Vincenzo nodded.

"Well, at least I can cut the umbilical cord," said Fobitano, getting his surgical scissors and making quick work of the process.

Dr. Fobitano took the child from Vincenzo, gave it a good slap on the rear, and the child let out a good, healthy cry.

"His mother should see him now," said Vincenzo. "A family should be together, always."

Vincenzo handed the baby to his mother. Mrs. Falcone looked weak, but happy as her son was placed in her arms.

"What are you going to name him?" asked Dr. Fobitano.

"Alessandro," she replied without hesitation. "It's the name of a good man."

* * *

A WEEK LATER Vincenzo was seated comfortably at Mrs. Falcone's kitchen table, sipping a bottle of Coca-Cola and eating a salami and provolone cheese sandwich. She'd given him the job of repainting the entryway and also given him the box of men's suits, which he'd taken to the tailor to be altered. Mr. Falcone was trying to get Vincenzo work on a construction site, but there had been more work at the Falcone's new building than anybody had expected.

At noon, Mrs. Falcone usually invited him to her apartment and fixed him a sandwich while she was taking care of the baby. Vincenzo knew the Falcones also had a small grocery store that Mrs. Falcone usually ran, but one of their regular employees had recently taken on the role of a manager. Mr. Falcone usually stopped by the store for an hour or two after his regular job to make sure things had gone well during the day.

Vincenzo found that Mrs. Falcone liked to talk about America and how it was different from the old country. He thought she sounded a lot like Mr. Patrio, and he could see how the older man had felt he could trust the young couple with a loan.

"Back home there are only two groups of people," said Mrs. Falcone one day while Vincenzo was eating lunch. "Those who have money and those who want it. And there's no good way to move between the two groups."

"And I was one of those who wanted it," said Vincenzo.

Mrs. Falcone smiled. "And if you want it over there and try to get it, you're probably a criminal. But here in America, it just makes you ambitious. Work hard and work smart, and you can make it. But you need to do both."

Vincenzo told her much about his life, shading some of the details. He told her that when he was very young his father had to go away, but he hadn't mentioned any details. He told her that his family was dead, but that they'd died after the Great War when Spanish Flu swept the island. Other stories contained more truthful elements.

He talked about running with a gang that he knew was nothing more than a training ground for young mafia members, but that he'd turned away from them. He talked about defending his younger sister, Angelina, from a bully girl named Livia, who wore men's clothes, smoked, and fought with anyone who looked at her oddly.

"Salvatore always protected me," said Mrs. Falcone.

"Your brother?"

She shook her head. "My father's servant. We always joked that he was the family watchdog."

"So you were one of those people in the old country who had money, not one of those who wanted it?" said Vincenzo.

Mrs. Falcone smiled ruefully and nodded. "But what does it matter what happened back there? Here we're all the same. And with the fascists in power now, well, whatever we once had is gone."

The buzzer rang. "I'm not expecting anybody," said Mrs. Falcone, then got up and pushed a button to unlock the front door.

A subsequent harsh knock came on the apartment door so quickly that Vincenzo thought the person must have practically flown up the stairs.

"That man!" said a husky woman's voice the moment Mrs. Falcone opened the door. The woman brushed by her into the apartment. She turned quickly, wild brown hair flying out like the snakes of a domestic Medusa. From the kitchen Vincenzo could just see her; younger than Mrs. Falcone, possibly even younger than himself. She was smaller than Mrs. Falcone, more vibrant, almost lustfully conceived. Her hair, hips, and breasts were fuller, her nose larger and more flared, as if she could just as easily be savage or sensuous. "He's such a skinflint!" she insisted.

"Who, Jacquetta?" Mrs. Falcone asked.

Jacquetta exhaled like a skittish horse. "Dante! All I wanted to buy was this little dress. It looked so cute, but he said it cost too much. It was only fifteen dollars. I mean, with all the money he has, don't you think he could spend a little on me?"

"Jacquetta," Mrs. Falcone said with disapproval. "I don't have any dresses that cost more than ten dollars. I can't see spending more than that on a dress. I agree with Dante—"

"Rosina, you're always taking his side!" Jacquetta said as she threw up her hands and walked into the kitchen. "I know you think I'm a complainer, but—"

She stopped talking when she saw Vincenzo sitting at the table. Vincenzo grabbed the back of the chair and stood up, inclining his head in a gesture of respect.

"I'm sorry," she told him. "I didn't know my sister had a visitor."

"You are sisters?" asked Vincenzo.

Mrs. Falcone took Jacquetta's hand as she walked into the kitchen. "Yes, this is my sister, Jacquetta Mercurio. She's just recently married so she's spending a little time getting used to it. Jacquetta, this is Vincenzo Nicosia. He's the man who helped deliver Alex." They had taken to using the more American version of the name.

Mrs. Falcone seemed amused to see her sister's anger defused so quickly. Vincenzo had a sudden flash of insight about the way the two acted with each other. Mrs. Falcone had always been the older, serious one, while Jacquetta was allowed to be the flighty younger sister.

"I did not know Mrs. Falcone had such a beautiful sister."

"She's married," Mrs. Falcone repeated with a smile, as if her younger sister often prompted such comments.

"He's charming," Jacquetta told her sister, touching her softly on the arm as if to say, *look at him.*

"A man should let his wife buy whatever she wants," Vincenzo continued. "He should always make her happy. If not, why reason to be together?"

Mrs. Falcone looked curiously at him, as if he'd suddenly transformed from a shy, young man from Sicily to a covetous wolf.

Vincenzo could read her expression, but didn't care. Her sister was a woman of fire. He stared at Jacquetta, smiling, and she smiled back.

This was the thunderbolt that caused a man to forget everything else.

Vincenzo thought he could spend years looking into those dark eyes.

"No reason at all," said Jacquetta, letting her voice trail off like a lovesick girl.

"Jacquetta," Mrs. Falcone admonished.

Jacquetta blushed and let her gaze move away. "I'm sorry. I didn't mean to stare. I was just so angry about Dante, and then I was surprised that somebody else was here."

"It fine," replied Vincenzo, keeping his eyes locked on hers, and smiling a deep, knowing smile.

Jacquetta blushed more intensely, and Vincenzo knew he had disturbed her. Vincenzo knew the bond between them went beyond physical attraction. There was a sympathy between them. They were both people of fire. Vincenzo felt as if God had suddenly shown him the missing half of his soul.

Mrs. Falcone spoke in a clipped manner. "My sister and I have a lot to talk about. I'm sure you understand."

Jacquetta whipped her head so quickly in Mrs. Falcone's direction that Vincenzo thought it might snap off. "That can wait!"

Vincenzo felt the shame of his poverty as he looked at this woman. He knew the situation with her was hopeless, but that didn't matter. The thunderbolt didn't care where it struck.

"Isn't that why you came over?" said Mrs. Falcone. "Because you wanted sisterly advice on how to deal with a husband who isn't paying you the proper attention? And she can give you that advice because she has a strong and happy marriage?"

"Well," said Jacquetta tentatively.

Vincenzo looked at Mrs. Falcone for a moment and nodded. "I go now." Vincenzo grabbed his walking stick and started to limp out of the kitchen. Jacquetta followed closely behind.

"Did you hurt your leg?" she asked.

Vincenzo had seen hospital nurses give less sympathetic looks to dying men. It made him happy to know that what he felt for her was returned in some measure. "Yes, but it seems like a long time ago, now."

"Does it hurt?"

"Not now," he replied with a smile.

"All right, Vincenzo," said Mrs. Falcone. "My sister and I really have to talk. Who knows what might happen to her if she doesn't have the benefit of my guidance?"

"That fine. I go finish up." He inclined his head to the two ladies and walked out, feeling as if he was floating on air.

* * *

Jacquetta returned to her house in Pacific Heights even angrier than when she'd left. Her sister had continued to insist that fifteen dollars was too expensive for a dress. While Jacquetta understood her sister's financial struggles, she didn't feel that Rosina understood her struggles.

Yes, if you were struggling with a new apartment building then a fifteen-dollar dress might be out of the question.

But Dante didn't have any money problems, and he didn't mind flaunting it. He'd spent five thousand on a LaFayette automobile, regularly bought fifty-dollar suits from England, and rarely purchased anything that was less than the finest quality. All a salesperson had to do to close a deal with Dante was to say the item was the best to be found. But when it came to Jacquetta's needs, he acted like he was a pauper. She felt like the most ill-cared for of his possessions.

Jacquetta rummaged through the pantry and kitchen for dinner. Even the icebox had been for Dante's convenience, providing for him, as he said, a restaurant's choice of meals. She wanted to make him his favorite meal that night, steak and spaghetti, so he'd feel guilty that even though he'd denied her a minor indulgence, she still gave him the best.

When Dante arrived home, she did not kiss him, but merely told him what was for dinner and waited for his reaction. He grunted and went upstairs to take a shower.

While he was upstairs Jacquetta found her thoughts drifting to Vincenzo. There was a feral quality to him, something danger-ous, and yet also something so protective. She found it a contrast to Dante, who was so civilized, so refined, and yet in many ways, so distant. Vincenzo would give her anything she wanted. And if he didn't have what she needed, he would figure out a way to get it.

Dante returned from upstairs, just as Jacquetta was putting the finishing touches on dinner. He passed by her, his cologne trailing after him, making her dizzy. There was something about a well-scrubbed man, the smell of cologne just splashed on him, that Jacquetta found intoxicating. He was a handsome man, tall and lean with dark black hair that he slicked back and a regal Roman nose, which gave him the appearance of a friendly eagle when he smiled. He sat down, picked up the paper she had waiting for him, gave her a slightly crooked grin as if to say he knew he looked good, and started to read the newspaper.

"I was over at my sister's today," Jacquetta began. "You should see little Alex. It seems like he's different every time I see him."

"Hmmn." Dante glanced at Jacquetta momentarily over the paper, his eyes then sinking back to the news.

"I also met the man who helped deliver Alex when Dr. Fobitano fainted."

"I heard he was some *dago* cripple right off the boat. Could barely even dial for the doctor. I wonder if it was the first time he'd ever used a phone. Probably doesn't have a nickel to his name." Dante gave a cruel little laugh to himself.

Why had she ever thought his cynicism was attractive? It had seemed funny when his barbed wit was pointed at others, but did he have anything else? Was there anything deeper to the man than contempt? He seemed to lord his American birth over everybody else, including her.

"He was actually very nice," said Jacquetta, feeling a strange need to protect Vincenzo.

"Why do these people come over here and expect to be somebody they never were in the old country?"

"You've never been there before. You don't know what it's like."

"Doesn't matter," Dante said, putting down his newspaper. "It's the same the world over. There are a small number of people who figure out what they need to do to get ahead, and the rest do just what they need to get by. Of course, you can be born into good fortune, and then, well, it's a little easier."

"He may not have a nickel, but he said he'd let his wife buy whatever she wanted."

"Not many dresses to be bought for less than a nickel," Dante replied with a smirk.

Jacquetta opened the oven door to remove the hot pan with the sizzling steak. Her hand slipped from the towel so her thumb touched the exposed metal.

"Damn!" she exclaimed, withdrawing her hand and putting her thumb in her mouth. The scorched spot burned, and she examined it. A small, white boil had appeared.

Dante put the paper down and looked at her with mild reproof. "Did you hurt yourself?"

"Yeah. It's fine. I'll get over it."

She thought of how much she wished she had a husband other than Dante, no matter how much money he had.

Chapter Four

VINCENZO STOOD AT THE PRECARIOUS SUMMIT of a skeletal six-story structure, which would soon become an office building halfway up Russian Hill. The sun was emerging over a bank of fog that stood like a castle wall against the coast. Below he heard the clang of trolley bells, motor engines starting up, and the clop of horses' hooves as fruit and vegetable carts made their way to market. He enjoyed the cold pinprick of the morning air on his face and the sound of the great hive of human activity as it awoke.

For over an hour, Vincenzo was the only person working on the building. As the sun rose higher, the other members of the crew started to arrive, stumbling to work, craning their necks to see a lonely figure toiling against the lightening sky.

The lift sputtered to life, bringing up the first group. Vincenzo knew he was different than the other laborers. They constantly worked less than Mr. Ireland required, stole tools from the site, and usually arrived Monday morning with red, rage-encrusted eyes caused by late nights at saloons that served alcohol in violation of the country's Prohibition laws.

Vincenzo couldn't understand why they worked so hard to throw it all away. When Mr. Falcone got him a job on this construction crew, Vincenzo had promised to give it his best. He had kept that promise.

"Ain't it a surprise who we've got here already?" Harry Rogers asked. He was a beetle-browed man, who liked to work with his shirt off, revealing the thick black hair that covered his chest and back. "Mr. Early Bird, catching his worm."

The two other men with Harry laughed. They were all like him, coarse and callous, with gorilla-like frames. Vincenzo hated them. "I come to do work," he said slowly, meeting Harry's gaze. "No man ever say I don't do my work."

"That's part of the problem, my *guinea* friend. I think you're doing a little too much of other people's work."

"I do work that needs to be done."

Harry pointed a finger at Vincenzo. "You just better watch yourself, now. You know what happens to the nail that sticks out? It gets pounded down."

"Maybe you break your hammer on me." Vincenzo turned and walked away. For the rest of the morning he ignored them. He kept assembling, board by board, the inner framework of what would become the individual rooms of the building. He enjoyed finishing a room. There was a beauty to this work, the creation of man's edifices. Although others would cover his labors with sheet-rock and paint and wallpaper, he could still imagine the outline of its final form. He could walk through what he knew would be a door, look at what he knew would be a sink where people would wash their hands, and sit where he knew some businessman would place his desk to get a view of the bay.

At twelve o'clock, Vincenzo rode the lift down for lunch. He always took the entire forty-five minutes given by Mr. Ireland. At a delicatessen a block away, he would sit at one of the few tables inside and try to read a paper to brush up on his English. Sometimes Pete Goodman asked him to lunch, but he usually liked to eat alone.

When the lift reached the bottom Vincenzo hesitated for a moment, wondering whether he should get his walking stick from Mr. Ireland's shack. He was accustomed to his limp and able to move around easily in a small area. But for a longer jaunt, the block to the delicatessen, he preferred to have his walking stick. Every day when he awoke, for a moment, he believed his leg was undamaged, and his family was still alive. Then he would try to move his leg, feel its unnatural heft, and remember all the people he loved were dead.

Something landed with a thump to his right. Vincenzo looked down to see a large hammer lying in the porous, gray dirt with a small cloud of dust hanging over it.

"Sorry!" an insincere voice cried from above.

Vincenzo saw Harry's face looking over the edge of the building. Harry had his shirt off. Men were beside him, hooting and hollering, even Pete Goodman. They reminded Vincenzo of a pack of monkeys in a tree.

"Guess you have to watch what you're doing or you might get pounded down!" Harry shouted.

Vincenzo picked up the hammer. In a steel garbage can was a refuse fire. Vincenzo looked at the men above him and took a step toward the can.

"Hey! What are you going to do with that?" Harry yelled.

Vincenzo tossed the hammer into the fire, the red flames crackling around the wooden handle.

"That's my own damned hammer, you *dago* bastard!" bellowed Harry. "Take it out!"

Vincenzo limped to the delicatessen without his walking stick.

* * *

When Vincenzo finally came down from the building at seven-thirty, the crew had long since departed. The light was still on in Mr. Ireland's office. Vincenzo knocked and entered.

"Come to pick up your walking stick?" Mr. Ireland asked, looking up from an accounting ledger sheet. He had salt and pepper hair, even though he was only in his forties, and a long, thin handlebar mustache he constantly twisted into shape. His hair spiked up like that of a well-plumed bird, and his large, alert eyes often had the surprised look of a bantam-weight fighting rooster.

"Yes, sir."

Mr. Ireland picked up the walking stick from where it lay against his desk. Vincenzo had purchased it with his first week's paycheck. It had a smooth, dark wooden shaft and a brass globe with the outlines of an old world map. When Vincenzo gripped it, he liked to think that someday he would have the entire world in his hands. "Working pretty late, aren't you?" Mr. Ireland handed the walking stick to Vincenzo.

"It not so late. You still working."

"Yeah, but it's not your business." Mr. Ireland twisted the end of his mustache. "I hope you realize I can't pay you for all the overtime you're putting in."

"I tell Mr. Falcone I work hard."

Mr. Ireland laughed. "You're sure as hell doing that. I wish I had an entire crew like you. I have to say at first I didn't think too much of you. You don't look much like a laborer, but you're surprising in many ways."

Vincenzo pointed to his forehead. "You work with brain, just as much as with muscle."

Mr. Ireland nodded.

"If you make me foreman, I make sure you have entire crew like me. I make sure you have no loafers, like now. They steal from you, Mr. Ireland. I know they do. Make me foreman, and I take care of those people."

Mr. Ireland twisted the end of his moustache and chewed. Vincenzo knew Mr. Ireland was considering what he'd said, but the spark to set the fire was missing. Without that spark, Vincenzo would remain just one of the workers.

"You've only been here six months," said Mr. Ireland finally. "I know you really give it your all, but you've got to earn your stripes. The other men won't respect a guy who's only been in the trade that long."

"But you no got anyone to be foreman since Ben O'Shea left," Vincenzo replied. "You try to run it all from down here, but it no good. You don't know what's going on up there."

Mr. Ireland's expression didn't change. "Can't really say there's anybody I trust enough to make a foreman. This way, everybody's a little afraid."

Vincenzo shook his head. "Not the way it should be. Must be one person they afraid of. Like a ship needs a captain, or it will not go. Need someone to give the orders."

"Well, I'm doing the navigating from down here. It may not be the best way to do things, but that's the way they'll run for a while."

Vincenzo knew there was nothing more to be said. He would continue working for Mr. Ireland and hope something would change his mind. "I go now," said Vincenzo.

"Don't be so impatient," Mr. Ireland told him. "I know you want to make something grand of yourself, but it will come. I ain't never seen hard work go unrewarded. You'll get what you're after."

As Vincenzo walked away from the site he felt happier than he had in years. He knew Mr. Ireland respected and valued him, even if he wasn't quite ready to turn over the keys to the kingdom.

In Sicily a man could not rise, not with landowners like the Duke or Signor Pellegrino keeping everybody down, or people even more ruthless, like Mussolini, who were busy consolidating their power. He read the Italian papers and saw how Mussolini was portraying himself as a law-abiding servant of the people. But Vincenzo had seen the tyrant's true face. He realized now it was foolish to get involved with the powerful.

No matter what they promised, the game was always rigged in their favor.

He headed for a streetcar stop just around the corner. Every time he saw the large, green and white buses with their antenna-like poles reaching for the electrical wires above, he was still amazed. Electricity had been unknown in Sicily when he was a boy. In America everything was electrified; signs advertising a man's suit for twenty dollars, houses stacked on the hills with their windows of comforting familial light, and even the buses that clicked and sparked their way through the darkened city.

Vincenzo turned the corner at a good clip. Harry Rogers stood directly in front of him, his huge arms flexing as he clenched and unclenched his fists. He was flanked by Frank McCarthy and Tom Edwards, the first tall and gangly with a huge Adam's apple, the other just slightly less simian-looking than Harry.

"If it ain't the nail that sticks up," said Harry Rogers. "I think maybe you need to be pounded down a little."

Vincenzo grasped the brass globe at the end of his walking stick, thinking a well-aimed blow could incapacitate or kill a man. "I going home and you not gonna stop me," he said.

He started to walk between Harry and Tom, knowing it would cause them a moment of indecision. They expected him to be frightened. They wanted to toy with him, like wanton children chasing a fearful cat. But he had claws they could not see. Vincenzo walked past them as if he was lord of the jungle. He heard their breathing, saw their heads turn in confusion as he went past.

Tom grabbed Vincenzo on the shoulder, more of a provocation than a threat. He knew they were trying to break his resolve, make him cajole, reason, or even beg to protect himself. Bullies didn't expect their victims to fight back. They didn't expect the sudden attack.

Vincenzo swung his walking stick. A sickening crunch came from the impact with Tom's head, like a watermelon struck by a baseball bat. Tom clutched his scalp, blood running between his fingers as he sank to the ground. Vincenzo turned on a surprised Frank McCarthy, holding the bloody walking stick like a baseball player ready to swing at the next pitch. Frank's mouth was open like a surprised clown.

From behind a muscular pair of arms grabbed Vincenzo, and his walking stick clattered to the ground. Vincenzo struggled to free himself, but realized he had made a strategic mistake. He had turned his attention to Frank, rather than Harry, the greater threat. Vincenzo struggled to free himself, but was as helpless as if in a straitjacket.

"You guinea bastard!" growled Tom, blood still dripping from his head as he got back to his feet. "I'm gonna squish you like a bug."

Vincenzo felt his arms slowly being pulled tighter behind him and knew Harry must be smiling as he gave the others an open shot at Vincenzo's vulnerable midsection. Tom approached Vincenzo slowly. "I'm gonna make you bleed."

Vincenzo struggled as Tom approached, but it was no use. Harry was holding his arms so tight he couldn't wriggle out. The upper part of his body was completely under Harry's control, but not his lower part.

As Tom approached, his fist drawing back, Vincenzo swung his legs up, and delivered a mighty blow to his chest. Vincenzo's shattered leg exploded with pain, but it was enough to knock Tom down and send Harry flying backward. The big man hit the ground hard, and Vincenzo rolled off of him. Vincenzo scrambled to get his walking stick. Before Harry could get to his feet, Vincenzo swung the walking stick, catching the man in the ribcage and sending him back down to the pavement.

Vincenzo turned to run, but then out of the corner of his eye saw Frank McCarthy, fists raised. Vincenzo's arms were at his sides, and the blow hit him like an anvil. He fell. The men were around him now, kicking his head, face, and back. Vincenzo thought the end had come and cursed himself for starting the fight. The worst they would have done was rough him up. Instead, he had let his pride get the better of him, and now he had roused a murderous anger in them.

"Hey! What in blazes do you think you're doing?" The question came in a thick brogue, followed by a police whistle.

"It's a cop!" yelled Harry.

Tom and Frank took a look at the stout, blue-suited policeman running toward them. The three of them started running as quickly as they could, vanishing around the corner of a building.

Vincenzo heard the fast click of the policeman's shoes on the pavement as he rushed by, then the clicks stopped. "Ah, I probably can't catch them boys anyway," the policeman said, almost as if speaking to himself.

"Help me," said Vincenzo.

The clicks began again, slowly heading in Vincenzo's direction. "You ain't looking so good, pal," said the officer as he bent down.

Vincenzo saw strange whirling clouds mixed with black. He felt the officer lift him into a sitting position. "You certainly got those boys riled at you," said the officer.

Vincenzo opened his eyes and gave the man a crooked smile. "Not half as much as they riled me."

The policeman laughed, then said, "Officer Frank O'Reilly, my bruised and battered Italian friend. You're going to be hurting for a while."

Vincenzo felt puffiness around his face and ribs that were probably cracked. He imagined his numerous bruises already turning colors. "I never think I very handsome before. Maybe I look better now."

"What the hell did they go after you for? Bootlegging deal gone bad?"

"No."

O'Reilly gave him a look of rough sympathy. "You can tell me. I don't have the heart to lock up a man roughed up like you for hustling some hooch."

Vincenzo shook his head. "I no bootlegger. I follow the law. I just try to do my job. People get mad when I work hard because I make them look bad. But I gonna turn it around on them. They no gonna get away with this."

He felt his hatred growing inside and knew it would give him the strength to recover. A man needed a reason to live. Hatred had sustained him before. It was a good friend for hard times. His hatred of the Duke, Mussolini, and now for Harry Rogers was like a salve to his soul. The anticipation of vengeance fulfilled made him almost dizzy with pleasure. He focused his mind on the thought, the sweet surrender of pure hatred, and knew it would save him.

"All right, pal," said Officer O'Reilly. "Let's stand you up now. I'll make sure you get home safe."

* * *

VINCENZO FELT THE moisture of the early morning fog working its way into his clothes. He'd tried to bundle up with layers of shirts and sweaters, but now he felt like a wet, shaggy dog. During the night, portions of his face had turned purple where he'd been hit, and his eyes had shrunk to tiny slits between folds of flesh. His back and torso ached from being kicked, and his stomach still felt nauseous.

Stubbornly he'd come to work at five in the morning, earlier than ever. Not even Mr. Ireland had arrived. Vincenzo left his walking stick next to the office door, determined to work harder than before, refusing to be defeated.

Not long after he reached the top of the building, the sound of the elevator descending startled him. He knew it couldn't be more than five thirty. The elevator dropped out of sight into a blanket of fog. He thought of hell, the devil himself soon rising from the depths. He was suddenly convinced Harry Rogers and his cronies were coming for him when nobody was around. On the steel girder and wooden-floored heights there would be no place to run. If they caught him he would be just another laborer who fell to his death while working. After all, another man previously fell and died on a nearby job.

Vincenzo picked up a crowbar and walked to the elevator. It was at the bottom now and he could hear somebody getting in it. The door clicked shut, and it started to rise. He pressed himself against the outside of the elevator shaft.

In the skeletal cage that was rising he saw only the gray and white top of a man's head. *Tom Edwards?* he asked himself. *Frank McCarthy?* Trembling with anger and fear, Vincenzo wasn't thinking straight.

He moved in front of the elevator with the crowbar raised. The door slid open, and he charged toward it with a yell.

"Vincenzo!" shouted Mr. Ireland. Vincenzo let the crowbar drop to his side. "What the hell are you doing?"

Vincenzo cringed with embarrassment, realizing that even if Harry Rogers meant to kill him, he'd never get up this early. The assault the previous night had been so simple, just a few hours waiting around after work. They probably even got sandwiches. He had credited them with far too much guile. They didn't have his foresight and planning. "I think somebody coming up here to get me," he said, trying not to sound like a crazy person.

"Does it have anything to do with this?" Mr. Ireland waved Vincenzo's walking stick. The globe on the handle was covered with dried blood. "If you've been brawling. . ." his voice trailed off. "My God, what happened to you?"

Vincenzo explained.

"You shouldn't even be working," Mr. Ireland stated in concern. "You look horrible. Let me take you to a hospital."

Vincenzo raised a hand. "I okay."

Mr. Ireland twirled his moustache and chewed one end. "You should be staying home at the very least."

"I feel better to work."

Mr. Ireland straightened his moustache. "I've been thinking about our conversation last night. The crew isn't doing very well. I try to supervise from the ground, but you were right. I need somebody in charge up here. I want to make you foreman."

"Really?" asked Vincenzo, stunned by this sudden turn.

"Yes. And I'm giving you full powers as boss. You can hire and fire whoever you want."

"I'll do what's right," said Vincenzo.

At eight o'clock, Mr. Ireland gathered the work crew of thirty men. Vincenzo looked carefully at the assembly. Most were taller than Vincenzo, and without exception all outweighed him. Harry Rogers hid in the back of the group, and his side still seemed to be in pain. Frank McCarthy's eyes were downcast, and Tom Edwards wore a winter cap, no doubt trying to hide his head wound. Vincenzo imagined the man must have a cracked skull, and it would still be slowly seeping with pus and blood tangling his hair. Vincenzo tensely gripped his walking stick, still stained with the blood of his enemies.

"I have an announcement to make," said Mr. Ireland. "It's difficult for me to run this operation from the ground. I know some of you men work very hard, but others do not. For that reason, I'm appointing Vincenzo Nicosia as your new foreman. You'll notice he's been a little roughed up. That's because he stands up for what's right."

"He ain't nothing but a baby hanging on the teat," one man complained.

"Works harder than you do, Burt," said another.

A few clapped but the majority remained silent. Mr. Ireland motioned Vincenzo to speak.

"I want to thank Mr. Ireland for giving me this opportunity," Vincenzo began. He sensed the men were examining his injuries. In the mirror that morning he thought he looked ghoulish, eyes blackened like a raccoon, his lips swollen and cracked as if he was dying of thirst. But he felt a power in his wounds, a badge of rank and honor as great as any military medal. There was an almost mystical aura in being gaped at and having the courage to stare back. His presence alone told them; I have the strength to take your worst and come back.

He continued. "It true I get beat up for working hard. I no ashamed of it. Because I stand up, I get to pull the strings now. I only want hardworking men on my crew. For that reason, I firing Harry Rogers, Tom Edwards, and Frank McCarthy."

"You *dago* bastard," snarled Harry. He pushed his way through the crowd and advanced on Vincenzo.

Mr. Ireland stepped in front of Vincenzo, reached into his jacket pocket, and pulled out a small silver pistol. He pointed it directly at Harry, who froze in his tracks. "I originally got this for my wife, but she said she wanted a bigger one. I'll grant you, maybe it's a little feminine, and I'm sure you do have a very thick skull. But take it from me—getting shot has a tendency to ruin any plans you have for the weekend."

"Come on, boss," Harry whined. "He isn't even one of us. He's a damned *dago*. I've heard you talking about how you don't like their kind, wish they'd just get back on the damned boat and leave."

"That'll be enough," Mr. Ireland cut him off with a glare, then closed one eye so he could better sight down the barrel of the pistol.

Harry narrowed his eyes and looked at Vincenzo. "I guess you've got protection now. That won't always be the case. If I were you, I'd keep watching over my shoulder."

Mr. Ireland walked over to Vincenzo and handed him the pistol. "I think you might need a little more protection, my friend."

Vincenzo sighted it at Harry, just as Mr. Ireland had done, then moved it slightly to the right and fired. The bullet passed about two inches away from Harry's head and buried itself in a plank of wood about ten feet behind him. "I a very good shot. I never miss. If I see you within a hundred yards of me, I won't even ask a question."

Harry realized there was nothing left to say. He turned to leave, Tom and Frank following after him like fellow renegade angels. Vincenzo watched them leave the site and knew they would not trouble him anymore.

Mr. Ireland put a hand on Vincenzo's shoulder. "I thought you had guts, but my God!"

"It your gun."

"That's true."

The knot of men started to break up and get to work.

"I not through," Vincenzo said in a loud voice. The men stopped.

Mr. Ireland looked at him. "What do you mean?"

Vincenzo slipped the pistol into his jacket pocket.

"More men I want to get rid of."

"But you said it was only three who attacked you."

"Is true. But you say I now foreman with responsibility for making good work crew. I know who not good. I get rid of them and get you good workers."

Mr. Ireland chewed again on his mustache. "I don't know about that, Vincenzo. These men have families who depend on them."

"If they have families, then they should work even harder. Not slack off, take from you, and show up late. If you have family, you must work for them. These men have no responsibility to family or work."

"I don't know," said Mr. Ireland.

"Do you give me responsibility or not?"

Vincenzo saw indecision in Mr. Ireland's eyes. His lips moved to speak, he stopped, and then finally he said, "All right, do what you want."

Vincenzo smiled, thinking this was the initial step. He had risen above the first rank of men, those who labored and toiled and cared only for their next paycheck. He had imagined this, and now it was happening. "I also fire Bob Knox, Kevin Shaw, and Pete Goodman."

The three men hung their heads and a tremor seemed to run through the others. They slowly moved away from the fired men as if they had a contagious disease. Vincenzo stared at the remaining workers, so there would be no doubt who was in charge. He wanted them to know he would never apologize for the pain he caused to make things run smoother.

"That's all for today," said Mr. Ireland. "The rest of you men get back to work." To Vincenzo he whispered, "I trust you'll get some replacements quickly. I don't get anything done without workers."

"Very soon," said Vincenzo.

Mr. Ireland walked back to his office.

The work crew beat a hasty retreat up the elevator to protect themselves from further retaliation by Vincenzo. The pain in his face and the rest of his body still throbbed, but a new feeling of power stimulated him like an electrical charge. Those who had mocked and attacked him now ran in fear.

Pete Goodman was the only one left standing there. He was an oversized, jovial man, who always reminded Vincenzo of a St. Bernard dog. Pete had been his first friend on the crew. Vincenzo even had dinner with Pete and his family in their small North Beach flat. In some ways it reminded Vincenzo of his own family, before his father had been taken away to prison. But after yesterday's events he no longer trusted Pete. Vincenzo started to walk past him.

Pete grabbed his arm. "Let me talk to you."

Vincenzo pulled away. "I said you fired. I have no more to say."

"But Vincenzo, I've been a good worker. I know I don't get here as early as you, but I'm always on time. You can ask anybody. And I ain't never stole anything."

"I see you up there laughing when Harry drop hammer and almost hit me," Vincenzo said fiercely.

"I was just walking by," Pete protested.

"Then why you laugh?"

"It didn't hit you or nothing. It was funny. You can't be getting rid of me because I laughed."

"Work an important thing. If you hang around people like Harry, you got no respect for work."

"Have a heart, Vincenzo. You know my family."

Vincenzo saw the defeated look on Pete's face. He was almost tempted to let him have his job back. But Pete had laughed. He wasn't a bad worker, but he let himself be swayed by those who were. Vincenzo would've strangled any bastard who tried to drop a hammer on his friend.

"I have heart," he told Pete. "And it for work. I have heart for Mr. Ireland, who give all of you work. I have no respect for people who take so much and give so little."

Pete gave him a pleading look. "I thought you and me were pals. Me and Sally had you to our place for dinner. You played with my kids, for Christ's sake. The other guys gave me grief for being nice to an Italian and all, but I told them to go stuff it. We were pals and that's what's important."

"I think you are a weak man."

Vincenzo turned his back on Pete and walked to the elevator. As he rode to the top of the building where his crew was beginning their day, he saw Pete Goodman's, shuffling, stoop-shouldered figure becoming smaller in the morning fog.

* * *

LATER THAT WEEK, Vincenzo went to Mr. Patrio's office on Columbus Street, across from Washington Park. His wounds had healed and were barely noticeable. He hoped his benefactor knew six good men who needed work. Through the stenciled glass doorway that announced The Patrio Company, Vincenzo saw Mr. Patrio sitting at his desk. He was sitting with a curly haired man in a suit who sat with his back to Vincenzo.

Just before he opened the door, Vincenzo noticed a battered old lantern on Mr. Patrio's desk. The opening of the door caused Mr. Patrio to look up from his conversation. A warm smile spread across Mr. Patrio's face, and he motioned for Vincenzo to come closer.

"What can I do for you, Vincenzo?" Mr. Patrio asked as Vincenzo approached the threshold of his private office.

"I no mean to interrupt," he replied. "I talk when you are finished."

"Nonsense. I can always extend some common courtesy. I'd like you to meet somebody."

The other man stood and turned to Vincenzo. He was a tall, young, Black man, dressed in a navy blue, double-breasted suit with a perfectly knotted red tie. Vincenzo had rarely seen a Black person up close, and certainly never dressed in such a fine manner. The man extended a well-manicured hand. When Vincenzo clasped it, he realized the roughness of his own hands in comparison.

"This is Abraham Washington," said Mr. Patrio. "His father and I knew each other when we were just young whelps running cattle on the Texas frontier. Mr. Washington, or Dr. Washington, I should say," nodding to the young man like a proud uncle, "recently graduated from Howard University and wants to start a practice here."

"Father always spoke about how much he loved the frontier life," said Abraham. "More civilized than any city he's ever lived in."

"Best life a man could ever have," said Mr. Patrio wistfully. "An empty country except for your buddies and a couple thousand cattle. A man knew where he stood. Sometimes I think all I'm doing here is trying to get back to the kind of clean, honest living we had out there."

Dr. Washington smiled. "Father told me you once saved the entire camp from a band of murdering Comanches."

"They were just starving boys," said Mr. Patrio, his expression darkening. "Not much of a raiding party."

"How'd you stop them?" Vincenzo asked. He'd always thought of Mr. Patrio as a denizen of the city, one who had never been forced to confront the outlaw places in the heart that either broke or made a man.

"Ah, you don't want to hear about it."

"Please."

Mr. Patrio gave a shrug. "Wasn't much courage to it. I always slept with my six-shooter next to me. I heard this yelling, the Comanche war cry. I looked around, and it was like things just got slower and I could see exactly what was happening. You see, most folks get flustered when there's some excitement. Not me. Just makes me clear-headed. I could see there were four of them, and I had six bullets. Got every one of them. One of them couldn't have been more than fourteen and a hundred pounds soaking wet.

The wars were supposed to be over. Made me sick. We'd killed off the buffalo, and their way of life was ending. They were a savage people, and I can't say I'm sad they're gone. Just made me wonder what we were doing on their land. Maybe it wasn't my place to have an opinion on it, good or bad."

Vincenzo listened in fascination.

"Well, my father was very thankful for it. Those Comanche boys would've murdered all of you, and we wouldn't be standing here."

"Boys killing boys, that's all it was. Got to be something better than that. I'm sorry to say, looking back on the history of the world, that's been the rule, not the exception."

"And we are changing it, are we not?" Dr. Washington held open his hands.

"In little ways, I guess."

Dr. Washington extended a hand. "Won't take up much more of your time today, Mr. Patrio. Father always said you were the best kind of man."

"Thank you. Got any patients, yet?"

"Well, n-no," stammered Dr. Washington. "I just got here from Philadelphia, and Cicely hasn't even had time to unpack."

"They teach you how to take care of old men at Howard?"

"Certainly. It's just that . . . the communities of which we're both a part might not. . ."

"You expect me to help a physician I wouldn't patronize myself?"

"Well, no."

"You're my doctor then. My previous doctor just retired. So, from this moment until they put me into the ground, I am in your hands."

"Yes, sir," said Dr. Washington with something of a sly, pirate smile. As he reached the doorway, he made a half bow to them and tipped his hat.

"Great young man," said Mr. Patrio after Dr. Washington had left. "Spends all that time in medical school and what does he want to do when he gets out? Help the poorest members of our society. That's the spirit I think we've lost."

"You help a colored man?" Vincenzo asked.

"I'll help anybody, Negroes, Chinamen, Jews. I know it ain't what some folks think is proper, but in the end, what the hell difference does it make? I figure the Almighty don't really care for all the trouble we make between the twelve tribes."

"My mother say God burned them black to punish them, just like he did to Sodom and Gomorrah."

"If it wasn't for the Africans, I doubt we Italians would have such curly hair. Just a hop, skip, and a jump across the Mediterranean." Mr. Patrio winked. "Now, what can I do for you today?"

Vincenzo puzzled over what Mr. Patrio had just said but wanted to remain focused on his task. "I need six men for construction who can do good work."

"I got twenty men who need work, all good."

"I only need six."

"And I need to help these men get jobs."

"I'm sure they all good, but Mr. Ireland. . ."

"Jim Ireland?" asked Mr. Patrio.

Vincenzo nodded.

"Well, I'll be damned! I gave him his first job as foreman after the '06 quake. I tell you, we put those things up quicker than you could blink an eye. Rome may not have been built in a day, but it almost seemed like we did it here after the Big One. One day the city was a smoking ruin, and the next, well, it's the Paris of the Pacific. Are you sure you couldn't take ten men?"

"No, we just need six men."

Mr. Patrio put a hand to his cheek and rubbed it. "I think I'll just give Jim a call." He picked up the phone, talked to an operator, and was put through to Mr. Ireland.

"Mr. Patrio!" Vincenzo protested. "I really no like you doing this. Mr. Ireland put me in charge."

"Jim?" said Mr. Patrio. "It's Gus Patrio. Listen, I've got Vince Nicosia down here, and he says you're looking for a few men. I was thinking of sending ten." He listened and nodded several times, and Vincenzo could see him moving in his chair, as if responding to what Mr. Ireland was telling him. "I know you're under a tight budget, Jim. But I've got some men who are really in need. Now if you have more men there, you can do things quicker. You make your bosses happy because the job gets done ahead of schedule, and you've given some good men valuable experience."

He listened for a few minutes longer.

"You can take eight? Splendid! Yeah, I'll have the whole crew there tomorrow. Early. I know you've got a number of things happening, but I really appreciate it. Give my love to Laura and the kids. Yeah, I'll tell Grace you say hello."

Mr. Patrio set the phone down and smiled proudly. Vincenzo was angry and knew it showed on his face. He'd been so proud of his promotion to foreman, a position of influence and respect, but Mr. Patrio's actions made him feel like little more than an errand boy. "I guess you always get what you want," said Vincenzo, struggling to remain civil.

Mr. Patrio seemed to find this remark very amusing.

* * *

THE EIGHT MEN were waiting in the cold and fog of a still, dark sky when Vincenzo arrived the next morning. They stood in thick coats, jamming their hands into pockets or rubbing them together and blowing into them with steam-filled breaths. Vincenzo talked with them for a couple moments, getting little more than their names before Mr. Ireland arrived.

"I get the men you wanted," Vincenzo told him proudly.

Mr. Ireland barely gave him a glance and walked to the construction shack. "I say I get the men you wanted," Vincenzo said again. "We can build to heavens if you want."

"I don't care about the heavens today," Mr. Ireland replied. "And I don't think they care much for me." He went up the steps to the porch to his office.

Vincenzo followed him. "What wrong, Mr. Ireland? I no see you ever act this way before. Did I do something wrong?"

Mr. Ireland turned around and put his hands on the porch railing. "Harry Rogers is dead. After you fired him, he was in a rage. Went on a bender and drank himself crazy. He picked a fight with a bigger son of a bitch, and the other guy cut his throat with a broken bottle."

Mr. Ireland slipped his key into the door and went inside, closing it with a mortal finality.

Jimmy LaRocca, one of the new hires, sidled up to Vincenzo. Jimmy was muscular with curly brown hair, a large hook nose, and hawk-like eyes. "This was a man you did not like?"

"Yes. He attacked me. And he was a poor worker."

"And now he is dead?"

Vincenzo nodded.

Jimmy grinned. "You are a man others will follow. And if they don't, let me know."

Vincenzo could see that the entire group was listening, hanging on their every word. He looked at Jimmy, gave him a slight nod and smile, and then turned back to the men. "All right, let's get to work. I'll show you new men what to do."

As Vincenzo started walking to the site, he noticed that the men fell in like soldiers behind him.

Chapter Five

JACQUETTA PACED IN THE LIVING ROOM and looked at her diamond wristwatch. Dante had given it to her on their first anniversary as a sign of his love, but in the years that followed it only served to detail his neglect. They were supposed to go to a formal Knights of Columbus dinner at seven, and it was already eight. She'd received Dante's permission to buy an expensive dress for the evening, black with red trim. Her other dresses were a little tight as she was three months pregnant.

But the master of the house hadn't arrived, and so everything had to wait.

Her eyes wandered across the thick, Oriental carpet, the expensive dining room set with its cabinet full of china, and the expensive chandelier that hung above it. Oil paintings and etchings hung from the walls, giving the feel of rich, comfortable elegance to the entire house. A woman's life wasn't necessarily bad, Jacquetta thought, as long as she had a good husband. While Dante might neglect her occasionally, he'd never been mean or physically abusive. In her charitable moods she thought of him like ether, a substance that was always present, but could never quite be grasped. In her dark moods she considered him a slippery snake, easily capable of minor deceptions, which she suspected of covering up more serious lies.

She heard Dante's fancy LaFayette automobile pull into the driveway. The damned car had cost more than five thousand dollars, but was still noisier than an eight-hundred-dollar Model-T. When Dante read with astonishment that the LaFayettes would cease production because of poor sales, it was all Jacquetta could do to keep herself from nagging him about his poor purchase.

The car door slammed, and she heard his steps coming up the walkway. Before he fully opened the door she asked, "Where've you been?"

Dante entered, dressed in his usual elegant suit. Jacquetta often wondered why a man who ran three pharmacies and even worked the front counter dispensing prescriptions should look so much like a stockbroker. But it was all in keeping with his image of himself as some sort of dashing figure. Angrily, Dante replied, "I had work to do."

"The store closes at six. It's eight now. What took so long?"

"I had to do inventory," he grumbled, then started to leave the room. "I'll take a shower and be right down."

"Wait," said Jacquetta in a softer voice. "Give me a kiss."

He looked at her almost fearfully, as if by coming close he'd lose some sort of mystical power. A slight, bemused smile then came to his face. H leaned forward quickly, gave her a quick kiss, and rushed up the stairs.

The tingling sensation on her lips made her happy, and she was ready to forgive his tardiness.

But a sudden thought shot through her mind.

There'd been another scent on him. She was sure of it. Not his cologne or the musty smell of pills, ointments, or gels from the pharmacy, but something very much like the mingled aroma of a woman's perfume and sweat. Jacquetta had noticed her own scent on Dante after one of the first times they'd made love, and it was bracing to realize she'd left such a mark of their passion.

But she hadn't been with him today.

Her legs felt weak, and she was barely able to make it to a chair. Was Dante really seeing another woman? She composed herself. Had she really smelled the scent of his betrayal? There were a thousand different odors in a pharmacy. Her mind started moving in the opposite direction, in defense of Dante.

He'd recently started stocking perfume in his stores and hired some young women to sell them. It was not unusual for him to spray on a scent to determine if it was something he wanted added to his merchandise. Jacquetta wondered if the rush of hormones from her pregnancy was making her irrational.

Jacquetta heard the shower going on upstairs. She imagined Dante had already slipped off his suit and was just waiting for the water to become warm before taking off his undershorts. He wasn't having an affair. She knew that to be true.

There'd been so much love between them, and it was still present.

He'd seen her first at church. Jacquetta always went to the eight o'clock service on Sunday morning. He was wearing an all-white suit when he came up to her, tipped his hat, and introduced himself. Jacquetta had to suppress a giggle. She thought he looked like the owner of a banana plantation. At the time, Jacquetta was living with the family of her cousins, Lucille and Jack Belevedere. Rosina and Nick were already married and living in a studio apartment.

Lucille was fifteen years older than Jacquetta and acted like a favorite aunt, never telling her what to do, only advising her and letting her make her own choices. Jacquetta was free to come and go as she pleased and had only a mild amount of household chores. For more than a week, Dante appeared at the house and asked Lucille for permission to take Jacquetta out.

Lucille's answer was always the same. "We're supposed to take care of Jacquetta when she's here, but we're not her parents. It's her decision." But in private she urged Jacquetta to go out with him. "He's a nice man," she urged, "and he comes from a nice family. So, he likes to look good. You'd always have a well-dressed man beside you."

Finally, she agreed. Dante took her to the symphony and since it was the night before Prohibition was to take effect, they went to a jazz bar afterwards. She remembered the musicians playing a few jaunty tunes, and then the band leader raised a drink to the assembled crowd, said a few words about the bleak, dry years ahead, and had the band play a slow, mournful ballad. The sadness of the upcoming years was softened by the chance for the couples to dance close. Jacquetta and Dante stayed out until two in the morning, and she surprised herself by giving him a very passionate kiss goodnight.

Maybe it was the champagne she'd drunk, but she didn't feel guilty the next morning.

Jacquetta heard the shower being turned off and imagined Dante toweling himself off. He was a man of such particular habits. Every part of him had to be dry before he stepped from the shower. He kept several towels in close proximity so he could discard a damp one and pick up a fresh one to more thoroughly dry himself.

In the weeks that followed the jazz evening they went out every night. He was fascinated by her stories of Sicily (since he'd been born in America), her father's prominent position, and her stories of their mansion on the Sicilian coast with servants. He affectionately took to calling her "the Princess," but she would rebuke him and say, "My father was not a Prince."

Within a month of their meeting at the church she'd slept with him, and after three months they'd had a large wedding at St. Peter and Paul Cathedral in North Beach. Dante's family had been in San Francisco for more than seventy years, arriving during the boom of the Gold Rush and establishing themselves deeply into the fabric of the city. His parents welcomed her into the family enthusiastically and even furnished their new house.

She heard Dante's footsteps coming down the stairs. He smiled at her. In his black tuxedo she thought he was the most handsome man in the world. Her stomach still fluttered when he smiled at her, and in the night when she lay close to his warm body it seemed almost like heaven. He reached the bottom of the stairs and extended a hand. "Are you ready?"

She rose and took his hand. "Do you still love me?"

"Of course," he replied in a slightly annoyed tone.

Jacquetta regarded him coolly, searching for any hint of deception. But there was none. She was foolish, she thought, to suspect him. It was as it had always been. They were the most elegant couple in the city. She smiled and bussed him on the cheek. There was only the scent of soap and cologne. "Well, I love you more than you can imagine."

* * *

IN THE THREE years since Vincenzo had become foreman, the fortunes of Ireland Construction Company had far exceeded the dreams of its founder. From a crew of twelve men on two jobs a month, the number of employees had grown five-fold and the work had grown even more. Vincenzo took justifiable pride in the growth of the company. In the second year he'd become a part-owner and bought a Ford Model-T, just like the one he'd had to abandon when he'd fled Sicily ahead of Mussolini's henchmen.

On the day they hired their twentieth employee, Mr. Ireland asked, "What did you do to them?" Twenty more men were waiting for the next opening.

"I gave them rules," Vincenzo replied, his English now much more fluent. He read the newspaper daily to improve his understanding of English and listened closely to nearby conversations of native-born speakers to comprehend the subtleties of the language. "An expectation that if they did as I told them, even better things were ahead. It's not just a job, but a place to belong. When you work hard, you take pride in what you do."

When a new man was hired, Vincenzo took him aside privately and explained if he ever caught the scent of alcohol on him (Prohibition was a joke in a port city full of Irish and Italian immigrants), he would be fired. If a worker was consistently late, he would be fired. If there was ever dissension in the crew, every man involved would be fired.

Morale improved dramatically.

The men often arrived early, knowing Vincenzo would always be there before them. They were well rested, clean-shaven, and enthusiastic to a degree that Mr. Ireland had never seen before. Half of every hour Vincenzo was prowling around the site, checking on the work. When a man did an especially good job, Vincenzo would praise the man in front of the other workers. He knew the words of praise, while costing him nothing, would ensure the continued efforts of the man for the next two weeks.

When a particularly difficult job was finished, Vincenzo would tell the men how much he and Mr. Ireland had made. "We made fifteen hundred on that job," he'd say, counting out that amount of money in ten-dollar denominations he'd brought along for that purpose. "And I'm taking twenty-five percent of that and dividing it up between you men for the good work you've done." Vincenzo had already calculated the extra bonus each man would receive (and sometimes he'd lowball the amount they'd actually cleared). But it provided the men with a clear demonstration that superior effort would yield superior rewards. He wanted each man to believe that if he worked hard enough, he, too, could be a king.

A cheer went up from the men when the numbers were announced. The wages were about average, but the bonuses made them among the best paid in the city. Vincenzo also calculated that being open with the men about their profits let them clearly know who was boss. And how much they could benefit by remaining in the service of an honest man.

Vincenzo wanted to leave early that day. It was Alex's fourth birthday. During his first year, he'd stopped by to visit Alex nearly every weekend. Since he had become foreman and then part-owner of the company, Vincenzo had been able to see Alex less often. Even though Vincenzo pretended his attachment to Alex was due to his help with the delivery, there was a deeper motivation. He wanted a son. And Rosina and Nick had made both Vincenzo and Mr. Patrio dual godfathers to Alex. In the Catholic faith this was a sacred, lifelong bond.

The birthday party was next weekend, but Vincenzo thought it important to present his gift on the actual day. Weeks before, he'd bought a wooden rocking horse, which had real horsehair in the mane. From the time his father had gone to prison, Vincenzo never had any presents. Yet it only seemed right the next generation shouldn't have to suffer in the way he did. The life of the next generation should be one without hardship, without suffering, and without the deformities of anger and rage.

The rocking horse was packed carefully into the back of Vincenzo's Model-T. He set it upright in the back of the car so its head stuck out the driver's side window like a curious dog. As he drove through the city, he'd eyed the little wooden horse in the rearview mirror. He laughed to himself, recalling that the first time he drove a Model-T he'd carried weapons to kill a man. Now he carried toys.

Vincenzo parked in front of the building and started to extricate the horse from the car.

"What did you get?" came a voice from above.

Vincenzo looked up to see Rosina leaning out of her window. Alex was also straining for a view, but his mother kept him back.

"Just a little something," he replied.

"What is it, Mama?" Vincenzo heard Alex ask.

Vincenzo saw Rosina turn to answer her son. "You'll see in just a minute, love." Rosina leaned out the window again. "I'll ring you in."

When Vincenzo staggered up the stairs with the heavy wooden animal, Rosina already had the door open. She was dressed in a blue skirt and white blouse, looking slim and stylish, but stood with her hands about her hips as if to demonstrate her overwhelming practicality. There was nothing false about her, and Vincenzo appreciated that.

Vincenzo brought the rocking horse up to the door and set it down. "Just a little something for my godson."

Rosina shook a finger at him in mock scolding. "You're doing even more than Nick and me!"

"You are good to your family all the time," Vincenzo said. "This is the only time I get to do something."

She gave him a serious look. "You should find yourself a good woman and settle down. Not many men care for children like you do."

"I have not found the woman I love. A man should not marry simply because it is his time. He must find the woman he would fight and die for."

"Like my sister?" she teased.

Vincenzo blushed. He went to say something when Alex came running up, dressed in a blue sailor's outfit. Vincenzo knelt and spread his arms wide. "Uncle Vin!" screamed Alex as he rushed into Vincenzo's arms. Alex felt unbelievably light, like a bubble that might float away if he wasn't careful. Every time he saw Alex, he seemed so different.

Vincenzo patted Alex on the cheek. He remembered how he had run into his father's arms as a child and felt completely safe in his embrace. His father would reach into his pocket and pull out a handful of hard, fruit-tasting candies and give them to Vincenzo.

"This is for you," said Vincenzo, pointing to the rocking horse.

Alex squealed in delight and clapped his hands. Vincenzo picked him up and placed him on the horse's back. Alex petted the horse's hair on the mane. "Soft," he said. He grasped the handles behind the head and rocked himself.

"This is too fine a gift," said Rosina.

Vincenzo smiled. "Nothing is too good for our children." He watched Alex, whose determination in rocking made him look like a future jockey.

"Well, the least I can do is get you a cup of coffee. Come inside."

Vincenzo took a seat at the small wooden table that faced the street, and they talked of the common problems of tenants and workmen. Rosina was the kind of person like Vincenzo who "took charge" with people, and he valued her insight.

The phone rang about ten minutes into their conversation, and Rosina went to pick it up.

"What do you mean, you can't find Dante?" Rosina said into the phone.

Vincenzo got up and walked into the hall to listen. He'd met Dante several times, tall and dark-haired with a large, beaklike nose, a man who acted as if the rest of the world did not pay him sufficient heed. At family dinners to which he'd been invited Vincenzo watched how Dante would disdainfully look at his wife if she held his hand or kissed him on the cheek. Jacquetta acted as if she didn't see the contempt, but when her eyes would catch Vincenzo's, there was something of a look that said, *I know.*

At those times, Vincenzo felt his anger stir and imagined doing terrible things to the man.

"You called at the store," Rosina said, "and they don't know where he is?" She listened for a moment. "You need to get to the hospital now, Jacquetta. I don't want you sitting there waiting for him to come home. Remember what happened to your sister?" She shot Vincenzo a quick smile and returned to the conversation. "Let me give Nick a call and see when we can get to you."

Rosina hung up and had the operator patch her to Nick's work. She talked quickly to him, explaining the situation, but it soon became clear it would take him more than a half hour to pick her up.

"I have my car," Vincenzo interrupted.

Rosina looked at him, then back to the phone. "Nick? Vincenzo's here, and he has his car. We'll pick her up. Meet you at the hospital."

She hung up the phone and grabbed a bulky black purse. "Get off the horse now," she told Alex, extending her hand as if he could reach across the room and take it.

"I want to ride."

"Now," she said sternly.

"Pleeeeease," Alex pleaded.

She walked over and regarded him silently. Alex looked up, stopped rocking, and reluctantly dismounted.

As they drove to Jacquetta's, the warm feelings Vincenzo had about wanting his own family hardened into concern. He drove quickly, and they rushed to the doorway of Jacquetta's house. Alex called after them from the car, but Rosina hushed him. The tiny front yard had a lawn and a small fig tree Vincenzo couldn't help noticing. Despite Rosina's excitement, he stared up at the two-story Victorian, painted sky blue and decorated with white trim. When he first arrived in America, it was a house whose price was far beyond him, but with how well things were going, he thought one day he might be able to afford it.

Rosina rapped on the door.

Vincenzo heard feet shuffling slowly across the wooden floor of the entryway. The door opened and Jacquetta appeared in white slippers and a blue night robe. As her eyes traveled from Rosina to Vincenzo, she looked placid, almost disembodied. "You got here very quickly. Would you like something to drink?"

Vincenzo was shocked by her appearance. Rosina's pregnancy had barely shown. Jacquetta's smaller, curvier figure had been swelled by at least fifty pounds.

"Jacquetta!" Rosina scolded. "Why don't you put on something a little more decent?"

"Nothing fits," Jacquetta replied in a scared little voice.

Vincenzo looked past her at the interior of the house. A large, Oriental carpet of bright blues and reds stretched under a long table with four chairs on each side and one on each end. On the table sat a centerpiece of red and white carnations. A burnished oak fireplace mantle held two silver candelabras reflected in a mirror. A large cabinet opposite was filled with plates and glasses and other utensils for sophisticated dining. It was a comfortable place to abandon a woman, Vincenzo thought.

"All right," said Rosina, still looking at her sister's peculiar choice of clothing. "We should get to the hospital."

Jacquetta nodded.

Vincenzo and Rosina led her to the car. Alex was still sitting in the back seat, pouting. Rosina told him to move up to the front seat with Vincenzo, so she could sit with Jacquetta. Alex climbed happily into the front seat. "We're the men, taking care of the women," Vincenzo said to Alex.

He laughed and repeated it to his mother. "Hey, Mama, don't worry! We'll take care of everything!"

Vincenzo started the car and pulled out into the street. Jacquetta sat quietly in the back, but gave off a disturbing sense of stillness. Vincenzo looked in the rearview mirror and saw Rosina holding her sister's hand and then heard her saying, "It's going to be all right."

Jacquetta looked blankly out the window. "He doesn't love me anymore," she said in a quiet voice.

Vincenzo drove as fast as he thought was safe to the hospital, honking at more than a few horse-drawn carts, autos, trolleys, and pedestrians. He was relieved that the carts were usually pulled by old horses that wouldn't have been frightened by the trumpets that toppled the walls of Jericho, much less an automobile.

One man ran out of the street so quickly his hat fell off.

Vincenzo didn't even brake as he ran over the fedora.

After they arrived at the hospital and Rosina was waiting with Jacquetta, Vincenzo went to find a pay phone to call Dante at the pharmacy. The assistant was unhelpful and seemed to laugh when Vincenzo demanded to know his whereabouts. A voice in the background whispered something to the assistant who suddenly became more attentive but was still unhelpful. "Let him know his wife is in the hospital getting ready to deliver his child," he said, before hanging up.

As Vincenzo hung up, he saw Nick walking toward him. He was out of breath, and his forehead was damp. The white dress shirt he was wearing with his gray suit was clinging to his chest. Vincenzo thought he must have run from the parking lot.

"Where's Rose?" Nick asked, his eyes darting from Vincenzo to the open doors of the long hospital hallway.

"With Jacquetta," Vincenzo replied.

Vincenzo liked Nick. He was a man who cared about his family. Nick was an engineer, but to Vincenzo he thought the man was more of an artist. Nick's father had been a sculptor back in Sicily, and he'd helped him in his studio. His mother and father had died young, and Nick had come to the United States when he was sixteen, settling first in Omaha, Nebraska, getting an engineering degree from Boyle's Business College, then heading to San Francisco where there were better opportunities. That was where he'd met Rosina, through some mutual friends. Nick had been so upset when Rosina had delivered early, and he hadn't been able to offer any assistance. He had taken to Vincenzo almost like a younger brother.

Nick's eyes focused on Vincenzo, and they seemed to lose their harried look. "I guess there's not much we can do now, huh?"

Vincenzo shook his head, and Nick smiled sheepishly. Alex came to his father and put an arm around his legs. Nick bent down affectionately and picked up his son. "How's my birthday boy doing? Not much of a birthday, is it?"

"It smells funny," Alex replied.

"That's because of all the medicines. But if you wait here a little longer, you'll have a new baby cousin for your birthday."

"I like the rocking horse Uncle Vinny gave me better."

Rosina came down the hallway toward them, looking worried. Nick was still holding Alex in his arms.

"How is she?" Nick asked.

"It's pretty hard on her. She's little, and they say the baby's big."

Nick drew Rosina close to him. Vincenzo knew Rosina wouldn't cry, but she needed reassurance. Nick held his wife tightly, stroking the back of her head. Vincenzo's father had held his mother in a similar manner when the police came to take him away. "We're going to have to wait," said Nick.

"You know how she makes me crazy sometimes, but she's my sister," Rosina replied, her voice becoming thick with emotion. "I remember when I was a little girl, wishing that something would happen to her because she always made me so mad. You don't think God finally heard those prayers and—"

"Don't think like that," Nick said in a soothing voice. "She's going to be all right."

For five hours they waited. Alex fell asleep on Rosina's lap. Nick told Vincenzo several times he could go home. Vincenzo nodded in acknowledgment but didn't leave.

"How can they make us wait like this?" Nick fumed at the six-hour mark. "Doctors are the most inconsiderate people on the face of the Earth!" He paced, as if he was the expectant father. Vincenzo shared Nick's nervousness. He could smell Nick's heavy perspiration and see the beads of sweat on his face. As Nick walked back and forth, he gripped and twisted his hands. Vincenzo suddenly remembered what Rosina had told him about Nick's family. Parents dead at an early age, sent off to live with relatives in the United States. Vincenzo wondered if Nick was reliving his own tragedies. He couldn't bear to think about his own family, the last image of them all dead in the front room. Did everybody have their own private hell they went to when they were most terrified?

"Have you tried giving Dante another call?" Rosina asked.

The question broke Nick's pacing. "Not for the past hour," he said.

"Why don't you?"

Nick searched through his trousers, and then looked at Rosina. "Do you have a nickel?"

Rosina opened her purse and rummaged through a morass of cosmetics, slips of paper with notes, and candies for Alex's restlessness. She finally produced a coin for Nick. He grumbled as he took it, but Vincenzo could tell he was feeling better. At least there was something he could do.

"Nothing," Nick said when he returned. "Now there's not even an answer at the store."

A doctor in a blood-spattered white smock came walking into the waiting room. He looked to be in his early forties and carried himself with the confidence of a professional, a man accustomed to discussing human afflictions in the dispassionate language of science. Rosina stood up quickly, almost spilling Alex onto the floor.

"I'm Doctor Sheffield," he said.

"Is she all right?" Rosina asked.

Her expression went from concern to desperation. Vincenzo could smell the sickly, copper odor of blood clinging to the man.

"There's been a problem."

"What?" she asked in a rush of emotion. Nick was patting her on the shoulder as if to say, *Wait a minute*, cara, *he'll tell us.*

"The baby died," Doctor Sheffield started to explain, "umbilical cord was wrapped around the neck. And your sister's had significant blood loss."

"Baby dead?" Rosina asked in a stunned whisper.

Doctor Sheffield nodded slowly.

"A boy or a girl?" Rosina asked.

"A boy."

"Jacquetta," Vincenzo said. "Will she be all right?"

The doctor looked at Vincenzo, assuming he was the husband. "If we can stop the bleeding. We've got it under control, now, but she shouldn't be moving around. The incision could easily rip open. And there's another thing. Her system's been through an ordeal, and there's been a lot of damage. I don't know if it's really advisable for her to have children in the future. It'd be very dangerous."

Vincenzo turned around and saw Dante standing behind him, wearing his white pharmacist's jacket. Even in professional attire, Vincenzo thought he still looked like a large, big-nosed bird with shellacked black hair—an arrogant, haughty raven.

"Where've you been?" Rosina demanded angrily. "Your wife has been here without you. You should be taking better care of her than having Vincenzo and me drive her to the damned hospital!"

"I had to go to Stockton to pick up some supplies," he replied quickly. "Now, where's Jacquetta?" Vincenzo knew Stockton was about a two hour drive from the city. Something wasn't adding up.

"In room 305," Nick responded.

"Are you Mr. Mercurio?" the doctor asked, his eyes shifting from Vincenzo to Dante.

"I ain't the man in the moon," Dante told him, and took off down the corridor.

"She's not supposed to see anybody now," Dr. Sheffield called out, starting after him. "Mr. Mercurio, she's resting now. You don't understand. She's had some problems. It's best that she's left alone. She's not feeling well, I assure you!"

Rosina, Nick, Vincenzo and Alex followed after the doctor, a human train of people chugging down the hall with Dante as the locomotive and Alex as the caboose. Dante turned into room 305, the doctor hot on his heels.

"Jacquetta, I'm here," Vincenzo heard Dante say when he was just outside the door.

Vincenzo entered and saw Jacquetta sitting up in bed, her bloated face a mask of anger. Her right hand was extended backwards, and she clutched a drinking glass. "Bastard!" she screamed.

Jacquetta threw the glass, and it shattered against the wall next to Dante's head. "You've been out with that salesgirl, Gina, haven't you? While I'm giving birth to your child? The reason he's dead is he didn't want you for a father!"

"I was on the road," Dante insisted.

"Liar!" Jacquetta screamed. "You were on top of that whore in some hotel! They couldn't find you because you didn't tell them where you were. But they all knew. And so do I."

"Mrs. Mercurio!" said Dr. Sheffield. He walked quickly to her bedside and pulled back the covers. She'd started to bleed again. "I'd like everybody to leave," he announced in an angry voice. "I told you not to come here. She needs rest."

Jacquetta lay back, drained by her outburst. Her face was pasty white, and her arms and legs looked paralyzed. Vincenzo had the awful thought that she looked like an empty bottle of wine. The doctor raised her gown over her knees.

"We should leave," said Nick. He put his arms around Rosina and Alex and herded them toward the door. Dante followed, reluctantly.

"I need some towels! Bandages and gauze as well!" Dr. Sheffield shouted past them.

A nurse appeared at the doorway, nodded, and rushed away. Vincenzo looked back at Jacquetta, covers pulled down, hospital gown pulled up, Dr. Sheffield's face stretched tight with concern as he pressed some sheets between her legs to staunch the flow of blood. The sight made Vincenzo feel that she'd been violated beyond reason, as the fascists had done to his sister.

He felt a cold wave of hatred wash over him and held in his mind for a moment, a comforting picture of Dante dead.

Chapter Six

IN THE FOLLOWING YEARS, VINCENZO SAW little of Jacquetta and Dante. He knew through Rosina they'd had no more children. He doubted Jacquetta would ever invite Dante into her bed, again. Dante prospered, and Vincenzo heard gossip that Dante had moved from shop girls to show girls, living on the edge of the Jazz Age. Vincenzo retained his tie to Nick and Rosina's family world in the tight-knit Italian community of San Francisco. He watched with pleasure and envy as Alex grew from a little four-year-old boy into a big boy of seven with an increasingly independent mind. Gradually, Vincenzo thought less about the terrible events that drove him to America. His parents and sister were still a burning memory, but more and more distant.

Vincenzo also prospered. When Mr. Ireland retired from the construction business because of his health, Vincenzo bought him out. He worked as hard as ever and allowed himself few luxuries. By 1929, Vincenzo's personal savings amounted to thirty thousand dollars. The city was rife with wild speculation, but he kept stacks of bills tucked in his mattress and a pistol on his nightstand. The stock market crash that October caught everyone by surprise.

Vincenzo was untouched by it, and soon realized the financial panic offered him opportunities. Desperate men in well-cut suits showed up unannounced at his office and pleaded for loans. He sent them all away and waited.

Finally, he heard a rumor that interested him.

A telephone call confirmed it, and a plan was set in motion. A few days later he set out with two friends, Tommy LaRocca and Paulie Spinoza, for the hills of Pacific Heights.

It was early evening when Vincenzo stopped by a large mansion that would have likely been the residence of a minor Duke or Count back in Italy. The three of them climbed a wide staircase to the front door. Still limping slightly, Vincenzo balanced his weight with a heavy satchel in one hand. "Knock on the door, Tommy," he said.

"Do you think this is right, boss?" Tommy LaRocca asked. Since the time Vincenzo became foreman, Tommy LaRocca had been his most trusted worker. He'd come from the poorest part of New York's Little Italy, a hustler, pool shark, and bag man for the local hoods until he caught the eye of a capo's girl and had to run. They called him "the sheik" because of his long eyelashes and full sensuous lips. Vincenzo found him useful.

"Sure it's right," answered Paulie Spinoza. "Vincenzo ever steered us wrong before?" Paulie was a wall of a man who could make a heavyweight fighter nervous. "You and me got nothing before him. Now look at what nice clothes we got." He touched the lapels of his gray suit and ran his fingers through his slick hair, unaware he looked like a gladiator dressed for a tea party. Vincenzo looked at the two men, realizing that hard work and the threat of menace were a hard combination to beat.

"Knock on the door, Tommy," Vincenzo repeated.

Tommy picked up the heavy brass ring, brought it down with three heavy clangs, and then looked nervously about. The exclusive Pacific Heights enclave where the captains and barons of industry lived was populated by politicians and lawyers as well, all living in great mansions that looked down on the Bay and the people below. In the early morning you could see the fishing fleets from Fisherman's Wharf, crewed mostly by Italians and Portuguese, heading out into the Pacific, and then returning in the afternoon or evening. The early evening air was bracing, cold, and wet. In the distance, a wall of fog swirled just outside the Golden Gate like a giant wave about to crash into San Francisco.

From inside, the click of fine shoes on marble sounded. The door was opened by a man of about fifty, dressed in a tailored English suit. Vincenzo smiled like a hawk fixed on a rabbit.

"My deliverance has arrived," said Mr. Ricci in a booming voice.

He reached out a hand to Vincenzo and shook it vigorously.

"Hello," Vincenzo replied.

Mr. Ricci looked at Tommy and Paulie, then barely at Vincenzo. "I thought we were going to do this privately. I don't really want anybody knowing about—"

"They won't talk."

Mr. Ricci looked again at the men and shrugged. "Please come in." Vincenzo motioned for Paulie and Tommy to precede him into the house. Vincenzo liked it that way, entering as if he was a king or priest proceeding to the altar. He looked around, noticing the Italian marble and large oil paintings of Paris and London on the wall.

"I almost thought you weren't coming," said Mr. Ricci. "You're over an hour and a half late."

"It took me a while to get the money," Vincenzo lied. The cash had been slipped from his mattress within a matter of seconds. It made him feel secure at night, knowing that any burglar would have to risk a bullet to the head to get the money.

Now he was going to buy something no thief could steal.

"I don't mean to sound ungrateful," said Mr. Ricci as he led them into the living room. "It's just that I've been so very worried. I know half a dozen wealthy men who will be absolutely wiped out in the next few days."

Vincenzo admired the room. The furniture was a mix of red, Victorian high-backed chairs, couches, and a life-sized wooden Indian with red war paint at a window facing the bay. Because of the steep elevation of the hill, the room appeared to be perched on the edge of a cliff.

Vincenzo liked the house very much.

He sat down in the center of the couch and spread his arms along the back like a great bird of prey. Tommy and Paulie took chairs on each side of the couch. Mr. Ricci looked for a place to sit. The only thing at hand was a small stool. He pulled it to the couch and sat down like a reprimanded schoolboy.

"Do you understand my situation and my needs?" asked Mr. Ricci.

"You had nearly thirty thousand worth of stocks that you purchased for three thousand dollars. It's the 'option' system where for a small price you own a large amount of stock. However, if the stock goes down, you need to cover it all. You've come up with about five thousand in cash, but that still leaves you exposed. They will take all your properties to cover the losses."

"I've spent my life building those properties," he said heatedly. "They're worth more than two hundred and fifty thousand dollars, and you know it."

Vincenzo nodded. "I do know that, especially since I built five of them."

Mr. Ricci gave him a look of gruff approval. "When Jim Ireland sold the business to you because of his heart condition, I wasn't too sure. But there isn't a better builder in the city or one who sticks to his price more than you."

Vincenzo smiled. He knew he was a good builder. There was something so redeeming about looking at a dusty patch of ground, imagining the foundations being laid and hardening in the open air; the posts sprouting like the first tender shoots of spring; the steel skeleton being assembled like a jigsaw puzzle; the flesh-like covering of wood and stone and paint; then having it burst forth from his imagination into magnificent reality. He tried to forget past successes and concentrate on Mr. Ricci. Yes, Vincenzo had built his reputation. Now it was time to cash in, as the Americans liked to say.

"I'm still confused though as to why you asked me for help," Vincenzo asked, stretching out the torture of the man. "Weren't there at least a few of your wealthy friends who weren't so foolish?"

"Well, to be quite honest," said Mr. Ricci, holding his hands together, "there's a certain way one acts around my group of friends. Now, don't get me wrong, they're a fine bunch of fellows, but if I was to go to them. . ."

"They would mock you."

"Something like that."

"It's pride that keeps you from going to them, yes?"

"Partly."

"And the other?"

"I don't know what they would do if they saw my vulnerability."

The realization came to Vincenzo, and he almost laughed. It was the same in every country. "Your friends are wolves, that's what you're saying, isn't it? They act like they're above it all, that they are of the highest class, and yet when the lights go out, it's still a knife fight. Am I right?"

Mr. Ricci changed the subject. "I've made a generous offer. Twenty-five thousand dollars and you get fifty percent ownership of my buildings until I can repay you. During that time, you'll also be sharing equally in all the rents. The moment I get out of this trouble I'll pay you back at the full price. You'll make five times your investment."

Vincenzo nodded toward the satchel he'd been carrying. Paulie picked it up and opened it. Mr. Ricci's eyes brightened.

Deliverance.

Vincenzo nodded again to Paulie, who snapped it shut.

"I was thinking last night this really isn't such a good deal," said Vincenzo. "At eight tomorrow morning, you'll have to show up with this money or they take everything. You'll be lucky to get a broken-down horse and wagon to sell rags."

Mr. Ricci's face took on a concerned expression, his white mustache twitching at the corner like a fussy house cat's whiskers. Vincenzo let the silence settle between them, as his eyes locked with Mr. Ricci's.

In an elevated tone, Mr. Ricci asked, "Do you mean to send me into ruin?"

Vincenzo felt Mr. Ricci was trying to act in the same way as when Vincenzo had been his paid worker. Asking for something different than the blueprints, asking if Vincenzo could make the change without raising the cost, and Vincenzo quickly trying in his head to figure out how to make it work and not risk a loss on the project.

Vincenzo sat forward on the couch. "I want you to keep this house. I've got thirty thousand in cash. That's five thousand more than you need. But you sign over all your properties to me. This is a purchase, not a loan."

"This is outrageous!" Mr. Ricci stood quickly and sent his stool flying backwards. Paulie and Tommy rose and moved protectively toward Vincenzo, but he motioned for them to sit down. They cautiously took their seats again.

"You told me on Friday evening that everything would be fine," Mr. Ricci continued. "There were other people I could have contacted. Now it's too late!"

"You know that's not true," said Vincenzo calmly. "Otherwise, you would have contacted them before calling me. All of you rich people have been very foolish. Now you're asking for my help. You treated me like I was a servant and now that you've fallen below me you want to be treated like an equal."

Mr. Ricci pointed a trembling finger at Vincenzo. "I've worked a lifetime for what I have!"

Vincenzo shrugged, as if Ricci had merely lost a two-dollar card game.

Mr. Ricci swung quickly at Vincenzo, striking a hard blow against his cheek. His head snapped back, but he remained sitting. Paulie and Tommy were up in a flash, pinning Mr. Ricci's arms behind him.

"Are you okay, Vince?" Tommy asked.

Vincenzo put his hand to his cheek. It felt as if his entire jawbone had been ripped out of its socket. Cautiously he moved his jaw back and forth. It still seemed to work.

"Hurts bad," said Vincenzo, still seeing stars.

"Well, I'm glad!" Mr. Ricci stared with the vehemence of a caged animal. "Damned thief trying to take what I made with these two hands." He tried to put them out in front of him but could only get them up halfway because of the grip the two men had on him.

Vincenzo stood up. He leaned closer to Mr. Ricci. "You've angered me," he said.

"Hah! I've angered you? Now, there's a laugh. You come here and try to take over everything I've built and say *I've* angered *you*?"

Vincenzo motioned for Paulie and Tommy to let Mr. Ricci go. "If you don't want my deal, that's fine with me."

With slow, deliberate drama, Vincenzo walked over to the chair with the satchel. He picked it up and walked back to Mr. Ricci. "But I want you to know something. I'm your best hope. Look out there." Vincenzo pointed at the glittering, darkened San Francisco landscape outside the window, half-concealed by the gossamer fog that had crept in. "Your only other chance is out there. Why don't you just go out there now? Knock on a friend's door. 'Oh, hello, Mr. Ricci,' they'll say. 'Why don't you come in and have a cup of coffee? Please, sit down, won't you?' And after you've mixed in your cream and sugar and taken a few sips, you'll sheepishly say, 'I've got a problem I need to tell you about.' And you'll tell them, and the wife will give her husband a look like you've announced you have some terrible contagious disease. And he'll give her a look that says, 'Don't worry, honey. I won't do anything foolish.' And you'll say, 'It's only twenty-five thousand dollars, and I know I can get it back to you very soon. I've always been a man of my word.' And as you're saying these things, you'll get a sick feeling in the pit of your stomach that they're not buying the bullshit you're selling. They'll offer you a room until you can get back on your feet, a week, maybe more if you need it, but they won't part with their money. They know they need it now, just as much as you do. So go! Go if you don't want my deal. Go out into the night and find your deliverance." He started to leave, with Tommy and Paulie following behind him.

"Wait!" Mr. Ricci cried.

"Yes?" Vincenzo stopped at the threshold of the living room.

"I'll get five thousand dollars out of this?"

"You'll be able to start over again. And I'm sure you'll find many ways to take advantage of the distress of others at this time of opportunity. We're not so different, you and I."

Mr. Ricci looked at him, then at the other two men. He appeared he had something he wanted to say, something high-minded like how the two of them were completely different, and yet the thought seemed to die inside of him, and he simply said, "Fine, I'll do it."

Vincenzo smiled. "You see, I've performed a great service. I've snatched you from the fire that is now consuming so many of your friends."

"Well, don't expect me to thank you too much. At least I'll be able to keep up appearances. Tomorrow morning, I won't lose my house like some people I know."

"What do you mean?" asked Vincenzo. "Your house is part of the deal. I haven't seen much of it, but I like it. I assume the rest will be to my satisfaction."

Mr. Ricci's face reddened, but Vincenzo knew his anger would not last. When a man's beaten, he thought, he stays beaten. "But you said I'd be able to keep my-my house," Mr. Ricci stammered. "What will Juliana say when I tell her we have to move? She loves this house." He began to shake so much that Vincenzo thought he might break down in front of him.

"That was before you struck me," said Vincenzo, rubbing his still aching jaw. "Besides, I'm certain there will be many suitable accommodations available to you at the current time."

"Okay," Mr. Ricci said in almost a whisper.

"Meet me at my attorney's office at seven tomorrow morning, and we'll get all the documents signed. You'll have your money by nine tomorrow."

This time Vincenzo walked out first, and Paulie and Tommy raced to keep up.

* * *

"I'M GLAD TO see you, Vincenzo," said Mr. Patrio.

Mr. Patrio was standing at the doorway of his castle-like home at one of the highest points of Pacific Heights. Vincenzo had heard the home was built shortly after the turn of the century by a flour merchant who was enchanted as a young boy by stories of knights, castles, and maidens in distress.

A week had passed since Vincenzo had gone to Ricci's mansion in the same part of the city. He wasn't sure why Mr. Patrio wanted to see him.

"I think you know my two men, Tommy LaRocca and Paulie Spinoza," said Vincenzo.

Mr. Patrio nodded to them but did not shake their hands. "Actually," he said, "I was hoping to speak to you privately. If you two gentlemen wouldn't mind, I recommend Donatello's at the bottom of the hill. Tell Luigi I sent you and put the meal on my tab."

Paulie and Tommy looked at each other, then at Vincenzo. He nodded at them to leave.

"The tortellini is excellent," Mr. Patrio called after them. "I suggest it with the pesto sauce."

Mr. Patrio ushered Vincenzo inside. The entryway was large, with a wide stairway leading to the second floor. The walls were lined with paintings of the American west and an arrangement of Indian arrows. One painting caught his eye, an Indian on a horse with his head bowed in defeat. The title was *End of the Trail*. "This is the first time I've been to your house," Vincenzo murmured. "It's very impressive."

"I invite you to my home because we talk as equals," said Mr. Patrio. "I think we'll be more comfortable in the parlor."

Vincenzo followed Mr. Patrio into a Turkish-style smoking room. He noticed the lingering aroma of expensive cigars. He'd heard Turkish parlors were popular among wealthy men, but he'd never seen one. The room had a life-size statue of a golden cobra with red, jewel-like eyes, the bust of a Turk in a red fez with a gold tassel, and a framed portrait of Queen Victoria. Resting on the player piano in the corner was a small Egyptian figure with a man's body and the head of a lion, sitting on a throne.

Mr. Patrio motioned Vincenzo to two, red stuffed chairs facing each other. Vincenzo had grown up in a small house, with stark white walls, thrown away furniture, and a dirt floor. As Mr. Patrio settled into his chair, he reminded Vincenzo of the Egyptian lion god sitting on the piano, his aged, yet clear eyes conveying the easy confidence of a ruler.

"I want you to know, Vincenzo, you've done a great deal that's made me proud to know you," began Mr. Patrio. "You work hard, you don't complain, and the men you employ do good work. You and I are a great deal alike. We're the kind of men who can change things. Most men sit on the edge of life, letting things be done to them. We're not like that. But the real question is: what do you want to do? What do you stand for?"

"I stand for myself."

"That way holds disappointment, madness, and ruin."

"You brought me here to talk about Louis Ricci?"

"Yes," Mr. Patrio replied. "He's been a good friend over the years. A man of the community. I wish he'd come to me first, but he was afraid of looking foolish. I would've helped. Maybe I still can, although I'm stretched pretty thin with the number of people I'm helping."

"He made an offer," said Vincenzo. "I suggested another. He accepted. That's business."

"That's not business," said Mr. Patrio, shaking his head. "You took advantage when a man had stumbled. There's no honor in that."

"Your words, not mine."

"When a man is young, he asks the question, what can I do? When he's older, if he's learned, he asks, what should I do? Can you take Louis Ricci's properties? Yes. Perhaps there is even some justice in it, as he invested in something risky. But is there another way? Instead of seeking to take advantage of another's weakness, can we figure out a way to combine our strengths? We are all weak, and in desperate need of grace. I've been worried about you for a few years, Vincenzo. Ever since I heard about you firing Pete Goodman. He was your friend."

"He wasn't a good worker," said Vincenzo.

"Do you know I started him in his own construction company? It's doing very well."

"Then it appears my firing him changed some of his habits. You should thank me."

"People like Pete, so easily liked. I don't know if that's going to happen to you."

Vincenzo stood up. He didn't want to be in this room anymore. It felt hot and close. The confidence of older men aggravated him. Even at his death, the Duke had been adamant about Vincenzo's eventual demise.

How could old men claim such foresight, he wondered, *when it was clear the world around them offered such little evidence?* If they were so wise, why was the Duke dead and Mr. Patrio trying to admonish him like an angry father?

Vincenzo knew the truth.

They were weaker than they believed, and he was stronger. It terrified them, and they sought to undercut his strength. Vincenzo replied, "If the only reason you've asked me here is to give me a lecture, I think I'll go."

Mr. Patrio got up and gripped Vincenzo's arm at the bicep. Even in his early sixties, Patrio had an iron-clad grip that was painful. "Goddamn it, Vincenzo, people like us have responsibilities. We're not thieves, we're businessmen. We should be like gardeners, trying to make the rest of the world beautiful. You'll make it a wasteland."

Vincenzo broke his grip. "It's not up to me to think for other people. I didn't tell Ricci to buy those stocks. I just saw an opportunity, and I took it." He started to walk out.

"I'll give you another opportunity," cried out Mr. Patrio.

Vincenzo spun around. "What? You want me to just give Ricci back his properties and work with him? Well, I won't. I made a good deal, and I intend to keep it."

"That wasn't the offer I was going to make," said Mr. Patrio. "I would've made that offer if I thought you were a different kind of man. But you're not. At least, not yet. No. My offer is this: Sixty thousand and you give Louis Ricci everything back, including his house. You worked six years to get your thirty thousand. It's been a week since you took his properties. You'll get to double your money for just stepping aside and being a decent human being. What do you say?"

Vincenzo was intrigued by the proposal. Mr. Patrio was wealthy, but certainly did not have an extra sixty thousand available for the benefit of his friends. "And what's in it for you?" Vincenzo asked.

"The truth is I don't want to see Louis ruined. We've talked about some arrangement where I'll get paid back when he gets on his feet again, but the particulars don't interest me. We are in dark times, my friend. We can be wolves, or we can be shepherds."

"Shepherds often fail. They lose members of the flock to predators, thieves, the weather, they can even die."

"So do wolves. But I would much rather meet my God as a shepherd, than a wolf."

"And is this fair for me?" Vincenzo asked. "Ricci so proudly told me his property was worth over two hundred thousand dollars. If you're being fair to me, that's what you should offer."

"The properties are not worth that anymore. They will not be worth that again for many years."

"I only ask for the value he claimed."

"I can offer you double your money for a week of doing nothing. And I've got something else for you." Mr. Patrio reached down into the coils of the cobra statue and pulled out what looked like a black accounting book. While Vincenzo had not seen it before, it did look familiar. "This is a copy of my address book. Every single entry is reproduced here. Grace spent many hours doing this. I can't tell you how much she complained. I'll give it to you and let you use my name with every single person. There are congressmen, senators, governors, and captains of industry. It's taken me nearly forty years to compile this list. They will do favors for you because of my name that they wouldn't do for any other person. That's what it means to have a good reputation. One finds others who value the same ideals. You do not have a good reputation yet. But you could choose a different path."

Vincenzo looked curiously at the book. He remembered the day he'd first seen the original book in Mr. Patrio's office and hungered for such a tool. But he'd been successful without it. He'd depended on people before, and his family had died because of his mistake. A wise man stands alone. "What use is a good name in a time of wolves?" he asked.

"Damn it, Vincenzo, what is this infernal thing that makes you so cruel? I've never seen it so strong in a person before. You could be a great man and yet you throw it away because of pettiness."

Vincenzo was becoming angered. Comfortable, old men sitting on plush chairs in large mansions could debate morality all day long, but they were hypocrites. They all made their money in the same ruthless way. And if in their later years they developed a conscience about it, well, everybody has their delusions. Vincenzo said, "You don't understand what terrible things happen to men who don't have power. To have power means to be safe in your own home. To have power means knowing tomorrow you'll eat. To have power means being able to protect the people you care about."

Mr. Patrio put a hand to his chin, a slight smile playing at the corner of his lips, as if he'd just cracked a very difficult puzzle.

"That's it, isn't it? You failed to protect somebody. That's the dark secret you're running from. A favorite brother? A falling out with a local Don in Sicily? A vendetta between families? I have my own darkness, Vincenzo, but I left it out on the frontier when I killed those Indian braves. I suggest you leave yours behind and concentrate on the here and now. Every saint has a past and every sinner a future. But you need to reach for the light; it won't come to you."

"They killed my entire family." The words slipped so quickly and angrily from Vincenzo's lips he was almost unaware of having said them until he saw the look on Mr. Patrio's face.

"Mother of God," said Mr. Patrio, his eyes widening.

Vincenzo felt tears welling in his eyes and a hot flush like shame coming to his face. In seven years, he had not cried. He had not cried since the day his family was slaughtered. And on that day, he had wept unabashedly, knowing those tears would turn to stone in his heart. He remembered how he'd wept over his mother, her body on the threshold between their dining area and the kitchen, shot in the back as she tried to flee. He recalled the oddly content look on the dead face of his sister, the first tender blossoms of her womanhood trampled underfoot. He remembered his father, seated at the head of the table on a throne of death with his blood splashed on the wall behind him. Vincenzo knew with clarity that they'd killed his father first, leaving his mother and sister without hope of a protector.

Every hour of every waking day these thoughts and many like them flashed through his mind, though he tried to forget them, to make them hazier. At night, they hovered on the edge of his dreams. Sometimes his mother would appear in his dreams and run her fingers through his hair as she had just before he fell asleep when he was a child, telling him everything would be all right. But she spoke in the same tone she'd used during the years of his father's imprisonment, when she assured him that his father would soon be home. He remembered speaking the same words he'd used those many years ago, "I'll protect us, Mama."

"I'm going now," Vincenzo told Mr. Patrio. He started to walk down the hallway, feeling the hot tears streaming down his face, and it humiliated him. Mr. Patrio was close on his heels. Vincenzo limped quickly toward the front door, extended his hand, and flung the door open. The bright sunlight, so unusual for San Francisco, assaulted his eyes. He felt like some nocturnal, unholy creature, unused to the garish daylight. With fast, uncertain steps, he headed for the street.

"I can help you, Vincenzo!" called Mr. Patrio. "Don't let this destroy you. I can help!"

Vincenzo knew he was beyond any sort of help Mr. Patrio could give. God Himself had set his feet on the devil's road.

Chapter Seven

DANTE CLUTCHED GINA PALONI'S HAND AS she rested against him. He knew Jacquetta would be expecting him for dinner. It was getting late, close to five thirty, but he knew he could be home within an hour. Early that morning he and Gina had left San Francisco for Carmel in his Model J Dusenberg. They arrived at the coast just as the sun was rising behind a thick banner of fog. They walked along the beach with its dark, crashing waters, working up an appetite while they huddled together against the cold Pacific wind.

At noon they had oysters for lunch at a small inn, and then took a room with a view of the ocean. They undressed so quickly and fell on the bed that they didn't notice an overproducing steam heater. Dante began to sweat, and it doubled his exertions. It was almost like making love in a sauna. Gina asked several times if he'd be more comfortable in another room, but Dante didn't want to stop. That was one thing about Gina he liked; she was always vitally concerned about his comfort. Jacquetta was always concerned about her own comfort. They slept a few hours, naked and clinging together, woke and showered together, tried another position, then dressed.

Dante did not love Gina, but he often found himself drifting back to her after his affairs with other women, usually shop girls, actresses, or dancers. She didn't mind not speaking for hours, just as long as she could be with him. And she was willing to do anything sexually that he asked. However, after a certain amount of time he felt he'd run through most of his fantasies and realized he was spending his time with a relatively simple and stupid woman.

He still loved Jacquetta, but like a childhood friend with whom distant feelings of intimacy can never be restored. His father told him he could never stick with anything, pointing out the jobs he'd drifted from until he put his foot down and said Dante had to come into the family business. He'd dedicated himself to the pharmacy, and yet he still felt like he was unmoored in the other parts of his life. Dante wondered if he was capable of true commitment to anything.

Half an hour later, with no more than a few words of conversation between them, Dante reached the bottom of California Street in San Francisco. She was dozing, her head resting in his lap, and his arm over her shoulder. Gina lived in an apartment on Russian Hill, the nicest place he could afford without raising Jacquetta's suspicions about the missing money. The amount he made each month from the sale of alcohol in "medicinal bottles" was more than enough to conceal Gina's expenses, but Jacquetta still suspected.

After the scene in the delivery room, Jacquetta had taken to sleeping in a different room of the house, and came to him only infrequently, when she needed to take the edge off her frustration. The next morning, she could not stand to look at him over the breakfast table, her face a scarlet mask of rage and shame.

Gina stirred against him as Dante proceeded into the intersection. He loved the silky feel of her skin. She had the most wonderful skin, soft and warm. The sensation of her cheek passing across his arm made him turn toward her. She looked up at him with that warm, vacant expression of hers and he smiled. She rubbed her hand along his thigh, stopping at his hardness and gently squeezing him.

"I want it again when we get to my apartment," said Gina.

He knew this was the currency between them, sex and caring for cash, the simulation of love and commitment, a fantasy that neither of them looked at too closely.

Dante kissed her full on the mouth, and she reached lower, squeezing his testicles and feeling his excitement quicken.

* * *

AT THE TOP of California Street, the driver of a large produce truck was unloading fruits and vegetables to the Fairmont Hotel. The driver had set the parking brake before leaving the cab but had not checked the brakes for ten months. They'd been worn thin by months of traveling up and down the city's hills and long sojourns to the Central Valley where dust bowl refugees picked California's bounty. The first sound that caught the driver's attention was the creaking of the truck as the parking brakes failed. The truck moved slowly at first, allowing the driver to jump onto the running boards.

He thought he'd be able to get into the cab and stop the truck in time. The driver had the door open and was about to get in, when the truck hit an intersection landing, breaching like a great whale. The driver was tossed from the truck and fell hard on the pavement, snapping his arm. The four-ton truck continued its headlong flight down California Street, the driver yelling in warning and pain, but the traffic continued on its unsuspecting course.

When Dante parted from Gina's lips, he saw the menacing grill of the leviathan truck, a cruel metal face thundering toward him at forty miles an hour.

It was the last thing either of them ever saw.

* * *

JACQUETTA FELT GOOD as she neared her house, her arms full from a day of shopping along Union Street. At first, it had given her little pleasure to know she could walk through the stores and purchase anything she wanted without raising Dante's anger.

She'd been the victor in the war over Dante's stinginess, but in the aftermath of resigned calm, it had been a cold peace.

He rarely came to her anymore, and she wondered if she went to his bed more than he came to hers. She missed that part of the marriage to which Dante had initiated her. Talking to other women didn't help. Most of them counted her fortunate to be done with that part of the marriage. But to Jacquetta it wasn't a blessing, it was a curse. She thought of her passionate nature, now so constricted and strangled, as she left that morning.

But then she'd seen a stylish red hat, a blue dress that revealed just enough to make her feel attractive but not wanton, and a gold necklace that completed the outfit. She pictured herself in the outfit and the jewels, walking down the street and attracting the attention of men who'd smile and tip their hats to her. And that would be enough for now. At their wedding, the priest said there would be a time for everything in their marriage. Jacquetta thought of this as the dark time of their love and hoped the sunshine would someday return.

As Jacquetta approached her house, she saw Rosina, Nick, and Alex standing at the front door. They were almost concealed by the hanging branches of the weeping willow that stood in the front garden. There was a small lawn in front of the house and a garden with rose bushes and trellises thick with vines. Although they'd had a much larger garden when she was growing up in Sicily, this seemed the perfect little city garden to her. In the early days of their marriage, Dante had put a table and chairs in the garden, and Jacquetta would serve a breakfast of eggs, Italian sausage, sourdough muffins, orange juice, and coffee. It had been a pleasant and restful time, the kind Jacquetta hoped might return.

Rosina often appeared at her door like this when Nick had a sudden desire to go out for a night on the town. Alex was always excited to go over to his Aunt Jacquetta and Uncle Dante's home, and, most nights, Jacquetta didn't want to let her nephew go. But something was different this time. Rosina's face looked pale and strained, and she clutched Alex's hand tightly.

"I have some terrible news," said Rosina as Jacquetta drew near.

A terrible coldness gripped Jacquetta's stomach. Jacquetta knew it wasn't something wrong with Nick and Alex because they were close beside her. "W-what?" she stammered.

"Dante," she said, her voice stiffening. "He's been in an automobile wreck. He's in the hospital. They don't expect him to. . ."
her voice broke off. "We've already called a priest."

The news produced only a dull response in Jacquetta. Maybe it
was shock, but she didn't think so. She suddenly knew she didn't
love her husband anymore. Passion had turned into comfort, then
boredom, and Jacquetta suspected betrayal. Death had been his
final escape. "Let me drop these things in the house, and I'll be
along." She handed one of the packages to Alex and looked for
her house key.

"There's more you should know," said Rosina.

A prickly feeling at the back of her neck told her she didn't
want to hear Rosina's news. Jacquetta found the key and opened
the door. In her mind, all things had been settled. Dante had been
a poor husband and was now going to die. She would give his memory the appropriate amount of respect, but in truth her heart would
be untouched. He'd left her long ago. When she turned to take the
bag from Alex, she looked at her sister and asked, "What?"

"Dante wasn't alone."

Jacquetta nodded. From the tone of her voice, Jacquetta knew
Dante had been with another woman. "Who was it?" she asked.

"Gina Paloni."

"Bastard," she murmured. Jacquetta had even hired the little
bitch for the pharmacy.

She'd been so sweet at first, then started asking personal questions, like why she and Dante didn't have any children, or giving
Jacquetta unsolicited advice on how to apply her lipstick and eye-
liner. "A woman should always be thinking of ways to be more
attractive to her man," she'd told Jacquetta in one of their early
interactions, as if they were the closest of friends.

But Jacquetta had seen a completely different person appear
whenever Dante was around.

Then Gina was attentive, sweet, and mildly stupid. But Jacquetta
knew it was an act, letting a man think there was nothing more in

your pretty little head than being around him. Within two months Jacquetta was demanding she be fired, but Dante just laughed at her. "The customers like her," he'd said. Yeah, because she smiled like a chorus girl, showed her cleavage, and shook her cheating little ass as much as possible whenever she pranced down the aisles as she was restocking supplies.

"We should be going," urged Rosina. "From what the doctor said there's not much time."

"I'm not going," Jacquetta answered.

Rosina's eyes grew wide. "What?" she asked.

"I'm not going," she said again. This time she felt a peculiar feeling of strength seep into her body. It was as if a great, crushing weight had been lifted from her and she felt . . . almost happy.

"But he's your husband, and he's dying."

"He was once my husband," Jacquetta said softly. "And I loved him then. But he left me." Her tone grew sharp. "I was supposed to have a life and all I had was a charade. It's been years since he's done a single kind thing. It wouldn't have taken much, a smile, a compliment, what does that cost? Dante once had a wife, but he couldn't keep her." Jacquetta pushed open the door, walked in, and dropped the bags on the floor.

"It doesn't matter what he did," argued Rosina. "That's in the past. He's dying. This is your one chance to say goodbye."

Jacquetta looked at her sister. Good Rosina. She was always trying to make people happy, to do the right thing. She couldn't understand there was nothing good here. "It does matter, Rose. He took a vow, and he broke it. I don't hate him. It's just that he means nothing to me. People die every day, and it doesn't touch us. He was just one of those people." She started to close the door.

Rosina put out a hand to keep the door from closing. "I'm going to the hospital to see your husband. Are you coming?"

Jacquetta shook her head. "I wish I could mourn for him, but I can't. Please leave me alone, Rose." She started to close the door again. Before it closed completely, Rosina stopped it. "We've got to go to the hospital, honey. I know you're upset, but even if you're not doing it for him, do it for yourself. You've got to say good-bye, make your peace."

"I already made my peace."

"We're going," said Rosina, releasing the door. "If you change your mind, that's where we'll be."

Jacquetta nodded to her sister and closed the door. She picked up her bags, walked down the hallway, and placed the bags on the dining room table. She pulled out the red hat and put it on her head, extracted the blue dress, and went to apprise herself in the mirror.

Yes, they'd go together beautifully.

* * *

Vincenzo sat in the back of the church for Dante's funeral. Tommy and Paulie volunteered to go with him, but Vincenzo wanted to be alone. He'd never forgotten the electricity of the first day he met Jacquetta. Her miscarriage had affected him deeply and made him keep his distance. In Sicily, there was a joke that a beautiful woman was more dangerous than any gun.

And yet, there was always something pulling him back to her.

They'd meet on the street, and she'd ask about his business, then tease him about whether he'd ever marry. Vincenzo considered himself slow, plodding, and uninteresting, always about the work. But with her he felt transformed.

In dreams, he often felt her lips against his, heard her deep, breathy voice speaking softly to him, and joined in the laughter of lovers discovering each other's secret lands. There'd been others in his life, but they were only fleeting encounters with women he imagined to be like Jacquetta, but who inevitably disappointed. These artificial courtships would end in a few weeks, and he'd soon see them on the arm of another and feel nothing.

He even told several women they were lucky to have escaped him for something better.

To his surprise, many remained friendly, and even seemed to regard him with an unspoken understanding, as if they too were irredeemably broken. One dark-haired, serious schoolteacher gave him a handwritten copy of her favorite poem. It was a sad verse, full of longing and unquenchable desires. He still kept it in his wallet, folded in sections where it lay nestled against his dollar bills.

However, today's grieving widow was the only woman on his mind.

The crowd at Saints Peter and Paul Catholic Church in North Beach was large, with men dressed in dark suits and bowties, women in dresses of somber colors, black or dark blue, and children who were having trouble keeping quiet. The casket at the front was surrounded by a jungle of flowers, as if Dante had been a favored son, but there was little weeping.

Vincenzo thought the attitude of the congregation was of interested sadness. Dante's death along with Gina's had raised suspicion to a near certainty. Everyone's eyes focused on Jacquetta in the front pew, dressed in black with a veil concealing her face, but apparently not crying. Rosina sat next to her, patting her hand, and whispering. Nick sat on Jacquetta's other side, trying to keep a squirming Alex quiet.

Gina Paloni's funeral had been held the previous day. Vincenzo heard it was a small gathering, the priest in a hurry to be done with the ceremony. It seemed hypocritical that the mistress received a hasty burial, but the adulterous husband was given all the honors of the Church. In the pew behind Jacquetta were three city council members, a congressman, A. P. Giannini, founder of the Bank of Italy, and next to him, Mr. Patrio. The two men leaned toward each other and talked in hushed tones of easy familiarity. Vincenzo knew they'd been friends since they were both young men. He envied Mr. Patrio for being A. P. Giannini's builder of choice.

The bishop of San Francisco appeared, a thin, frail scarecrow of a man in white robes. He recalled Dante as an altar boy when he himself was a young parish priest, and how God had called Dante to serve at the greatest altar.

At the end of the eulogy the congregation seemed to exhibit little emotion. A man lived and a man died, seemed to be the feeling in the church. In a regular funeral, the bishop's words would calm the troubled souls of those left behind, one might hear the quiet sobs of friends or family members, but few seemed disturbed. Dante was disliked by most people, even some of his customers at the pharmacy.

Mourners began to file past the body. Vincenzo could see that Rosina had to prod her sister to stand beside the casket. Jacquetta stood defiantly beside her husband's lifeless body, refusing to bow her head to say a prayer. Vincenzo watched with admiration as she ignored disapproving stares, then after a few moments took her seat again.

A reception was held at Jacquetta's house and somber people milled about with small plates of food.

Vincenzo ran into Mr. Patrio at one of the food tables and they had a pleasant conversation, but Vincenzo knew the old man was just being polite. A bond had been broken between them and could not be repaired. Mr. Patrio informed him that he was helping Mr. Ricci start a new construction company with Pete Goodman, as if he was talking about the travails of a local sports team.

On a high-backed Victorian couch in the living room, Jacquetta received mourners. They'd take her hand and pat it while saying kind words about Dante, then move on. Vincenzo waited in line, and finally reached her. Her face was barely visible under the veil, but he thought he saw a brightness in her eyes as he approached and an attentive tilt of the head, possibly even the hint of a smile.

"It's a great tragedy you've suffered," he said as he took her hand. "I'm very sorry."

She pulled him closer so she could whisper in his ear. "It's a trag-edy I have to go through this masquerade," she said. "You know how a man should treat a woman. Is this the way a husband should die on a wife?"

Vincenzo was both surprised and thrilled. "Normally a man cannot choose his end," he said. "It simply comes to him."

"He was always careless," said Jacquetta.

Vincenzo nodded politely, then began to pull away. She did not release his hand but drew him closer. "Don't leave," she said.

"Many other people want to see you."

"I don't want to see them. I have to put on a false face, act the tearful widow, when all I really feel is that bastard deserved it. Just sit next to me. Tell me what's been happening with you. Distract me." Jacquetta patted the section of the couch next to her. "I've been thinking too much about myself these days. I want to know what's happening with other people."

Vincenzo sat next to her as more funeral guests expressed their condolences. A few looked askance at him, but most seemed to regard him as a good friend providing comfort.

Alex came racing into the room, pursued by Francis Tortelli, one of Jacquetta's cousins from Dante's side who always drove other children to be on their worst behavior. "I'm going to get away from you!" Alex was now eight years old and the largest boy in his class.

At ten, Francis had already been expelled from three schools for unruly behavior and pursued Alex with the fury of a hunting hound. Alex looked back and then ran into the corner of a long, dark table. It caught him mid-chest, and he fell to the ground as if shot. Jacquetta jumped up and ran to him, Vincenzo trailing behind her. Alex was clutching his chest and crying. Vincenzo crouched over him, checking his chest to see if there was any-thing cracked.

"Don't be a baby!" said Francis. "You knew I was going to catch you!"

"Francis! Go away now!" said Jacquetta sharply. She turned back to Alex and cradled him in her arms. "Are you all right?" she asked in a soothing voice.

Rosina came rushing out of the kitchen and said, "Alex! What do you mean running around like a madman? This is a time to behave! How can you treat your aunt like that?"

"But Francis started it," Alex complained.

"Oh? And you'll finish it? Couldn't you have just refused to play?"

"Rose, he's not bothering me," said Jacquetta. She helped Alex to his feet. He massaged the center of his chest where the corner of the table had struck him.

"Well," Rosina told him, "I don't want you doing anything more today." She motioned to a chair. "I want you to sit there and not get up for the rest of the time."

"But Mama!"

"Don't say anything to me. I wasn't running around here like a crazy person. You need to learn there are times when you need to be still, take other people into consideration. Just because somebody provokes you doesn't mean you need to respond."

"I'll watch over him," said Vincenzo. "Keep him out of trouble."

Rosina looked at him and nodded.

After she left, Vincenzo and Alex exchanged a look. "Thanks," said Alex.

Vincenzo leaned close. "Mothers often don't understand how much energy their sons have."

The three of them sat together through the rest of the event, talking intermittently with mourners who slowed to a trickle. Rosina was in the kitchen, making sure the guests had enough food and drink, and even Nick came over to sit with them for a while.

Finally, the guests started to leave, Rosina and Nick finished cleaning up in the kitchen, and the house started to empty. Vincenzo remained in the background, walking through the other rooms. He spent some time in Dante's study, looking at a large bookcase full of books, their pages not even cracked, as if it had been put up for show. Along the shelves and counters were framed pictures of Dante and Jacquetta at various social events. They'd been a handsome couple. He saw the desk where Dante had paid the bills for the pharmacy and almost assuredly had written out the payments to his dead mistress.

Jacquetta entered the study. "Well, the circus is over," she said, "and I've received enough dinner invitations to last a year."

"I was wondering if you'd still like some company."

"I'm pretty tired," she replied, reaching up to take off her veil. Her wild, black hair tumbled to her shoulders. Vincenzo was startled to realize that not only had she regained the vitality she'd lost during her pregnancy, but there was something even more vibrant and alive in her.

"It's not good to be alone at a time like this," he said. Part of him felt almost unable to speak with her, as if his words came out halting. "The most terrible thoughts can come into your mind."

"I'm not really sad," she replied. "Things are honest now, maybe for the first time in years."

"Then maybe you'd like somebody to talk to about these new truths."

"The truth is I'm hungry. But I don't want funeral food. Too sad. What about you?" asked Jacquetta. "I can fix us something."

"Let me do it."

"You can cook?"

"If I couldn't," he said, "I would've starved a long time ago. Sit down and I'll fix something."

Jacquetta sat down at the kitchen table and watched as he went through the drawers and cupboards. He eyed her and thought it felt good to take care of her. When a woman stayed over at his place, Vincenzo always made sure she left in the morning with a full stomach. While she was sleeping, he'd slip out and buy some freshly baked bread and fix a full breakfast with eggs and bacon or sausage, so she'd awake to the smell of delicious food.

Within minutes he had a pot of water boiling and had selected some pasta, cheese, onions, and a long link of spicy sausages. He warmed sauce from a large pot that seemed to be a part of every kitchen he'd ever known. Jacquetta looked down at her black mourning gown, as if thinking she should change into something else.

"My father taught me to cook when I was very young," he told her, trying to be conversational. "He thought there might be a time when I needed to cook for a large group of men."

"During a *vendetta?*" she asked, using the Italian word for what loosely translated into English as a feud between families, often over a question of honor, or to avenge a killing.

"Yes."

"Did you ever have to fight in one?"

Vincenzo thought for a moment. When he killed the Duke, it had been something cold and calculating, not a *vendetta*. And when he was betrayed by Mussolini's men and on the run, he was not interested in killing, just escaping. "No," he finally said.

"I know many people in the old country did bad things. Sometimes there was no other way. My family was not part of that world. But I don't pretend to be above it."

"In Italy the little criminals steal in the streets and the biggest criminals are in the government."

"But that's not the way it is here," said Jacquetta.

"No, perhaps here we can be better people. Life will not crush us."

"Did you ever have to do bad things?"

"Bad things were done to my family, and I did bad things to others. I don't apologize for it."

"Who did bad things to your family?"

"The fascists. Before Mussolini took over. Before he marched on Rome and the King and the government welcomed him with open arms."

"Is that how you hurt your leg? Fighting the fascists?"

Vincenzo nodded. He remembered the stranger in the *pensi-one*, who must have been a secret fascist, the jump from the high window, the snap of bone. *Fighting the fascists* sounded so roman-tic, especially to an Italian woman in America, obviously from a wealthy family, who had never had to deal with such things. But it was true enough.

"The fascists took my family's property when they came to power. But it was okay for us here. My father had given us money for Rosina to start buying property. She was always so good with those things, even back in Sicily, keeping accounts and things like that. Me, not so much."

Vincenzo was close to finishing the pasta. He drained the water, mixed it with the sauce, threw in a few spices, and then took a bit with the spoon and offered it to Jacquetta. "Tell me how it tastes."

She blew on it, then took a bite. "Still needs a little something."

Jacquetta rummaged through a cabinet and came back with a small medicinal bottle.

"What is it?" he asked.

"Cough syrup," she said, uncorking it and putting it into the pot. "Actually, it's red wine. That's the way Dante was able to sell it."

"Jacquetta Mercurio," he said with mock gravity. "I never fig-ured you for a lawbreaker. A bootlegger. Don't you know alcohol is destroying the moral fabric of America?"

"Dante was the bootlegger. Or at least the distributor for them. As for me, I was just the lucky beneficiary."

"Got any more of that 'cough syrup?' Might go well with our meal."

"I think I can find a bottle or two."

As they ate, their conversation turned to more mundane sub-jects. Jacquetta gossiped about Rita Benedetti trying to find a hus-band, Laura Lazio not wanting to have another child after her fifth, even though her husband said it was unnatural for a woman to stop having children, and Laura telling her friends that if she got preg-nant a sixth time, she'd arrange a convenient fall down the stairs.

Jacquetta complimented Vincenzo's cooking several times, and the new familiarity between them felt good.

After they finished dinner, she picked up their glasses and walked into the living room. "I want to look out the window and see the city lights in the fog," she said.

Vincenzo followed along and noticed a fireplace in the room, a stack of newspapers and wood next to it. "Fire?" he asked.

"Sure."

Within minutes he had a warm, crackling fire going. Jacquetta handed him his glass of wine, sat down, and looked out the window. The lights of the city twinkled like stars in the velvet of the night sky. Ghostly wisps of fog sailed past, dimming, shrouding, and then uncovering the lights.

"I used to sit like this with my family and watch the fishing boats come in at night," said Jacquetta. "They had lanterns hung from their bows, and if it got late, the fisherman's families would light bonfires to guide them in. From our balcony, we'd hear them laughing and singing in the night. I thought that someday I'd do the same with my own family. But now I know I'm meant to be alone."

"A woman like you won't be alone for long. Unless you want to be."

"Oh, you think so?" Her reply was disbelieving, a mocking tone, and she raised an eyebrow. "You men are a complete mystery to me. I remember the first boy I ever kissed, Enzo Romano. I was thirteen. We'd been playmates since we were children. One day we climbed up to the old Greek theater overlooking the Bay of Naxos. I thought it would be nice to watch the sun set. It was beautiful, the sun an enormous, brilliant ball of yellow fire, the water such a deep blue, the warm breeze. I was so happy that I slipped my hand into his without even thinking about it. He stroked my arm in a way that made me tingle like never before, and he looked at me like a man, not a boy anymore." She shook her head. "Then he kissed me full on the lips before I could even react. He sat back and looked at me. I was shocked beyond belief. I'd seen lovers kissing in the streets, but did I ever think that would happen to me? No, I did not. 'Did you like that,' he asked me? I started to shake my head, but he kissed me again and this time I did. I thought there was nothing more wonderful than a kiss, no art, no statue, no food, no wine. We stayed until night. I simply kept looking at the stars and resting in his arms. That night I felt the stars had been hung just for me."

"What happened to Enzo?" Vincenzo asked.

Jacquetta ran her finger around the rim of the wine glass. "I'm not sure. After that he didn't talk to me much. Something had changed, but I didn't know what. Some of the other boys teased me, asking if I wanted to go to the 'theater.' I don't know if he told them, or they just guessed. He went off to war a few years later. Died in France. That's the way it is with men. They leave you alone, either before they die, or when they do."

Her eyes gazed dejectedly into her glass. Vincenzo thought she looked like a child, legs drawn up close to her body, and eyes about to tear. He reached out and put a hand on her cheek. She moved into it, like a cat hungry for a kind human touch. She rested her hand on his and pressed it against her face. Vincenzo moved his face closer to hers. She touched her cheek to his own and stroked the back of his head. He pressed his mouth to hers and they kissed. He felt an initial acceptance, a moment of belief and faith, but then she pulled away as if horrified.

"We can't do this!" she said.

"We're not children, Jacquetta. We know what things mean."

"I think you'd better leave."

"Why? Because you honor the memory of a man who kept his mistress right under your nose, who paid for her with checks he wrote in this very house?"

"This is wrong."

"I know what it's like to lose," said Vincenzo. "To find yourself in the dark lands, doubting you'll ever find the sunshine again.

I don't want to go back. Let life be good to you. Let me be good to you."

He leaned forward and kissed her again on the lips. He hoped it felt like the second time she'd kissed Enzo, a sensation greater than any other in the world. She seemed to relax, to let sorrow and shame fall away from her. He kissed her again. She responded, pressing herself against him as if she could drive out the darkness and anger in her soul.

Vincenzo slid the black mourning gown off her shoulders, running his hands along the contours of her waist and hips. His fingers felt almost electric. She unbuttoned his shirt and ran her hands over his lean and muscular chest, and he shivered with delight.

He motioned for her to lay down on the pillowed couch, pulling at the buttons and ties of her undergarments until he felt her warm skin against his own. He felt himself swelling against her and the delicious yielding of her flesh. His hands and mouth moved quickly across her neck and breasts, kneading and grasping, kissing here and nibbling there until he knew Jacquetta was lifted to the level of his own hungry passion. He seemed to be starving, and she was his only food. Her legs parted willingly.

Vincenzo pushed against her, feeling the fleshy wetness of her as he entered, a moan escaping from her lips. He felt her wrap herself around him as he began to thrust, begging him to go even deeper. "More, more," she whispered, as if it was possible to fuse their two bodies into one. Vincenzo thought of Sicilian legends of ghostly lovers, able to slip their vaporous essences into each other and achieve a communion undreamed of by mortals.

Jacquetta's fingers grasped the skin of his shoulder blades so tightly as to almost tear the flesh off his bones. She dug her nails into his back, and then pulled his buttocks to drive him even deeper into her. He exploded, gave a final moan of pleasure, then kissed, kissed, and kissed her again as he continued to pour into her. Finally, he rested his head on her shoulder as she ran her fingers through his hair.

"My beautiful man," said Jacquetta.

"*Mia bella donna*," he whispered. "Was there ever a woman so perfect?" He lifted his head to look into her eyes.

Her expression stiffened. "I've done a terrible thing."

"You've turned sadness into joy."

"Maybe."

"This is not a mistake. I think everything that happened was the way it had to be. Dante had to go away for us to be together. You said it yourself. He'd already left. I know I can make you happy in all the ways he never could."

She took his face in her hands. "Good and true, Vincenzo, I know you feel that way. But I don't know about tomorrow. I half expect Dante to walk in on us, and then what will I say?"

"Do you want me to leave?"

She shook her head. "No. Stay tonight."

* * *

AT TWO IN the morning Vincenzo felt restless. He looked at Jacquetta, curled up like a child next to him, her wild black hair concealing her face. With her features hidden, he thought she could be almost any woman, but Vincenzo knew she was the only one he'd ever really wanted. He buried his face in her dark hair to smell its sweet perfume and stroked a hand along her bare, smooth back. She stirred for a moment, then fell back to sleep.

Vincenzo got up. He felt self-conscious being naked in a dead man's house, so he slipped on his trousers and went to the kitchen where he'd left his jacket. He fished for his wallet, and took out a folded piece of paper. He realized he'd been drawn to it like a spell. He unfolded the paper and began to read. The calligraphy was still as beautiful as when she'd written it for him years earlier.

"What are you doing?" Jacquetta asked.

Vincenzo looked up, seeing Jacquetta standing in the kitchen doorway. She'd wrapped a white sheet around herself, and he couldn't help but think she looked like some holy woman.

"I was reading something."

Jacquetta took a seat at the table. "What is it?"

"A poem by a man named Rilke. It was given to me as sort of a farewell present."

"By a woman you loved no doubt. I think I should be jealous."

Vincenzo shook his head. "A woman who wished I loved her. She said she could see me for who I was and that the poem was about me. The part that was incomplete. Would you like to hear it?"

"I don't know. I might want to go find her and scratch her eyes out."

Vincenzo began to read the poem in a soft voice:

You who never arrived
in my arms, Beloved, who were lost
from the start,
I don't even know what songs
would please you. I have given up trying
to recognize you in the surging wave of the next
moment. All the immense images in me – the far-off, deeply
*   felt landscape,*
cities, towers, and unsuspected turns in the path,
and those powerful lands that were once
pulsing with the life of the gods – all rise within me to mean
you, who forever elude me.

Vincenzo hesitated, recalling someone who understood him enough to see beyond the surface, who knew there was anger in him, burning ambition, and even violence, but there was also something else. He felt sad he'd been unable to love the schoolteacher. In another life, perhaps, but not this one. He continued:

> *You, Beloved, who are all*
> *the gardens I have ever gazed at,*
> *longing. An open window*
> *in a country house -, and you almost*
> *stepped out, pensive, to meet me. Streets that I chanced upon, -*
> *you had just walked down them and vanished.*
> *And sometimes, in a shop, the mirrors*
> *were still dizzy with your presence and, startled, gave back*
> *my too sudden image. Who knows? Perhaps the same*
> *bird echoed through both of us*
> *yesterday, separate in the evening.*

He looked up at Jacquetta. Tears streaked her face. She extended her hand across the table. "That's so terribly sad. What's it called?"

"'You Who Never Arrived.'"

Vincenzo violently tore the paper in half, then in fourths, and finally into tiny pieces.

"Why did you do that?" she exclaimed.

"I don't need it anymore. It's for the person I used to be. Sad. Tortured. But things have changed. You've arrived."

* * *

MUCH LATER THAT night, Jacquetta awoke with a start, jabbing Vincenzo in the ribs as he lay spooned beside her. He moved groggily as they turned toward each other, locking their warm bodies together. She dragged her long fingernails softly down his back, sending tiny shivers through his body.

"Good morning," he whispered, his vision surrounded by her wild, black hair.

"I had a bad dream," she said as she pulled him closer to her.

"I had only good dreams," he replied, running his fingers through her tangled hair.

"It was about my father," said Jacquetta.

"I imagine he wouldn't be happy with what we did last night. But he doesn't have to know."

"He's dead," said Jacquetta. "My mother, too."

"Rosina mentioned that."

She waited a moment before speaking again. "I worry that when he was alive I was too hard on him. Rosina worshipped the ground he walked on."

"I'm sure he knew you loved him."

"I hope so."

"Tell me about the dream."

"It's probably just stupid. Nothing to think about."

"No, tell me," said Vincenzo.

"I was back at our family's house in Taormina. My father called me to talk to him, and he was furious. In a way I'd never seen before. As if I was in great danger and he wanted to warn me away from it."

"You're from Taormina?" In America, many immigrants never named the town of their birth. Like others he'd avoided the subject, as if he'd run from something evil, and the less he talked about that accursed land, the better. He did not 'long' for the old country.

"Yes," she said. "Why?"

"Nothing," he replied, feeling a knot in his stomach. "Why do you worry you were hard on him?"

"You know we had money, right?"

"Yes."

"You might also say my father was in the government. He administered our local area, making sure crimes were punished and whatever meager amounts of money were provided by the government in Rome were fairly distributed. I'd say to him, 'Papa, the people are so poor. How can you judge them when they're just trying to survive?' I know it hurt him when I'd say that. But he knew I was right."

"He was a judge?"

Jacquetta laughed. "You might say he was a bastard and you'd be just as right. The bastard son of our great king, Victor Emmanuel II, unifier of Italy. Of course, they gave him a title, Duke du Taormina, and a position that he tried to fulfill with honor. But how can you be a man of honor in an unjust system? As you said, the biggest criminals in Italy are in the government, even before Mussolini took over. He knew that, but didn't want to admit it."

"Your father was Alessandro de Leone, Duke du Taormina, the Lion of Sicily?" The tension in Vincenzo's throat made his words tight.

"Yes."

Vincenzo felt as if his heart had been ripped from his chest. He'd waited for years for Jacquetta, only to find she was the daughter of the man he'd murdered. His life had been a terrible, downward spiral since that day: the massacre of his family, the deaths of Roberto and Michael by the stranger in the *pensione*, his crippled leg, and finally at the moment when all that darkness seemed ready to lift, it was revealed to be a false dawn.

"My family knew your father well," he said bitterly.

She didn't reply, as if confused by his tone. He threw off the covers, feeling ashamed to be naked in front of this woman, and quickly pulled on his trousers. Jacquetta watched from the bed as if terrified, the covers drawn up close to her. "What is it, Vincenzo? I want to know. We can tell each other anything."

Vincenzo quickly left the room, and, as he went out the front door of the house, he thought he could hear her crying.

* * *

VINCENZO KNELT IN the confessional of Saints Peter and Paul Church in North Beach. With the exception of the funeral of Dante the day before, he'd rarely attended a church service after he'd left Sicily. However, after leaving Jacquetta's house he'd become very confused. He boarded a streetcar and headed for North Beach where he hoped Father Cristiani, the priest who'd given him food and lodging when he arrived, would be hearing confessions. The plaque on the outside showed that Father was hearing confessions, so Vincenzo entered.

"It's been nearly eight years since my last confession," he began, recalling it had been the Easter service in the spring before he'd murdered the Duke.

"That's a long time to be without God, my son," said Father Cristiani. "What do you have to confess?"

"May I ask a question, first?"

"Of course."

"Can the dead come back and speak to us?"

"No, my son. When a person dies, his soul leaves our world. Only our Lord Jesus Christ was allowed to come back and show us God's power. That's why his reappearance was such a miracle. If this was not true, there would be no basis for our belief, nothing that was miraculous."

"Maybe then everything would be miraculous."

"That is not the way of things," Father Cristiani replied in a matter-of-fact voice. Vincenzo remembered Father Cristiani as a good man, but strong-minded in matters of religion.

"I had a brother who died before I was born," said Vincenzo. "My mother told me he often appeared to her in dreams. He'd tell her about his friends in heaven, the wonderful candies they had, and that she should not worry about him."

"Your mother was in pain. Sometimes we have such fantasies to help with the sadness, and perhaps God will not condemn us too much for having them. But your actual brother never appeared to your mother in her dreams. Now, what have you come to confess?"

Vincenzo did not respond. On the other side of the grate, the priest was just a shadow. He doubted if Father Cristiani even recognized his voice.

"What is it, my son? God already knows."

"I killed a man and slept with his daughter." His voice was calm, and he was amazed he was able to say it so clearly. At times, he'd hidden his murder of the Duke even from himself. It was a dark well into which he did not look.

"Go on, my son," said Father Cristiani. Vincenzo knew the priest must be shocked, but in a lifetime at the confessional he must have heard the confession of many horrific deeds.

"I killed him because he harmed my family. Me and my sister were left without a father and my mother without a husband. She did things with men for money. I spent years hating that man. Then there came an opportunity to take revenge. To make things right."

"And did things go right?"

"No," Vincenzo replied. It had all gone horribly wrong, but he couldn't bring himself to believe he'd done anything wrong. The Duke had been the destruction of his family. Vengeance was owed to him. Mussolini had betrayed him. That was his only mistake, his only sin, trusting Mussolini.

"And this woman," Father Cristiani said. "Did you sleep with her out of spite, or because of a higher emotion?"

"I did not know I'd killed her father until after I'd slept with her."

"Then it is some higher emotion that brought you two together?"

"Yes."

"Perhaps you've been sent to this woman to cleanse yourself of the sin you've committed against her family. The ways of God are many and His methods sublime."

Vincenzo said nothing.

Father Cristiani continued. "You have confessed your sin, but now you must ask for forgiveness. Do you ask the forgiveness of our almighty Lord?"

Vincenzo remained silent for a moment and then spoke. "I don't know that I need forgiveness, Father. I do not regret what I have done."

"You took a human life, my son. Does that not weigh heavily on your conscience? I don't think you can ever be truly free until you ask to be forgiven."

Vincenzo suddenly felt foolish to have come to the church. It felt hot and close inside the confessional. "I do not feel I have done anything wrong, Father. It is unfortunate, and bad things flowed from it, but it was not wrong."

"Do you know the story of the scorpion and the frog?" Father Cristiani asked.

"No."

"Once a scorpion wanted to get across a stream, and he saw a frog swimming close by. He asked the frog, 'Will you take me across the water?' The frog replied, 'But you are a scorpion. You'll sting me.' The scorpion answered, 'Why would I do that? I would also sink and drown.' The frog thought for a moment, then told the scorpion to climb on his back. When they were in the middle of the stream, the scorpion stung the frog. As the poison set in, the frog started to sink and cried out, 'Why did you do that? Now we're both going to die.' The scorpion replied, 'Because it's in my nature.'"

"Why are you telling me this, Father?"

"I've known you since you first came here, Vincenzo." Hearing his name spoken violated the anonymity of the confessional, and Vincenzo shrunk back. "I know the cruelty of which you are capable. God gives men free will, unlike the animals. You are telling me you choose to be the scorpion. If you do not reach toward God, then He will not reach toward you. However, I will continue to pray for your soul, that you may see the error of your ways."

* * *

JACQUETTA ANSWERED THE knock at her door. Again, she wore her black mourning dress. Tradition required she wear it for at least a month. Vincenzo thought he saw a hesitation in her eyes, as if she didn't know whether she'd forfeited the right to wear it because of what had happened the previous night.

"I'm sorry I left so abruptly this morning."

She regarded him with faint guilt. "I'm assuming my father went after somebody in your family?"

"Yes."

"Cousin? Brother? Father?"

"Father."

She nodded. "And you suffered greatly?"

"Yes."

"I've met others who don't have the kindest of words for my father. It's why Rosina and I don't talk much about him to outsiders. You just never know who you're talking to."

Vincenzo nodded.

Jacquetta started speaking, slowly at first, then quickening her words. "I think there's so much about the old country that's not worth thinking about. It's something best left behind. We're here in this new country because we hope for something better. I hope for that with you. But if this thing that happened before . . . if it makes you feel it would be something permanently between us . . . well, I understand."

"No." Vincenzo shook his head as if his very soul hung on the answer. He knew the answer had to be, could never be anything but, *no*. It was an answer that rejected everything in the past, a rejection of the sterile, passionless life he'd led since the murder of his family. Jacquetta seemed to offer the forgiveness of all things, the magic wand that drew the poison from his heart. He moved to embrace her.

She let him wrap his arms around her, making a sound of deep satisfaction, and then moved away from him. "There's still a dark road I must travel from Dante's death. But you've let me see there's an end to sadness. I hope you'll stand beside me as a friend while I grieve, and when that is finished, a new life can begin."

"I will wait as long as it takes."

Chapter Eight

JACQUETTA WAITED AT THE WINDOW FOR Vincenzo, twisting a lock of her long black hair and placing it in her mouth. Three months had passed since Dante's death. She and Vincenzo had not been lovers again. She had little strength for such things, and he never brought it up. He'd become her caretaker, and while she knew Vincenzo was waiting for the day she could love again, she often wondered if it would ever arrive.

He always arrived promptly at seven, dressed in a handsome three-piece suit. He'd make coffee and breakfast for her, they'd talk about things, then he'd leave by eight-thirty, not returning until about six, when he'd fix her dinner, clean up after, and then leave. She couldn't help but notice his limp, which he never complained about. It was noticeable to Jacquetta because even though Vincenzo was in his early thirties his frame was still slight, his features were sharp, and he looked like a young boy. When he arrived, removed his jacket, and rolled up his sleeves to prepare breakfast, he reminded her of a dutiful son tending to his ailing mother.

At times, Jacquetta was ashamed of the way she'd acted since Dante's death. She'd become withdrawn and reclusive. Their wedding had been a lavish affair, attended by several hundred people, and on that day, she'd felt like a royal princess. In those days, she'd been happy to walk down the streets of North Beach, Russian Hill, or Pacific Heights, and have men tip their hats to her. She'd meet other recently married women in the stores or on the street and share intimacies about the thrill of married life, or ask how to compete with the memory of a mother-in-law's cooking. As she became doubtful of Dante's fidelity, her interest in seeing people waned. She was happy to let months go by without talking to her friends. After the funeral, when it became clear she'd been made a fool by him, she felt like stopping all contact.

Jacquetta's physical appearance had also deteriorated. She barely combed her hair, instead letting it hang loose. She didn't have her nails done, and if some event forced her from the house, she found the most unattractive dress to wear. She didn't want men to tip their hats to her anymore. She didn't want women to share recipes or confidences of a life that included a decent and faithful husband. She simply wanted to be left alone in her shame. Her skin had become pale, and at times she thought she could spend the rest of her life in this house with just Vincenzo and her sister coming to visit.

Vincenzo lived only three blocks away. Every morning Jacquetta fixed her eyes on the corner where he would first become visible. It was a cold morning, as Jacquetta could feel when she placed her hand on the foggy glass. Sometimes in the morning, when the fog was thick, all that could be seen was the garden and the large weeping willow trees. It was almost possible to believe she was the only person in the great wide world.

Jacquetta heard a car motor starting up, saw a middle-aged man walking a petite white poodle—obviously his wife's— and then from around the corner came Vincenzo. His hands were shoved deep in his pockets, and his breath was a fine mist. A tremor of excitement sparked through her. In the past few weeks Jacquetta had noticed a change in herself.

Previously, she'd looked at Vincenzo as if he was almost a servant, almost like her family's servant, Salvatore, but now she saw him as something more. She was genuinely touched by Vincenzo's patience and acts of kindness. Once a week he brought flowers and put them in a vase on her nightstand so their beauty would be the last thing she saw when she closed her eyes and the first when she awoke.

She watched as he came up the walkway, heard his footsteps on the landing, the jangling of the keys, then the opening of the door. "Jacquetta?" he called.

"Yes," she answered from the living room. This was where she always waited for his arrival.

He slipped into the room with the easy grace of one who was well-acquainted, rubbed his hands together, and asked, "How are you doing this morning?" This is how it always was between them, the elaborate courtesy that had become a ritual.

"Fine," she replied, as she always did.

"Any bad dreams?"

"Nothing that I can remember." Aside from the dream about her father, which she'd only had that one time, she often dreamed she heard Dante's voice calling her. In her dreams, he wasn't dead, but had simply gotten lost in some room of the house. She'd hear his voice calling her and then dash frantically from room to room looking for him. When she woke, it would take a minute or two for her to realize he was gone, and she'd often break down into tears. Rosina had spent several nights with her in those first few weeks, before Jacquetta finally felt foolish about her emotional rollercoaster and told her sister to go home.

"Good." Vincenzo removed his jacket, rolled up his sleeves, and went into the kitchen to make breakfast.

Jacquetta had noticed that for some reason food was tasting good again. For months it had been a labor to eat, and her weight had dropped shockingly, but now she found herself anticipating the next meal. When she woke now, she'd lie there and wonder if Vincenzo was going to fix scrambled eggs, or maybe some hotcakes dripping with butter and maple syrup.

Vincenzo quickly had a carton of eggs out on the kitchen counter and the stove lit. He took out a few bowls, along with items wrapped in paper he'd just taken from the icebox. It also went without saying that he did all the shopping for her. "What are you making for us today?" she asked as she took a seat at the table.

"Omelet with cheese, Italian sausage, and mushrooms." He cracked eggs on the lip of a bowl and stirred them.

"Where'd you learn to cook like this?"

"I worked at a boarding house when I was ten years old," Vincenzo explained. He cut off a wedge of butter, dropped it into the pan, waited for it to start sizzling, then swirled the pan to spread the butter, and poured in the eggs. "I arrived every morning at five o'clock. The owner's name was Antonio. He was a large man." Vincenzo spread his arms out wide. "And he liked his meals to be large."

Jacquetta laughed.

He looked at her curiously. She rarely laughed, but things were changing. She seemed to be coming back to herself. Vincenzo continued, "If somebody wanted an omelet, it had to be made with four eggs, and if he wanted bacon or sausage or anything with it, it had to be a good amount. I remember the cups he used were so big that when I drank from them, I felt like my face had been swallowed up." Vincenzo smiled at the memory.

"How long did you work for him?"

"Two years." He noticed the eggs were getting done and quickly added cheese, sausage, and mushrooms. He frowned as he tried to get all the ingredients together. When he was satisfied, he continued, "Every day for payment he gave me six eggs, usually some bacon, and some pears and oranges. He put it in a little bag for me, and I remember walking home with it clutched to my chest like it was a king's ransom. It was enough to feed my mother, my sister, and me."

The omelet was ready. Vincenzo took plates from the cabinet and placed them on the table. Coffee was brewing on the stove, and he poured a cup for Jacquetta and himself. He transferred toast from the toaster to a small plate, slathered them with butter and jam, and served the slices to her.

"You mentioned your family a while ago," said Jacquetta. "I know they're gone, but do you ever dream of them? Like I dream of Dante?"

"I used to," he said. "But I'm starting to forget their faces. Isn't that terrible? More and more, I feel I've always been alone."

Jacquetta extended a hand and placed it on top of his. She wondered whether it was better to remember or forget those one once loved.

* * *

AFTER VINCENZO LEFT, Jacquetta showered, then sat herself down in front of her vanity mirror to take the first hard look at herself that she had in months. Occasionally, she'd glanced at herself as she pulled a brush through her hair, or washed her face, but she'd lost her previous pride in her appearance. Her cheeks were a little thinner and her skin had an unhealthy pallor, but she thought she hadn't deteriorated past the point of no return.

She reached into her makeup drawer, pulled out a tube of bright red lipstick, applied it, pursed her mouth, and then smiled. Okay, that was a little scary, but it offered something to work with. She pulled out her base powder, applied rouge to give her cheeks color, a touch of eyebrow pencil, curled her hair, and spritzed on some perfume. Dante had never liked it, so she applied even more.

Jacquetta went to the closet and pulled out several dresses, pressing each against her and examining it in the mirror. Finally, she saw a box on the closet floor. It was the dress and hat she'd bought on the day of Dante's death. With a flourish she pulled out the coquettish red hat and placed it on her head, then held up the blue dress to view in the mirror. The bright colors seemed to wash out the remaining color in her pale skin. She'd be the fragile spring flower, bursting out of the winter ground. Yes, this was the outfit she'd wear today. She dressed quickly, then, before leaving the room, took a deep whiff of the flowers Vincenzo had left at her bedside.

She approached the front door with trepidation. In her bedroom, it had seemed such a simple thing to do, to begin again. But when confronted by this portal to the outside world, she hesitated. Outside the door were people who knew of her failure, her humiliation. They knew of her pride in her attractiveness, while at the same time knowing her husband had been with another woman. In their eyes, she must appear foolish.

That didn't matter, she decided.

The question was whether she was going to lie down and die, or start living again. She reached for the door handle and turned it.

The morning fog had burned off and the brightness of the sun momentarily blinded her. Her eyes slowly adjusted as the sky faded to a deep, brilliant blue with a few fluffy white clouds on the horizon. A slight breeze ruffled the weeping willows in her garden, and the ivy covering the ground moved like a sea of grass. In the distance, she could see the bay with its whitecaps and ships nearing the end of a long voyage in Oakland or San Francisco, or starting their journey of several thousand miles to Hawaii, Tokyo, Hong Kong, or perhaps even India. The low sound of a ship's horn caught her attention, as did the singing of birds and a dog barking several blocks away.

She closed the door behind her and proceeded at a brisk, business-like clip down the walkway and through the front gate. She nearly collided with a stout man in a navy-blue suit and bowler hat. He tipped his hat to her and said, "Please accept my apologies, beautiful lady."

"No harm done," she murmured, a smile forming at the edge of her lips.

Jacquetta wanted to walk so she could feel the earth beneath her heels. She wanted to go where people were living, talking, laughing, arguing, and loving. Suddenly, she saw Dante as simply a man, and her relationship with him as just a mistake, like choosing the wrong type of jacket for a cold day. She had loved him, married him, and he'd betrayed her. What fault did she bear in that equation? None. Dante was the one who should feel ashamed. He was the one who'd gone to his grave with everybody knowing he was an unfaithful husband.

From her house in Pacific Heights she walked all the way to Fisherman's Wharf to watch the boats coming in. They were small craft, many not longer than thirty feet, brightly painted and stenciled with names like *Angelina, Santa Lucia, Bella Donna,* or something humorous like *My Other Wife.* Muscular men in thick sweaters unloaded boats filled with crab, salmon, shrimp, abalone, Petrale sole, sand dabs, and various types of rockfish. The sharp tang of sea life assaulted Jacquetta, reminding her of Taormina, a comforting memory of home.

From Fisherman's Wharf, she walked to North Beach. Aromas from bakeries and Italian groceries with vats of olives made her senses come alive. Baking sourdough bread, cappuccino and espresso, fancy pastries in the window, cannoli with ricotta cheese or chocolate pudding sprinkled with powdered sugar, cured ham, salami, and prosciutto, all combined to make her delirious. This is what it meant to be Italian, to live in a vivid sensual world, rich with emotion. She walked through nearly every store on the street, just to regain her sense of the overwhelming variety in even the smallest corner of the city.

Life was a banquet, even if your dead husband had been a cheating son of a bitch.

On the edge of North Beach, she walked into an art gallery. There were statutes of cherubs for fountains, heroic-looking warriors of old, and statesmen of the Roman Republic, but it was a painting that caught Jacquetta's attention and sent a chill through her body. Two figures, the first being an angel with a body like a boy, brilliant white wings, curly hair, and eyes looking heavenward. In his arms, he held a woman whose feet hovered mere inches off the ground, her arms folded against her breast, and her head resting against his shoulder. Her eyes were closed and from her expression the woman trusted the angel completely. No matter how far he flew, or how great the height, she was safe. Both were naked, except for the thinnest of purple gauze shrouds concealing their intimate parts and billowing behind them like a great cloud.

"It's a beautiful piece, no?" asked a woman in a lilting French accent. She was tiny and thin with white hair pulled back in a bun.

"It's magnificent," Jacquetta replied. She leaned closer to examine the detail. "She's got wings, too!" she exclaimed in surprise. They were almost hidden by the billowing shroud, but were clearly visible. They were smaller than his wings, as if newly sprouted.

"Yes, she does have wings," said the French woman. "Someday she will fly like an angel, too. The picture is called *The Abduction of Psyche*, a copy of the painting by the great French artist, Bouguerau. It's based on the Greek myth of Psyche and Cupid. Do you know the story?"

"No."

"Psyche was a beautiful princess. Venus, the goddess of love, was insanely jealous of her. She sent her son Cupid to shoot her with an arrow and make her fall in love with a monster. Instead, Cupid fell in love with her, defying his mother. They went through many trials because of their love. Eventually Cupid convinced the gods to turn her into an immortal so they could be wed."

"That's quite a story."

"It tells us we never know what the future brings when it comes to love. We think we want one thing, then the heart speaks and tells us it wants another. Do you wish to buy it for your husband? Is he so good that you can call him your angel?"

"My husband passed away." For the first time, Jacquetta felt no shame. It was simply something that happened.

"I'm so sorry, my dear." The old woman laid a hand on Jacquetta's arm. "I've buried three husbands. Two were saints, one was a devil. Men are like the bright shooting stars that fill us with hope, but often vanish too quickly. We women are like the moon, forever in the heavens, waiting for the next flash of excitement."

"I don't know if I'm waiting for the next flash of excitement."

The old woman looked at her closely. "I know the stages of what you're going through, and it seems you have made it through the darkest of those times. When you looked at that painting it wasn't with desperation, with loss, but with hope. There is one who makes you believe the pictures on the canvas are not a fantasy. There is one you think of as an angel, and yet you are worried you do not have the strength to fly so high."

"There's been a man who's helped me," she began. "I feel I should do something to thank him."

The old woman nodded. "Is he a good man?"

"Yes. I think so. Maybe not always. But now, yes."

"Men and women do not play at love like children. If he's been around to help in your time of need, it's been because he has feelings for you. If you have allowed him to help, it's because you also have feelings for him."

"I don't know if I can love, again. My husband, he cheated on me, with many women I believe."

"And now he's dead," the woman said in a cold, icy voice.

"Yes."

"Why do you let the dishonored dead have any hold over you? To love is to live. If this friend who helped you is a good man, you should go to him. I did not marry Francois until I was fifty-six, even though we'd known each other since we were five. We only had eight years together, but they were the best of my life. I had other loves in my life, but it was Francois who loved me best. I think I would have looked at that painting the same way you did when Francois first made his intentions known to me. Let him know he is your angel. The rest will take care of itself."

"Okay, I'll take the painting. I'd like it to be wrapped and sent to my house, too."

"Very well, dear. I'll take care of it."

* * *

JACQUETTA WAS EXCITED for Vincenzo's arrival that night. Normally she was, but there was something different that night. She was taking control of her life.

He usually came at six, so fifteen minutes before he arrived, she had candles on the table and dinner cooking in the oven. It was the first significant meal she'd prepared in months. The painting had arrived about four, and she'd placed in on the entryway table where it would be immediately visible. At five to six, she stood to wait at the window, as she always did. Vincenzo always drove his Model-A to his house, then walked over to Jacquetta's, so as not to draw unwanted attention. She caught sight of him, walking with his slight limp. She wondered if he was tired of being her caretaker, although there was nothing in his stride that suggested it. But he was in for a surprise.

She saw his head tilt upward to the house and fix on her. His expression was startled, as if he didn't believe his eyes. That afternoon she'd had her hair styled, nails done, and with her blue dress and slim but buxom figure, she thought she might look like a fashionable department store mannequin. She saw him smile and walk at a brisker pace. She rushed to open the door.

He placed his hands to his heart in a dramatic gesture. "The beauty has returned," he said.

"I'm better now, I think." Jacquetta nodded. "Come in. I want to show you something." She took his hand, led him in, and pointed to the picture. "I bought this for you." She told the story of the picture as the older French lady had explained it to her.

Vincenzo's eyes welled with tears as she finished. "The priests know nothing of the world," he whispered.

She wasn't quite sure what he meant, but instead found herself swept up in her own emotion. "I wanted to get something that let you know. . ." Jacquetta wiped a tear from her eye. "You've been very important to me. I never could've made it through this time without you. You've been like the angel in that picture to me, a savior."

"I have not been an angel, but you make me want to be one."

They made love for the first time since the funeral. When she woke next to him in a cocoon of warmth, it was as if a new life had begun for her. She did not realize what a hold Dante had upon her, even before she'd know for certain of his infidelity. Why was it a woman felt so vulnerable to the man in her life, even if he didn't deserve that importance? She ran a hand across Vincenzo's chest as he slept, knowing that of all the wonders of the world, none was greater than the human heart.

They were wed one year to the day after Dante's death. Vincenzo told her, "Good can be built on what was once bad. I want you to remember this not as the day you lost a husband, but the day a new life started for you."

* * *

KARL MUNDT WAS the most feared boy at St. John the Baptist Grammar School. For a ten-year-old, he wasn't exceptionally large. In fact, Alex was taller and probably had about five pounds on him. But unlike most young boys who might threaten a fight, Karl was always ready for one. He'd bloodied the noses of several boys for real or imagined insults, despite the best efforts of the nuns and priests to moderate his behavior. Violence came naturally to Karl. His father was a longshoreman who'd moved up into union leadership, and often came home too late at night during the week to be much of a threat to his family. But the weekends were a nightmare, and Karl often suffered the brunt of his father's frequent wrath.

Lately, Karl had discovered a way to make his violent nature profitable. The blue-suited young boys or girls in ankle-length, black and white checkered skirts and blue sweaters who passed through the school gates every morning usually had nickels or dimes given to them by their mothers for the day's lunch or an after-school treat while walking home. Karl charged them a toll to walk past him and onto the school grounds.

"Falcone!" Karl shouted, leaning up against a pillar. "I heard you were taking your little cousins to the movie after school. Mommy probably gave you a whole quarter for that."

"I'm not giving you any money," said Alex. He thought Karl had a face like a flattened bulldog, it was so ugly. Students whispered behind his back that he had lice because he rarely washed his stringy black hair.

Karl motioned for Alex to come close. Karl acted like he was going to whisper something to Alex, and foolishly, he leaned forward. Karl's fist slammed into the side of Alex's head, a glancing blow that made his head ring. Alex staggered, expecting Karl to have his fists up, but he was back to leaning against the pillar.

"What'd you do that for?" Alex asked.

"Cause and effect, Falcone. I ask, and you respond. The wrong answer gets you a punch to the head."

"I'm not giving you any money," said Alex.

Karl's fist flew at lightning speed into Alex's gut, doubling him over. "Second wrong answer gets one to the stomach. Third one is to the face, I think."

Alex held a hand up in surrender. He fished into his pocket and gave Karl the quarter.

"Easy money," said Karl, flipping the coin in the air. He gave Alex a look. "Now beat it. I've got more to collect."

* * *

WHEN ALEX WALKED in the door at three, his mother said, "I thought you were taking your cousin to the cinema." Alex knew his mother wasn't expecting him home until at least five-thirty or six. He'd considered staying out until then, and for a moment he wished he had.

"I don't have my money," he said.

"What happened to it?"

"I lost it," he said, hoping that would be the end of the conversation. But no ten-year-old in history ever escaped additional questions from his mother when his explanation didn't make sense.

"How did you lose it?" she asked. He felt like he knew what was going to come next. She'd say he had to be careful with his money. Even in Sicily, his grandfather had been a wealthy man, but he'd always taught his daughters the value of money. And when Mussolini took their family's properties after the death of her parents, it was a good thing she and Jacquetta knew how to take care of themselves. Everybody needed to know how to take care of themselves, both men and women.

"It wasn't my fault," Alex protested.

"I guess it just walked out of your pocket?"

Alex looked at the floor in shame. "Karl Mundt stole it from me."

"Who's he?"

"A boy at school. He says we have to pay him a toll to go through the school entrance."

Rosina dropped to her knees and caressed his face, as if he'd been injured. He didn't mention the slap to the side of the head or the punch to the gut. He felt he'd failed her.

"Did you report it to the principal?"

Alex shook his head. "No."

"Why not?"

"Karl's not the kind of kid you tell on. I hear his parents give a lot of money to the school. His dad's a union leader."

"Well, they're not going to let this go on if I have anything to say about it."

"No, Mama. Please don't. It'll make things worse."

Rosina picked up the telephone. "If you let a bully get away with something like that, he'll just keep doing it."

Alex listened as his mother talked to the school receptionist and vented her anger. He felt almost sorry for the woman on the other end of the line. He could almost hear her saying, "Yes, ma'am, yes, ma'am," as his mother continued her tirade. Rosina demanded a meeting with the principal, and the receptionist scheduled it for the next morning before school.

"You see?" said Rosina when she hung up. "Everything's going to work out," she promised. "Your father will also come to the meeting. We'll work this out."

* * *

Father Timothy Rappa was standing at the gates of the school like a sentry when Alex arrived. Father Timothy was tall with a shock of greased black hair and a plank-straight back that would have qualified him for the military if he hadn't chosen the priesthood. He was the school disciplinarian and when he peered over his bifocals and spoke in a low voice, the children knew to be quiet. Alex tried to enter the grounds unnoticed, but he was half a head taller than most of the others.

"Alex!" shouted Father Timothy. His voice wasn't angry but demanded response.

Alex stopped as the stream of children flowed around him. He knew it would be whispered around the school that he'd talked to Father Timothy, and it would get back to Karl. Father Timothy motioned for Alex to come over. Alex took a deep breath and approached him.

"I heard you had a little trouble the other day," said Father Timothy.

Alex had at least convinced his mother not to accompany him when his parents came to talk to the principal. "I didn't have any trouble," he replied.

"Oh no?" Father Timothy asked, peering over his bifocals. "Your parents had a different story."

"I don't want to talk about it," he said, looking at the ground.

Father Timothy tipped Alex's face up to look at him. "There's right and wrong, Alex. You must understand that. If somebody takes money from you, then he's a thief, and he should be pun-

ished. When somebody does something wrong, you report it to the
authorities, and they'll do the right thing. Now, some boys might
have tried to take matters into their own hands, gotten into a fight
about it, but you didn't, and that's good. You did the right thing
telling the truth. We'll take care of it from here."

"You're not going to make things better," said Alex in a defeated
voice. "You don't know him. You can't watch him all the time.
I wish my mother had never said anything."

* * *

KARL MUNDT AND his gang caught Alex that afternoon about
three blocks away from school. There was some pushing and shov-
ing, a punch or two to the gut, but nothing that would leave much
of a mark. What was truly terrifying was how they circled around
him, taunting him like a pack of wolves, enjoying the psycholog-
ical torture even more than the physical harm. By the end, Alex
was thoroughly traumatized and felt like throwing up.

Aunt Jacquetta and Uncle Vincenzo's house was only a few
blocks away, closer than his own, so he headed to it as a place to
recuperate before going home. He wanted to conceal the event
from his mother but knew he couldn't do it if he was visibly upset.

Alex remembered their wedding, a little more than a year after
Dante's death. Alex was the ring-bearer. Uncle Vincenzo was in a
buoyant mood, a little drunk, and at the reception he'd taken Alex
aside. He draped an arm over Alex's shoulder and said, "Do you
know this wedding is your doing? If you hadn't been so restless at
Dante's funeral, I don't think I'd be married now. You set events in
motion, and I owe you for it. Anything you need, you just tell me.
We're family now, and that can *never* be broken."

The house his aunt and uncle lived in was a mansion, and he'd
heard Vincenzo bought it from one of his former clients after the
stock market crash. There'd been some controversy about the purchase, but none of it made any sense to Alex. People bought and

sold things. If you didn't want to sell, then don't do it. Adults often made things very confusing.

He knew his aunt and uncle would be calmer than his mother, and if he asked them to keep quiet, they would. Besides, Vincenzo had made him a solemn vow, and for some reason, he trusted his uncle would know how to handle this kind of situation better than his own father.

* * *

VINCENZO DIDN'T LIKE being home in the middle of the afternoon, but Jacquetta was ill, so he'd come home after lunch to check on her. Paulie and Tommy were competent to run the job site, but Vincenzo chafed over being at home while others were at work.

His thoughts could run dark when he was in the home alone, with Jacquetta sleeping upstairs, as if things might suddenly be taken away from him.

Vincenzo opened the door and saw Alex in his navy-blue school suit. He hated the uniforms, thinking they made ten-year-olds look like accountants. Alex's face was ruddy, as if he'd been crying, and his pants were streaked with dirt.

"What happened?" Vincenzo asked.

"Some boys beat me up. Not really, but they—" he struggled to find the words.

"Why?"

"One of the boys took some money from me. I told my parents, then they went to the principal. They said they'd make it better, but they didn't."

"Come on in. I'll get you cleaned up."

Vincenzo's mind was already turning to the question of what sort of punishment would be best for the hooligan who'd harmed his nephew. Alex was larger than any other boy in his class, and Vincenzo knew that was why he'd been picked on.

The bully knew the way to win over a group was to defeat their champion.

But Alex didn't consider himself a champion.

He was a quiet, thoughtful boy, helpful, who tried to stay out of the way of others, but his stature made that impossible. In many ways, Vincenzo thought Alex was his grandfather's double, but he lacked the old man's bravery.

Even at the point of death, the Duke hadn't feared Vincenzo. You had to admire an adversary with such courage.

"Please come in. Let's sit. I want you to tell me more about this boy."

Alex nodded, came inside, and they took a seat at the table. Vincenzo listened as Alex told him all about Karl Mundt, and what he heard confirmed his suspicions about how to deal with him.

"I know how to stop him," said Vincenzo with confidence.

"How?"

"It's a way your parents and your aunt won't approve. So, if I tell you, it must be our secret."

Vincenzo waited to see how Alex responded. He watched the turmoil in the boy's expression, the emotions that played so visibly across his face, weighing the need for the approval of his parents versus the nightmare he was facing daily. Finally, he said, "Okay."

"This is not a promise you break. You do not speak to your family of what we talk about. Not ever. Do you understand?"

"Yes," Alex replied, and Vincenzo saw the young boy's expression harden in resolve. Maybe someday he *would* be as brave as his grandfather had been.

* * *

KARL'S NEW BUSINESS venture was three weeks old. Alex was his most compliant customer. He did as Vincenzo told him, giving Karl the money, acting reluctant but resigned to the inevitable loss. Since Alex's claim about Karl taking money from kids on school property became known and Father Timothy would be watching for it, Karl moved his operations about two blocks away from school, his fellow ruffians often guarding the other approaches.

"Got some money for me today, Falcone?" Karl asked.

"None, today. Sorry," he said cheerfully. In his pocket he fingered the zip knife Vincenzo had given him.

"You always have to be willing to go one step further than the other guy," his uncle had told him. "If he punches you once in the stomach, you punch him twice in the face."

"No money?" Karl said with visible annoyance.

"Completely out. Will you take a check? Money order?" Vincenzo had told him to say something cheeky, a challenge, which would anger and draw him in. Violence should be swift, brutal, and demoralizing.

Karl advanced on him as Alex expected. He'd seen the move before, Karl getting right up into somebody's face, yelling and swearing, spit flying out of his mouth.

Karl's face was no more than three inches from his own, his expression screwing up in anger. Alex eyed a spot on the center of Karl's forehead. A swift, bare-knuckled punch to the forehead his uncle had told him.

Alex felt the slight movement of his right shoulder, knowing it was bringing up his fist, and POW! The punch hurt less than Alex thought it would, and Karl was tumbling backward. Karl seemed to fall in slow motion, his hands reaching down to break his fall, but still tumbling onto his back, hitting his head on the sidewalk.

Alex was on him in a flash. Karl still didn't know what had happened to him. Alex grabbed Karl's tie with one hand and with the other drew out his knife, dramatically showing it to Karl, smiling as he pushed the button on the handle and the blade shot out with an audible *click!*

"Don't do anything to me, Alex," Karl pleaded. "I never meant anything by it. You and me, we're pals, right?"

The other kids formed a circle around them. They'd cheered Alex when he punched Karl but fell silent when he produced the knife.

"You've been an ass to everybody," said Alex.

"Yeah," Karl replied, nodding vigorously.

"I want to hear you say it."

"I've been an ass. I've been an ass."

"And you're going to pay everybody back the money you stole."

"I spent it all."

"I don't care," Alex said in a voice so low and threatening it surprised him. Karl's eyes grew wide with fear. Alex pulled his tie a little tighter and let the blade rest on Karl's neck. A strange feeling of power came over Alex, as if he merely had to push the blade in a few inches and he would have done something good for the world, rid it of a piece of human trash.

"All right! I'll give back every penny."

"I don't know if that's enough." Alex let the tip of the knife dig a little into Karl's neck, a small drop of blood welling up from it. Vincenzo had suggested this. Karl must not only be defeated, but he also had to be humiliated.

"Please! Please! Don't cut me," Karl begged in a pitiful voice. "I just want to go home." Karl started to sob and wail, and Alex let him.

"He pissed his pants," cried one of the children.

Alex saw the left side of Karl's trousers, wet from his crotch to almost his knee.

"Karl pissed his pants! Karl pissed his pants!" the schoolchildren jeered. "Karl needs diapers! Karl needs diapers!"

"If you ever try to take something from anybody again, it will be even worse. Understand?"

"Yes! Yes!"

"I don't know if I believe you."

Alex gripped the tie even tighter, lifting his head up. Alex slashed with his knife, and Karl fell backwards onto the pavement.

Alex stood over him, clutching the tie he'd sliced off. Karl's hands went to his throat, feeling only the stump of his emasculated tie. He scrambled to his feet and ran away crying.

The children looked at Alex with the blue cloth in his hand as if he'd just slain a lion. This was what it meant to be a champion, a defender of the weak. His gaze rested on Jessica Dubrovnick, a small blonde-haired girl whom Karl had taken money from the previous week.

"Take this," he said, handing her the severed tie. Then he looked at the group of kids around him, using his zip knife for emphasis as he spoke. "Nobody breathes a word of this to any adult," he said. "I'll never be like Karl, but this can't come back on me. Understand? You'll always be safe, but I need to be safe, too."

"If Karl says anything," volunteered Jessica Dubrovnick, "I'll say he's a liar."

Several other kids chimed in, saying they'd take Alex's side over Karl if he claimed anything. His uncle had told him this might happen, but Alex hadn't believed it. With a single act of violence, he had the people on his side.

It was a lesson he wouldn't forget.

Chapter Nine

JACQUETTA WAS ACTING STRANGELY. IN THE early morning, she'd leave their bed and not return for hours. At times, she was giddy and happy, and Vincenzo felt as if he was basking in the bright, warm rays of the sun.

But at other times she was depressed and moody.

When he asked what was wrong, she'd come up with some evasive story, like needing to go to a neighbor's for something she'd forgotten, but he knew that wasn't the real story.

In the two years they'd been married, their life had been sweet. Vincenzo's business had boomed. He found that because of Jacquetta he had the energy of two men. At work, he was more productive than ever, and it seemed as if the crew was actually starting to like him.

He'd nearly forgotten his fatal connection to her family.

Maybe the priest had been right; there was some sort of balancing going on.

One morning after Jacquetta left their bedroom early, Vincenzo decided to wait for her. He watched the clock move from 5:30 a.m. until well past the time he was expected at work. When she returned, she was surprised. "Aren't you supposed to be at work?"

"Yes," he replied, giving her a challenging stare.

"Why aren't you, then?"

"Something's wrong and you're not telling me."

Jacquetta smiled, lifted the bed covers, and lay down next to him. She was cold and shivering. Instinctively, he embraced her. "You're going to be a father," she said. "You know how many miscarriages I've had. I wanted to make sure this one stayed."

"How long?"

She'd been pregnant by him once before, and he'd learned there were several miscarriages with Dante. "Three months. That's usually my danger time. It's only the second time I've made it beyond that time."

"And what are you doing in the morning?"

"An old woman told me to follow a special regimen every morning. I drink a special tea, walk to the church, light some candles, and say some prayers. Sometimes I just forget where I am."

"And then you get back into your night clothes?"

"Oh Vincenzo, I didn't want to tell you until I was even farther along, but now I'm glad you know. This makes us complete."

"Am I . . . going to be a father?" Vincenzo whispered. He could not believe it. He thought of his own father, having him at nineteen, and at twenty-seven looking at many years in jail, then a violent death. Vincenzo was now thirty-three years old. He'd chosen violence at a younger age than his father, and his family had paid a terrible price. When he was a child, he often thought of his father as weak, wasting away in a jail cell, but now he viewed his father differently. He had wanted so much, and yet those dreams were beyond him. No wonder he had lashed out at the jeweler who disrespected him. Jacquetta often talked about the hopelessness of the old country, the leaders pitting people against each other, and how something different existed in America.

Perhaps this was the place where somebody could be better, where one could escape the past.

"There's something I'm worried about." Jacquetta looked directly at him. "When I lost the child at the hospital. . ." she looked away. "I had a lot of damage. The doctor didn't think I'd be able to have any more children. And if I did . . . I might not make it."

"That won't happen," Vincenzo promised. He immediately remembered how he'd promised to protect his family in Sicily and what had happened. But surely, that lightning bolt would not strike him again.

"I want to have your children," said Jacquetta. "I didn't want to have Dante's. I think that's why the one time I came close, the baby knew he shouldn't live. But I worry I killed him with my hatred for Dante. And that because of that hate, God punished me, wounded me."

"You can't think that."

"But I do. I'm worried I've damned myself."

"Then we will be damned together," he said, pulling her tighter.

* * *

AN HOUR LATER, Vincenzo was at the job site under a menacing sky. Rain was several hours off, but the heavens had an unsettling darkness. Only a few men were working on the four-story apartment building he was constructing on the lower heights of Nob Hill. They appeared like phantoms in the fog, barely floating in and out of view above the earth.

Vincenzo wondered if a workman had been injured. It looked like the crew was only about a third of its expected size. The men above stared down at him. Vincenzo went to the small office on site to talk to Paulie.

"What happened to the crew?"

Paulie's blank look telegraphed the bad news. "They said they got a better deal. Ben Kingsfield, Jerry Slovonia, Tim Robbins, Burt Grossman, and Dave Rubino."

"Who?"

"New company started by Goodman and Ricci."

Vincenzo cursed under his breath. Men quitting didn't bother him. But those men were skilled and would be difficult to quickly replace. Yes, there were millions out of work, but this needed to be done by men who knew what they were doing. It was also a blow to his pride, having men taken by somebody he'd once fired. "Did you offer them more money?" Vincenzo asked.

"They said it wasn't about money."

Vincenzo's expression darkened. In the beginning, it had been much easier. There were rules; no alcohol, no arguing, and no lateness. The men seemed eager to follow the rules, Vincenzo telling them he was making them the best workers in the city. But inevitably they started slipping, and Vincenzo wasn't hesitant to send a worker packing. At first it worked, but then for every one he fired it seemed two or three became surly or hostile. Sometimes it seemed he was replacing a full crew every year.

"We keep the ones who know how to bend the rules," said Paulie, "but not break them."

"Is that why you're still here?" Vincenzo snapped and walked out.

The day looked like an infernal twilight with dark clouds blotting out the sun. He doubted whether even a rooster would crow at such a godforsaken sky. He knew the news about Jacquetta's pregnancy should fill him with excitement, but after he left her presence, he couldn't help but feel a deep sense of foreboding.

Ominous signs were all around him. He felt he needed a walk, to get out of his office, and out of his tortured brain.

Trouble with business, the oppressive weather, even people in the street seemed like specters. Cars moved almost soundlessly, as if carrying away the souls of the damned.

Vincenzo realized he'd walked all the way to North Beach, the Italian heart of the city.

Old men on a bench in Washington Park played checkers. The scent of sourdough bread and garlic wafted through the air. Vincenzo felt a pang of memory as a horse-drawn cart with fruits and vegetables passed him, one of the few remaining in San Francisco as Model A's and lumbering Ford trucks sought to replace them.

Vincenzo drew closer to Mr. Patrio's office, and he wondered if this was where his mind had been taking him all along. They'd last seen each other at Dante's funeral. He'd sent the old man an invitation to their wedding, but he hadn't come, or even acknowledged it.

Light shone from inside the glass windows of the Patrio Building Company, almost like a comforting campfire on a dark night. Twelve years earlier Vincenzo had come to this office as a refugee from the fascist assassins who'd killed almost everybody he knew in Sicily. Then he'd been a determined young man for whom no obstacle was too great. Those were the days when his unyielding fury made him as dead to the world as a Trappist monk. There'd been a purity to his drive at that time, an inhuman force that would never flinch from the most difficult of tasks. That hatred had served him well, and yet he was wondering if it had started to master him. He went to Mr. Patrio almost like a penitent to a priest, asking for a curse to be lifted.

Vincenzo pushed open the door and saw Mr. Patrio sitting at his desk on the far side of the room, deep in conversation with another man. Mr. Patrio stopped talking and squinted to see who'd come in. Vincenzo could see his face was more deeply lined with wrinkles and only a thin fringe of white hair crowned his head.

"It's Vince Nicosia," he said, waving a hand as he limped over to the desk.

Mr. Patrio regarded him suspiciously. "Hello, Vincenzo," he said with detached politeness. "I think you know Mr. Giannini, president of the Bank of Italy." He quickly corrected himself, "I mean, Bank of America now."

Giannini stood and extended a hand to Vincenzo. He was roughly the same age as Mr. Patrio, but taller and more robust. His dark charcoal grey suit and gold watch hanging from his vest gave him an air of elegance. "I certainly know Mr. Nicosia by reputation," he said. "They say you're the best builder in the city, after Augustus here, of course." He glanced at Mr. Patrio.

Vincenzo released his hand. "That's a great compliment coming from a man like you." A. P. Giannini was a legend in the Italian community and was quickly becoming known across the country. This grocer's son had founded an immigrant's bank thirty years ago, convincing everyone from Central Valley farmers to factory workers that their money was safe in his bank. After the 1906 earthquake, when San Francisco had been burned to the ground, Giannini had traveled through the smoldering ruins in a horse-drawn wagon, bearing gold coins so people could rebuild their shattered homes and businesses. Whenever somebody said people were not to be trusted, Giannini pointed out that every single dollar he'd lent after the disaster had been paid back. The bank was also funding many Hollywood movies and giving loans to farmers so California could become the breadbasket of the nation after the disaster of the Dust Bowl. Vincenzo knew Mr. Giannini was currently lining up investors to build a bridge across the Golden Gate that would link San Francisco to Marin County.

"I believe what I've heard is true," Mr. Giannini replied to Vincenzo.

Such honest praise warmed him. "Thank you. Your work and bank are well-known. But why are you changing the name?"

Giannini's expression darkened. "Too many people thought we were supporting Mussolini because of the Italy name." He shrugged in a way familiar to most Italians when a situation cannot be changed by reason. "And to be honest, America is an Italian name, so it's really not much of a change. I bought a small bank with that name, and I'm transferring all the assets into it. But to our longtime customers, we will always be the Bank of Italy."

Vincenzo felt his face redden. He remembered the young Mussolini, the forceful man whose arguments had persuaded him to assassinate the Duke. Mussolini had filled him with such hope, such promise, but when Vincenzo had completed his task Mussolini's men struck back with brutal vengeance. "He's an evil man," said Vincenzo.

"Yes, indeed," said Mr. Giannini. "He's a tyrant and far too many Italians are paying attention to him, even in this country. We Italians have an unfortunate flaw. As much as we say we believe in the glorious Roman Republic, the Roman Senate, and its ideals of democracy, in our hearts we still believe a little more in Caesar."

Vincenzo nodded.

Mr. Giannini continued in a passionate tone. "And now we've got that little Austrian corporal taking power in Germany. His first trip was to see Mussolini, like he's an uncle or his older brother in crime. Calls him the 'Great man south of the Alps.' Those two men will be the ruin of Europe."

"I hate him in a way you can't even begin to imagine," said Vincenzo. He felt his hands tingle with the desire to hold a gun.

Vincenzo watched as a flicker of fear crossed Giannini's face. Vincenzo knew he had to let his anger go in front of these two men. They talked of things in a general way. For Vincenzo, it was a visceral hatred that comes only from being betrayed. "I was poor in Sicily," Vincenzo said in explanation. "The fascists made promises. When they took over, it was worse."

This seemed to mollify Giannini. "Yes, you have seen the devil up close."

"I have."

"Is that why you fear banks? You're one of the few who does it the old way, keeping his money somewhere safe."

"Yes. But I know how much they say you are a banker to the people, a man to be trusted. You have small offices you call 'branches' close to the regular folk, and you stay open late, until nine or ten so simple working men can visit after their day is done, while the other banks like to close at three or four."

"I could help with capital, or loans, if you were one of my customers. Go after some of the bigger jobs."

"I'm fine the way I am," said Vincenzo.

Giannini nodded. "Very well. I need to be going now." He shook Vincenzo's hand, then turned to Mr. Patrio and said, "Thanks for breakfast, Gus."

Mr. Patrio stood and came around the desk. He clapped a hand on Mr. Giannini's shoulder. "Always happy to spend time with you, my old friend." He started to walk Giannini out.

At the door, Giannini turned back toward Vincenzo. "You know, Gus here has bought some of the bonds I'm selling for our new bridge. The Gateway Bridge, or Golden Gate Bridge, I don't know what they're going to call it, but we're planning it to be one of the great architectural wonders of the world. It'd be a real safe place to put your money."

"It's a grand plan," said Vincenzo. "But I may be too simple a man for it."

Giannini smiled, still selling as he was getting ready to walk away, and said, "It's going to be a sight to see."

Giannini left and Mr. Patrio turned to Vincenzo. "What can I do for you, today?"

"I'm going to be a father," he replied.

Mr. Patrio's expression softened. "Well, that is a change, Vincenzo. I congratulate you. Children are a blessing to a man. They're the best reason to be a better person because we leave them our reputation."

"Yes," said Vincenzo quickly. "Jacquetta and I are very excited, but it could be dangerous for her, according to the doctor."

"You two will have my prayers," said Mr. Patrio.

Vincenzo nodded. "Thank you. But the real reason I'm here is something else. I'm having some problems with the business. Men leaving. I'm not sure they were good, but they got things done. It's an inconvenience. I think you could put a stop to that."

Mr. Patrio stroked his mustache. Vincenzo knew his meaning was clear. He was asking for an end to the undeclared war between the two of them. "I never had problems with my crews. I always had more men wanting to work for me than I could employ."

"Then you must be a smarter man than I," said Vincenzo.

"I am."

Vincenzo saw a steeliness in Mr. Patrio's eyes he'd never seen before. The jovial man who at times could be mistaken for a fool had a core of iron inside him. Vincenzo could easily imagine the young Mr. Patrio coolly dispatching the four young Comanche braves who'd attacked his camp.

"I've offended you," Vincenzo began. "We had some cross words over Mr. Ricci, but—"

"Conscience getting to you, Vincenzo?" Mr. Patrio had an enigmatic smile on his face and a slight tilt to his head. "That's the thing men like you never consider. You think you've left it behind. But it's with us as long as we're alive. You're not really worried about replacing the workmen Goodman and Ricci took from you. That's a simple matter. You worry what it says about you as a man. Yes, you sign the checks for these men, but you don't have their hearts. Loyalty is earned. Remember what I told you when we met? I have more than two thousand people I can call on, each considering me a friend. How many do you have, Vincenzo?"

"I want this anger to be a thing of the past," said Vincenzo. "Let me live in peace to run my business as I see fit and I'll do the same. And just tell Goodman and Ricci to stop poaching my workers."

Mr. Patrio narrowed his eyes. "Something's different about you. You're scared."

"I'm not scared."

"Let's see if we're talking about the same person. When Jim Ireland made you foreman, the first thing you did was fire your best friend. The first time you had any real power, you ruined one of your benefactors. And when your nephew Alex was bothered by a bully, you taught him to gain respect with the blade of a knife."

Vincenzo couldn't conceal the shock on his face, and Mr. Patrio clearly saw it.

"Yes, I know about your little indoctrinations of Alex. You forget that children talk and that reaches the ears of people like me." Mr. Patrio smiled coldly. "Remember, he's my godson as well, and I take my responsibilities seriously. I swore an oath in God's house that I'd guide him on a righteous path, not the one you've got him on."

Vincenzo swallowed. He wanted peace, even if it cost him some of his pride. "Maybe I was too strong with Alex."

Mr. Patrio walked around to his desk and sat down. "I can't figure you out, Vincenzo. You're a ruthless son of a bitch. You take advantage and don't stop until you've got what you want. That's not uncommon. I see guys like you all around. It's just that I don't have any time for them. Let God sort out you bastards. But then you seem to keep fighting against your nature." He leaned forward and put his hands on his desk. "Now, why are you really here?"

"I've made mistakes and people suffered." He thought not only of his own family, but of the stranger in the *pensione* with whom he shared the truth, who then killed his two friends and permanently crippled him.

"It's your child, isn't it?" Mr. Patrio said finally. "When we first met, you said your family was killed by the fascists. I don't think you meant to tell me that, but you did. And I'll make a guess. You were not blameless in the matter. You did something to bring the darkness to your family. And now you're worried the darkness in your soul will do the same thing to your new family."

"Yes." Vincenzo was surprised by how easy it was to admit this truth. But it was also a simple exchange. He'd ask for forgiveness, and Jacquetta and his child would live. He'd take a different path, have a different intention, and his family would live.

"The devil has a soul, eh?" Mr. Patrio raised an eyebrow. "Penance is possible, but it comes at a price."

"What?"

"Give Louis Ricci back the buildings you stole from him. He'll give you the same sixty thousand I offered you."

Vincenzo laughed. "You expect me to give up half the properties I own? That's more than a quarter million dollars. This is not a fair exchange."

"You've used those properties to buy even more. You won't be left destitute. You'll still have more money than you need, and you'll also have a good reputation. There's much that is commendable in you, but there's also a darkness that needs to be extinguished. I believe in the possibility of your redemption."

Vincenzo was quiet.

Mr. Patrio continued. "When I lived on the frontier, there was a law about horse thieves. We hung them from the nearest tree. A good horse meant life or death for a man. He might starve or be attacked by Indians. You did the same thing to Louis. It's a damned miracle that man had the strength to start over again at his age. You see, I'm letting you off with a light sentence. If we'd ever caught a horse thief, and he tried to give back what he stole to avoid a hanging, we would've laughed ourselves silly."

"Perhaps we can work something out," said Vincenzo.

"I gave you the deal. It's a yes or a no."

"It's a bad deal."

"I think it's very generous."

Taking a deep breath, Vincenzo rose from his chair. His injured leg had gone to sleep. He limped to the door and then paused at the threshold. "I was very interested in working things out with you."

"Only on your terms," said Mr. Patrio. "We don't get to negotiate our redemption. We surrender to it."

Without a backward glance, Vincenzo left. Outside he saw the overcast sky had become even darker.

* * *

Six months later, Vincenzo paced in the hospital waiting room. Since he'd seen Mr. Patrio, he'd obtained men from other sources. Not as good as he wanted, but adequate. Jacquetta's pregnancy had been without incident. She hadn't gained fifty pounds as before and seemed as happy as he'd ever seen her.

Early that morning she'd awakened him and said, "It's time."

Vincenzo had everything packed and ready to go. It meant a great deal to go with her, unlike Dante who'd been with his mistress while his wife was in labor.

But the doctor's warning terrified Vincenzo. The delivery could kill her. He looked at Nick, Rosina, and Alex on the hospital waiting room couch and felt vaguely cheered. He'd called them at five in the morning, and they'd come within the hour.

"Do you want a cigarette?" asked Nick. He pulled out a pack of Lucky Strikes.

Vincenzo accepted a cigarette and a light. Taking a deep breath, he let the smoke snake down into his lungs. "She means everything to me," said Vincenzo. "I told her I didn't care if we had kids as long as I had her."

Rosina gave him a fond look. Vincenzo knew she approved of the way in which he'd taken care of Jacquetta in comparison to Dante. At one family event, she'd taken him aside and asked, "How is it living with my sister?"

"Great," he'd told her.

"She's not too much?"

"No, she's just right."

Dr. Sheffield approached, looking much older than when Vincenzo had first met him. His hair had thinned, and his eyes were sunken like a corpse. Vincenzo wondered if the man would live out the year. He put a hand on Vincenzo's shoulder. "There's a problem," he said.

Vincenzo felt his legs go weak. No escape. He cursed himself, thinking he should have taken Mr. Patrio's offer. If he'd done so, the doctor would not have the look of death on his face. Vincenzo would've undergone any form of unimaginable torture to have prevented this moment. But he had to know, like Pandora had to investigate the evil box and release untold woe on mankind. "Is s-she. . .?" was all he could force himself to ask.

"She's unconscious," said Dr. Sheffield. "She lost a great deal of blood, like she did in her last delivery, but it was worse this time. She will not be able to have any more children."

"But will she survive?"

Dr. Sheffield looked down. "Nobody can say. Sometimes they pull through, other times, well, they. . ." He let his words hang.

"And the baby?"

Dr. Sheffield's expression brightened. "You have a beautiful baby daughter, Mr. Nicosia. I was just going to have the nurse bring her to you."

"No," said Vincenzo. It felt wrong to see his child while his wife lay fighting for her life. "I will not see my child until Jacquetta is well."

"But Mr. Nicosia, that's not necessary."

Vincenzo gave him a look like a wolf ready to pounce, and the doctor quickly backed off. "All right. If you want, I can take you to see your wife."

"Yes. Even if she's unconscious, she'll know I'm there."

Dr. Sheffield motioned for Vincenzo to follow him down the hallway to Jacquetta's room. As he walked, he wondered why God had led him once again to such a precipice. Hadn't he already been pushed off one cliff?

Inside her room the first thing he noticed was the overpowering stillness. The curtains were drawn and a small lamp next to her bed cast a pale light onto her face. Her eyes were closed as if in death, but the slight rise and fall of her chest let him know she still lived.

Vincenzo pulled up a chair next to her bed. He knew she was fighting for her life, but she looked so calm in repose. He couldn't help but feel she was being punished for carrying the seed of her father's murderer in her body, but it made him curse God even more. She was an innocent. If there was any punishment to be made, it should be against him.

He took her hand and rubbed it. "I'm sorry I've done this to you," he began. "I know it's my fault." Tears slipped down his face. "You shouldn't be with me. I've always tried to protect the people I love and done a bad job of it. But please, don't leave me."

He put her hand to his chest. "There's a true heart for you. Even you, who knows love so well, would be surprised at the feeling I have for you. If I had to lose everything, even my life, I'd willingly give it for you."

All day Vincenzo stayed by her bedside. In the evening, Dr. Sheffield told him it was time to go home. Vincenzo glared at him and refused to leave. "It's really against hospital policy," said Dr. Sheffield, but left without attempting to enforce the edict.

Vincenzo didn't care about any rules. He would not break faith with her. God would look down from on high, see his devotion, and withhold His vengeful wrath. Holding Jacquetta's hand, he fell asleep in the chair. When they slept together, he always had to be touching her, as if to reassure himself she was real, and not a dream.

He awoke with a start at about three in the morning, certain of what he should do. He kissed Jacquetta gently on the lips and went out. The night nurses were moving quietly through the halls and a pretty, young blonde one gave him a friendly smile that he interpreted as a sign of divine favor. The spirits of his family were watching over him.

Outside, the stillness of the city at such an early hour unnerved him. He could hear, on some nearby street, a car sputtering along, even discerned the sound of its wheels rushing across the pavement. He had no direction in mind but knew he could probably find a church nearby in which to confront God on His own ground. The night was cold, and his teeth chattered.

He finally found a Catholic one after passing numerous Protestant houses of prayer. Once he'd gone to a Protestant service, and the easy familiarity of the parishioners shocked him. He did not like their aggressive friendliness, sincere earnestness, and light-filled house of worship that reflected belief in a God of goodness. Vincenzo craved the reserve of the Catholic mass—darkened cathedrals with spare shafts of daylight barely illuminating the interior, and the fragile flames of votive candles supporting the prayers of the faithful. This was the lair of the real God, if He even existed, hiding in the darkness like an all-powerful beast. The lair of a God who'd driven humanity out of Paradise for wanting knowledge, drowned his creation in a great flood, destroyed cities with fire, and sent His own Son to die in agony on the cross.

Inside, the only light came from the votive candles near the altar and faint moonlight. Vincenzo knew this was the home of the true God, the one who killed Job's family to test his faith, the God who looked down upon countless acts of cruelty and did nothing.

Vincenzo knelt before the candles, remembering how many times he'd done so as a young boy, praying for his father's release. It seemed several lifetimes ago. In those days he'd known how to pray, to seek the blessings of the divine, and believed his faith would be rewarded. He folded his hands, recited the Our Father, and then said, "The most important thing in my life is in danger. You have the power to make her well if that is your will. I wish there were things I could atone for, but I don't believe I've done anything wrong. Everything I've done is because you've put me in a position, and I had to react. But I don't want to argue about that. Here is simply what I want to say. I would give up my life for Jacquetta, and if you want it, you have only to ask."

In sudden agony, Vincenzo looked upward, "Do you hear me?" he shouted. "Strike me down now, and I'll praise you forever in hell. Strike her down and let me live and there'll be no darker soul on the face of the Earth."

He waited for a moment, made the sign of the cross, and left the church.

* * *

It was near five in the morning when Vincenzo arrived back at the hospital. The streetcars had started running at four, loaded with janitors, maids, and many others going to early jobs. A large Black woman in a white maid's uniform walked with him into the hospital and then disappeared. Vincenzo hadn't noticed it before, but there were many Black people in the hospital, carrying bed-pans and changing sheets, all the jobs nobody else wanted. They moved silently, attracting little attention, and he wondered if they felt as cursed as he did.

In Jacquetta's room she lay still with her eyes closed. Apparently, there'd been no change. Vincenzo took her hand. "I've been to church, *cara,*" he whispered. It seemed as if she could not hear him. But in some inner recess of his soul, it felt better to speak to her. "I told Him to take me instead of you." Vincenzo brought her hand to his face and moved it across his cheek as she'd done so many times before, an intimate gesture that never failed to thrill him. "I could stand anything, except something happening to you." He felt tears running down his face onto her hand. "I know I have a wicked soul, but you're the light for me, the only thing that keeps me from falling into darkness."

Vincenzo remembered what his mother had said when he'd shouted at the Duke after the sentence had been pronounced against his father. "Forgive him. He loves his family too much."

Yes, Vincenzo thought, that was true. He'd always loved his family too much. And now Jacquetta was that family. At times he cursed the cruel twist of fate that made him love the daughter of the man he killed. But most of the time she made him feel such joy in being alive and on the earth that he'd willingly suffer any imaginable torture to be with her.

Exhausted, he slumped down in the chair. A part of him wanted to stay awake, to watch every minute, but the events of the previous day had worn him out. He folded his arms across his chest and fell asleep.

Sometime later a familiar voice came. "Vince?"

He opened his eyes. The curtains were still closed, but their thin material was illuminated by brilliant yellow sunlight. It had to be late morning. He looked at Jacquetta. Her eyes were open, and she had a weak smile on her face.

"Have you been here all night?"

"Yes."

"You were that concerned about me?"

"Very much." All he could do was stare, for he was looking at a miracle.

She took his hand and rubbed it against her face. "I lost the baby, didn't I?"

Vincenzo shook his head. "No."

Jacquetta's eyes grew wide. "We have a baby?"

"A baby girl."

"Where is she?"

"I didn't want to see her until you were awake."

She chuckled and made a slapping motion toward him. "Get the nurse to bring our baby!"

Vincenzo laughed. "Okay."

He lifted himself stiffly out of the chair and hobbled out into the hallway to flag down a nurse. A few minutes later Vincenzo saw the nurse coming back down the hallway with their daughter. Before the nurse entered Jacquetta's room, Vincenzo looked at his daughter. Her features were small and pinched, but she already seemed to have a personality. She was calm, almost at the edge of sleep, and occasionally opened her mouth to yawn. When he put a finger close to her hand, she reached out for it.

He walked with her into the room and put her into Jacquetta's arms.

"She's perfect," said Jacquetta.

"Yes, she is."

"What should we name her?"

"I was thinking of Angelina, after my sister." Yes, he wanted to name his daughter after his murdered sister. Jacquetta knew his family had been killed by the fascists, but not the chain of events that had brought them to his door. That would stay forever hidden.

"Angelina Nicosia," she said, her eyes warm with approval. "You live again. And may this be a better life for you."

Chapter Ten

VINCENZO WAS AMAZED BY FATHERHOOD. ANGELINA could cry for hours, angering him so much he wanted to toss her out the window. But the moment she stopped and smiled, all was forgotten. During the first year, she often woke howling four or five times a night. Jacquetta quieted her most of the time, but Vincenzo also spent time pacing with their daughter. Jacquetta had always been scattered, as if trying to be in seventeen different places at once. But Angelina gave her a sense of singular purpose that Vincenzo envied.

It was like a fairy tale to watch their baby take her first steps, speak her first words. *Children are a rebirth*, he thought. It was the most profound feeling to realize there'd once been another Angelina Nicosia who'd been loved by her parents. Another Angelina Nicosia had crawled along the ground, struggled to stand erect, and was confounded by the complexities of speech, but prevailed. Another Angelina Nicosia had been excited by the sound of her father's voice, helped her mother set the table for the evening meal, and gave mischievous looks to young boys. But that was all dead and buried now like stories of long ago, except that Vincenzo remembered. At times when he watched his daughter, thinking about all that lay in front of her, tears came to his eyes because it was all so beautiful.

She was the reason he'd escaped, so the Nicosias would not all die. He could recreate them. His father lived in him, his mother, his sister, and all of the generations before them, and now they had a new life in her. Vincenzo wondered, as his daughter gazed at the chandelier in their dining room or slept in the softest blankets money could buy, if she knew it had all been for her. The crimes he'd committed in Sicily, the men he'd fired when he became foreman, taking advantage of Mr. Ricci in the wake of the stock market crash; it had all been for her. Like John the Baptist, he'd prepared the way for her arrival, and nobody would ever take that from him.

* * *

"I WANT YOU to come with me this afternoon, Alex," said Vincenzo.

"What for?" Alex asked as he put down his carpentry tools.

They were in the final stages of putting up a four-story apartment building in the Mission District. Alex was seventeen now and had been working for Vincenzo for the past two years. During school, he worked in the afternoon and on weekends when most of the regular crew took off. In the summer, he worked full time, fifty to sixty hours a week. He'd put away a fair amount for college. Vincenzo knew education was important for the next generation, but hoped his nephew wouldn't become one of those snobby college types without an ounce of common sense. Even at a young age, Alex seemed to have a powerful sense of right and wrong, and maybe that was okay in a more balanced world.

Alex was tall like his grandfather and carpentry had made him strong. He was well-liked by the other members of the crew, even more so than Vincenzo. They knew Alex had influence, and he'd intervened a few times to keep Vincenzo from firing men. Productivity had increased since then, and they were keeping workers for a longer period of time.

"I'm going to bid a job today for Antonio Cesari."

"Of Cesari Meats?" Alex asked. The company had been founded in 1897 by Antonio Cesari Sr. and was sold in four western states. Almost every delicatessen in San Francisco offered their fine hams, sausages, and other meats. Alex grinned. "He's a very wealthy man. Are we moving up, Uncle Vince?"

"Perhaps," said Vincenzo, resting his arm on Alex's shoulder. Even though Alex was not an actual blood relation, since Jacquetta could not have any more children Alex was the closest thing to a son he would ever have. At times, he felt somewhere between an uncle and a father to the young man, especially since he'd helped him come into the world. In the past few years, Alex had spent more time with Vincenzo than his own father. Vincenzo told Alex to be careful what he told his parents as he knew they wouldn't approve of some of the lessons he might teach. Alex had a good, calculating mind and was an avid student. After beating up Karl he'd become the most popular boy in school, never had to fight again, and had been elected class president. Vincenzo continued. "We've got some competition. Another firm is bidding against us."

"Do we know their bid?"

"No," said Vincenzo, shaking his head. "We'll be there with Mr. Cesari sitting in judgment, holding all the cards."

"Sounds like an auction."

"And we're on the selling block? But it's very important, and I'll tell you why." He liked giving this kind of information to Alex because he ate it up. "Cesari is not just rich; he's at the very top. They're like royalty. Their money can make things happen. There are the kinds of people I've dealt with, and then there's a level above. I want to crack that level."

"What would you do if you did? Ten years of making all the money you ever wanted?"

"Maybe I'd go back to Sicily. I know it's probably different than when I was there, and I wouldn't go back with Mussolini in power, but ten years from now, who knows?"

"My parents don't like the old country very much," said Alex. "I hear them talk about it sometimes. They talk about the corruption and the poverty and how it all stays the same."

Vincenzo nodded. "There is, but there's also something else. Spirit. Do you know how long the Sicilians have been a conquered people?"

Alex shook his head. Vincenzo smiled. The Duke would have known.

"It started with the Phoenicians, Greeks, Romans, Turks, Moors, the Vikings, and even, for a time, the French. There are no people in the world who've been more conquered, sitting at the intersection of Europe, Africa, and Asia. She's the prize over which everybody fights. Yet there are no people more hopeful for the future, more protective of their families, and more appreciative of the daily goodness of life. It's a beautiful land. The gentle Mediterranean sun, golden fields of grass, and everywhere around it the bluest waters you've ever seen. Nearly eighteen years since I last saw it and, if I close my eyes, I can still remember how the wind rustled the olive groves, the donkeys fought with their cart drivers, and my mother making sure we were clean for Sunday mass. I don't know if you'll ever understand what it's like to love a place so much."

Vincenzo looked at his young apprentice who seemed speechless. The young did not know what loss meant, and perhaps that was the way it should be. Vincenzo tried to bring the mood back to the present. "Okay, let's think about this meeting. Mr. Cesari is very clever. He had more than twenty firms wanting to do the work, and he's chosen two for the final meeting. He won't tell me who the other one is, but I have an idea."

* * *

"Isn't this a surprise?" asked Mr. Cesari.

Vincenzo saw by the amused expression on Mr. Cesari's face that it was no surprise. He liked playing the part of a common man, but he was as cunning as the best of them. "I advertise for bids and the two lowest I get are from companies who've had, shall we say, a certain history?"

Pete Goodman and Louis Ricci sat in the other chairs, with Alex filling up the uncomfortable distance between them. As much as he felt like lunging across the table at Mr. Cesari, he knew it was the kind of response he intended to provoke. Get angry, get rattled, and promise things Vincenzo could never deliver if he wanted to make a profit. Some developers acted as if contractors should pay for the privilege of building their projects. Vincenzo calmly folded his hands in a steeple and stared at the meat baron.

"If I remember correctly, Vince," said Mr. Cesari, "you and Pete worked for Mr. Ireland until you became the new foreman and fired him. Up until then, you two had been the best of friends."

"It was a long time ago," said Pete. "Ancient history."

Vincenzo looked him over. Pete was less the outgoing callow youth he remembered, not as fat, and now there was a steely determination in his eyes. Getting fired appeared to have had a beneficial effect on him. Pete's wife was said to be sick. Vincenzo was saddened to think of the hale, hearty woman who'd fed him when his ribs stuck to his skin, lying in bed at home. It was yet more proof that God did not punish the wicked and reward the virtuous.

Mr. Cesari regarded Pete like a child who'd failed to deliver his lines at the proper time in the school play. He gave an indulgent smile to Pete, then turned his attention back to Vincenzo and continued twisting the knife. "And I believe you built some projects for Louis Ricci until the Depression hit, and you acquired his properties at, shall we say, a greatly reduced price?"

"He stole them from me!" shouted Mr. Ricci. "I trusted him with everything. When I was down, he struck like a snake!" Vincenzo couldn't help but have a grudging respect for Mr. Cesari for unbalancing Mr. Ricci. Vincenzo tried to think how he could turn that to his advantage.

Alex looked warily at Louis Ricci, who'd lived at the Falcone apartment building after Vincenzo evicted him from his own house. Mr. Patrio had arranged it. Alex had told Vincenzo that even though his parents had given him the apartment rent free for two months, Ricci still complained constantly. The steam heater was loud and knocked, the room was stuffy, and the bathroom, which had recently been painted, supposedly gave him headaches. Several times Rosina and Nick wanted to turn him out onto the street.

"I don't know why you're working for this man, Alex," said Mr. Ricci. "Aside from the fact he's your uncle. I always thought you were a pretty nice kid, but your reputation will be dirt if you work for him."

"Please, I don't want to turn this into anything uncivilized," said Mr. Cesari, although that had been exactly his intention.

"Who had the low bid?" Vincenzo asked. "That's what matters." He couldn't imagine he didn't have the low bid. When he ran the numbers he saw he'd take a significant loss, but the prestige of building for Cesari Meats would make up for it in the additional projects that were likely to be funneled his way.

"Oh no," said Mr. Cesari, raising a finger like a schoolteacher pointing out a minor error in a student's answer. "I'll grant that's important, but there are many things to consider. Like labor costs. I know you often have trouble keeping workers, whereas Goodman and Ricci don't have such problems."

"Yes, because they keep the troublesome workers, rather than firing them."

"And apparently they know that," said Mr. Cesari, "which is why they don't stay with you very long."

"Our men stay," declared Mr. Ricci, "because they know we will stand up for them."

"And they walk all over you," said Vincenzo. "Of course they love you. You let them waste time. I complete my jobs much quicker than you do. I don't tolerate lazy workers. I don't think you do, either, Mr. Cesari."

"We've been doing a good job with worker retention," Alex interrupted. "Turnover the past two years has been very low. We've kept more than seventy-five percent of our workers."

Vincenzo knew it was because he'd placed Alex to be the good cop to his bad cop. It worked well, because whether he knew it or not, all the other workmen considered Alex to be an extension of his uncle. It was almost like having a spy in their midst.

Mr. Cesari ignored Alex's contribution. Vincenzo knew this was a game being played amongst men, not boys. Instead, Mr. Cesari turned toward Louis Ricci. "Vincenzo has a point because his jobs are done quickly and generally at a lower price. It's very rare for him to have a cost overrun."

"Because if he comes up short he steals it from the workers and subcontractors."

"And is that better than stealing from me?"

"I'm an honest man," said Ricci. "What do you want me to say?"

"Both of you have very fine companies, and I'm sure that whichever one I choose will be more than sufficient."

"You have your own plans of which we're both in the dark," said Mr. Ricci. "You know we have the best reputation. What else is important to you?"

Mr. Cesari regarded him with the pleasure of a director who finally got the actor to hit his lines. "I know you have an outstanding reputation for honesty, Louis, but your price is too high."

Vincenzo sat back in his chair and smiled. He glanced at Alex who was also smiling. They had this thing. The real price for the building should be four hundred thousand. They'd bid three hundred and eighty, knowing Goodman and Ricci wouldn't go lower than three ninety.

"How much did they underbid us?"

"Ten thousand."

"And you want me to match that?"

"I want you to beat it," said Cesari.

Goodman and Ricci looked at each other, some sort of understanding passed between them, and then Goodman said, "We can go to three seventy-five. And there won't be any cost overruns."

Mr. Cesari looked at Vincenzo. "Can you match that?"

Vincenzo was burning with fury, but he wanted this deal. "Three seventy," he said. Sources told him Goodman and Ricci couldn't afford to lose more than ten or fifteen thousand on the deal. It would hit Vincenzo deeper than he'd planned, but he could weather it.

Mr. Cesari looked back at Pete Goodman. "Three sixty-five," he countered.

"I can't match the offer," said Vincenzo.

Mr. Cesari nodded. "Very well, then. The job goes to Goodman and Ricci."

Alex leaned toward Vincenzo and whispered, "How could they make an offer like that?"

"I don't know," said Vincenzo. "But I have an idea."

* * *

As VINCENZO DROVE to North Beach, he clutched the steering wheel so tightly he thought it might break. Was there anything so low as underhanded betrayal? He thought of the anger he felt toward Mussolini for slaughtering his family. He knew this was different, but it felt just as raw.

Vincenzo pulled his car in front of a fire hydrant, rushing out so quickly he forgot his cane, hobbling to the front door of the Patrio Building Company. He flung the door open and it banged against the wall.

Mr. Patrio was sitting alone at his desk, reading a letter. Vincenzo knew immediately from the calm look on the old man's face that he'd financed Goodman and Ricci and was probably expecting his arrival.

"Did you keep me from getting the Cesari job?"

"I have the most amazing letter here." Mr. Patrio held up a sheet of paper. The letterhead bore the crest of the White House. "It's from President Roosevelt. I met him recently when Grace and I were back east on a trip to visit relatives. It says, '*Dear Augustus: It was a genuine pleasure to meet you and your lovely wife, Grace, in the Oval Office. I hope your stay in the east was an agreeable one and that Grace's cousin, Frank, has better luck with the new store than with the previous one. I enjoyed hearing your strong opinions on my social programs, and must tell you that a number of the members of my own family share your opinion. In my defense, I can only say that if all businessmen were as concerned with the general welfare as you and your good friend, A. P. Giannini, few of my programs would be necessary. Sincerely, Franklin D. Roosevelt.'"*

Mr. Patrio shook his head with a trace of a smile on his face. "I've voted for every Republican since Ulysses S. Grant, but next time I'm probably voting Democrat."

Vincenzo didn't care if Mr. Patrio was on good terms with Saint Peter himself. "Did you offer Goodman and Ricci the money they needed for the Cesari job?"

Mr. Patrio put the president's letter down and pointed at Vincenzo. "I'm still a pretty good gunfighter when I need to be. Yes, I did."

"Why?"

Mr. Patrio motioned for him to take a seat. He refused.

Mr. Patrio shrugged. "You're an affront to everything I believe," he began. "When you came in here looking for work, I didn't ask what you could do for me. I wanted to know what I could do for you. That's called being civil. It's where we get the word 'civilization.' It means we live in a society where we're decent to each other. I don't suppose that has much value to you, but it does to me. From the lowliest shoeshine boy to the president of the United States, I've got a good reputation. If anybody's in trouble, they know I'll try to help out. It gives my life meaning, being of service to others."

"And it's certainly made you very wealthy," snarled Vincenzo.

"Yes, it has," agreed Mr. Patrio. "My success has led to the success of others. Together we have a common vision for the improvement of humanity."

Vincenzo felt an anger building in him as strong as anything he'd ever known. "Everything a man does, he does alone." He thought of his father wasting away in his prison cell, no friends coming to see him, and even pleas to the local mafia boss did nothing. "The only thing of value in a man's life is what he accomplishes on his own. Anything else leads to treachery and betrayal."

His words seemed to have no effect on Mr. Patrio, and he felt foolish for saying them. Instead, in a soft voice, he said, "You're broken in ways I don't think I can fix."

Vincenzo slammed his fist down on the table. "You are the one who's broken! You know I'm stronger than you, which is why you use these underhanded methods to keep me from success. You do not play fair. And a time will come when you pay for it! I've killed men before." Vincenzo wanted to see the fear on Mr. Patrio's face. Whenever he raged at a workman, the others moved away because they'd heard the story of how he supposedly killed Harry Rogers. They didn't know the men he'd really killed.

"So have I," replied Mr. Patrio coolly. "I warn you, Vincenzo, I'm a good friend to have, but I'm an even worse enemy. I have no wish to tangle with you. I gave Pete and Louis the money because they said they might need it. No other reason. It was a business decision. I really haven't given five minutes' thought to you in the past ten years. That's what I do with people like you, those I consider outside the group with whom I wish to associate."

Vincenzo felt that was the unkindest cut of all. He could've accepted it if Mr. Patrio said he'd hated him, had connived and planned with Goodman and Ricci for years. But it hadn't even entered his mind.

"I won't forget this," said Vincenzo as he stood and started to limp out of the office. Suddenly he felt very old and tired. "I just want you to remember you're the one who violated the rules a man should live by, not me."

Chapter Eleven

VINCENZO LEANED BACK IN HIS OFFICE chair in the early morning and felt a rare sense of satisfaction in his accomplishments. He was nearing forty years old in the summer of 1941, had a successful business, and a family he loved beyond measure. Only occasionally did his mind wander back to the dark road he'd traveled as a young man, his father's imprisonment, and his mother's wretched life in the years after. The other unpleasant memories had slowly faded.

Even though Mussolini was still as securely in power as he'd been since 1922, Vincenzo often found himself dreaming of taking his family one day to Sicily and living for a few months, if not a year, in his old hometown. But there were other distractions now, his beloved wife Jacquetta and their daughter Angelina, who was nearing the age for confirmation. Even though he couldn't really muster up much of a belief in God, he found himself comforted by the rituals of the Church. He felt comfortable acting as if he believed. Although he lamented that Jacquetta would never give him a son, he took solace in the fact that Alex was almost like a son to him.

When Vincenzo's thoughts turned philosophical, he considered his life almost as a two-faced mask. One side was dark and brooding like tragedy, containing all the things that shamed him. The other side was light and happy, filled with everything that gave him pride: his family and the hard work he'd done to create a successful business. He was proud of the fact that he had the strength and ruthlessness to do unpleasant things. But the need to do many of those things had faded. He hoped in the future to concentrate on the better angels of his nature.

Vincenzo heard the opening and closing of the front door. His morning reveries had come to an end with Alex's arrival. It was summertime, and Alex, getting ready for his senior year in high school, always came in about seven, barely half an hour after Vincenzo. The young man was a good worker with natural leadership skills. He was affable to other members of the construction crew, and they respected him. He was tall like his grandfather, carried himself with an almost aristocratic grace, and was always courteous, but his mind was sharp enough to know when such pleasantries were unnecessary. Vincenzo could see the cunning in Alex's eyes, and it was something he encouraged. Since conquering the bully at school, Alex seemed to feel there wasn't anything he couldn't do, and Vincenzo even imagined him one day taking over the business.

"Ready to go out to the Gilmore job?" Alex asked, leaning into Vincenzo's office. The company had been constructing a small three-story apartment building in the Western Addition, and the owner, Frank Gilmore, was difficult. Vincenzo wondered why he'd taken on the job when he already had so many projects, but was faced with the simple fact that he hated to turn down work. There was also the threat of increasing competition, much of it coming from Goodman and Ricci. As he expected, Patrio's help had put Goodman and Ricci into a new stratum, but from what Vincenzo heard, there were many complaints about their work.

"I'm not going to the Gilmore job today," said Vincenzo.

Alex raised an eyebrow. "Mr. Gilmore isn't going to like that. You know how he always wants to make sure we're watching over things. And with Paulie and Tommy working on the South Bay project—"

"You're going to be the foreman today," Vincenzo declared.

Alex's eyes grew wide. "But I'm just a kid. I'm just seventeen."

"You've been working with me for three years now. I was with Mr. Ireland for only six months when he made me foreman. Of course, I had to get beat up to do it." Vincenzo smiled, remembering how Harry Rogers had opposed him. After Harry's demise, the workmen became suspicious; opposing Vincenzo meant death. And Vincenzo did not try to convince them otherwise.

"I don't know if I'm ready."

"Consider it a challenge," said Vincenzo. "I'm turning forty next week, and it's making me think about a lot of things. Everything feels right. Do you know how that feels?" He immediately felt foolish for asking such a question. How could his nephew possibly know?

Vincenzo was unsurprised when the young man sheepishly said, "Not really."

"It's probably better that you don't understand. It means you haven't known loss. You have only known victory. Like with Karl Mundt. Be bold, hit fast and strong, and never take any half measures. Friend or foe, love or hate, that's all there really is in this life."

A sharp rapping at the front door made Alex look over his shoulder. "Expecting anyone?"

"No." Vincenzo motioned for him to get the door. "Maybe it's a new client, or Mr. Gilmore sent somebody to complain."

Vincenzo heard Alex open the door and a strangely familiar voice ask for him by name. Alex led the man into his office. The stranger was tall and muscular in a thuggish way, bald, and had a pockmarked face that reminded Vincenzo of rotten fruit. The man smiled, revealing several golden teeth, and extended a hand. "Vincenzo, it's good to see you after all these years, doing so well and being so far from our home."

Vincenzo did not accept the hand. "Do we know each other?" he asked.

The man looked at Alex. "Do you mind if two old friends catch up with each other?"

Alex looked to Vincenzo, who nodded that it was okay. "I'll get going to the Gilmore job."

After Alex left, the man said, "I can't believe you've forgotten me. Perhaps this will help you remember." He pulled up his shirt and pointed to a six-inch scar that ran across his stomach like a bolt of red, jagged lightning.

"Lorenzo De Bruzzi." Vincenzo remembered the young Sicilian bully who'd spoken so disrespectfully of his mother's nights in the streets. It was the first time Vincenzo had held the life of another person in his hand, and it had been an intoxicating brew. Although the look on Lorenzo's young face when he'd stabbed him had thrilled Vincenzo, it also filled him with revulsion. He'd won that battle but turned away from bloodlust until Marcello had revived that demon in his soul.

"You do remember," said Lorenzo, tucking his shirt back into his pants. "I thought you might. I have never forgotten you. A scrawny little boy who suddenly evened the odds by using a knife. We were only children then, but you thought of a way to make me pay. When I was young, I was angry with you for it. But over the years I've come to admire that cunning. It does not surprise me to find the man who was once that boy doing so well now."

"And what is it that you do these days, Lorenzo?"

"Unlike you, I have taken the path of working with others. More of a family thing, offering protection and advantages to businesspeople like yourself."

"I don't pay for protection," said Vincenzo. The West Coast didn't have the large mafia organizations like New York and Chicago, but branches of the families still made occasional forays into the area. Tommy and Paulie were usually all he needed to send their kind packing.

"Yes, what we offer probably isn't necessary for your line of work. You've been successful without the assistance of people like me. Normally, I'd cross you off my list, but when I saw your name, I did a little more investigating. Wanting to know what you've made of yourself out here."

"And what did you find?"

"Many interesting things."

"Such as?"

Lorenzo let the question hang for a moment, a smile playing at the corner of his lips. "Your nephew is a handsome young man. Almost the very image of the pictures I saw of his grandfather at that age. The Duke du Taormina always cut such a dashing figure. Could almost make you believe in the nobility of man."

"And why would that interest me?"

"Because I know of your special affection for Alessandro de Leone, the Lion of Sicily, who was instrumental in putting your father in prison."

Vincenzo shrugged. "My father committed a crime and was punished. What does that have to do with me today?"

"That's not the way you felt when you were in Sicily. Then you burned with hatred for the man. And that's why I told Marcello you were the man to put down the Lion of Sicily."

Vincenzo remained still but felt his blood run cold.

"I know what you're thinking, Vincenzo. Both you and I trusted the fascists. They turned on me, and I had to flee for my life as well. I think it's important you know Marcello did not escape the fascists. Marcello was a stupid animal. He did not realize when Mussolini told him to kill your family, that he would surely be next. I would not have made that mistake."

"What do you want?"

"We are two of a kind, you and me. I tire of working for my bosses back east. They will only let me rise so far. But I see you, here in San Francisco, and I say to myself, this is the place to make something of myself."

"And you think I would do this even though you've just told me you were responsible for the death of my family?"

"Mussolini killed my family, as well. I share your grief. We were young and did foolish things. Let us not be foolish again. We should be the ones in charge."

"And if I say no?"

"To keep a continuing secret requires a continuing payment. One way or another, we will work together."

"Get out of here," Vincenzo said in a tone of cold fury as he rose from the desk.

"And where will I go? To your lovely mansion on Green Street where I'll have a word with your wife, the daughter of the Duke? Or should I just send her a letter with all the relevant details?"

"If you do that, I'll kill you."

Lorenzo rose from his chair. "It's a funny thing, but the older we get the more we want to keep living. And the more we want to be respected in the eyes of our family. I've given you a good deal to think about. I'll be back in touch when you've had some time to think over my proposition. We are not young men anymore. We do not have time for useless fights. We should simply think about ways we might improve our lives."

He tipped his hat to Vincenzo and left the office.

Vincenzo felt the anger slowly draining out of him. In its place was calculation and plans to fight. It wasn't in Lorenzo's interest to ruin him. He remembered how Lorenzo liked to play with his victims, break them psychologically so he didn't have to do as much physically. There was a way to fight this man. He just didn't know what it was, yet.

* * *

"Papa, why do people do bad things?"

It was early Sunday afternoon, and Vincenzo was walking hand in hand with his daughter, Angelina, through Golden Gate Park. They'd attended eight o'clock mass, had breakfast where she'd wolfed down an entire order of French toast thick with whipped cream and strawberries, and then gone to watch the toy sailboats on Stow Lake. Later, they planned to see an afternoon movie. She looked up at him with dark, questioning, seven-year-old eyes. In those eyes Vincenzo saw all the innocence of his sister until the day she was murdered. On that day, his sister's eyes held terror and fear, but also the pain in her soul of something that had been profoundly broken. He wanted to protect his daughter in a way he hadn't been able to protect his sister.

"I don't know, honey. There are lots of reasons. Why do you ask?"

"There's this girl in school who does mean things. I'm always nice to her, but she frowns at me and says nasty things. The other day we were standing in line, and she pinched me real hard."

Vincenzo thought for a moment. He always tried to answer Angelina's questions as honestly as possible. A few months ago, she'd asked where babies came from. He didn't say they came from storks, or that they were found by their mothers under cabbage leaves, but told her directly how a baby grew in its mother's womb and was delivered. He felt it was important not to lie to children, and that sometimes their questions had no good adult answer. "Sometimes people are just bad," he said. "And other times it's just temporary. They're growing up and what makes sense to them one day seems foolish the next. I think the problem with this girl is probably temporary."

Angelina's face became sour. "I don't think so. She just seems real mean. She scares me."

Vincenzo tried to figure out what to do if this girl continued to bother Angelina. With a boy like Alex, it was easy to solve. But females were different. Angelina didn't have to worry so much about being beaten up by another girl, only annoyed. However, with girls, that type of social shunning was often more traumatic than boys getting into a fight. The thought of anybody upsetting his daughter caused him deep concern.

"Look at that, Papa!" Vincenzo felt a sudden tug on his hand. Angelina pointed toward the shore of the lake. An old organ grinder with a small monkey was beginning to play. The monkey was on the old man's shoulder, holding a tiny cup. Children were starting to gather. The organ grinder wore a red vest and gestured to the children that they could pet the monkey.

Angelina broke from her father's grasp and ran toward the old man.

"Angelina!!" Vincenzo cried out, but she didn't stop. He started to walk quickly, then slowed and smiled. She'd reached the organ grinder and was peering curiously at the monkey. The old man dropped to one knee so Angelina could get a closer look. She reached out, and the monkey cautiously wrapped a hand around one of her fingers. "Papa, the monkey's shaking my hand!" she said with excitement, then turned her attention back to the tiny primate.

Vincenzo felt somebody behind him then, a large man, and a familiar voice whispered in his ear. "She reminds me so much of your sister. They both had such an innocent view of the world." Vincenzo turned to see Lorenzo behind him. "I don't think your sister ever knew what her mother did during those years she was a baby. You protected her from finding out. It would be good if your daughter never knew what her father had done."

"What are you doing here?" Vincenzo asked furiously. "I'm with my daughter. Have you no respect?"

"I wanted to see if you'd considered my idea of us going into business together."

"It's too bad Mussolini didn't kill you like he did Marcello."

"He tried to get rid of me, just as he did you. You see, we are very much alike, you and me. We're both very hard to kill."

"We're nothing alike."

"I didn't have to work very hard to find the wolf behind that calm exterior. You put on a charade that you have become a good man in this country. I have no such illusions. I know I am a bad man. And I know that you are still one, too."

Vincenzo decided to play along. "Let's say I'll consider it. What's your idea?"

"I am offering my friendship to you. In fact, I would be a secret friend to you. Nobody would know about it. Your enemies would simply find unpleasant things happening to them. I know men who would do these things, but they would never be traced to you."

"What kind of things?" Vincenzo asked.

Lorenzo laughed. "That is the Vincenzo I knew. Still the wolf. It would depend. We wouldn't want to get predictable. For one it might be a labor shortage, another man finds himself in the middle of a scandal, and maybe somebody's building burns down, just after the insurance company has canceled their fire protection. For myself, I'm always partial to a good fire."

"We may have something to discuss," said Vincenzo. "But not here."

Lorenzo spread his hands in a gesture of acceptance. "I will leave you to your daughter on this fine Sunday." Lorenzo offered his hand once more.

Vincenzo did not take it. Lorenzo smiled and withdrew his hand. "Until we meet again."

Vincenzo watched as Lorenzo walked away.

"Papa, come over here!" said Angelina, still entranced by the monkey.

Vincenzo took a moment, letting the fear and anger drain out of him as Lorenzo vanished into the crowd of families. He thought of what he might do to Lorenzo, how to spring the trap, his mind working through the details, until it all clicked into place. With his plans set, Vincenzo felt himself return to the world.

He smiled and walked toward Angelina.

* * *

JACQUETTA WAS DEEP into spring cleaning on the second floor and going through some old dresses when she heard the front door open and close.

Her heart skipped a beat. Her husband and child were home. Even after nine years of marriage, she felt a great attraction and love for Vincenzo. He was still so kind, bringing flowers every week, shaving when he came home from work so his face would be soft to the touch when they lay in bed. There were a million kind things he did for both her and their daughter, like taking Angelina to the park so Jacquetta could have a few hours to herself. Most Italian men balked at helping with their children, but to Vincenzo it seemed the reason for life itself.

It surprised Jacquetta that she could feel so strongly for any man. With Dante there had been love and the discovery of sexuality, but in the later years it was always like an ill-satisfied hunger. She wanted and desired, he gave himself grudgingly, yet the encounters ended without any feeling of fullness. She'd hated, then needed at the same time, and despised herself for not being able to sort out her feelings.

With more hatred of Dante than need for Vincenzo, she'd slept with Vincenzo that first time. She'd intended it as an offense against Dante, against herself, and most of all, against the God who had been so cruel to her.

But there'd been no punishment for her transgression.

Only love grew out of her grief and hatred. Vincenzo had been so kind to her in the months that followed, but most of the time she was numb to it. At first, she did not think there was a chance for something good, merely a bittersweet farewell to a part of her life that had ended with Dante's death.

However, when she awoke from her sleep of grief, he'd still been there. The seed that had been planted at the first snowfall of winter bloomed with the thaw of spring. The need was as strong as ever, but without the hate or confusion. He became an obsession to her. At family dinners or in public, it was torture to look at him and be unable to do the things she wanted at that very moment. She wanted him to come to her, be inside her, to be both lost and found in him.

"Vince?" she called out.

"Could you come down here, please?" he asked.

"Is everything all right?"

"We need to talk. Quickly." His voice had a nervous tone she'd never heard. He was always a pillar of confidence. Jacquetta left the pile of dresses she'd been going through and hurried to the stairway.

At the top of the stairway, she could see that Angelina looked calm, but Vincenzo's features were drawn tight. "What's the matter?" she asked as she reached the bottom of the stairs.

"We saw a monkey at the park, Mommy," Angelina interrupted. "Can we get a monkey?"

Vincenzo patted Angelina on the shoulder. "Why don't you go wash up, honey? Mother and I need to talk."

She smiled and looked up at her father. "Are you going to talk about me getting a monkey?"

"Among other things," he said. "Now go."

She raced up the stairs.

"What's wrong?" Jacquetta asked.

"I want you to go and stay with your friends in San Jose for a few days," Vincenzo said flatly. "I need you to leave within the hour."

"What is it?"

"Something from Sicily followed me."

He'd told her about part of his past, and she didn't seem to mind that he kept other parts from her. To her, he was a child of the Sicilian streets who'd made good in the United States. She'd been wealthy, but still able to see the desperation in which so many lived and not judge what others had done to survive.

"Are we in danger?" she asked.

"Yes." Jacquetta saw Vincenzo visibly relax. It had always calmed him to tell the truth.

"I want to stay," said Jacquetta.

"No. I lost my entire family in Sicily. I need to know you're safe, so I can be strong."

"I don't want to lose you."

Vincenzo smiled. "I'm hard to kill."

"When you do this thing, will it be over? Truly over?"

"I have a plan. It's a good one. But one never knows."

Jacquetta nodded. He'd told her a hard truth, but she accepted it. "I have loved you like no other," she said.

"As have I."

She put a hand to his face. "Come back to me, Vincenzo Nicosia."

"I'll do my best."

She could feel tears forming in her eyes as she leaned forward to kiss him. They kissed for a moment, she felt her hot tears fall upon his face, and then she turned away from him to get things ready for their departure.

* * *

VINCENZO WAITED IN his office with five thousand dollars in a briefcase. At precisely 7:00 p.m. he heard the door open and a moment later Lorenzo walked in.

"Can I get you anything? Tea, a coffee, maybe some water?" Vincenzo asked.

"Your kindness is appreciated, but no. I'm fine." Lorenzo eyed the briefcase and sat down. "I see you have my money."

"Yes. On the phone you explained it was to get us started."

Lorenzo motioned for the briefcase.

Vincenzo nodded and handed it over to him.

Lorenzo opened the briefcase and smiled when he saw the money inside. "This all seems in order."

"What now?" asked Vincenzo.

"We start from the top. Augustus Patrio. I know you harbor some ill feelings toward him. Then once we have him, we start working on his friend, A. P. Giannini and the Bank of America. Guys like us haven't gotten into banks, but it's the sensible play. Like when they asked that bank robber, Willie Sutton, why he robbed banks. He said, 'That's where the money is.' You know the bankers are the real criminals."

"Patrio doesn't get intimidated."

"You know what they say about people who play with fire? Well, I'm one of them. Patrio might be a little more amenable if some of his buildings started burning down."

"What about the New York people?" Vincenzo asked. "Seems like they'd want some of this."

Lorenzo shifted in his seat. "This is something we would be doing without them. By the time they realize what's happening, we would already be established."

"Let me set up a meeting with Patrio," said Vincenzo. "He's a tough old bird, but we might be able to persuade him if we had the appropriate muscle." Vincenzo motioned to the briefcase he'd given Lorenzo. "That will be used to hire the appropriate men?"

"Yes," said Lorenzo. "I will get started on it first thing tomorrow." He seemed almost giddy. "I had thought it was so fortunate when I saw your name among the city's leading men. We fought in the streets of Sicily, but here in America we are joined in business."

Vincenzo nodded, and Lorenzo took that as his cue to leave.

When the front door closed, Vincenzo went to the window and watched Lorenzo cross the street. Paulie walked by the window with a subtle nod to Vincenzo, who flicked a finger toward Lorenzo. Vincenzo couldn't help but think that Lorenzo was making the same mistake he had when they'd met as children in the street: he'd let his guard down.

* * *

VINCENZO SHIVERED AS he stood on a grubby street in the Tenderloin.

He watched the light in a seedy flophouse room flicker off. Paulie had followed Lorenzo here, bribed the manager to admit him to Lorenzo's room, and discovered several containers of diesel fuel. It was a good choice. Better than gasoline because it burned longer and was less explosive.

Apparently, Lorenzo liked to be prepared, and low-profile, which probably explained why he was staying in this area of town. But he also had a fondness for drink. Paulie had tailed him to several bars that night and by the time he arrived back to the flophouse he'd barely been able to get through the door. Every man had a weakness. One just had to find it.

Paulie and Tommy were on the opposite side of the street, and Vincenzo nodded to them. They made their way to the flophouse. Vincenzo waited. He knew Paulie had made a copy of the key and could easily gain entrance to Lorenzo's room. The signal for Vincenzo was when the light in Lorenzo's room came back on.

After a few minutes the light flicked back on, and Vincenzo made his way into the building. The door to Lorenzo's room was slightly ajar and Vincenzo went inside, closing it behind him.

Paulie and Tommie had Lorenzo tied to a chair, a towel gag in his mouth, and a can of diesel next to him.

"You didn't think I had a little muscle of my own, did you?" said Vincenzo. "That's the thing about a Sicilian. We may go years without being violent, but we are always ready for it. These are some of my best workmen, but they're also killers when they need to be."

Lorenzo struggled to say something.

"If you promise to speak very softly, I will take the gag out of your mouth. Do we have an agreement?"

Lorenzo nodded. Vincenzo nodded for Paulie to remove the gag.

"It wasn't me who was responsible for your family, Vincenzo. It was Marcello and Mussolini. We should leave that behind in the old country. Mussolini killed my family, as well."

"It seems we have all suffered for our choices," said Vincenzo.

"Yes! Yes! I had three brothers and five sisters. All dead."

"But you were the most responsible. You pointed the evil eye in my direction. Took advantage of my weakness."

"What we have is not weakness. It is strength. We are the men who bend the world to our will."

Vincenzo motioned for Paulie to put the gag back on him. Lorenzo struggled, but within a moment it was back in place.

"It's time for this to end."

Vincenzo motioned to Tommy who picked up the can of diesel and poured it over Lorenzo. Vincenzo reached into his jacket pocket and brought out a matchbook. "You were wrong about me,

Lorenzo. I will not enjoy your death. I am merely indifferent to it. No one will mourn you. Your bosses in New York will hear of your loss and simply shrug their shoulders. Another idiot who brought his own death upon himself."

Vincenzo struck the match, and then threw it into Lorenzo's lap. The flames quickly kindled, and Lorenzo squirmed, his eyes going wide with terror as Vincenzo caught the whiff of burning flesh. Vincenzo wished he could feel something for this man about to die. But he had been a thug in Sicily, and he was a thug in America, bringing only death in his wake.

Vincenzo watched the flames grow higher, heard Lorenzo's muffled screams through the towel, watched his struggle, but couldn't tear himself away.

This was the justice God should have delivered, and yet it was left to Vincenzo to carry out the sentence.

"Boss, we got to go!" said Tommy.

Vincenzo looked at him. "Yeah. Make sure people know there's a fire. Only the guilty die this time."

The three left the room, shouting and knocking on doors, "Fire! Fire! Everybody needs to evacuate!" before racing out of the building.

The residents would never know their names, but in the stories they told their families, the three of them were angels who sounded the alarm and rescued them from a burning building, then vanished into the night.

* * *

WHEN VINCENZO ARRIVED home, he picked up the phone and called the house where Jacquetta was staying. The phone rang twice, and then was picked up.

"Hello," said Jacquetta's sleepy voice.

"It's me," said Vincenzo.

"Are you okay?"

"Yes, I'm fine."

"Is it over?"

"Yes."

"Will you ever be able to tell me about it?"

"No."

"But it's really over?"

"Yes."

Vincenzo hoped it was true. In his mind, there was only one man left in the world who drew his hatred. But this man lived in Rome, surrounded by armed guards in black shirts supporting a government that was nothing more than unprincipled barbarism. This man ruled Italy with a stronger grip on power than any in the past thousand years. He'd taken over the ancient Roman possessions in North Africa, signed a pact of steel with the German dictator to the north, and even made peace with a Catholic Church alienated from the Italian state since the first king of a united Italy had assumed the throne more than seventy years earlier.

The ruler was distant, but in Vincenzo's heart there was only hatred for the man called *Il Duce*, Benito Mussolini, the Italian dictator.

* * *

AFTER SHOWERING AT home, Vincenzo went to the office.

It would be a few hours until Jacquetta and Angelina arrived home, and he wanted to feel the act he'd committed slip away from him in the mundane details of his business. He focused his mind on the tasks of the day, rather than what he'd done the previous night. It was important not to feel guilt. In the days after the murder of his family he'd felt enormous guilt. Not for what he'd done, but for his failure to anticipate how they might come after his family. When one became older it was important not to make such mistakes.

"The Gilmore job is done," Alex announced proudly when he walked into the office. "Put the final touches on it around eight last night."

"Three hours after the end of the workday," Vincenzo said with pride.

"The day is over when the work is done," Alex replied. "Not before."

"Good boy. Now we just have to get Mr. Gilmore to make the final inspection."

"He did that at eight-thirty." Alex held up the final signed completion document and a check from Mr. Gilmore, which he handed to Vincenzo.

"Impressive," Vincenzo said, looking at the check. Gilmore was rarely satisfied with anybody's work. Vincenzo always planned an extra week or two in the schedule to take care of the inevitable additions.

Alex seemed to be bouncing on his toes with excitement.

"Let's get some breakfast," said Vincenzo, grabbing his jacket. "Celebrate the completion of my nephew's first big job."

"Really?"

"Yes."

"Okay."

As they walked out of the office, Alex asked, "Hey, did you get together with that old friend of yours?"

"He was not a friend. Just a mistake from my past."

"He looked mafia," said Alex.

"Yeah."

"Is he gonna be trouble?"

"I don't think so." Vincenzo looked at his nephew as they walked to the restaurant. He held his gaze for a moment, and then said. "I'd appreciate it if you never said anything about him to anybody."

"Why?"

"When you're older, you'll realize one of the most important things a man can do is keep those he loves from worrying about things. Men take care of things. Then we do not talk about them. And that is the burden we bear to protect others. Do you understand me?"

"I do, Uncle. I think I do."

"You're a good man, Alex. You'll go far."

Book II

Return of the Lion

Chapter Twelve

"CAN I TALK TO YOU?" ASKED NICK FALCONE.
Alex looked at his father. It was the morning of Angelina's confirmation, and Alex was getting ready in his room. Alex was in his final year of high school, planning to go to the University of San Francisco, a good Jesuit institution, to study business in the fall of 1942. His thick, dark hair was almost like a mane, and his strong jawline, perfect nose, and languid eyes combined to give him a regal, almost unearthly appearance, like a warrior angel one might see in a Michelangelo painting. Over the past year, Nick had noticed his son often checking himself out in the mirror, and Nick could imagine the questions running through his son's mind.

Am I handsome?

Will girls like me?

Alex worked so hard at school, team sports, and in his uncle's business that he didn't realize he was the subject of many a young woman's fantasies. At six foot two, he was taller than most of his classmates and working construction had made his chest broad and his arms thick. The previous Thanksgiving, with absolutely no prompting from his parents, he'd gone to a tailor and bought a fine, pin-striped three-piece suit and imitation gold watch. At the time, Nick and Rosina had thought their son was trying to match the sartorial elegance of his wealthy uncle, but now it came in handy for the confirmation ceremony.

Yeah, sure," Alex said to his father.

Nick was silent for a moment, gathering his thoughts. He knew his son didn't look up to him as he did to his Uncle Vincenzo. Nick thought about how Alex had come to him and

Rosina when the bully, Karl Mundt, had been going after him. They'd tried to handle it the proper way, but knew it hadn't gone well. He suspected Vincenzo had stepped in, because after that his son's confidence had gone up significantly. Alex had started going out for school sports; he had a keen eye in baseball for the perfect pitch to hit, as a running back on the football team he danced and weaved through defensive linemen, and in basketball he had beautiful hand-eye coordination and could sink a shot from anywhere and hit nothing but net. Of course, he'd also been elected class president. He was the kid nobody worried about, but Nick worried.

"I want to talk to you about working for Vince," he said. Nick saw his son visibly stiffen. Nick never referred to him as Uncle Vince, and Nick knew it bothered his son. In his defense, Nick always spoke well of Vince as a husband to Jacquetta and a better family man than Dante had ever been, but it was clear there was no real affection between the two men.

"What about it?" Alex asked.

"I don't think it's good," said Nick, who could look severe with his high forehead and thick glasses. "I hear bad things about him. He hires former crooks and Mr. Patrio, your godfather, thinks he's a violent man. Now, I haven't seen any of that behavior, but I don't think that's an environment you should be around."

"You also made Vince my godfather," Alex reminded him. "And he is my uncle, as well."

"We did make him your godfather. He was there when your mother went into labor with you, and I'm eternally grateful for that. But I can't dismiss what somebody like Mr. Patrio tells me."

"Mr. Patrio doesn't like Uncle Vince because he's a better builder than Patrio," Alex replied angrily. "He gets the job done quicker and for a lower price." Privately, Alex worried about the "friend" who had come to visit his uncle. How had Vince been so certain he would not be a problem? Alex knew that in discussion with Vince and his favorite workers, Paulie and

Tommy, there were looks between them that conveyed more than their words.

"That may be true," said Nick, "but I've always trusted Mr. Patrio's judgment."

"He's wrong this time," Alex said.

"I know you hear me, even if sometimes you want to make me think you don't. I'm just telling you to be careful. Sometimes people aren't who they appear to be."

"Uncle Vince is exactly who he appears to be," Alex replied.

Nick exhaled deeply, knowing the conversation was over.

Alex almost felt sorry for his father. He knew his father would not fight him. He was not a man who liked confrontations. At times, Alex almost felt as if his father was a powerless man, somebody who made little difference to the world, but that wasn't the way people treated him. If anything, Alex was often surprised at how much others sought him out for advice. When Alex had overheard people talking with his father, he noticed his father generally remained quiet, letting them spin out their stories, and then he might ask a series of questions, at which point the person would respond. Often at the end of these conversations, the other person would ask his father, "What do you think I should do?"

Normally his father would say something like, "If you genuinely consider the questions I've asked, you'll know what to do. You understand your life better than me."

Alex was aware of more than a few adults who held his father in exceptionally high regard, impressed with the fact he'd gotten a degree in mechanical engineering and had recently gotten a job with the Army Air Corps at Moffett Field in the south bay to work on their airplanes and dirigibles. But these things did not draw Alex's admiration. Like his uncle, Alex enjoyed working with the earth, stone, metal, and wood—creating something out of nothing. As far as Alex was concerned, his father worked in the rarefied air where his planes and airships flew, while his uncle worked among reality and the things of the ground.

"You'd better finish getting ready," said Nick finally, and left his son's room.

* * *

VINCENZO SAW SUNDAY, December 7, 1941, as a day full of omens.

Not only was the seventh his murdered sister's birthday, but it was also his daughter Angelina's confirmation. Angelina was now eight years old, slender, and dark-haired like her mother, with dark almond eyes, but she was less fiery. She had more of her aunt's calm temperament.

Angelina's eyes looked modestly down as she stood before the altar in her white dress and pledged to be free from sin, follow God's teachings, and have faith in the face of any adversity.

These were the same words he'd spoken as a boy in Sicily, even though his mother was still walking the streets at night. She had made sure Vincenzo was confirmed, but to him it had all seemed a charade. He'd remembered the priest at his confirmation, talking about the fall of Lucifer. The renegade angel's sin had been pride, disbelieving in the wisdom of God. "But all things serve Him," the priest said on the day of Vincenzo's confirmation. "Even Lucifer serves God's plans by showing the majesty of our Lord."

After the service, guests arrived at Vincenzo and Jacquetta's house for a festive brunch. Jacquetta was happy to have many glasses of champagne waiting for them. That availability had become a private joke between her and Vincenzo since their first drink together had been when alcohol was still illegal. Prohibition had ended just as the Depression was beginning to hurt the public. But Vincenzo had weathered that storm.

Jacquetta had hired waiters in tuxedos, and after church the house was quickly filled with people. Vincenzo had turned on the radio to get some music, but on a Sunday morning there were only religious sermons and religious songs. He'd wanted to get the

Victrola and put on some music, but Jacquetta told him to simply leave the radio on at a low level. "I think after twelve o'clock we'll get some regular music."

"It's a proud day for you," said Nick to Vincenzo. Alex walked up to the two men, a glass of champagne in his hand, and an impish smile as he took a drink. He had recently celebrated his eighteenth birthday.

Vincenzo nodded. He liked Nick, but knew the feeling wasn't mutual. Vincenzo was always deferential to Nick, but could sense the man's distrust of him. Still, this was family, and he knew he must put on his best face.

"I can't believe she's as old as she is," said Vincenzo, sticking to safe topics. "Next thing you know, she'll be getting married."

"I don't know, Uncle Vince," said Alex. "I heard she really got into all the church stuff during her confirmation lessons. Maybe it'll be the convent rather than the altar for her."

"If she goes into the convent, it'll be over my dead body," Vincenzo joked. "I want grandchildren someday, a lot of little ones running around calling me *nono*, or grandfather."

The religious broadcast was interrupted, and an announcer broke in. With a shaky voice he reported, "The Japanese Empire has attacked Pearl Harbor in Hawaii, sinking several American battleships. More than a thousand men are believed to be dead. The attack was completely unprovoked. It's a terrible, terrible outrage." The radio announcer seemed to have trouble continuing to speak and another announcer took over.

Conversation stopped at the party as everybody strained to hear what was being said.

President Roosevelt was calling a special session of Congress the following Monday. There were radio reports from Pearl Harbor, describing the carnage.

"There's going to be war," said Nick. "Soon we'll be up against Germany and Italy, as well."

"They didn't attack us. Just Japan did," said Alex.

"I hear a lot of talk at the base," said Nick. "This is what Roosevelt's been trying to get us ready for. The only question is whether we've done enough." Nick shook his head. "Attacking Hawaii, that was pretty bold. Might put us out of action in the Pacific for a year or two."

"I want to enlist," said Alex.

"Don't be in such a hurry," Nick replied. "I remember my friends going off to fight in the Great War. Didn't expect to see so much dying in the trenches. War's a brutal business. I got called up, but my date for enlistment was one day after they signed the Armistice. Later I talked to my friends who'd been over there. Wasn't what they'd expected."

"But we've got to do something," Alex protested.

"Remember, Alex, I work for the Army Air Corps. I am doing something."

Vincenzo could see that Nick had diminished himself in his son's eyes. Alex was similar to how Vincenzo had been as a young man, full of the desire for adventure, to strike out against something. He remembered the exhilaration of meeting Mussolini, planning the assassination of the Duke, and the oath he'd sworn with Michael and Roberto, that they'd always live as men, unafraid to face any foe. However, with the passage of time he'd realized Nick's perspective was the wiser one.

"They promised us that the last war would be the last one, the one that would establish peace and democracy throughout Europe. Millions died. And for what?"

Alex ran his hand through his hair. Vincenzo could feel his frustration. "We can't just do nothing," he said in exasperation, as people continued listening to the radio broadcast.

* * *

VINCENZO FOUND ALEX later that day, sitting outside on the curb, looking out at the San Francisco Bay and the Golden Gate Bridge to the west.

"The danger is out there," said Alex, motioning to the Pacific Ocean. "Just a few thousand miles away. We have to stop it."

Vincenzo sat down next to him. "You know your father is just worried about you."

"I know."

"And you could die. I know you don't think that, but there's no reason it couldn't be true."

"You're taking my dad's side?" Alex asked.

"No. Just telling you the way things are."

"You don't think I should enlist?"

Vincenzo took a deep breath. "Sooner or later all the young men will go. I don't think you'll have a choice."

"I want to go."

"I know you do. But when you do, I think you should have a different purpose than you do now."

"What's that?"

"Right now you hate the Japanese. A lot of people hate Hitler because of what he's done in Europe. But the person you should hate is Mussolini."

"Mussolini?"

"Yes. Blood should be repaid in blood. I know your parents have talked about your grandfather's death, wondering if it was a mafia killing, maybe bandits, but there was more to it. I know. I was in Sicily at the time." Vincenzo paused, wanting to proceed cautiously, not wanting to give away too much. "Your grandfather was encouraging the king to stand against Mussolini and his black shirts. He might have been planning a coup against the king with some of the generals if the king didn't agree with him. But somehow Mussolini got wind of his plans. Mussolini gave the order for your grandfather to be killed. Mussolini is the one who perfected the strategy of the dictators, followed by Hitler and the Japanese."

Alex was quiet, stunned by the revelation. "And Mussolini had my family killed as well," Vincenzo added.

"Were they working with my grandfather?"

"No," said Vincenzo. "Different reasons. But their existence was also a threat to him."

"You think Mussolini is the one I should hate?"

"I think it is your destiny to kill Mussolini," said Vincenzo. "I've been thinking about this since we heard the news from Hawaii. I have this overwhelming feeling the two of you are destined to meet. I want you to watch as the light leaves his eyes. You will kill Mussolini for your family and for mine."

* * *

"PLATOON HALT!" SHOUTED Sergeant Orona, nicknamed the "Spanish gentleman" by his troops, although when he wanted he could swear with the best of them.

"We're almost in Taormina," protested Alex, now Private Falcone, "and we've still got a few hours of daylight. I'm sure the Germans have already bugged out to Messina, trying to get back to Italy."

"You want to fight like Patton," replied Orona, with a smile. "But unfortunately, I'm in charge here, and I say we wait."

The other troops cheered Orona, and Alex knew the platoon was tired and needed a rest after weeks of heavy fighting.

Alex had signed up the day after Pearl Harbor and left for boot camp six weeks later. Nick turned white when Alex told him about the enlistment, but by the time he departed, his father had reconciled himself to the inevitable. Before he left, though, his father gave him a medallion of the warrior archangel, Saint Michael, depicting him defeating the devil in the War in Heaven.

"Saint Michael has two aspects to him," said his father in presenting the medal to Alex. "He's the leader of the heavenly host, God's mightiest angel, whom he picked to lead the angels against Satan and his demons. But there's also another tradition from the Middle Ages about Michael, that God put him in charge of weighing the souls trying to get into heaven. And the story is God keeps getting mad at Michael because he lets too many people into heaven. Michael is God's greatest warrior, but his compassion toward our flawed humanity surpasses even that of our Lord. I want you to be like Michael in all that you do in this war."

Alex had been overwhelmed by his father's gift and told him he would try to follow Michael's example.

Boot camp was harder than Alex had expected and each night he collapsed into bed feeling like every part of his body had been abused. But he did well in his unit and finished first in basic training, marking him as future officer material.

Their platoon had been part of the second wave in North Africa, fighting against Rommel, and in the first wave with Operation Husky, the amphibious landing in southern Sicily in the early morning hours of July 9, 1943.

While they'd been fighting in Sicily, more than five hundred Allied bombers struck Rome. On July 22, Patton took the Sicilian capital of Palermo, and three days later King Victor Emmanuel III arrested Mussolini and had him placed under custody, but declared their alliance with Hitler remained intact. After taking Palermo, Patton was determined to beat the British general, Bernard Montgomery, to the other side of the island, where the Germans were seeking to evacuate their forces from Messina to the Italian mainland.

"Looks like you lost that battle with the sarge," said Alex's friend, Bill Squire, as he set up his bedroll for the night. Bill was a corn-fed Nebraskan, a son of Middle America, with blonde hair and a gunfighter's blue eyes. He also had a fatal weakness for Sicilian women, having proposed to two different women in the four weeks they'd been fighting on the island. Luckily, they lived in different towns.

It hadn't been difficult to fall in love with the Sicilians. They hated their German occupiers, and when the Americans marched into town they hung out of their windows, cheering, waving, and smiling, many of the townspeople bringing out wine and food for the soldiers, wanting the Americans to stay and have a meal with them. Alex was sure the army was leaving a trail of American babies in their wake.

"We should go into town tonight," said Alex. "Do some reconnaissance."

"You're just upset that the king arrested Mussolini before you could kill him, aren't you?" Bill teased.

Alex tensed. Yeah, sure he'd told Bill about wanting to kill Mussolini. Hell, even Patton said he wanted to be the one to blow Hitler's brains out. A lot of guys imagined they'd be the one to finally put an end to all this carnage. Why was he so different?

"Taormina's where my family is from," Alex answered him. "I want to be the first one to walk back in since Mussolini took it. Is that so strange?"

"Am I going to have to follow your stupid ass like in Algeria when you charged that machine gun nest?"

"I didn't tell you to follow me."

"What kind of a friend would I be if I didn't? So, what's the plan?"

"Maybe leave around midnight," said Alex. "Two, three hours investigating the town, then get back here by sunrise?"

"Means I can get a few hours of shut-eye," said Bill, laying down on his bedroll, his helmet serving as a pillow.

* * *

As THEY MADE their way along the coast to Taormina, a quarter moon hung low over the Mediterranean, bathing the landscape in a pale light. Alex could hear the crashing of waves a hundred feet below and, in the distance, could see the white stucco buildings and red clay roofs of Taormina, the jewel of Sicily.

The ocean brought up a cool breeze as they trudged toward the village, keeping a sharp eye out for any German soldiers. Alex suddenly felt disconnected from reality. He didn't have to be an American soldier advancing on a fascist town. He might as well have been a Roman solider fighting off Hannibal's armies. Maybe a Norman knight whose castles still dotted the landscape. Or perhaps a Viking, a Barbary Pirate, a Moor, a Saracen; all of them had once held sway on this island. Alex was just passing through history, but Sicily was history.

"Do you really think we should be doing this?" Bill asked.

"Yeah," Alex replied.

"I got a bad feeling about this."

"You should have had a bad feeling about that last woman you proposed to. Her father almost shot you when he found you in the shed with her."

"Takes a good amount of skill to run away with your pants down around your knees," Bill said with a smirk.

They were coming close to the town, climbing up to the main road, checking for anybody, but it was silent. The scent of manure from the horses and donkeys who pulled many of the island's carts was still pungent, and someone in the town was baking bread. At the outskirts they encountered the first buildings, no more than two or three stories tall, the doorways decorated with elaborate carvings of vines and grapes, or floating cherubim. The Italians loved their wine, and they loved their religion.

Alex had the sense of a place where people had lived for thousands of years, as if the accumulated memory of generations was part of the architecture. He knew that people were in the town, but it seemed as if everybody was waiting, not knowing what was coming next. Windows were tightly shut, streets were empty, and the noise of living human beings was absent, as if the very land was holding its breath.

They crept quietly into town, moving from the shadow of one building to another. Alex wanted to hear the sound of a voice, a lover's quarrel, the threats of an angry mother, or someone laughing at a joke.

Turning a corner, he almost ran into a young woman dressed in black like an old woman and wearing a shawl around her head.

She couldn't have been more than seventeen years old and looked shocked to see them. But underneath the shawl Alex saw she had blonde hair and pale skin, uncommon among Sicilian women. Was she a German agent? The platoon had been warned the Germans were resorting to all sorts of deceptions to slow the Allied advance.

She started walking quickly away into town, but Bill pursued her.

"*Signora, Signora,*" said Bill in butchered Italian.

A short distance away from them she stopped and looked at them.

"*Americano, Americano,*" said Bill as he continued to walk toward her.

Her eyes darted to a rooftop, then back to them. "Run, American!"

Alex looked up to see a German sniper on the roof, taking aim at Bill. The bullet struck Bill before he could even bring his rifle up, and he crumpled to the ground.

Alex had the terrible sensation of everything happening in slow motion. He tried to lift his rifle into firing position but knew the sniper already had a bead on him.

A sharp pain erupted from his left shoulder, and he sank to his knees, a shroud of darkness slowly descending over him. Out of the corner of his eye he saw the blonde woman. *Why was she pulling a pistol out of her dress and firing at the roof?*

Another rifle shot cracked and struck Alex in the right thigh, causing him to fall the remaining distance to the ground.

This is the end, Alex thought. He felt no pain, just a great tiredness. *Maybe they'll capture me, maybe they'll just kill me.*

Alex was aware of more gunfire, but it didn't seem to be aimed in his direction. He looked to one side and saw the blonde woman, still firing her pistol. But several young Italian men were also racing to her side, armed with rifles, firing at the roof. They were yelling in Italian, but he also thought he heard German.

He was in the middle of a fight that made no sense to him.

Alex reached to his chest to feel his Saint Michael's medallion. He'd been a fierce warrior and done nothing in a year and a half of fighting to dishonor himself. He thought of his father, worried in December 1941 about this very moment in August 1943, and his Uncle Vince, telling him he had a duty to kill Mussolini, and believing he'd failed both men.

I've come to the town of my grandfather only to die was his last thought before his body went limp.

Chapter Thirteen

ALEX WOKE WITH THE FEELING THAT all the liquid had been drained from his body.

His limbs were heavy, and it took a great effort for him to lift his head off the pillow. He saw his left shoulder was bandaged and pulled the sheets back to reveal the wound to his right thigh, which had also been treated. Since he didn't see a splint on his leg, he assumed the bullet hadn't struck bone. With gathering strength, he looked around the room. He was not in an army hospital. More like the private residence of a wealthy man. He lay in a large feather bed, with a marble table directly across from it and a mirror over it. On the table sat a small Chinese vase with freshly picked flowers and a fine porcelain figure of a Roman woman reading while a man painted her. Red wallpaper depicted the Greek god Mercury with his physician's staff, fleeing from Zeus. On one wall was a tapestry of Saint Sebastian depicting his martyrdom, tied to a tree with arrows puncturing his flesh.

"I know how you feel, buddy," said Alex to the tapestry.

"How are you doing, my brave American friend?" asked a voice in stilted English from the doorway. Alex saw an older, muscular, balding Sicilian man, maybe in his late fifties or early sixties, standing with a tray that contained a pitcher of water and a glass.

"*Va bene,*" Alex replied. "*Grazie.*"

"Ah, you speak the language," said the man in Italian. "I thought you looked like a southerner. Even through the bad American accent I could hear the hint of Sicily."

"I'd love some of that water," said Alex.

The man brought it over to Alex and poured a glass, which he took and drank greedily. The man poured another glass for Alex, and he drank about half of it.

"The Germans are still a day or two away from fully evacuating Taormina, so we must still keep you hidden," said the man.

"How's my friend? The other soldier?"

The man was silent for a moment and then said, "I'm sorry. There was nothing we could do for him. His body has been taken to the undertaker. When the Americans arrive, he will be properly prepared for return to his family. It is the least we could do."

The news struck Alex hard, and he felt tears coming to his eyes. Bill had been his best friend since basic training. They'd battled across North Africa without a scratch, fully believing they'd get through the whole damned war without a single problem.

"In the battle against evil," said the older man, "there will always be casualties."

"What happened?" asked Alex. "I remember walking into the town, a young woman, she was blonde, then the firing started."

"We expected the Americans to start making probes into town, to see if the Germans had left. Most of them had, but they left many snipers behind. The young woman you spoke of, we thought she would be the least conspicuous person to be out in the open. We were keeping out of sight, close to buildings and in alleyways."

"She saved me."

"She did. But unfortunately, she did not save your friend. Our partisans felt very bad about that. We did not want the Germans to get any of you. Please accept our apologies."

Alex could not keep it together any longer. He started to weep, a loud, crying jag, of which he was unashamed.

The man put down his tray, pulled up a chair, sat down, and took Alex's hand in his own. "It is good to cry for lost friends. I will cry with you, for my own lost friends, so that you will know that even though we are in pain, we will get through this."

Alex continued to cry loudly, while the older man wept quietly, and after Alex had cried all his tears, he fell into a deep sleep, the older man still holding his hand.

* * *

ALEX WOKE THE next morning to the sound of distant gunfire.

He bolted upright in the bed, seeing the old man had placed a pair of crutches next to his bed in case he needed them. Alex gingerly moved out of the bed, taking care not to injure his left shoulder, while also not placing too much weight on his right leg.

As he was navigating to the window to take a look outside, the old man entered. "Ah, I see our activity has wakened you. The partisans have decided the German forces are weak enough that we may now attack them. Still, I advise you stay away from the window."

"Probably good advice," said Alex.

"I realize I have not introduced myself," said the older man. "You must excuse my bad manners. I am Salvatore Cristiani, at your service."

"Alex Falcone."

Alex was starting to get accustomed to walking around on the crutches, but he knew he was out of the war for at least a few weeks in spite of being anxious to get back into the fight. As he hobbled around the room, his eyes fell on what he took to be a bust of some medieval prince, an older man with long hair down to his shoulders.

"And if it's not prying too much, *Signor* Falcone, why was it only two of you sneaking into town? I'd heard that American reconnaissance units usually have more men."

"Honestly, it was unsanctioned. I just wanted to be the first to walk back into Taormina."

"Ah," said Salvatore, "you are like Patton, wanting to beat Montgomery to Messina, huh? Another American in a hurry?"

"It's a little more personal than that."

"Oh?"

Alex sat back down on the bed. That was enough therapy for the day. He felt exhausted. "My mother is from here. She left before the fascists took over. But she always told me stories about this place."

"What was her maiden name? Perhaps I can put you in contact with some of your cousins."

Alex shook his head. "Nobody's left as far as I know. She and her sister left. There were just my grandparents. Their last name was Leone. They say he was some kind of minor nobility. Supposedly got killed by the fascists."

The color drained from Salvatore's face, he seemed unsteady on his feet, and he struggled to find a chair in which to collapse. "Are you speaking of Alessandro de Leone, the Duke du Taormina, the Lion of Sicily?" he finally asked in a quivering voice.

"Yeah. I'm named after him. My full name is Alessandro de Leone Falcone. My mother's name was Rosina de Leone."

"I was his servant for twenty-five years. I helped raise your mother and your aunt Jacquetta. Does she still have such a fiery temper?"

"She does," said Alex.

"And your mother was always the calm one. Very smart. Good with numbers."

"Still is."

"I was the last person to see your grandfather when he left for Rome to urge the king to stand against Mussolini."

"So, is it true? Mussolini had him killed?"

"Yes."

The room was quiet as the weight of the news sunk into Alex. "If your grandfather had been able to convince the king, Mussolini would never have come to power," Salvatore continued. "Just as if Hitler had been confronted, when he marched troops into the Sudetenland. When evil men rise, it is important to confront them."

"How can you be sure Mussolini gave the order?" Alex asked.

"I was here when your grandfather's body came back, as well as the two men who were protecting him. If it had been just bandits who killed him, or mafia, the authorities would have acted in a certain way. They would have been in mourning for a great man who always stood for the people of Sicily. Instead, they brought him back as if he was a criminal they'd killed. Your grandmother was devastated, but none of the public officials comforted her. They actually took control of your grandfather's property, claiming it now belonged to the state. She died a few days after he did; a broken heart. I saw how the authorities were looking at people like me, those they knew who were loyal to your grandfather. I disappeared in the night. We Sicilians know how to anticipate trouble, to vanish into the countryside. And that's where I met your grandfather's killers."

"You met them?"

"Yes. Mussolini betrayed them as well. He tried to kill them, but they escaped. There was a small *pensione* in the interior of the island, well-known to those who need to hide. There were three of them. Roberto and Michael, and a third one. He didn't give his name. I always thought of him as 'the quiet one.' You could tell he was the leader. Didn't need to talk. Said it all with his eyes. And he was always watching. The others talked. Bragged about what they'd done. I waited until they'd fallen asleep. Shot one, then the other, but I should have started with the quiet one. He escaped, jumping off the balcony. Must have broken his leg in the fall because I saw him limping away as I tried to shoot him. But I'd drawn too much attention with the shots, so I couldn't pursue him. But I can't imagine he survived. Mussolini's men were everywhere in Sicily."

"And what happened to you after that?" Alex asked.

"I remained hidden for a few months, and then came back to Taormina," Salvatore explained. "Mussolini was in power and trying to make peace with everybody. Technically, your grandfather's property was owned by the royal family, so it reverted to them, this building, the shops down below, the vineyards and orchards owned by your family, but nobody had been running the properties. I resumed my role, but instead of the money going to your grandparents, the money went into the king's coffers. I wrote to your mother, asking whether she wanted to contest it, but she said to let it go."

"Did you tell her what happened to her father?"

"I hinted at it in letters but was worried the authorities might be monitoring my mail. Besides, what good could it do?"

"My uncle said the fascists killed my grandfather. Said it was common knowledge in Sicily."

Salvatore shrugged. "We Sicilians are a suspicious lot. Your grandfather was a well-known opponent of Mussolini. We do not listen much to what the authorities say, but instead see who benefits from a certain series of events."

"I wish I'd known him," said Alex.

Salvatore brightened. "You have already been spending time with him." He motioned to the bust of who Alex had thought had been some medieval prince. "That is your grandfather. Sculpted about two years before he died. If you look closely, you will see how much you resemble him."

Alex looked at the bust with a newfound sense of appreciation. "What can you tell me about him?"

Salvatore was quiet for a moment and then said, "All good men are the same. They do what is expected of them by their families, their friends, and their God. They are gentle, strong, and fierce when needed, quick to forgive a slight, find humor in their flaws, and provide the roof under which everybody else can flourish. The good that a man does in his life lasts a long time, even longer than the wickedness done by other men."

"Sounds like a lot to live up to," said Alex.

"Let me show you something." Salvatore motioned for Alex to follow him over to a large chest. Alex hobbled over on the crutches, and Salvatore opened it. There were hundreds of gold and silver crosses and medallions with the images of saints. Alex picked a few up to more closely examine then. There was a medal of Saint Christopher carrying the Christ child across a river; a medal of Saint Jude, the patron saint of lost causes; and a medal of the Virgin Mary, Mother of God. Many of them were fine pieces with exquisite detail, while others seemed to be quite simple.

"What is all this?" Alex asked.

"The love of the common people," Salvatore replied. "These were anonymous gifts given to your grandfather by Sicilians over the years to let him know how much they appreciated what he had tried to do for them. He was not always successful in helping people. In fact, he failed many times more than he succeeded. That is the fallen world in which we live, and Sicilians know that better than most. All anybody can ask is that a person try, which your grandfather always did. In Italy there is the tradition of 'tribute,' for what you owe to the rulers. It was done with the Caesars, the mafia, but it was always enforced. Not with your grandfather. Many times, his tribute was not a religious artifact, but rather a basket of fruit, or meat, or cheese. The best of whatever they might have had is what they gave to your grandfather. They always placed it on our doorstep in the middle of the night. They wanted him to be strong in his righteousness and not grow weary."

"That's quite a legacy to live up to."

"I know you will meet that challenge. It is why God placed you exactly where He did, so that you would come to this place and learn of your grandfather."

"I don't know if my sergeant will see it like that."

Salvatore smiled. "I will see to it that you do not get into any trouble. I still have deep contacts with the anti-Mussolini politicians. I can tell you as we sit here that the Americans are already negotiating with the new Italian government to join the American side. We Italians have known empires and republics, and we are on the side of freedom, not the German dictator. There is no joy in the dictator's soul, and we Italians are full of joy."

"The girl," said Alex, "the one I saw before I got shot. Is she still around here?"

Salvatore shook his head. "She has already gone north to Rome. She was sent here to observe the fighting between the Americans and the Germans. She is reporting this information to the government, stiffening their spine to turn their back on the Germans."

"Can't say I put on much of a show for her. She had to save me."

"The Americans have come here twice to fight wars we should never have had," said Salvatore. "She is nothing but grateful."

Alex recuperated for a few more days, by which time the Americans had entered the town. Sergeant Orona came with a detachment of men, and although he cursed Alex out for what he'd done, he also made sure he was taken to the local army hospital to recuperate. "Don't think this gets you out of the war," said the sergeant. "I expect you to be back with us in a few weeks."

Before he left, though, Orona gave Alex a few minutes with Salvatore to say their goodbyes.

"The Lion of Sicily marches with the American army," said Salvatore. "I have relayed that message all through our network in Italy. Already you are a hero to our people."

"Sounds a bit much for simply getting myself shot."

"There is much more to your destiny, Alex. God will reveal it to you soon enough."

* * *

ALEX WAS ASSIGNED a bed at the army hospital in Messina. His injuries were almost healed, and the doctors estimated that within a month he could rejoin his unit.

The Allies had crossed the Messina Straits and were advancing against light resistance up the boot of Italy. On July 25, 1943,

Mussolini had been called to a meeting with the king, who had him arrested and placed in a rotating series of safe locations to elude the Germans.

As Salvatore had predicted, on September 8, 1943, General Eisenhower announced the Italian Premier, Pietro Badoglio, had surrendered all the Italian forces, and many captains in the Italian fleet were already in the process of turning their ships over to the Allies. The Nazis were furious at their former allies and promised to continue fighting the Allies in Italy, along with as many of the Italian soldiers who would remain with them.

With all the good news from the Italian campaign, it was possible to believe all of Italy might fall to the Allies in a short time.

The army hospital was housed in what had been the city hall and was staffed with many locals, who were only too happy to work with the Americans. Although most of them were anxious to practice their English, Alex asked that they speak to him only in Italian. He was surprised to realize his Italian came back to him so quickly and was diligent in practicing his pronunciation, the slang, and even the mannerisms of the locals. A couple times one of the Sicilians would approach him and say, "Is it true you are the grandson of the Lion of Sicily?"

"Yes," he would reply, and a look of admiration would come across their face. "But that was my grandfather," he'd add. "I haven't done anything to make you compare me to him."

The person would usually smile, as if Alex was being modest, and add, "The Lord is with us in this fight. God bless the Americans for bringing you here."

Alex wasn't sure how he felt about being treated as a folk hero.

On September 13, 1943, just as he was finishing up his convalescence, an orderly brought him an Italian newspaper with the banner headline, "MUSSOLINI ESCAPES!"

Alex could not believe the story. The former dictator was guarded by more than two hundred Italian policemen in a mountain facility north of Rome. But apparently a team of Nazi special forces had swept in on twelve gliders, taken the guards by surprise, and loaded Mussolini onto a plane and flown away.

Mussolini would no doubt be meeting soon with Hitler and promising to continue the fight. Alex realized the Italian campaign had just become a great deal more difficult.

With Mussolini on the loose, Italy was looking not just at a fight with the Germans, but also a civil war among the Italians themselves.

* * *

"Good to have you back," said Sergeant Orona when Alex returned to his unit.

"Thanks," Alex replied. He waited, but nothing was said about Bill Squire.

The unit was on the Italian mainland, advancing toward Naples, where fierce fighting raged between the Allies and the Germans. Most of the Italian army had already surrendered to the Allies, but the Germans were more than making up for the loss. Alex's unit had taken heavy casualties, more than they had in Sicily. It was almost as if the loss of their Italian allies made the Nazis even more determined. Orona had written many letters home to grieving families.

"As you know, the Italians are now on our side," said Orona, "and that's great, as we always have them coming up to us with information. But nobody here speaks much Italian. I understand when you were in the hospital you spoke nothing but Italian. Feel pretty comfortable with the language now?"

"Yes, sir," said Alex.

"All right. In addition to your other duties," said Orona, "you're the unit interpreter."

* * *

While Alex expected their drive through Italy to go quickly with the Italians on their side, with the escape of Mussolini, it didn't go that way. The Nazis knew the danger posed by the Allies being in Italy and flooded the country with their soldiers. The fighting quickly bogged down.

Despite the fact that the Germans were the enemy, Alex understood the unusual position in which they found themselves. Although the government in Rome had changed sides, the Italians had been partners with the Nazis for years. Many probably still supported them. As reports of atrocities by the Germans in other countries were reported, nothing like that had taken place yet in Italy. Might the Nazis hope to win the Italians back to their side? As long as the Italians stayed mostly on the sidelines of this fight between the Nazis and the Allies, the Germans seemed to ignore the Italians.

For the next five months, Alex and his unit were held up with thousands of other Allied soldiers at Monte Casino, which had at its peak a Benedictine monastery that had been built in 529 AD. From that commanding position, the Germans directed their mortar attacks with deadly efficiency throughout the valley, holding what became known as the Gutsav Line.

In January 1944, the Allies landed a large force at Anzio Beach to the north, hoping to cut the German lines in half, but the effort was nearly a catastrophe. It probably would have been better if the Allies evacuated the beach, but they continued to fight. Although the Allies eventually gained control of the beachhead and made some progress inland, the German supply lines remained strong.

On February 15, 1944, Allied bombers reduced the Monte Casino monastery to rubble. However, what the Allies didn't know was that the Germans had not occupied the monastery (perhaps in deference to the Italians who remained fighting on their side), just the area around it. The monastery had instead remained in control of the monks and several terrified townspeople who'd fled the fighting.

Monte Casino and the Gustav Line were not breached until May 1944, with the road to Rome finally open to the Allied Forces.

Since the loss of Bill Squire, Alex found it difficult to get used to the newer members of the unit. Many of the guys he'd known had been injured and taken out of the fight, and Alex didn't like the idea of getting close to other soldiers who might also be taken out. He started to feel like the ghost of the unit. For nearly a year, they hadn't taken much real estate, just had to deal with nearly daily bombardment by the Germans, and a few small actions here and there. But nothing that made them believe they were making much progress. About the only social contact Alex had was with the Italian soldiers and citizens who often came into their camp with information, which often wasn't very helpful. Most of the information seemed reliable, but they couldn't act on it.

On June 4, 1944, just as Allied soldiers were boarding ships in England to prepare for the D-Day Invasion, Alex and his unit entered the eternal city of Rome. He'd later learn that Hitler ordered his generals to blow up the historic bridges over the Tiber River and fight the Allies block by block in the city. But the generals disobeyed him and ordered a general retreat, planning to fight on a better battlefield in the north, perhaps in the Italian Alps. Only a few snipers remained in the city, and many of them were quickly dealt with by the Roman citizens or Allied soldiers.

Alex marched with Sergeant Orona through the streets of Rome in what became a de facto victory parade as the citizens of Rome lined the streets and hung out of windows to welcome their liberators. Alex looked at their ecstatic faces, reminding him so much of the Italians he'd grown up with in San Francisco. There were old men waving their arms in welcome and young girls leaning out of windows and tossing kisses to the American soldiers. Every block it seemed as if a middle-aged woman ran into the ranks of the soldiers and embraced a solider as if he was her own son.

A portly nun rushed into the street and, taking Sergeant Orona's face in her hands, gave him a passionate kiss on the lips. In an excited and stammering voice, she said, "G-good Americans!

Good Americans! *Bona serra*, American soldiers!" before disappearing back into the crowd.

Sergeant Orona blushed. "Maybe don't tell my wife about that."

"Your secret's safe with me, sarge."

"They seem to be pretty good people," Sergeant Orona remarked to Alex as they marched down yet another street filled with cheering Romans.

"They've had enough of tyranny," Alex replied. The pride of what his grandfather had died fighting for swelled in his chest. "Millions left for the United States in search of something better. Now it's time for them to fix their own country."

"Yeah, well not too long ago they were cheering for somebody else." Orona pointed to the balcony of a large red building. "Remember seeing it on the newsreels? Mussolini would come out on that balcony and jump around like a little marionette? I always wonder why dictators get so emotional when they talk? I mean, can you imagine Roosevelt getting all hysterical, waving his hands around?"

Alex kept his eyes on the balcony as they approached. It was not large, perhaps twenty feet long by six feet wide. Despite the celebratory atmosphere, Alex couldn't help but feel the lingering evil of Mussolini. This had been the center of the Roman Republic and the Roman Empire, a place of both democracy and learning, as well as brutality and corruption. This was the Italy of da Vinci and Michelangelo, as well as the Italy of Nero and Caligula. Whatever you believed about humanity, either good or bad, you could find abundant evidence of both in the history of Rome.

His mind drifted to the carnage of North Africa, the screams of injured men, the night sky aglow with tracer bullets and exploding mortar rounds like a demonic Fourth of July. He thought of the Sicilian campaign, the months of fighting at the Gustav Line, and the pointless destruction of the monastery at Monte Casino. All of that had begun here, and if Alex was to believe Salvatore—on the night the King welcomed Mussolini to join the government to speak for the first time from this balcony.

A single decision, to surrender rather than fight, had changed the history of the world.

They paraded down a few more streets, and then Orona pointed toward something in the distance. "What the hell is that?"

Alex looked in the distance and saw what had drawn Orona's attention. Standing more than two hundred feet tall and five hundred feet long, made of gleaming white Brescia marble, dubbed by the locals "the wedding cake," it was the largest and most magnificent monument in all of Rome. It was fronted by a massive colonnade like that of an ancient Roman temple and on each side was a winged figure driving a chariot with four horses. Steps leading from the front were decorated by mosaics of fighting soldiers, depicting Italy's glorious past and their various wars for unification, which, depending how you calculated, started in 1815 and ended in 1861, with the exception of the Papal States, which did not fall until 1870.

However, Alex's attention was riveted to the figure at the front of the "wedding cake," the thirty-five-foot-tall bronze equestrian statue of his great-grandfather, King Victor Emmanuel II. The King was mounted in front of the temple façade, his erect military bearing and deep-set eyes conveying the image of a man of action.

During his time with Salvatore, the servant had told Alex much about the first king of a united Italy, and how with the help of his prime minister, Count Camillo Cavour, and the Sicilian patriot, Giuseppe Garibaldi, the three had forged the Italian nation. Each had been hard, calculating men, and Salvatore had told the famous story of an English woman, who had remarked upon meeting the King, that he was the only royal she'd ever met who looked like he could defeat a dragon. In the battle for unification, the King often fought alongside his troops. In later years, the King often said he slept better on the hard ground during a campaign than he ever did in a soft palace bed. In addition to his martial prowess, the

King had a roving eye and fathered so many children out of wedlock (such as Alex's own grandfather) that he was jokingly referred to as the actual "father of the nation."

As Alex stood in front of the monument, he felt insignificant. Yes, he had been a soldier in this war, but he had done little that was notable, other than survive.

And Mussolini was still at large.

* * *

"Get up, Falcone,' said Sergeant Orona. "We've been called on again."

Alex blinked and focused on Orona. It was the morning of their second full day in Rome. The sun was just a dull glow on the horizon of the eastern sky. Most of the soldiers had spent the evening drowning in red Italian wine and flirting with the beautiful Roman women, but Alex felt separate from it. "What is it, sarge?"

"There's a situation outside of Rome," he explained. "We're supposed to get there ASAP. They've got a jeep waiting for us."

Within an hour they found themselves in rocky, scrub-covered country to the north of Rome. They jostled as the jeep took them over an unpaved road and stopped at the base of a small hill. A few other military personnel were present, along with some Italian policemen. Alex could see a partially covered entrance to a large cave.

At first Alex thought there must have been a landslide, but later he'd learn the Nazis had dynamited it. Several soldiers at the top of the debris pile threw rocks down to the bottom. Alex saw the soldiers were all wearing handkerchiefs around their mouths.

Alex and Sergeant Orona exited the jeep. A tall, thin, blonde soldier approached Sergeant Orona and saluted. "I'm Colonel Wyatt. Good to see you sergeant, private," the colonel nodded at Alex. "You speak Italian?"

"Yes, sir."

"Good. We've got a witness, but I can't understand him."

"First one coming out," cried a soldier from the rubble.

Alex saw the first body, a middle-aged man, come out. There'd been a massacre at the cave. The only question was how many had been killed. Alex walked quickly to the base of the rubble and helped the soldiers. The dead man had the physique of a military man but was dressed in civilian clothes.

The second body pulled from the cave made Alex gasp. It was a blonde-haired young woman. Alex watched two soldiers carry her out and lay her next to the first victim. For a moment, Alex thought she was the woman who'd saved him in Taormina. Her hair was about the same length, the same height, and her figure looked almost identical. But when Alex inspected her face more closely, he realized it wasn't her. This woman had a prominent Roman nose and sharp features. The woman of Taormina had delicate features and a small nose. He'd glimpsed her haunted visage nearly a year ago, and yet it remained burned in his memory.

An old Italian man was brought to Alex. Alex translated for the officers on scene. The old man had been walking through the hills to his home when several trucks pulled up. He hid among some rocks to observe the scene. The trucks were filled with former Italian army officers who disagreed with Mussolini, Italians imprisoned for petty crimes, and seventy Jews. The Gestapo trucked them to this lonely place, unloaded them, stood them together, and machine gunned them, before placing their bodies in the cave and dynamiting it.

The previous restraint the Germans had shown to the Italian population prior to the fall of Rome seemed to have ended. Later, Alex would learn the Germans initiated this massacre for attacks by Italians on Germans prior to the fall of Rome, which killed thirty-two of their soldiers. That appeared to be official German policy now in Italy. For every German killed by an Italian, ten Italians would be killed.

Eventually all the bodies were brought out of the cave, laid on the ground, and photographed, and reports were written up. As it turned out, many Italians had observed various parts of the massacre, and it was Alex's job to interview them and write up a report, for later prosecution of the soldiers and officers involved, if they survived the war.

It turned Alex's stomach as he put the report together. He thought of all the lives that had to intersect for this atrocity to take place. He thought of the Italian soldiers with the courage to defy Mussolini and who were imprisoned for their principled stand. He thought of the petty criminals, understanding their punishment might be jail, but not death. He thought of the Jews, who had been Hitler's main target in this war. And he couldn't help but think of the German soldiers, many of them not older than him, who had followed orders, even though they knew they were dishonoring themselves and their families. Killing in war was one thing. Killing helpless civilians was quite another.

You brought me to this place, God, Alex thought, remembering the words of his grandfather's servant, Salvatore, *what do you want me to do?*

Chapter Fourteen

For six months, God gave no answer to Alex's question.

In the Apennine mountains, guarding the Po Valley in Northern Italy, his unit battled the Germans and their Italian allies under Mussolini, to a standstill. The Allies held several high ground peaks, and the Nazis held several others. Yet in the fall of 1944, it seemed as if both sides forgot about this theater of the war as the real fight was the dash through France and into Germany.

The Po Valley was eighteen thousand square miles in size, mild even in winter, with abundant rainfall for agriculture and a cornucopia for the German forces that occupied it. Six rivers flowed from the snowy heights of the Apennines to the south and the Alps to the north. The Po Valley contained the large cities of Milan and Turin with their vital industrial factories, which were still serving the German war machine. The mountains to the south and north allowed the Germans to deploy their winter warfare units, which were among the best in the world. The Germans had done a great job confining the American forces to the Apennines, where they'd fought the war to a stalemate.

The United States had created their own special mountain war-fighting unit, the US Army 10th Mountain Division, and Alex had been assigned to them, primarily because of his language skills, as well as his growing folk status among the Italians as the "Lion of Sicily." The story had apparently spread widely among the Italian soldiers who were still working with the Nazis, as well as the Resistance forces, with whom Alex also interacted as part of his job gathering intelligence on the German forces.

The winter of 1944–1945 had been a nightmare of frigid conditions, as the Allies fought a number of small skirmishes among the peaks and passes, never gaining what they needed to send large numbers of troops into the fertile valley below. The 10th Mountain Division boasted the highest number of college graduates, usually rich kids from the Ivy Leagues, who'd skied in the 1930s at the few resorts on the East Coast, or in Europe. Alex didn't mix well with them and continued his solitary ways, earning him the nickname of "the monk." Most of the 10th hadn't seen near the fighting that Alex had, and they seemed to be drifting through the war as if it was some extended European holiday.

The spring of 1945 brought new hope, along with the news that the Allies had advanced across the Rhine and into the German heartland. This was especially good news, as in December 1944 the Nazis had launched the Battle of the Bulge through the Ardennes Forest, nearly breaking the Allied lines before Patton's counterattack and the clearing of clouds, which had prevented Allied air attacks. But with the failure of the massive German counterattack, the Allies slowly made their way into Germany. Italian partisans, taking advantage of the crumbling of the Axis powers, engaged in fierce guerilla campaigns in the Po Valley, but the Germans were still in undisputed control of the region. Alex figured it was possible the Allies might eventually take Berlin without the Po Valley ever being breached, and he'd spend the rest of the war freezing in the Apennines.

At least being stuck in one place allowed his mail to easily find him. "My dear son," a letter from his father began. "I'm so happy you're stuck in the mountains where the greatest threat is frostbite. The war nears an end and hopefully that comes to pass without you firing another shot. Please do not do anything rash, as you did when you enlisted so quickly. Perhaps you have seen enough of suffering that you understand one should not rush toward it. I look forward to seeing you soon." The letter continued on with more news of home, and Alex found himself deeply missing his City by the Bay, family, and friends.

However, a letter from his Uncle Vincenzo contained a different message. "The jackal is still on the loose," he wrote. "Mussolini attacked both sides of your family and yet he still walks free. It is for you to avenge us. It is time for you to leave those cold mountains and find him. The two of you have been left alone for this moment. It is your destiny to look upon his dead face."

Alex thought about what the partisans had been telling him. The defeat of Germany was inevitable, but the Po Valley was still held by the Germans and their fascist allies. The people had been quiet, but they were getting ready to revolt. The Italians were an incredibly practical people. They wanted to rise at the right time to kick out the Germans.

For the last several months, Alex's home was a relatively sheltered area of the Apennine Mountains with sixteen other members of the 10th Mountain Division. They'd make patrols of the peaks, often having spectacular views of the green and lush Po Valley beyond, but knew the Germans controlled the lowlands heading into the valley. The constant word was that they were going to get fresh troops for an eventual assault on the valley. But Alex had long stopped believing these reports. The real action was the race for Berlin and Hitler, not the race for Milan and Mussolini. They slept in small, triangular tents on the hard ground, often dealing with the biting wind that whipped through the mountains.

When they'd first arrived, members of the Resistance visited often, usually arriving on horseback to give their group the latest intelligence. Alex knew they visited more often than they would have otherwise because of his folk hero status as the "Lion of Sicily." They treated him with a great deal of respect, often asking his thoughts on the war, and when he'd complimented them on their riding skills, they asked if he rode horses in America.

"Sorry to disappoint you," said Alex. "But I'm pretty much a city boy. Never been on a horse in my life."

"We must teach the American how to be a cowboy," said one of the Resistance members, and the others laughed.

And that's how Alex learned to ride, saddling up with members of the Resistance and getting to know the area around his camp. Being in the presence of these men had been the most enjoyable time he spent in those cold mountains, but as the months passed and no further assistance came from the American side, the Resistance members lost interest in coming so often to their camp, only to leave disappointed.

On April 12, 1945, the Resistance came to their camp to express their sorrow over the death of President Franklin Roosevelt and stayed for several hours. Alex could feel the war slipping away, especially with the news a few days later that the Ruhr Valley in Germany had been captured, along with more than three hundred and seventy thousand German soldiers.

Their unit was kept supplied by a nearby mountain village and a young boy named Giancarlo, who trekked the ten miles on his burro every other day to keep them supplied with cheese, milk, and wine, as well as some simple delicacies prepared by the local women. The slender fourteen-year-old wanted to be a soldier like the Americans. Sometimes to amuse the unit he'd dress up in a spare uniform that hung on his thin frame like a circus tent, and he'd do his best impression of an American singer, like Frank Sinatra. The Germans had killed his father as the Americans were making their push into the Apennines because they suspected him of being a member of the Resistance, which he was.

When the Americans arrived at his village, a few weeks later, Giancarlo was terrified of the soldiers, thinking they'd be like the Germans. Alex had spoken to him in Italian and handed him a chocolate bar from his knapsack.

That was all Giancarlo needed to be convinced the Americans were the greatest people on the face of the Earth.

This time, when he saw the teenager coming up the slopes with his loaded burro, he had an idea. The rest of the unit was used to Giancarlo's comings and goings and did not pay much attention to him.

"I've got a favor to ask," said Alex.

"Let me tie up Lucinda first," said Giancarlo. "If she is not tied up, she runs toward the valley. She does not like the mountains."

"Neither do I," said Alex, taking Lucinda's reins and tying them to a tent stake.

"What do you want, Signor Falcone?"

"I was wondering if you could get me some regular clothes? So I'd look like an average Italian man?" He paused for a moment, realizing he'd have to provide the young man something of an explanation. "My superiors want me to sneak into the valley. Assess German troop strength."

Giancarlo thought for a moment. "My father's clothes are still in his closet. He was not as large as you, but they would probably fit."

"And I need you to get in touch with the Resistance for me. Let them know what I need to do."

Giancarlo smiled. "The Lion of Sicily leads us to victory," he said. "You think this is the time to strike?"

"It's getting close. Can you do this for me?"

"Of course," said Giancarlo. "It has been my great honor to assist the Lion of Sicily."

* * *

GIANCARLO RETURNED THE next night with his father's clothes. Alex had told him to come after nightfall, while Alex stood guard. Alex thought of the men in his unit, Kowalski, Henry, Danner, Fitzpatrick, and the others, from whom he stood aloof. He knew all the men in his North African unit like brothers—their home-towns, their sweethearts, and what they hoped to do after the war. But when so many of them died and he knew those futures were never meant to be, he found he did not want to know these new soldiers.

"Did you have any trouble?" Alex asked when Giancarlo drew close.

"No. I would be surprised if there are any Germans left in these mountains. And besides, they can't be quiet like Italians. They like to be loud, so everybody knows they are coming."

From a knapsack Giancarlo pulled out a white shirt and black pants. He looked away as Alex exchanged his uniform for the civilian clothes. The shirt fit Alex well, and the pants, while short in the legs, were comfortable around the waist. Despite the food provided by Giancarlo's village, Alex and most of his unit had lost substantial weight. In the mountains the soldiers had let their hair grow, as well as their beards, and the men had a grimy appearance.

Giancarlo handed him a jacket and cap, which he put on. "Think I can pass as an Italian peasant?" Alex asked him.

"If you stand still and do nothing," Giancarlo replied, "then you can pass as an Italian. But the minute you move, they will know you are American."

"How's that?"

"You walk too proud and smile too much to be an Italian peasant. If you want to avoid capture, don't swagger. It annoys the Germans because they believe they are the lords of the Earth."

"Got it."

Giancarlo sketched out the route Alex should take down the mountain, assuring him that most of the German camps had been evacuated in the past few weeks. At the first small village there would be a barn and a man waiting outside. His name was Leonardo and was a partisan Alex had met before. "He will take you where you need to go."

"I can't thank you enough, Giancarlo," said Alex.

"You Americans have shown great courage in freeing us from the Germans. It is we who owe you."

They said their goodbyes, Giancarlo headed back to his village, and Alex started down the mountain to his destiny.

* * *

Leonardo met Alex at the barn at about four in the morning.

Although Giancarlo had assured Alex the Germans had fled the mountains, he didn't want to take his chances and took a longer route avoiding the known encampments. However, the intelligence seemed to be accurate as Alex did not see signs of any Germans on the northern side of the Apennines. For a moment Alex considered simply walking back up to his camp, informing them that the Germans had fled, and abandoning his mission. But he knew Mussolini was somewhere in the valley and the Germans were withdrawing for the final battle in Berlin against the Americans and British on one side, and the Soviets on the other.

There was no time to waste.

"Where does the Lion of Sicily wish to go?" Leonardo asked, a hint of a smile on his face. It was a little embarrassing to Alex to be referred to by this name, but he'd long ago accepted it.

"What do you know about Mussolini's whereabouts?"

"He's supposed to be near the village of Dongo on Lake Como. It is some distance away. I have a cart with horses for us to drive, loaded with hay. It will be much less conspicuous than two men walking on their own."

Alex thought that sounded like a good idea. Sitting on a cart he wouldn't have to move much, which according to Giancarlo would quickly identify him as an American. During the months in the mountains none of the group had cut their hair, and Alex couldn't help but realize his hair was the same length as his grandfather's bust at the family estate in Taormina. He would be able to observe things as a typical Italian.

Motor cars were a rarity, aside from those owned by the military or the German automobiles driven by Nazi drivers or their fascist allies. As they made their way further into the valley, they encountered an abundance of horse-drawn wagons, a few supply trucks, and of course the railroads, which seemed to connect all the towns. One of the things the fascists had done well was build an excellent system of roads, although most of the traffic was still horse-drawn carts.

On the outskirts of Vigevano, they stopped to watch a German unit being attacked by partisans who shot at them from a nearby rooftop, then vanished. Two Germans were wounded, but the commander, a tall Prussian man with a long scar on his left cheek, simply shouted at his men to gather up the wounded soldiers and continue along the way.

Leonardo leaned over to Alex. "The partisans are losing their fear. The Germans will not stay behind to conduct reprisals, for fear of making themselves vulnerable to further attack."

They traveled on for some distance until Lorenzo saw a familiar face along the street. It was an older man, well into his eighties, with a full head of white hair and a hand that quivered on his walking stick. He pulled the cart to a stop, jumped out, and embraced the older man.

"How are you doing, Signor Rollo?"

"Very well, Leonardo. You?"

"Excellent," he motioned to Alex. "My friend and I are traveling north to Lake Como to see if we can get in some trouble."

Signor Rollo looked at Alex, his expression brightened, and then he turned his attention back to Leonardo. "Have you not heard the news?"

Leonardo shook his head.

"Mussolini has been captured. He was trying to escape to Vienna, driving in a German convoy. He even hid his uniform under a German overcoat and was driving one of the vehicles as if he was a German officer. But he was observed by an Italian customs guard who reported it to the Resistance, which took swift action. They are taking him to Milan for public trial, at the Piazza Loretto, where the fascists recently murdered fifteen patriots."

"How far is Milan from here?" Alex asked.

"About thirty miles."

"We need to get there, fast."

Leonardo looked at the horses, then at Alex. "I have packed saddles in the hay. Do you still remember how to ride, city boy?"

"Yes."

"Time for us to go cowboy then, American."

Lorenzo jumped down from the cart and pulled the saddles, as well as rifles and revolvers, out from the hay. Alex helped him and within about five minutes the two had the horses ready.

The old man watched them as they saddled up, making sure their guns were safely secured. "Thank you, Signor Rollo," said Leonardo.

Alex nodded at the old man in thanks as well.

"Good luck to you, Lion of Sicily," he replied. "I know that God is truly with us, now."

Alex and Leonardo kicked their horses into action and took off toward Milan and the Piazza Loretto.

* * *

THE TWO RIDERS raced through the Italian countryside as if carried on angel's wings.

Most of the areas were calm, but when they heard gunfire, they detoured around it. They caught distant glances of retreating German forces and Italians dancing on rooftops, brandishing their guns. Alex wasn't sure how many of the Italians knew Mussolini had been captured, but it seemed to be the majority because they were coming out of their homes and, even in the quiet areas, they saw Nazi and fascist flags ripped and lying on the ground.

Even without the long-promised Allied forces to drive the Germans out of their last hideout in Italy, the Italians had finally risen up and were kicking out the Nazis and the fascists.

When Alex and Leonardo reached Milan, they were only able to ride their horses until about a half mile from the Piazza Loretto because the streets were so jammed with people. They dismounted from their horses, taking their rifles and revolvers, and joined the crowd, which was surging toward the square.

As Alex walked with the crowd he sensed the hostile mood, as many were carrying rotten fruit and eggs with which to pelt the dictator. Several people saw the guns they were carrying, identifying them as members of the Resistance, and smiled at them or patted them on the back.

"I think Mussolini is going to try and give one last speech when they put him on trial to rally his followers," said one man.

"Ha!" another man replied. "Do you think he has any more followers other than his little whore mistress, Pettachi, who was always by his side?"

Alex and Leonardo were swept along with the crowd to the square. As they got closer to the center of attention where there was a raised stage and the girders of what looked like a bombed-out filling station, Alex lost Leonardo as he sought to get as close to the stage as possible. He put his hand into his jacket and felt for his revolver. If they allowed Mussolini to speak, Alex wanted to be the one to put a bullet right between the dictator's eyes.

The fascists had erected the stage months earlier and often used the girders to hang the bodies of Resistance fighters. Several men were already on the stage, and it looked like they were busy with something Alex could not see.

One of the men looked up at the girders, threw a rope over it, and began to secure it. After a few minutes, the man looked at the crowd and said, "You will like this, my fellow Italians!"

The man made a signal to a few others behind him and they began pulling the rope. Alex saw the lower part of a man's body being pulled up, then the military uniform he knew so well from the newsreels, and then the bald head of Mussolini, his arms hanging down. A cheer went up from the crowd. Alex saw that a spike had been driven through the dictator's heels. Alex looked at the dictator's body, the tips of his fingers just a few inches above the ground.

"He's dead?" Alex blurted in Italian.

"Dead and disgraced," said a man next to him. "As all tyrants should be."

"How?" Alex asked in English.

The man looked at him. "You are American?"

"Yes."

"Tell this to the Americans, then. Mussolini was held by the non-communist partisans at first, then the communists stole him away. Made Mussolini think they were fascists, coming to rescue him once again. Even at the end, I hear he was promising them an empire. They say he died like a man, though, opened his jacket and told them to shoot him in the chest. But his mistress grabbed the gun before they could shoot and was shot herself. After that the blood flowed freely. They killed everybody in Mussolini's party they captured."

Alex stared at the dead dictator's body, now tied off. The crowd seemed momentarily silent, not sure how to react. "American, there are some things you need to know," the man next to him said. "I am happy that the communists killed Mussolini, but that is not how things should have gone. I do not want the communists to be the heroes of this war. They will be the ruin of Italy, just as the fascists were."

The next dead body they hoisted up was that of Clara Pettachi, Mussolini's longtime mistress. She was a petite woman, her hair hanging from her head in little ringlets, as if the rush of war had caught her unaware while she was arranging her makeup in the powder room.

In short order, the communists strung up the other ten fascist officials who'd been captured with Mussolini, their bodies dangling just above the stage. Alex watched all of this with grim satisfaction. These were genuinely evil men, and their deaths the result of righteous justice. There were scattered shouts of approval from the crowd, and one man even darted onto the platform and gave a savage kick to Mussolini's head. "Mussolini is now in hell!" the man shouted.

The crowd roared its approval, as if it was finally finding a way to fully express their emotions. Several other men climbed onto the platform to spit on the dictator or kick him in the head.

After a few moments a middle-aged woman took the stage, pulled a revolver out of her shawl, and said to the crowd, "My five sons died in this war!" then shot Mussolini's body five times, the report of each shot echoing across the Plaza. "Five shots for my five assassinated sons!"

Alex realized he had perhaps not been too late to deliver some measure of justice to Mussolini. He hopped onto the stage and addressed the crowd. "I am an American soldier, but my grandfather was Alessandro de Leone, the Lion of Sicily, who died trying to stop this man from taking power." The crowd cheered wildly. "Both sides of my family suffered from this man. And on behalf of my family, and the entire Italian nation, I deliver my sentence upon him."

Alex took out his pistol and shot the dictator twice.

"The Lion of Sicily has returned!" the crowd cheered. "The Lion of Sicily has given us justice!"

Alex reveled in their applause for a few moments, then slipped off the stage, to hearty backslaps and embraces from men and women alike.

As Alex exited the stage, a young man clambered onto the platform. He took off his shirt, rolled it up into a ball, and lit it with a lighter, placing it under Mussolini's face, trying to set the dictator's body ablaze. But the flames started to burn his hand, and he dropped the shirt. After a few fruitless attempts to pick up the burning shirt, he stalked off the stage in disappointment at having failed to make his grand statement.

A woman who looked to be in her mid-thirties took the stage and approached Il Duce's body. She turned toward the crowd, lifted her dress, squatted, and began to urinate on Mussolini's face. There was almost a childlike rapture on her face, and when she finished and pulled up her skirt, the crowd cheered wildly.

Several other women took to the stage and did the same thing, each being applauded by the crowd. A few men also took the stage, unzipped their pants, and did the same to the dead dictator.

"This is savagery," Alex whispered under his breath.

A young, haggard partisan took the stage, began kicking Mussolini's head, then as the dictator's body swung away from him, took out his rifle and started smashing the dictator's head with his rifle butt.

An older partisan commander rushed over and said, "Enough!" The young partisan paused for a moment, then returned to smashing Mussolini's face.

The commander turned to his men behind the stage and shouted an order. Ten partisans took out their rifles and fired shots into the air, attempting to restore order. But the crowd continued to curse and call for new indignities to be heaped on the dead dictator. Alex saw how quickly this was turning into a volatile situation.

From the back of the enormous crowd, Alex could see several Carabinieri policemen trying to disperse the crowd, but the crowd started attacking the policemen, forcing them to retreat.

The sound of a truck horn blaring loudly echoed across the Plaza, and the crowd parted to let the vehicle pass. It was filled with partisans, as well as a lone prisoner, an older man shackled and guarded by men with guns who stood next to him.

"That's Achille Strace, Mussolini's secretary," said a man next to him.

The truck made its way as close as possible to the stage, and then Strace was hustled off the truck and onto the stage. Alex was no more than twenty feet from the man and saw him as he took in the scene. Strace's eyes wandered over the bodies hanging in the square, people he knew well, with whom he had argued, talked, and laughed, then at Mussolini's body, now riddled with bullets, beaten, urinated upon, and his face partially burned.

But Strace refused to be cowed. He turned to face the crowd, looked at them with contempt, his lip curled in disgust, and gave the fascist salute, modeled after the Roman salute given to Emperors, his left arm over his heart, his right arm fully extended at an upward angle, facing forward, palm down, and fingers touching. "Long live *Il Duce!*" he shouted.

The guns of the partisans blazed and Strace fell with a thud on the platform to the cheers of the crowd. Several partisans walked over to his prone figure and shot him several more times. Then they tied rope to his legs and pulled him up to join the others.

The execution of Strace seemed to finally satisfy the bloodlust of the crowd.

The church bells of Milan began to ring, as if officially announcing the liberation of the city. People continued to stare at the hanging bodies, but it seemed as if the horror of the past several years was at an end. The Resistance members untied the ropes and hoisted the bodies higher, so more people could see them, but also to prevent further desecration of the dead.

Alex noticed several people begin to exit the square, many taking one last look at the scene, making the sign of the cross, and then departing. The evil that had once ravaged their land had been driven from it, and they could get back to rebuilding their lives.

* * *

A FEW HOURS later, Alex ran across a British patrol that had just entered the city.

Despite the fact that there were few Allied forces in the Apennine Mountains, the uprising by the Italians had been the signal for them to enter the valley. Alex waved down the unit.

The middle-aged British sergeant stepped forward. "What can I do for you, my Italian friend?"

"I'm American," said Alex. "Tenth Mountain division," he paused, thinking he needed to explain himself. "I've been detached to work with the Resistance. Wanted to observe what was happening on the ground."

The sergeant looked at him suspiciously. "Name, soldier?"

"Alex Falcone."

The sergeant motioned to his men to take out their side arms. "We got a bulletin a couple hours ago about an American deserter by that name. Got to take you in, son."

Alex put up his hands to show he wasn't a threat. "I went toward the fighting. Not away from it."

The British soldiers relieved him of his weapons and put him into handcuffs. "Desertion's a serious crime, son. Court-martial is a certainty, if not worse."

They loaded him into the back of their truck, and Alex found himself thinking, *If only I'd listened to my dad, none of this would have happened.*

And yet he didn't feel sorry for listening to his Uncle Vincenzo. He hadn't made the safe choice but had fought the war until the very last minute.

Justice had been delivered.

Chapter Fifteen

WHILE ALEX WAS HELD IN A military jail in the bowels of the Milan City Hall, Russian forces made their way to less than five hundred yards from Hitler's bunker in Berlin, where on April 30, 1945, the Fuhrer committed suicide along with his wife, Eva Braun. On May 2, Berlin surrendered to the Russian Army, and on May 7, the new German president, Admiral Karl Donitz, authorized the unconditional surrender of all German forces.

The war in Europe was over, but Alex rotted in jail as a deserter. When he asked his guards what was planned for him, they told him things were so chaotic it might be a month or so before anybody actually took a look at his case.

The guards were American soldiers, veterans of what had been a relatively low-intensity conflict in Italy for the past year and didn't mind chatting with him. They'd asked why he was arrested, he told them, and they thought his incarceration was a bit of a travesty. "Man, you pumped a couple bullets into Mussolini?" one of them said. "They should be giving you a medal for that, not keeping you in here!" The guards made sure Alex had enough food, handed him their copies of the *Stars and Stripes* newspaper after they were done reading it, and one even gave him an old copy of *The Count of Monte Cristo* by the French writer, Alexandre Dumas.

Alex devoured the tale of the falsely imprisoned nobleman, Edmond Dantes, who escaped after seven years of imprisonment, fled to the Orient where he discovered a treasure, which enabled him to return to Paris in disguise as the fabled "Count of Monte Cristo," where he sought vengeance upon the men behind his unjust imprisonment. But in the book, the Count is not a genuine

hero, as he seems to have little regard for the guilty or the innocent. Alex had seen the 1934 movie and loved it but noted the
Hollywood version was much different. In the Hollywood version,
the Count was a genuine hero, not the conflicted character from
the book.

In mid-May the guards told him he had a visitor. Alex couldn't
guess who it might be, although he knew a letter had been mailed
home to his parents letting them know he'd been arrested. The
guards had been good about letting Alex bathe and shave, but
his hair still hung down to his shoulders. Although there wasn't a
mirror in the cell, Alex ran his fingers through his wild hair, trying
to make himself look a little more presentable. Since he'd been
captured in civilian clothes, and there wasn't a priority in getting
his uniform sent from his camp in the Apennine Mountains, he
remained looking like an Italian peasant from the mountains.

A door clanked open and down the hallway Alex saw Salvatore
Cristiani, his grandfather's servant, walking behind the guard. "My
young master," cried Salvatore, racing ahead of the guard to reach
through the bars to grasp Alex. "I'm blessed by the sight of you. How
many nights I laid awake wondering if a stray German bullet had
found you. But I held onto my faith, that the same God that had led
you back to me would not let you be so cruelly taken from this world."

Alex found himself welling up with tears. What he'd seen in
the war hadn't given Alex much faith in a God who watched over
people. And still, that desperation made him ache even more
painfully to believe in a God who ordered the world. "H-how did
you manage to find me?" he finally asked.

"I heard stories that the Lion of Sicily had been there when
Mussolini was hung. Even that you put a few bullets into his lifeless body. But then I heard that the Americans had taken you into
custody and knew I must find you and help you."

"Probably not much you can do for me," Alex replied. "The
army says they want to charge me with desertion. Looking at a
dishonorable discharge at the very least."

"You were not a deserter," said Salvatore. "There are many people in the Italian government with who I am in touch. I am sure we can get something worked out."

"Can't say I have a lot of hope, Salvatore."

"Of course not," he said with a smile and a wink. "You are young, and everything seems dark and overwhelming. But when you are older, you see there are many possible paths."

* * *

A WEEK LATER, Salvatore returned with an American military man, a colonel in his early fifties, with blonde hair and blue eyes, and walking with an easy, nonchalant grace, as if nothing bothered him.

Again, Salvatore walked in front of the man, reaching out and grabbing Alex's hands through the bars. "I have brought a friend," he said. "Alex, let me present to you Colonel James Iselin."

Alex stood at attention and saluted. "Sir!"

Colonel Iselin stood in front of the cell and looked Alex up and down. "Where's the uniform, son?" Alex would later learn Iselin was a Harvard graduate, class of 1921, had worked in New York finance for many years, and then joined up at the start of the war for a very special detachment.

"Hasn't made its way to me yet from my base."

"And the hair?"

"Kind of let it grow when I was stuck in the Apennines, sir."

Salvatore intervened. "In light of what we talked about, Colonel, I think it might be better to let his hair stay that length. Given his resemblance to his grandfather and the effect that might have on others."

The Colonel looked mildly amused. "What do you have to say about it, Alex?"

"Me?"

"Yeah. I'd like to know what you think."

"You let me out of here, and I'll shave my whole body. Or if you want, I won't shave for a whole year."

The Colonel chuckled. "Okay, Falcone, let me lay out the situation. I'm with army intelligence, Office of Strategic Services. I'm sure you've heard of us."

Alex nodded. They'd performed a good deal of the spy work during the war, getting information about German forces from partisans and dropping people behind enemy lines—often the kind of stuff the members were sworn to secrecy about for several years. It made sense for the spy agencies to now take on diplomatic duties since they already knew much about the local players.

"Even before the war was over, we started making plans for the future of Italy," the Colonel explained. "Us and the Italian government. It's called the 'Allied Control Commission.' Nobody's quite sure how this is supposed to work, but when the Americans leave this time, we don't want to come back in another twenty years to fight another war. Understand?"

"Yes."

The Colonel motioned to Salvatore. "Mr. Cristiani has explained to me your family's rather unique history and suggested your presence on the commission, as my aide, of course, might be looked upon favorably by many members of what we hope will be the new Italian government."

"I won't be court-martialed?" Alex asked.

"That depends," said the Colonel.

"On what?"

"On you not doing anything stupid again."

"No more stupid from me, sir."

"But to be fair," said the Colonel. "Many of the world's great accomplishments wouldn't have been possible without the stupidity of young men. It's just that now you'll be working for me, and I don't accept any of that shit."

"I'll follow orders."

Colonel Iselin nodded. He paused for a moment, then with a half grin asked, "Tell me, how did it feel to put a couple slugs into that son of a bitch?"

"It felt good, sir," Alex said. "Very good."

* * *

AN HOUR LATER, everything had been processed. Alex had been provided with a new uniform, and he was on a train with Colonel Iselin and Salvatore bound for Rome.

For most of the trip the three men were quiet, looking out at the calm Italian countryside, people going about their business much as they'd done for centuries. Alex found himself considering the people as the train thundered toward the south. Did any of them genuinely want war? For that matter, did the regular people of Germany? Of Japan? He thought of the people he'd met in North Africa, Sicily, and Italy. None of them appeared to be evil when you met them. They were just trying to get through life as best they could. Why throughout the centuries had governments felt the need to put their men into uniform, name an enemy, and send them into battle? Maybe there was a time when war made sense from a purely materialistic point of view, when you could steal treasure or land, but hadn't the last war shown the terrible cost of that strategy? Why did it seem the people never wanted war, but their leaders were always pushing them toward it?

When they arrived in Rome, Colonel Iselin said, "Alex, Salvatore's going to take care of you. I understand he's already found you a place to live, and knowing the uniform is all you have, he's going to take you to get some clothes."

Alex looked at Salvatore. "You don't have to do that."

"It would be my honor," he said. "I was always in charge of your grandfather's wardrobe, and there was no better dressed man in all of Sicily."

Alex followed Salvatore to a tailor's shop he apparently knew well and introduced him to the tailor, Carmello, a man who looked a few years younger than Salvatore, but whom he resembled in looks and build. "This is my brother, Carmello. We often argue about who is younger. I say I am the younger brother, but Carmello seems to think it is the opposite."

Carmello looked at Alex. "He always used to say I was the younger brother, but he was the better looking one. Now he wants to be the younger *and* better-looking brother."

"You look so much alike I figured the two of you must be twins," Alex replied. "Any difference of age must simply be that of a few minutes."

Carmello looked at his brother. "I like this one. A diplomat."

"And you have even more reason to like him," said Salvatore. "This is Alex Falcone, grandson of the Lion of Sicily."

Carmello regarded Alex. "I thought there was something familiar about you. I made several suits for your grandfather when he traveled here with my brother. I am happy to serve your family once again."

Carmello took his measurements, showed him some styles, and told Alex to come back the next day and he'd have two suits ready for him. In the meantime, Alex bought some other clothing items, talked some more with Carmello about how the Italians were feeling about their future with the fascists gone, then left with Salvatore, who wanted to show him the apartment he'd rented for Alex.

Salvatore had secured a fully furnished apartment for Alex just off the *Via Del Fori Imperali*, near the ancient Roman Forum, seat of the Roman Republic. Nearby were the Temple of Castor and Pollux, the Palatine Hill, the Tiber River (just a few hundred yards away), the Roman Colosseum, and the Pantheon, the oldest free-standing structure in all of Rome, built between 113 and 125 AD. It was a spacious apartment with two bedrooms, and Alex couldn't help but feel embarrassed that he would be living in luxury while so many of his fellow soldiers were sleeping in tents all across Europe, or even worse in the Pacific. "How much is all of this going to cost?" Alex asked.

Salvatore waved him away. "The Allied Control Commission will pay. And if not, some of my friends in the Italian government. You do not need to worry about these things."

"This is a lot better than a jail cell," said Alex. "But why do I feel like I'm still in some form of captivity?"

Salvatore smiled. "Think of it as a much more comfortable incarceration. You should simply consider that you have been placed in a different manner of service."

"How long will this last?" Alex asked.

He shrugged. "As long as you can be of service. Does it really matter? You are in the greatest city in the world, you have a beautiful place, and you are a young man. What could be better?"

"Why do I feel like I'm a pawn and you're the chess master?"

"We are all pawns of God," Salvatore replied. "Being moved in ways we do not understand to serve His plans. However, some of us try to move God's plans along. I will leave you now as I have some of my own affairs to attend to. I suggest you relax here, or maybe take a walk around the city and familiarize yourself with your new home."

"I want you to know how much I appreciate what you've done for me."

Salvatore smiled. "I am happy that I have been able to assist you."

After Salvatore left, Alex thought it might be a good idea to take a walk around Rome. He'd been there briefly after liberation, but that was nearly a year ago. The more natural city rhythms had returned, and he wanted to discover them. As far as he could determine, life in Rome was a mix of planned anarchy, blustery bravado, and family devotion. There was no possible way to feel lonely in this city because people were always talking to each other. He saw it in the Piazzas where boys sat whistling at pretty girls who walked by, in the cafes where old men debated the meaning of a

Verdi opera, or in the streets jammed with carts, mules, motor cars, and pedestrians.

Alex observed the entire chaotic, crazy fabric of Roman life, but also couldn't help but notice a certain calm and tranquility beneath it. The Romans seemed to understand that tomorrow was likely to be just the same as today, and few things were necessary to worry about too much, as expressed in the Latin proverb, *Vivamus, moriendum, est*, or "Let us live, since we must die." There was a jauntiness and confidence in the Romans, and the sense that every person was an actor, playing their part with maximum emotion, but knowing the next day would be a different scene in the ongoing drama. As he walked down the street in his uniform, he couldn't help but notice the smiles he got from many, along with many calling out in broken English, "I love America," to which he smiled and waved back.

Alex thought back to his experiences in the war with captured Italian soldiers. Most were only too happy to provide information about the Germans but were often equally vocal about the idiocy of their commanding officers. Often this commanding officer would be present as the soldier attacked his decision-making, and the two men would argue with such vigor it often had to be broken up by Allied soldiers. By contrast, captured German soldiers rarely volunteered information and never criticized their commanding officers. From other soldiers he heard that the Germans were much easier to administer, staying in their camps and doing what they were told, like a group of well-behaved, but silent and sullen sheep. The guards Alex talked with all liked the Italians much better.

The captured Italian soldiers were always bumming cigarettes from the Americans, asking to join the American army, or simply sneaking out of the camps in the middle of the night while the Allied soldiers looked the other way. They knew the Italians wouldn't be returning to the battlefield. Even when they were fighting on the German side, Alex got the impression the Italians soldiers had fought just enough to keep themselves from being shot by the Germans behind them. He often wondered how the Germans and Italians could have ever formed an alliance with such wildly different national characters.

Alex found an outdoor café and ordered some dinner as well as a glass of wine. As he ate his dinner and sipped his wine, watching the swirl of Roman life around him, he thought to himself, *I could get used to this.*

* * *

A FEW DAYS later, Alex was scheduled for his first meeting of the Allied Control Commission, as Iselin's aide, and if necessary, interpreter.

Salvatore had insisted that Alex dress in his civilian clothes, taking the time while Alex changed to inform him of some of the more delicate provisions of the September 23, 1943 Armistice with Italy and Instrument of Surrender, which had established the Allied Control Commission. The Italian part of that Commission had been established on November 10, 1943. Alex realized that at the time the Commission came into existence, he was still stuck behind the Gustav Line near Monte Casino.

"That's been nearly two years," said Alex. "How much has been accomplished?"

"Not much," replied Salvatore. "But we should go now."

They left the apartment and walked about half a mile to the headquarters of the Allied Control Commission in Italy, housed in the *Palazzo Marcello alle Colonne*, a mid-sixteenth century villa. The Marcello family was one of the great families of Rome, and the villa reflected this history. The front portico had six majestic Doric columns, and two heroic statues framed the entrance to the courtyard: a nude bearded male (a philosopher allegedly trying to understand the meaning of life by giving away all his possessions) and a mostly intact bust of an imperial Roman soldier. There were also several Roman monuments with Latin inscriptions.

"The Marcello family claims descent from the House of Julian," Salvatore explained, "which produced many emperors. They wanted to recreate a villa in which a patrician of the Roman Empire might feel at home. Some might say the strong attachment of Italians to the past is a bad thing. But I think it is a good thing. Whenever one has a question, it is often good to look to the past and see what people did. But in the end, every time is unique, and to some extent we are always making our decisions in the dark."

The entrance doors to the villa were made of dark wood and boasted a finely inlaid design of vines and grapes. Flanking the doors were two life-sized busts of Roman senators.

Salvatore motioned to them. "These are new. Only about a hundred and fifty years old."

Alex heard the sharp click of a man's shoes approaching the door across the marble floor, and Colonel Iselin opened it.

"Why isn't he wearing the uniform?" Colonel Iselin asked.

"Well, actually, it's my fault," Salvatore explained. Alex couldn't help but note the older man's combination of charm and humility. "We Italians are a proud people. I thought it might help the negotiations if they were conducted in a manner more like friends getting together to discuss a problem, than a military occupation. Especially given this young man's family history. I thought it would be a good gesture."

"You want the Italians to think Alex is on their side?"

"I prefer to think of it as there being no sides."

"Well, there are. Now, go home and come back in uniform," said Colonel Iselin and closed the door.

Alex couldn't help but feel a flash of anger at Iselin, not just for how he treated him, but the disrespect he exhibited toward Salvatore. He looked at Salvatore, but before he could say anything Salvatore put a hand on his shoulder and said, "I know you wish to fight him, but keep your anger to yourself."

"That guy is an asshole!" Alex replied.

Salvatore guided him away as they made their way onto the street. "A bull will rarely catch a person unaware, but a cat waits for the perfect moment to strike. We must do the same thing. Colonel Iselin is really nothing. He thinks he is in control, but the truth is that none of us are. There are forces at play more powerful than any of us, but we might be able to guide them. Your armies will one day leave Italy, and it will belong to the Italians. If we must endure a few humiliations until that time, that's a price we must be willing to pay."

An hour later, Alex and Salvatore returned. Colonel Iselin greeted them a little more cordially, and Alex reciprocated because he wanted to follow Salvatore's advice.

The three of them went to a nearby street and Colonel Iselin handed Salvatore the keys to the car. Salvatore and Iselin climbed into the front of car and Alex took the backseat, as if he was their child. But as they began their drive, Alex couldn't help but smile, as if instead of a child, one might think that Salvatore and Iselin worked for him.

Colonel Iselin started talking as they drove. "The man we're going to visit, Giorgio Sachretti, is a high-ranking member of the Christian Democrats. Mussolini nearly wiped them out. Sachretti is looked upon as the grand old man of the party. When Mussolini marched on Rome, Sachretti kept calling on the military to stop the fascists. When they took over, Sachretti withdrew to his villa outside of Rome. During the war he slipped us a lot of information, and he was one of the key leaders of the Resistance, although we don't want that to be widely known. In fact, a lot of what you're going to be hearing in these meetings is to go no further. Understood?"

"Yes, sir."

Colonel Iselin continued. "I'm here to make sure that this country doesn't fly apart into civil war or go into the communist camp. I don't want us Americans coming over here for a third time this century."

"We are in complete agreement about that," said Salvatore.

They pulled up to a small nondescript building just outside the Aurelian Walls, the original center of Rome, which enclosed roughly thirty-five hundred acres, including the fabled Seven Hills of Rome. Alex couldn't help but notice the building looked squat and toad-like among the more beautiful buildings surrounding it. When they approached, Alex saw the stone door frame had carved cherubs and seraphim, and the wooden part was scratched and seemed to have marks that he thought might be bullet marks.

Salvatore stepped forward and knocked on the door.

A young woman opened the door, taller than most Italian women, her rebellious blonde hair was wild, like Medusa's snakes, her eyes sharp-witted and observant. Alex felt a thrill of recognition.

She quickly appraised Salvatore with a look that suggested familiarity and then shot a quick dispassionate glance at Colonel Iselin and finally a glacially cold stare at Alex. "Salvatore, I see you brought us our American overlord and the stupid soldier who thought he could so casually stroll into Taormina."

"It was you," said Alex, remembering that terrible night in Sicily.

"Of course it was me," she replied. "Although I expected more from my first meeting with an American than one so foolishly putting himself at risk."

"Dianna," Salvatore said sharply. "You must be more hospitable to our American guests."

"Guests?" she said with anger. "We have shed blood with the Americans against the Germans for years, and yet they still treat us like children who need to be managed."

"We lost a lot of American boys in this country," said Iselin, matching her emotion. "We wouldn't have needed to do that if your king had a little more guts than letting Mussolini just waltz into power. It might have helped if your people hadn't been cheering him for twenty years."

"Gentlemen," said an older man's voice from the hallway. The three of them turned to see a thin, expensively dressed man with an air of Old-World elegance in the way he moved come toward them. He was fair skinned for an Italian and blond, which immediately marked him as a Northern Italian, close to the border with Austria, where such a light complexion was more common. "Please forgive my granddaughter," he said with an amused expression. "You know how strong-minded the young can be about things. All who enter this house are friends."

"Signor Sachretti," said Colonel Iselin.

Sachretti warmly greeted Salvatore. "How are you, my old friend?"

"Quite well. Especially since I learned that God has protected this young man," he said, motioning to Alex.

"Alex Falcone," said Signor Sachretti, taking both of Alex's hands in his own. "I am also glad that God has protected the grandson of my good friend, the Duke du Taormina, the Lion of Sicily. Do you know the history you represent, young man?"

"Salvatore has told me much about my grandfather."

Sachretti nodded. "Yes, it is good to hear stories, but they are nothing compared to actually having known the man." He paused for a moment, releasing Alex's hands, then placing a hand on Alex's shoulder and drawing him close. "He was a beacon of integrity. I am not sure what it is that makes certain men so good that they cannot even consider the slightest bit of dishonesty. I would tease him sometimes about how he didn't mind offending politicians and bureaucrats, and he would always say 'The only words of praise I want to hear are when I meet my Maker and He says to me, 'Well-done, my good and faithful servant." That is who your grandfather was."

"That's a high standard to live up to," Alex replied, deeply moved by the words about his grandfather.

"It is. After all, we are but flawed humans, forever in need of grace," Sachretti replied.

"And yet I believe God still watches us and intervenes in our affairs in times of need." The older man motioned to Dianna. "What are the odds my granddaughter would be in exactly the right place she needed to rescue you from the Germans?"

"Grandfather," said Dianna, "if he hadn't disobeyed orders, I wouldn't have had to save him. It was only luck that his stupidity didn't kill him!"

Signor Sachretti seemed amused by his granddaughter. "You may not know this, but Dianna joined the partisans when she was only thirteen years old, carrying out missions for them. For her it seems as if she's been at war for a long time, and she's anxious for the last vestiges of it to be removed from us."

"I am tired of all this talking," said Dianna. "It's time for us to say goodbye to our American friends and let us Italians sort things out." She started to walk out of the room.

"Dianna, before you leave," Sachretti said, "I was hoping to ask a favor of you."

She stopped and spun around. "Yes, Grandfather?"

"When we are done here, I was hoping you might show our young American friend around Rome. Let him see the Eternal City through Italian eyes."

"I'm not the diplomat you are, Grandfather."

"We must all make our sacrifices."

"Yes, Grandfather."

"*Grazie*," said Signor Sachretti.

And with that she left the room.

Sachretti turned his attention to Alex. "I understand you are a skilled translator."

"Yes, sir."

"My English is good enough, but it tires me. I would like to speak in Italian, if possible, and have you translate for me."

"I'd be happy to."

"Good."

The three of them sat at a table, a servant came in asking if they'd like something to drink or eat, and they got themselves situated.

For the next three hours, Signor Sachretti talked almost nonstop, and Alex found himself struggling to keep up with the translation. Italian had a greater sense of irony than English and many of his statements could be taken to mean the Italians were wise, or sometimes the greatest of fools. Alex was fairly certain he was properly conveying the ideas, as often when he finished, he'd look to Sachretti, who would normally smile and nod his head. A few times Sachretti would break into English to more completely convey what he meant, and then switch back to Italian once the point was made. The thrust of Sachretti's comments was to understand that Italians were a particularly argumentative people, which suited them well for democracy, but they also had an unfortunate tendency never to come to an agreement. Talk was good, but there needed to come a time when decisions were made.

"What about the monarchy?" Colonel Iselin asked. "Should it be retained?"

Sachretti paused, then resumed in English. "It's my impression that people are evenly divided on this issue. Personally, I think things should remain the way they are. There are many monarchists among the people. But we cannot get around the fact that in the minds of many the King is associated with the fascists. Those who were anti-fascist may grumble about the monarchy being retained, but it will keep quiet those who may have been allied with the Germans."

"Perhaps a referendum on the fate of the monarchy might be a good choice?" suggested Colonel Iselin.

"Yes, it is good to let the people decide these issues."

"Can the people be trusted?" Iselin asked.

"The people can always be trusted," said Sachretti.

"They cheered when Mussolini walked in," said Iselin.

"This is true," Sachretti agreed. "But the first thing he did was dismantle the opposition. That is a not the sign of a leader secure in his power. We all have a little of Mussolini in our souls and must be sure to fight him, in others and in ourselves."

Colonel Iselin glanced at his watch, then stood up and extended a hand to Sachretti. "It's been very nice to have this discussion. Your reputation as a wise man about your country is well deserved. I hope when the election comes the voters will be farsighted enough to give you back your old position as chairman of the House of Deputies."

Sachretti smiled and shook his head. "It's a job for a younger man. I'm just an old dog trying to keep the young curs from playing too roughly with each other. They're much quicker than I am, but I am older and can therefore usually outthink them."

"But certainly, there's a role for an elder statesman," observed Colonel Iselin.

"Perhaps."

"We should be going now," said Colonel Iselin. "Thank you very much, Signor Sachretti."

"But of course, Alex will be staying behind, won't he?"

"Yes."

Colonel Iselin left. Alex observed Sachretti watching Iselin walk away, then after he was sure that Iselin was out of earshot, turned to Alex.

"What do you think of politics so far, young man?"

"There's a lot to think about."

"Your great grandfather, King Victor Emmanuel II, was a remarkable military leader, but left politics to others. Your grandfather had both physical and moral courage, a rare combination in a public figure. Our present king, Victor Emmanuel III, has none of these traits. He is like many today, a fearful man, always trying to prevent the next disaster, and in the process bringing about something even worse. What do you think you are, Alex?"

"I'm not sure."

"I know you are a solider, at the very least. Going into Taormina, sneaking into Milan and putting two bullets in the dictator's corpse. What I'm wondering is if you can be something else as well. Something more, perhaps."

"What would you have me be?"

"These times require both goodness and cunning. A soldier, politician, a diplomat, and perhaps a miracle worker as well."

Dianna entered the room. "I'm not taking him out in his military uniform," she said.

"Why not?" Signor Sachretti asked.

"People will think I'm just another young girl trying to get a soldier to marry her and give her big American babies."

Signor Sachretti looked at his granddaughter in exasperation.

Alex intervened. "I've got some civilian clothes back at my apartment."

"We'll have a car take you there and bring you back," said Dianna, spinning on her heels and starting to leave. "Let me know when he returns," she said to her grandfather, giving a quick glance back as she left the room.

"No matter where we are," said Signor Sachretti to Alex, "we men always live under the tyranny of women. Is it not true?"

Alex had to agree with the elder statesman.

* * *

WHEN ALEX RETURNED in his civilian clothes, Dianna gave him a quick appraisal.

"Salvatore got those clothes for you, didn't he?" she asked.

"Yeah. Why?"

"They're the clothes of an old man. Yes, I'm sure they would meet with the approval of people like my grandfather, but not those of anybody younger."

"It's all I got," said Alex.

She shrugged. "All right."

They walked past the Aurelian Walls and toward the center of historic Rome. As they began their walk, she moved quickly, as if angry she'd been forced to spend time with him. Alex decided the best course was simply to keep up with her and wait for an opportunity to speak. From working at his uncle's construction company, he'd learned that when dealing with irate people, it was best to let them speak first, then simply respond. After about ten minutes, it seemed as if some of her anger had dissipated, and she asked, "Where are you from in the United States?"

"San Francisco," he said, not adding any other details.

That seemed to catch her attention. "Not New York," she said with an intentionally nasally pronunciation, as if she was from the Bronx, or New Jersey.

Alex laughed. "You've got an ear for accents," he observed.

"When you're in the Resistance you learn that listening is more important than speaking."

"I had a lot of interactions with the Resistance," Alex said. "They seemed like good people. Brave."

"We have a lot of communists in the Resistance," said Dianna.

"I've heard that."

"They want to take over just like the fascists did."

Alex nodded.

"I worry for Italy. We like to argue, but we don't really like physical confrontations. Enjoy the good life. Laugh, drink, chase women. But the communists are not like that. You look into their eyes and know they mean business."

They eventually found themselves in front of the Trevi Fountain, completed in 1762 and made of Travertine stone that had been quarried near Tivoli, a little more than twenty miles from Rome. The name came from the Latin, *Trivium*, meaning the intersection of three roads, specifically *De Croichi, Polli,* and *Delle Muratte* streets. The theme of the fountain was the "Taming of the Waters," and depicted the Greek god Oceanus, a Titan son of Uranus and

Gaia, who ruled over the rivers. Oceanus rides in his chariot pulled by tritons, a grip of fish-tailed, half-human sea creatures who were often in the employ of the sea god, Poseidon, and who were in the midst of taming hippocampi, the half horse, half fish of the deep.

Dianna explained the background of the sculptures, and then said, "The Tiber River has given both life and death to Rome. It is what rivers do all around the world to the people who live near them. But the hope is that we can tame their destructive force."

"Big ambition," replied Alex.

As they stood watching the fountain, Dianna asked him about his life in San Francisco. He found himself talking more than he had since Bill Squire's death and was surprised at what came out of his mouth. He realized he had great pride in his family, what his parents had accomplished, as well as the work he'd done with his Uncle Vincenzo in the years before the war. *Perhaps*, he thought, *you never see people and places clearly until you are away from them.*

"You are not what I expected, American soldier," said Dianna after he'd talked for a while.

"What did you expect?" Alex asked.

"Well, first there was the stupid American soldier who walked into Taormina," Dianna replied. "Then there was the legend Salvatore created of the 'Lion of Sicily' who marched with the American army. I can't tell you how many times I heard other members of the Resistance whisper your name with great reverence, as if that proved God was on our side. Next was the story of how you slipped away from your unit in the mountains, traveled with the Resistance, and got to Milan just in time to see Mussolini's dead body strung up. It was as if Salvatore's tale had a ring of truth about it. Then I met you and listened to your stories of life in America, and I find myself confused. In a way you're all those things I thought, but in another you're none of them."

"Maybe you shouldn't be so quick to judge."

She laughed. "It is the Italian nature, especially of our women. You see exactly how we feel on our faces."

"And if you're wrong?"

"It is not impossible to get us to change our minds."

"Good to know I may not always be the stupid American."

Dianna fished in her purse and pulled out a few coins. "There is a tradition here. You put three coins in your right hand," she said, dropping them in Alex's palm, "turn your back to the fountain, make a wish, and then throw them into the water over your left shoulder."

She got him properly situated at the fountain, then got herself ready with a few coins. "Let's do it at the same time. One, two, three!"

They threw the coins into the fountain and heard their satisfying splash. "What did you wish for?" Dianna asked.

"Peace," said Alex. "I've seen enough of the bad stuff. I don't want to see any of it anymore. I just want a quiet life from now on."

"You make a big wish for your first time at the fountain," she observed.

"And you?"

"A smaller one." She fingered the lapel of his jacket. "You look like an old man in these clothes," she said, releasing it with disgust. "If you're going to be a young man in Rome, you should dress like one. Maybe you should wear these clothes for the Commission because it is filled with old men. But you should let me take you shopping, pick out some better clothes for you."

"I'm in your capable hands," said Alex. "After all, you did save my life. I guess I could endure the torture of a few hours of shopping."

"Maybe if you Americans listen to us Italians," said Dianna, "it will not be too bad to have you here for a time." They turned away from the fountain, and she took his arm as they walked away to find a tailor.

Chapter Sixteen

IN THE NEXT FEW WEEKS ALEX spent a great deal of his free time simply walking around Rome and taking in the history of the city. His work for the Commission involved constant political infighting, and he sometimes struggled to translate certain Italian curse words into English. It often seemed that little progress was being made, but Alex enjoyed it nonetheless. Often, he'd be introduced as the grandson of the "Lion of Sicily," there would be some kind words directed to the memory of his grandfather, and then the politicians would go back to their same arguments conducted at a high decibel level.

In August, atomic bombs were dropped on Hiroshima and Nagasaki, and shortly after those game-changers the War in the Pacific came to an end. Japan signed a formal surrender, and General MacArthur arrived in Tokyo to take on his role as American Viceroy over the defeated enemy. Alex noted that one of the first things MacArthur did was to reassure the Japanese people that the emperor would retain his throne and the monarchy would continue in the future.

In summer the Tiber was a slow-moving river, and Alex found he liked to rise early in the morning and watch the city come to life as the rising sun revealed warm shades of brown and orange, touched by the silver-gray of church and palace stone.

Alex liked to begin his day with a walk through the *Forum Romanum*, where the Senate of Rome once stood. Stones from the Roman Senate littered the ground. Alex wondered if a similar fate might one day befall his own country, a far distant future when its former glory would be remembered. Occasional columns stood throughout the site like petrified trees. On the Imperial Road, the great arch of Constantine, the emperor who converted the empire to Christianity, rose into the morning sky, the majesty undimmed by its dirty whiteness. The city itself almost seemed like a museum, and Alex spent hours studying the statues of emperors, barbarians, and scenes of battles fought more than fifteen hundred years ago. Even though the scenes depicted warriors carrying spears and swift chariots rather than rifles and tanks, Alex couldn't help but imagine himself in the pictures. The life of a soldier in World War II, despite the difference in technologies, would be quickly recognizable to a soldier in Caesar's army. Alex struggled with the question of whether it would ever be possible for humanity to avoid war. Would war come every few years with each generation touched by fire, or would it be a rare occurrence, like the appearance of a great comet, which only the oldest of living eyes had glimpsed before?

The barbaric energy of the Colosseum drew Alex almost as much as it repulsed him. The roots of the catacombs underneath the arena had long since given way, allowing a view of where war prisoners, animals, and early Christians were held before the cruel games in which their lives would be taken from them. Alex could not decide whether he felt shame as an Italian or pride as a Christian. Alex considered the imprisoned Christians fervently praying in their cells before their deaths, and the unlikely event that transpired where this Empire that once killed Christians would eventually surrender to the Christian religion.

Only in the Vatican did Alex find a sense of peace, which made all things whole and good. He could almost feel God in the way the shafts of light sliced through the open windows to illuminate the darkness of the cavernous structure, creating pools of shadow and light. It was as if there was a great slumbering divinity in the hushed silence of Saint Peter's, the reverence of the parishioners, priests, and nuns as they prayed to the Almighty. Statues of saints placed all about the great cathedral reminded him of the struggles endured for the sake of their simple faith. But Alex also recalled how certain popes in history had suited up for battle like a general or sold indulgences to pay for their grand cathedrals. However, even with this knowledge, Alex felt this great building was not about the sins of mankind and their failures, but a symbol of the forgiveness God offers to every human being.

Alex often wandered to the small chapels that flared off from the center of the building. In the grandness of the Vatican, there was still room for the intimate, the private moment of reflection and prayer. Alex often stopped to look at those who were sitting alone, either kneeling in prayer, or on a pew looking at the flickering votive candles lit in remembrance of the dead. Several times Alex would take a candle and do the same in memory of his good friend, Bill Squire, who'd been killed on that haunting night in Taormina.

One Saturday morning, he strolled past one of the side chapels and saw a familiar figure, kneeling in front of a row of candles. Her head was bowed, but her profile and outline were unmistakable. It was Dianna. He'd seen her at meetings a few times briefly since their night out, which had ended in a tailor's shop with him purchasing several pairs of pants and shirts, as well as some stylish shoes. The country might still be dealing with deprivations from the war, but somehow, they still found a way to look their best. That was the night Dianna had explained to him the Italian concept of *bella figura*, translated as "the beautiful figure." It meant that whenever you went out in public, you looked your very best. That meant certain things if you were a woman, and even if you were a man with just one good set of clothes, you made sure your jackets and pants were clean and smoothed of any wrinkles.

Rather than draining him, the constant bickering of the various factions with which he had to contend during the day put him in something of a playful mood when he was away from it. He walked to Dianna's pew, entered, and took a seat uncomfortably close to her. "And what are we praying for today?" he asked her.

"I wasn't praying for somebody to disturb me," she said, but there was a hint of a smile on her face.

"Do you want me to leave you alone?"

She shrugged. "You can stay. Besides, all are supposed to be welcome in the house of God."

"Even a stupid American soldier?"

"Perhaps he needs it most of all."

"Then I will attempt to pray very deeply," Alex replied, going down on his knees and assuming a prayerful position.

After a few minutes, Alex sat back on the bench, perfectly comfortable to sit with Dianna in companionable silence. Dianna leaned over to him and said, "I like the silence of a church. So much in my life is noise, people talking, not listening to each other; then I come here, it's quiet, peaceful, and I can hear my own thoughts."

"And what are those thoughts?"

"I should be happy," she said. "The tyrants have been defeated. But I have to wonder if it's the people who have the problem. I dislike your Colonel Iselin a great deal, but part of me worries he is right. Can we Italians be trusted to make our own decisions without the guidance of others? For thousands of years, we were the ones telling the rest of the world what to do. Then we had centuries where we were at the mercy of other countries, each having a piece of us, or we were small warring kingdoms, grasping greedily for whatever they could. Perhaps man is God's great mistake, and we should simply accept that."

"I don't believe that."

"Oh no?" she said, with a wry smile. "And what does the American soldier believe?"

"I think a lot of the world is messed up," he replied. "But your average person is pretty good. I look at what happened in Europe, and I think you did everything wrong. You didn't protect what we in America feel is our birthright, freedom of speech, the right to bear arms, and religious freedom. We don't like our leaders, we can shout that from the rooftops, vote them out, and even if they stay, we still don't have any problem talking about how much we don't like them."

"And if you really don't like them," she whispered, "you have your guns."

"We keep our guns holstered pretty well," Alex replied. "Only time we've taken them out was for our Civil War to free the Blacks. I won't apologize for that. I'm not saying we don't have our problems. I'm just saying we're unlikely to have Mussolini or Hitler-sized problems."

Dianna seemed to brighten. "So, you're not so pessimistic about our chances?"

"No."

"The Germans executed my parents," said Dianna.

"I'm so sorry."

She nodded, not looking at Alex. "It was right after the King arrested Mussolini and switched sides to the Americans. Everybody in the Resistance was so excited we got reckless. They were making contact with military commanders in the field, urging them to turn their guns on the Germans. I'm not sure what we expected; maybe that the Germans would simply leave our country, let Italy be free. But that was foolish."

"There is evil in the world," said Alex. "Of that I have no doubt. I've done a lot of fighting, through North Africa, Sicily, and in Italy, but none of that really convinced me. But then I got called in to take evidence for the massacre at the Ardeatine Caves, more than three hundred civilians. If I hadn't really believed in the devil before that day, I believed in it after."

"But what if that evil is in me, as well?"

"What do you mean?"

"That night you were shot in Taormina. You don't know what happened afterward. We chased him down, cornered him. He was trying to surrender, and the partisans shot him dead. And I felt good about it. What does that say about me?"

"A sniper left behind like that knows his life is a short one. He wasn't expecting to make it through the fight."

"If I'd had my gun out, I would have shot him dead as well."

"He was an invader in your land."

"When my parents were killed, I wondered if it was God's judgment being placed upon me."

"It doesn't work that way," said Alex. "We're all sinners. Besides, you're forgetting something. That sniper was lying in wait, all on his own. He made the decision to pull the trigger and kill my friend. He could've simply surrendered to us, as he knew our army was coming, and we would've treated him well. He chose to kill with stealth and got killed in return. I call it a righteous kill. And as for your parents, no shame, just pride. They knew the dangers and chose to proceed. Nothing could be braver."

Alex could feel Dianna looking at him with genuine regard. "So, is that how you Americans think? Always putting things in the most positive light?"

"Why do you have to put it in the most negative light? What does that get you?"

"I don't know," replied Dianna. "Maybe I just wanted to feel sad today."

"You can be sad if you want."

She looked him up and down. "It looks as if you liked the clothes we got."

"You said if I was going to be a young man in Rome, I shouldn't dress like an old one."

"I don't think I want to be sad today," said Dianna. "Do you have any plans?"

"No."

"Good," she said, standing up from the bench and offering him a hand up. "You almost pass as a young man of Rome, so I want you to see it as we Italians do."

She took his arm as they walked out of the small chapel, and Alex found himself liking the feeling of her arm against his side. He was amazed at how good it felt.

* * *

DIANNA POINTED THEM towards the Tiber River, which they crossed and eventually found themselves at the Spanish Steps. The Spanish Steps were completed in 1725, rising from the fountain at *Piazza di Spagna* to the *Piazza Trinita dei Monti*, which was dominated by the *Trinita dei Monti* church.

Alex wanted to lounge around the fountain at the base of the steps, but Dianna insisted they climb the 135 steps to the top, which gave them a lovely view of the Vatican from which they'd come, as well as much of historic Rome.

Dianna pointed to a house on the *Piazza di Spagna* where the English Romantic poet John Keats lived and died in 1821. "If you want to understand what it is to be an Italian, you must come to the Spanish Steps," said Dianna.

"Why?"

"Watch," she replied.

For more than two hours they stood at the balustrade of the Spanish Steps, watching Rome unfold on the steps and plaza below. And Alex felt he saw it. He focused first on an older woman, walking with a bag of groceries. As she made her way up the steps, Alex counted her greeting no fewer than twenty people as she made her way up the 135 steps, and two younger people offered to carry her bag. There were innumerable groups of young men and women, eyeing each other, flirting, and interacting. And for the great middle, the men and women who were most likely married, with kids and jobs, were constantly interacting in large and small groups. He occasionally heard them talking about food, their health, politics, or the weather, or gossiping about a person they knew in common.

"I see it," said Alex, leaning close to Dianna.

"Do you?" she replied.

He moved closer and kissed her. She didn't withdraw, but wasn't enthusiastic, either.

"What was that for?"

"It's a complete life, here," said Alex. "That's what you showed me. Beginning to end. The good, the bad, and everything in between. Life can be terrible, but it can be wonderful, as well."

"I think I am turning you into a Roman," she said, and kissed him passionately, then drew back, smiled, took his hand, and added, "Let's continue our day."

* * *

THEY HAD LUNCH in the Prati neighborhood, then explored *Castel Sant' Angelo*, which had originally been built as a mausoleum for the Emperor Hadrian in 139 AD. However, it was eventually turned into a military building and castle. The building was cylindrical in shape and for centuries held the ashes of the Emperor Hadrian in a treasury room. In the fourteenth century, it was connected to the Vatican by a covered, fortified corridor, and it was a refuge for Pope Clement VII in 1527 during the Sack of Rome. Later it was used as a prison. Among its notable prisoners was Giordano Bruno, a seventeenth-century scientist and mystic who not only predicted what Galileo would confirm years later, but also claimed the universe was filled with other intelligent beings. In the small courtyard, Bruno was burned at the stake.

"Again, Rome shows her brutal and beautiful side," said Dianna after they'd toured the castle. "But there is no better place in Rome to watch the sunset than here."

They sat on a bench near the Tiber River and *Castel Sant' Angelo*, watching the sun set and occasionally kissing. Alex couldn't help but note she hadn't let go of his hand since they'd first kissed on the Spanish Steps. The reddish stone of *Castel Sant'*

Angelo took on an almost magical appearance in the fading light, and Alex couldn't help but feel this might be the most pivotal day of his life.

They had dinner at a small outdoor café on the *Piazza Navona*, drinking many glasses of red wine and talking so easily that hours seemed to pass like minutes. "Walk me home?" she asked when the night had turned late.

"Yeah. Where do you live?"

"I have an apartment at my grandfather's villa."

"I remember," said Alex. "That's where I met you."

"Yes, or as I like to call it, 'When Dianna Lost the Battle of the Military Uniform.'"

"Yeah, but look at me now," Alex replied, pointing to his clothes. "Seems like you won the war."

"Women always win the war," she answered. "It's just that most men don't realize it."

They walked together through the late-night Roman streets, a smattering of people still out late talking, drinking, and laughing, and Alex couldn't help but imagine he was living in a moment outside of time. He felt truly happy, walking down these pathways, Dianna next to him, her warm hand in his own.

When they reached her apartment, she paused. "Want me to come in?"

"We're not done with each other, are we?"

"I don't think we're going to be done with each other for a long while."

Alex thought he caught a glimpse of a smile on her face as she pushed the door open, entered, and waited for him to follow.

He had been with other women, fleeting wartime romances, the ever-present specter of death imparting a vividness to life that those who had not experienced such times might never understand. Alex even imagined he'd been in love a time or two but found such feelings fading quickly with the distance he put between them. He figured she'd probably lived a similar life in the Resistance, but here they were now, a lifetime of experiences behind them, and yet so much left on the road ahead.

They took it slow, the Italian way, savoring the moment, entwined with each other as they lay on her couch talking. They kissed several times then fell to talking again, and after about an hour, he began to lift off her blouse. She raised her arms to help it slip off more easily, shook her blonde hair free, laid back against him, and cocked her head to catch his eye. "Like what you see?"

"Very much."

"I like it when a man looks at me. Means I have his attention."

"You certainly have mine."

She turned over in his arms. "An Italian woman is comfortable with her body. You are not too American, are you?"

"No, ma'am," he replied.

"Let us find out." She tugged at his shirt, and then when that was off, had him stand, unbuckled his belt, drew his pants to the floor, and removed his shoes. He stood naked before her. She walked around him, a single fingernail tracing a line around his body.

"Like what you see?" he asked.

"It's acceptable," she replied. "But you forget, I have seen it before."

"In Taormina."

"Yes." She was quiet, continuing to walk around him and stopping at the scar on his shoulder. "I remember how bloody this was. The men did not think you were going to make it and suggested we should let you die. I was so angry at them, yelling at the top of my lungs like a madwoman." She ran her finger up and down the scar, sending shivers through his body. "I remember cleaning it out, stitching it up, then going to work on this." She touched the wound on his thigh. "You were lucky it did not hit bone. But there was so much blood. I was covered in it. But I would not let you die." She brushed a cheek against his bare shoulder, and Alex could feel a warm tear wet his skin.

"I didn't know."

"I stayed by your bedside for two nights, listening to you breathe, shallow at first, then with growing strength. I stayed longer than I should have; it made the crossing back to Italy more dangerous, but I had to know you would survive."

"I survived all that and more," he said, taking her face into his hands and kissing her.

"I'm tired of blood," she said after he kissed her, letting her skirt drop to her feet, stepping out of it, and pressing herself into him so he could feel her heat. "We like to think the evil is out there, in men like Hitler, Mussolini, and Stalin, but that's not true. It's inside us, waiting for the key to be turned, like a motor car, and then we are on the road to ruin."

"We can choose the road," said Alex.

"Do you think so?"

"Yes."

He dropped to his knees, kissing the edge of her lovely hips, working his way into her center, inhaling her deep wonderful musk, and feeling her surrender to his touch. She took his hand firmly, led him into the bedroom, and slipped beneath the warm covers, delighting each other in all possible ways, the grasping, squeezing, licking, and laughing until they could stand it no longer. Her legs opened wide to accept him, and he entered her.

But it was the look of utter bliss on her face as they made love that drew him most, making him realize this was the most important moment of his life.

Chapter Seventeen

"Ever since I was a young boy, I've always liked taking a walk at dusk by the Tiber," said Signor Sachretti. "Many times, I walked here with your grandfather, and we talked about how to make our government as good as its people."

They strolled along a sidewalk close to the banks, with drooping shade trees. Twenty feet below the river flowed slowly. Alex had been spending most nights with Dianna, often seeing the older man, but none of them spoke of the reason. Alex understood it was a form of discretion on the part of the older man, pretending not to see their relationship. Catholic Italy didn't approve of young people living together, even in the aftermath of war, Instead, Sachretti treated Alex like a member of the family, trying to educate the young man.

Sachretti continued. "Maybe it is how all honest men feel when they see behind the curtain of what happens in their country."

"And what did my grandfather think?"

"He was an optimist," Sachretti said with a laugh. "He always told me I was thinking too hard, seeing darkness everywhere, and ignoring the light. 'Leave it to the people,' he'd say. Don't think you have to fix everything. You are one person, and what you see is limited. Be humble in the world."

"And which one of you was right?" Alex asked.

"It was a conversation we started forty-six years ago, and I still don't have an answer."

"When did you meet him?"

"July 29, 1900, the date of the coronation of our current king. I was a young member of Parliament. He took a liking to me. We took this very walk. They were troubled times, much like today."

"Why?"

"A new century. So much promise, but so many dangers. Our previous king, Umberto I, was struck down by an assassin, an Italian-born anarchist who had just returned from America. Just like your President McKinley was killed by an anarchist six weeks later, paving the way for Teddy Roosevelt to become president. We both entered the century in anarchy."

"I didn't realize our countries shared that much," Alex answered.

"We're an old empire, weighed down by the centuries. You're a new empire, full of energy and purpose, so much ahead of you, and yet you do not know the things we know."

"Such as?"

"The dangers of ambition. To assume that because you are strong, you are wise. Those are two different things."

"And do older empires make such mistakes?"

Sachretti laughed. "Of course, they do. What was Mussolini, but a Caesar in training? He wanted us to become an empire again; he said so all the time. Why else did he go into North Africa, Albania, Greece, even France? It was madness at the time, but so often we forget."

"Can the United States avoid those mistakes?"

The old man shrugged. "Who can say? You are such an interesting experiment; your founding principle is you want to be left alone. But power is such a temptation. When it seems you have the world in your hand, who among us would not seek to grab it?"

"We don't want to stay in Europe a second longer than we need to," Alex replied.

"I'm sure that's what your fellow soldiers think, and even probably most of your countrymen. But it's always others who decide. Sometimes those decisions are made by men of courage. Other times not."

"Were you part of the group working with my grandfather to prevent Mussolini from coming to power?"

The old man's expression grew more animated. "You speak of what I tried to do almost a quarter of a century ago and failed. Who knows if it would have worked, even if your grandfather had not been killed. But yes, I was an intimate part of the plan. I remember telling your grandfather he needed to be ruthless if the King did not yield. But he would have no part of it. 'I will go to my nephew and tell him what he should do,' he said. 'Even offer to lead his army in battle against Mussolini. But I will not raise a hand against my King.' When you hear this of your grandfather, then look at what came after, is that a decision that fills you with pride, or something else?"

"He would not have opposed the King? He would have let Mussolini come to power?"

"He told me he would try everything possible to convince the King. And if it did not work, he would take whatever part of the army that would follow him and march out against the fascists. 'Even if it's just me with a single rifle,' he said to me, 'I will fight the fascists. But I will not point a rifle at my King.'"

"You would have gone to violence against the King?"

"I would have done whatever was necessary to keep Mussolini from coming to power. Nothing that happened was a surprise to me. We were not ready to fight, and as a result we let the wolves free among the sheep."

Alex considered the older man's words. He looked at the Tiber, indifferent to humanity, then at the people who walked along its banks—children, young lovers, middle-aged parents, grandfathers and grandmothers—hopeful that their rulers would leave them alone and not call them to a foolish battle. "It's all so fragile," he said in almost a whisper.

"Now you know what keeps old men up at night," said Sachretti.

* * *

"WON'T BE TOO long before we're all able to go home, Falcone," said Colonel Iselin to Alex. Salvatore had joined them as they were sitting at an outdoor café in the *Piazza Navona*.

It was a warm spring day in late April, with a blue and white cloud-spotted sky. In the eleven months since the war in Europe had ended, it seemed as if a new world had been born. Romans went about on the streets smiling, and even though the politicians for whom he translated argued as much as before with Iselin and the Allied Control Commission, they didn't seem to have the same energy. It seemed to Alex that the people were tired of strife, and in the Italian manner of accepting things they couldn't control, just wanted to move on.

Even Colonel Iselin had relaxed over the past months, though he always insisted Alex wear his military uniform when working on behalf of the Commission. When Colonel Iselin had given him a Christmas present the previous December, a copy of Michelangelo's *David*, Alex had been deeply touched. As he looked at the copy, Iselin had remarked, "It's something for a young man. Notice how Michelangelo made David's hands and head so large, in proportion to the rest of his body. It's as if he was trying to say, 'he's growing into his greatness.'"

It was odd for Alex to consider how he'd first met Iselin and found him such an imposing figure, but now considered him almost like an older uncle.

"I figure after the referendum on the monarchy is complete, we can ship out of here," said Iselin, as he finished a glass of red wine.

"Did we really do anything here?" Alex asked.

Both Colonel Iselin and Salvatore looked at him curiously.

"What do you mean?" Salvatore asked.

"We came here, the sides had already been chosen, maybe we kept things from getting out of hand a few times. But the King is the one who let the fascists in, allowed Mussolini to run the place for decades, and when the referendum is over, the King will probably still be on the throne. They called us the 'Allied Control

Commission,' but it didn't seem like we controlled anything. It's all going to just go back to the way it was. Thanks so much for playing the game."

"The country was on the edge of fracturing," Iselin said. "Holding it together is something I'm proud I had a hand in. And we clipped the old King's wings. Since October of '44 he hasn't been in government councils and his son, Umberto, is head of state. Victor is just a figurehead."

"To the people it all looks the same. It's holding together because nothing's really changed. Most of the fascists kept their jobs, and we let them do it if they'll simply promise to be better next time."

"It is difficult to make judgments of people in such challenging times," Salvatore added.

"It seems to me that's just the time when we should be making the clearest of judgments about people. It's the time that matters most of all."

"This isn't a perfect word, Alex," said Iselin, "But it's a pretty good one."

"Why? Because we kept the communists from coming to power?"

"Look, we did a much better job in Italy than they're doing in Greece," Iselin replied. "There's a war coming there and we—"

"Did you ever think that part of the reason the communists are so popular is because people see people like us, the Allied Control Commission, not really interested in changing things? We're just interested in 'stability' and not upsetting the apple cart? Let the corrupt politicians go back to their usual way of doing things, the rich get to keep their money and not do anything to help the poor, and the one good thing Mussolini did do was drive the mafia out of Italy, but now with freedom I'm sure they're coming back. Not much of a victory, if you ask me."

"You know, Falcone, you're starting to sound like an anarchist," said Iselin.

Salvatore intervened. "My young master is not an anarchist. If anything, he sounds much like his grandfather." He turned to

Iselin. "You do not understand this about us Italians. We like to think out loud. Say everything that is on our minds. It is better to let it out, rather than keep the poison hidden deep within our bodies, as our good friends from the more northern climes often seem to do. You never have to ask an Italian twice to tell you what he thinks."

"Sometimes there's an advantage to keeping your mouth shut," grumbled Iselin. "You Italians seem crazy to me, more often than not."

"I understand it appears that way to you," said Salvatore. "Which is why when I'm with you, I do my best to speak in a way that feels most comfortable to you, and that you can comprehend."

"I think he just called you an idiot, sir," said Alex with a half-smile.

"Oh, I'm certain he did," Iselin replied, choosing to look at a pretty girl walking by instead of his companions. "It was just done so diplomatically I decided to marvel at it, rather than be offended. Tell me, Alex, have you convinced your little Italian fireball to follow you home when you leave?"

"What are you talking about?"

Iselin looked to Salvatore. "Young guy thinks we old guys don't see things."

Salvatore chuckled.

Alex shrugged. "I thought we were keeping it pretty quiet."

"It got reported to me," said Iselin. "Possible fraternization with the enemy, and all."

"The enemy?" Salvatore asked.

"Don't worry," Iselin replied. "I'm keeping it under the hood. You see, I can keep a few secrets. I don't always share all I know. Just don't go native on me, Alex."

"Dianna isn't the enemy."

"Look, I get it," said Iselin. "Resistance family and all that. Don't have a single bad thing to say about Dianna or her grandfather. Hell, he's probably going to become the new prime minister after this referendum. But the fact is—our interests might diverge. And that can become as big a problem as having an enemy. You have to remember, I've been in the room when General Eisenhower was meeting with our allies, they left, and the General shook his head and said, 'I wish I was just fighting the Germans.' This is a difficult thing we're doing. Negotiations. Determines what happens here for the next fifty years. Are American boys going to be fighting again over this same real estate in ten, twenty years? I like to know all the little details, because that's often where things go wrong. You got something going on the side, I want to know how serious it is. If she's gonna follow you home, I got fewer worries about it."

"She doesn't want to leave her grandfather."

Iselin shrugged. "We still got problems, then. She's choosing an old man over a younger one. Got to work on your negotiation skills, Falcone."

Alex felt completely dressed down.

"Don't look so sad," said Iselin. "I've got a surprise for you before you leave."

"What?"

Iselin waited for a moment, a small smile playing on his face, then said, "I was speaking with the King yesterday and mentioned my interpreter was a cousin of his. I think I got your grandfather's name correct. Alessandro de Leone, Duke du Taormina, right?"

Alex nodded.

"Well, when I mentioned this to the King, he went crazy. He wants to meet with you. When he asked why I hadn't introduced you, I said it was because he speaks English so beautifully that I had no need of an interpreter."

"I don't want to meet him," said Alex.

Colonel Iselin's jaw dropped. "The King of Italy has made a formal request for your presence. And you're refusing?"

Alex folded his arms. "I've got no respect for him. I think he's a coward. He allowed Mussolini to come to power, and only turned against him when it was clear the Allies were winning. He's led this country to ruin, and he's going to remain. I can't do anything about that. But I can choose who I want to see. And I don't want to see him."

Iselin's expression became clouded with anger. "This isn't a request, Falcone. I assured the King you would accept. You will accept."

"I don't want to meet him," Alex said again.

"Perhaps it would be good if you did, my young master," offered Salvatore. "The King was a dear friend of your grandfather. And you might judge the man too harshly. If you had been here in the twenties, seen the chaos, you would see things differently."

"You're going to visit him and be pleasant," commanded Iselin, closing discussion on the matter.

"I'll visit, but I'm not promising pleasant." Alex took a sip of his espresso and found solace in the fact that in a few weeks he wouldn't have to take orders from anybody else.

* * *

ALEX LAY IN bed with Dianna beside him. He raised himself on one elbow and gazed at her. It was early morning, and she was still groggy, but Alex felt he had to talk.

"Why don't you come to America with me?" Alex asked.

Dianna lay on her back with her tousled, blonde hair arranged around her face like the petals of a flower. Her awakenings were not slow, languid occurrences, but sudden bursts into conscious-ness. Her eyelids popped open. "We've talked about this before," she said with the tone of a person who suddenly felt guilty. Alex felt her warm body tense against his own.

"Your grandfather can fend for himself. He's probably going to be running the country. He'll be fine."

"Why don't you stay here?" Dianna asked. "You are the American conqueror. Perhaps you will become the 'King of Italy,'" she teased. "You are royalty after all. Must I curtsey to you?"

"I don't want anything to do with that. I've had enough of politics for a lifetime. I can't believe they're forcing me to sit down with that son of a bitch."

"Why don't you stay here? All the important people know you. They like you. Doors would open. And I know your heart. You would take the right path. You would not be corrupted."

"They don't see me," Alex lamented. "They see the memory of my grandfather. A man I never knew."

"But you have heard stories of him from those who knew him best. From Salvatore, my grandfather, from your own mother. What is a man except for the decisions he makes? And he lives on in your family. You may not think you know him, but you do. You can claim that heritage."

"I don't want it," he replied. "I want to be who I am, not my heritage. In America you can forge your own path. I know this place tires you out. Don't you want to create something new, not just be the granddaughter of somebody else?"

"Is America as good as you say?"

"It isn't perfect. But it's free. Vote for whoever you like, criticize whoever you like. Rome is beautiful, but San Francisco is something else. The Pacific Ocean, the bay, the fog; there's nothing like it in the world. Big Italian population, as well. You'd never feel alone."

"And would I be the Queen of San Francisco?"

"I'd work every day to make sure you were."

She snuggled into him. "Let me go back to sleep and dream about it. The Queen of San Francisco or the King of Italy. These are not such bad choices."

Within a few minutes she'd fallen back asleep, and Alex thought to himself, *Maybe I'm a better negotiator than Iselin thinks I am.*

* * *

AT SIX O'CLOCK the following evening, Alex arrived at the Quirinal Palace in full military uniform, on the direct orders of Colonel Iselin.

The palace was built on the Quirinal Hill, the tallest of the fabled Seven Hills of Rome. Built in 1583 by Pope Gregory XIII as a summer residence, it was a way for the pope to remain in Rome during the humid summer months, perhaps catching a cool breeze, but away from the Tiber River's unbearable smell during the sweltering heat of July and August. The palace contained 1,200 rooms and more than a million square feet. In his short reign over Italy, the Emperor Napoleon had chosen it as his residence *par excellence*. Despite Napoleon's brief occupancy of the palace, it had been the playground of popes for nearly three centuries, until Alex's great grandfather had driven the pope from the residence in September 1870 and the pope took to the Vatican, where he would remain until the Catholic Church's deal with the devil, Mussolini, in 1922.

The palace was built around an enormous central courtyard, and in addition to the royal living quarters, there were many government offices and apartments for high-ranking officials. The Pauline Chapel in the palace was built to the same size and shape as the Sistine Chapel at the Vatican and had been the location of the selection of four popes.

Alex was told he would be meeting with King Victor Emmanuel III and Crown Prince Umberto in the Great Hall of the Cuirassiers, the largest room in the palace, capable of seating 350 guests, where the king often received ambassadors and foreign dignitaries.

Although he was dressed in his military uniform, his shoes buffed to a glistening, mirror-black shine, he couldn't help but feel intimidated as he walked through the grand palace. The ceilings were generally at least twenty feet high, religious and historical tapestries graced the walls, and great chandeliers hung from the ceilings. Every place his eye landed there was a piece of artwork, either some statue of antiquity from the Roman empire, a reproduction from the Middle Ages of the glory that was once Rome, or a representation of one of the Christian saints, usually enduring their martyrdom, such as arrows being shot into their flesh, being roasted over an open fire, or facing a lion in the Colosseum. It was almost an assault on the senses, an overwhelming display of both beauty and wealth, and he couldn't help but compare it to the poor humble dwellings he'd seen in his native Sicily. How could there be such opulence and such poverty in the same country?

A guard led him into the Great Hall of the Cuirassiers and Alex saw a table had been arranged and three chairs situated around one side, two of them occupied by the King and the Crown Prince.

"Alessandro de Leone Falcone, the American," announced the guard, giving his full name.

Alex had been instructed as to the etiquette with which he was to greet the King and Crown Prince. As an American, and the subject of no king, he was not to bow to them. He could slightly incline his head in greeting to the King, and refer to him as "Your Highness," but should not refer to him as "Your Royal Highness." He did not need to incline his head to the Crown Prince, as he was not the ruling monarch (even though he was officially head of state) but was also instructed to refer to him as "Your Highness" or "the Crown Prince."

The King and Crown Prince stood from their chairs, and Alex walked about halfway into the room.

"Your Highness," said Alex inclining his head, then turned to the son, "Crown Prince." He walked further into the room and up to the table.

The King's lip trembled, and his eyes welled with tears. He reached out a hand and touched Alex's cheek. "It's like seeing my dear uncle alive again. I see him in you as if I was staring directly into the eyes of the 'Lion of Sicily.'"

Alex was shocked at how small the king was, barely five feet tall. Alex understood why many jeeringly referred to him as the "dwarf king," or "Little Saber" though many Italian men weren't much taller.

The Crown Prince seemed almost a giant next to the King, standing about five-foot-eight.

The King's tears flowed freely, and he embraced Alex, who at just a shade under six-foot-two, had to bend down to not make the encounter so awkward. This hadn't been part of any etiquette instruction Iselin had given him.

"My father can get very emotional," said the Crown Prince, a smile upon his lips.

The King broke from Alex. "Forgive an old man his tears," he said. "The older I get, the more easily I seem to cry."

"I understand," Alex replied.

"I think you're even taller than your grandfather," said the King, "and to me he always seemed a giant among men. A gentle giant, but a giant nonetheless."

"Shall we sit?" asked the Crown Prince, motioning to the table.

The two of them looked at him and nodded.

After Alex sat, he felt his nervousness begin to ease.

"Would you like something to drink?" the King asked.

"No, I'm fine."

The King motioned for his guards to leave. "And please close the doors," he said.

The two guards nodded, left, and shut the door behind him.

"And now we may speak freely without uninvited guests listening in," said the King.

"That's a problem?" Alex asked.

"An occupational hazard, you might say," said the Crown Prince.

The King began. "I should perhaps apologize it took us so long to meet. I learned of you many months ago, asked Iselin about it, but he discounted the story. Then just a few days ago he brought it up again and said we should probably meet."

"Colonel Iselin usually seems to have his own agenda," Alex replied. "And he often doesn't share that agenda with me."

The King and his son shared a glance and smiled. "Yes, we have noticed that as well," said the King. "What is that American expression, 'he does not show all his cards?' Do you know he was on the official negotiating team, which they call the 'Italian Surrender' and we call the 'Changing of Sides,' and it was he alone who demanded I have no role in the government? He did not like it that I wanted Italy to be respected." The King motioned to his son. "Umberto was supposed to be 'Head of State' but they do not listen to him, either."

"They don't let me into those discussions," said Alex.

"Of course, they don't," said the King. "Because you would see the unfairness of it. The three of us are the ones without power. So let us be honest with each other."

"Certainly," said Alex.

"I believe your mother is Rosina, and your aunt is Jacquetta." The King seemed to be trying to remember something. "I recall your mother was the calm one, and your aunt, she was the more fiery of the two."

"You have that correct."

"I met them just once," the King continued. "Your father brought them to court, along with your grandmother. But every time we met afterward, he would speak of them. It's amazing how you remember somebody as a child, and then when they are older, they still have the same personality."

"Yes."

Alex felt his eyes wandering around the room, taking in the magnificent gold and blue ceiling, with intricate designs of crosses, eagles, and dragons.

"You are a bit overwhelmed by the room?" asked the King.

"A little," said Alex.

"Let me explain it for you," said the King. "You know this Palace was built by the Catholic Church, then taken over by the Italian government, or more particularly by my grandfather, your great grandfather, in 1870?"

"Yes."

"And this room," continued the King, "was designed by Pope Paul V in the early 1600s, who favored depictions of eagles and dragons, as well as angels. These are symbols of earthly and heavenly power. When our family took it over, we added the symbol of the cross and shield, the emblem of the House of Savoy, from which we descend. That is what you see on the ceiling."

The King motioned to another area of the room. "And on these walls are frescoes depicting seventeenth-century visits from our flock in the east and from the African continent." Alex looked closely and saw figures that were Slavic, Middle Eastern, and Black depicted. "To be Catholic means we are all children of Christ, regardless of how we may look."

The King pointed to the floor. "As the ceiling represents the heavens, the marble floor is the earth, and the geometric designs reflect many of the designs above our heads."

"Thy kingdom come, thy will be done, on earth as it is in heaven," Alex said, reciting the Lord's Prayer.

"Correct," the King replied. "We seek to have a harmony between what is asked from above, and that which we do here on Earth."

"But this palace no longer belongs to the Church," Alex observed. "It belongs to the state. To the royal family."

"We are still dedicated to doing God's will."

"Is it God's will to have such an extravagant building?" Alex asked.

"It was the Church who built it. When we took it over, it became the people's property."

The Crown Prince intervened. "I understand how this might look to an American."

Alex shifted in his seat, wanting to be diplomatic. "Yeah, we're not that comfortable with kings or opulent palaces."

The two of them laughed, then Crown Prince Umberto said, "Do not think of us that way. We are family. And I understand.

This palace is twenty times the size of your own White House. But you see, neither my father nor I built it. We're simply the stewards of it. This is tradition."

"I've seen enough of the country, the poverty. That's the tradition you embrace. It's why so many millions of Italians left for America. How is it being in charge of a country so many people want to leave?"

"And you think America is so much better?" Umberto challenged him. "With your history of slavery, your greedy capitalists, race riots, your murder of the Indians?"

"We fix our problems. Slavery? Yeah, we had it. And we fought a Civil War to get rid of it. Did you fight to get rid of Mussolini? No, you didn't. You even joined with Hitler. You even sent some of your Jews to his gas chambers." Alex knew he was escalating the situation, but couldn't help himself.

"It was not that simple," said the King.

"Yes, it was," Alex shot back. "My grandfather saw how easy it was. All you needed to do was confront Mussolini and his Brown Shirts when they marched on Rome in 1922. They would've run like cowards. Did you know Mussolini had my grandfather killed? I'm certain you must have suspected it at the time. And yet you shook hands with the man, invited him into the government. And a few years later, Hitler looked south and saw what Mussolini had done in Italy and figured he could do the same in Germany. Do you understand that will be your legacy? Every single death in this last war should be on your head."

"You did not know the carnage of the First World War," said the King in anger. "We had five million men in uniform. More than five hundred thousand men died. There was sorrow and suffering in every Italian village. You have no right to judge me."

"I can judge you all I want," Alex spat out with righteous anger. "I spent two years fighting in your goddamned country, lost friends, and for what? So people like you, in palaces twenty times bigger than the White House, can go on making bad decisions that other people pay for? I'm sick of all of you."

"You will not speak to my father that way," the Crown Prince said, rising from his chair, his hands clenched into fists.

Alex didn't even bother getting up from his chair. "You gonna take a swing at me, prince? I've got six inches and forty pounds on you, besides being probably thirty-five years younger than you."

"Enough!" shouted the King. "I will not have such unpleasantness in my family." He stood from his chair. "I had hoped this would be a pleasant reunion. Share love with the grandson of my beloved uncle. But it has all turned to disaster. Everything I try to do, disaster. I am sorry you feel that way, Alex. But I understand it. There is judgment upon me. I know it. But please, do not think so badly of me. I tried to do the best I could, given what I knew. May you never be in such a position where so much rests on your shoulders. I leave you now but know that I do it with love and affection for your family."

The King quickly strode out of the room on his little legs, the Crown Prince following him. "Papa! Papa! Wait!"

Alex was left alone in the Great Hall. "That went well," he said to the empty room.

* * *

AN EARLY MORNING pounding on Dianna's door woke the couple. "Alex, get the hell out here!" shouted Colonel Iselin.

Alex quickly threw on a pair of pants and went to the door. "What is it, sir?"

Iselin threw a newspaper at him. "Read about it yourself. The King has abdicated. Decided to resign last night. Right after you had that big fight with him." Iselin was quiet for a moment, gauging the young man's reaction as he looked at the headline. "Yeah, that's right. I heard about it. What were you thinking? Blaming him for Hitler?"

"It's true," said Alex.

"Just because something is goddamned true doesn't mean you ought to be saying it. Haven't you learned anything while being here? Do you know how much this complicates things?"

"I didn't expect him to abdicate."

"That's because you're one stupid son of a bitch."

Dianna had put on a nightgown and folded herself next to Alex so he knew she was on his side.

"I'm sorry, sir. Is there anything I can do?"

"He's already flown to exile in Egypt. There's no taking your crown back after you've abdicated. Shit, Falcone, we're thirty-two days away from a referendum and now this! The people remember the old king from before the fascists. There was genuine fondness for the old man. They look at the son and see a fascist stooge. Goddamned, I was so stupid to let you meet with him."

"What do you think will happen?"

"I don't know," said Iselin, shaking his head. "This is unprecedented. A royal abdication just before a referendum. We'll try to spin it as the King wanting to give the Italians a fresh start, promote Umberto as the savior of Italy, but I don't know if it's going to work. All the fascists, communists, monarchists, and democrats have been pretty quiet, but this might be a flashpoint."

"The flashpoint of what?" asked Dianna.

Iselin looked from one face to the other. "Civil war." Iselin pointed a finger at Alex. "And if that happens, it's on your head."

Chapter Eighteen

TO THE SURPRISE OF EVERYBODY, NEWLY crowned King Umberto II threw himself into campaigning with the energy that might be expected of an American politician.

In the industrial (and formerly fascist) north, Umberto worked hard to gather support, as most of them were ready to be done with the monarchy, especially because of their betrayal of Mussolini. Umberto campaigned on a platform of education for all Italians so they could take their place among the developed nations of the west. The King also vowed better civil rights protections for all groups, and an Italy at peace with the world. The north also had stronger socialist support, which Colonel Iselin believed was communist inspired.

In the rural (and formerly mafia) south where the Allied and Axis armies had wrought so much destruction, the crowds were more enthusiastic. Iselin and Alex were part of the King's traveling entourage, often meeting behind the scenes with local leaders and businesspeople to gauge political support. Most of the time the group traveled by train. On a long train ride from Bari, on Italy's southern Adriatic coast, a messenger came into Iselin and Alex's compartment, requesting Alex to join the King.

Alex looked to Iselin for a response.

Iselin shrugged. "I guess you can't screw it up worse than you already have. Just try to be nice. Remember, we're supposed to be diplomats here."

Alex followed the messenger to the King's private compartment. When Alex approached, he nodded to the two guards at the entry, who waved him past, entered, and saw the King was sitting quietly by the window, watching the Italian countryside go by.

"Your Highness," said Alex when he entered.

"Hello, Alex," the King replied, motioning to the seat across from him, "please sit."

Alex slowly eased himself into the seat, and the King resumed looking at the countryside for a moment. "It all looks so peaceful from here," began the King. "I sit here as the train goes through cities and towns, getting a look at people going through their daily lives, and think I know them. Sometimes, when I see some of them, a glimpse through a window of a family sitting down to dinner, two young lovers sharing a forbidden kiss, I wish I could simply stop the train, spend a few minutes with them, ask about their lives, tell them I care about their situation, and maybe, if asked, give some fatherly advice."

"But you can't," Alex replied. "Because if you decided you wanted to stop, it would take more than a mile, and all the time the brakes would be screaming, terrifying everybody who heard it."

The King nodded. "Exactly. And that would ruin the fact that all I wanted to do was share a quiet moment with one of my subjects. Do you understand this is one of the drawbacks of being a ruler? It's so rare that I can have genuine interactions with my people."

"Your Highness," said Alex. "I wanted to apologize for my behavior when we met last time. I should not have said those things to your father. It was unkind."

"But you were accurate and truthful in your words," said Umberto, looking directly at him.

"Yes," said Alex, "that's true—but still—"

The King smiled. "You see, we are having a genuine interaction."

"Hopefully more pleasant than the last time."

"Let me tell you what you missed about my father. He was a genuine man of his word, even when it did not make sense. He had made a deal with Mussolini, and that's the way he saw it. I tried to convince him we needed to switch sides and join the Americans. But in his mind that was a betrayal of his word. Do you understand that? How it is possible to be both terribly wrong and honorable at the same time?" the King asked.

"Yes, I do," said Alex.

"I know that Iselin blames you for my father's abdication, but he is just as responsible," said Umberto. "It was Iselin who decided my father would have no role in the councils of government after our switch in 1944, but simply be a figurehead. All his life my father was told he was smart and wise. Do you know what it does to a man like that when he is told he has no power? My father's abdication had as much to do with what Iselin did as what you told him that night.

"It is so strange," Umberto continued. "In the public's mind, I am a former fascist, and my father, well, he somehow floated above it." He shrugged. "My father thought the military would be good for me, get me away from court life. But when Mussolini took over, well, I was along for the ride, like I am on this train. Even though I was one of the first to make contact with the American side, even before the invasion of Sicily, the Americans do not trust me. Not really. They are keeping me on a short leash, although they say it is for my own protection."

"I'm sorry to hear that."

"Is it true that you rode from the mountains to Milan to put a bullet in Mussolini's dead body?"

"Two," said Alex.

The King laughed. "You are more Italian than American."

"You don't feel bad about your former leader?"

"He brought it upon himself," said Umberto. "From the start he was bad, but we did not see it. We saw only the problems of the day, not how Mussolini was deceiving us. Then, when Hitler came upon the scene, he thought he'd found his soulmate. There is a certain kind of Italian, the Caesar, who thinks if he can simply control all things, that there will be paradise, a new Roman Empire, instead of the Roman Republic. No, I don't feel bad about what happened to Mussolini. But I am upset that the communists executed him before he could be brought to justice, made to stand before his people and defend what he had done."

"You don't think that might have divided people even more?"

"Perhaps," said the King. "But I think it would have been better for the people. Let Mussolini be condemned, hear the list of his crimes, then hear him try to defend himself."

Alex nodded, and there was silence between the two men for a short while as the countryside flew by.

"The railroads were supposed to be the savior of Italy, did you know that?"

"No."

"It was a mistake. We should have invested in roads, like you or the Germans did. But it was thought the railroads would bring about managed growth. Instead, it was simply the rich who took control, just as they always do."

"Sometimes you just have to trust people," said Alex.

"I am an Italian, and I don't necessarily trust Italians. What about you? Do you trust all Americans? Even Iselin, who keeps you here in Italy, a year after the war ended, even though you long to be home?"

"He did get me out of a jail cell," Alex said in his commanding officer's defense.

"You were not a deserter. You went toward the battle. Not away from it. He liked you because you hated Mussolini so much you put two bullets in him, even though he was dead. He saw someone like himself, who could do the hard things that needed to be done. Trust me, Iselin could have set you free long ago. He rather likes you. Sees promise in you."

"Should I gather from this that you don't trust the Americans?"

The King gave a slight smile but did not answer. "Then to the east I have Stalin, stretching his tentacles into Italy. During the war

they were happy to call themselves communists in the fight against
Hitler. But with the Americans here they change their stripes, call
themselves socialists. Even swear on the Virgin Mary they have
never been communists. But the communists are atheists, so what
does it matter if they swear upon the mother of Christ?"

"You didn't answer me about the Americans."

The King was silent for a moment, and then said, "I understand
how Stalin will try to move against Italy. They want the hammer
and sickle flying over the Vatican. Our Lord Jesus broken and forgotten. The Americans, I'm not sure. One day they want to leave,
the next they want to be in control. Are they friends, enemies, or
something in between?"

"And what about me?" Alex asked. "Do you trust me?"

"I don't know you," said Umberto. "From what I saw of you with
my father, you are an honest person. You say what you think, but
there is more to a person than what they say in the heat of anger.
I would like to know who you are, because it seems you might be
just as much of a prisoner in this drama as I am. And we prisoners
should be honest with each other. We are also both descendants
of the House of Savoy, founded nearly a thousand years ago. This
tie is even stronger than blood because it means the people have
looked to us for centuries for guidance, as they would a shepherd.
So, tell me, Alex, who are you? Not the grandson of the 'Lion of
Sicily.' Not the soldier. But the person you were in America before
you became a soldier, before you became the young man who put
two bullets in Mussolini."

Alex was quiet for a moment. It was a challenging question.
After four years of war, who was he? Who was the person he'd
wanted to be? "I was getting ready to go to college. I was planning
to go to the University of San Francisco, a Jesuit school."

"Were you planning to be a professor? A man of letters?"

Alex shook his head. "I was planning to study business. From
the time I was fourteen I worked with my uncle, a builder. He
has one of the largest construction companies in San Francisco.

I started as a regular laborer, and then just before the war was promoted to supervise a crew. Happiest day of my life."

The King nodded. "A builder. We will have need of builders
in Italy."

"I want to get back to America," Alex said. "That's where my
life is."

"I understand you have an Italian girlfriend," said the King.
Alex laughed. "Yes."

"Women do not usually leave their family," he said. "It is the
men who leave, who establish themselves in a new place."

"Maybe."

"I'm going to win this referendum," the King declared, "and
I would like you to stay. You would have my favor, and that
would be a powerful thing. This is not a corrupt thing I suggest. You would have to prove yourself, but I have no doubt
you would. However, in return I expect you would be somebody
I could call upon for advice, somebody who would never lie
to me."

"I will always tell you the truth," said Alex.

"But I cannot tempt you to stay?"

"I'm not sure. Let me think about that."

"Would you have any objection to simply keeping me company
on this train ride? We will not talk of grand things, but the simple
things of life."

"I'd like that," said Alex.

* * *

A political campaign is like a traveling circus, a self-contained
bubble moving across the countryside. Then the whole world
enters and overwhelms your senses at the rallies. In total, even
with security, the group traveling with Umberto never num-
bered more than fifty people, and Alex was a trusted member of
the entourage.

Umberto had suggested Alex mingle in the crowd, before, during, and after the speech, then report back to the King what he'd heard. Alex agreed.

"I'm looking for you to get the mood of the crowd," the King had told him. "Are they excited, angry, indifferent? Just by being there you'll pick up things."

Alex did as asked, first walking through the crowd during a speech in Naples, then reporting back to the King. He was glad to be able to say the crowd was more enthusiastic than he'd seen in a lot of northern Italy, especially in the larger urban areas.

"The common people of the south appreciate the consistency a monarchy brings," said the King. "The progressive areas of the north, they are ready to abandon tradition, go off into dangerous territory. The communists hide among them, making them angry, causing trouble. It is a narrow path I walk; don't you think? I must want change, and yet I want things to remain stable."

"It sounds difficult," said Alex. "And there's little room for error."

"And yet this is the life God has given me," said the King. "We cannot see the road ahead, yet must keep our faith."

After Alex left the King's compartment, Iselin cornered him. "I hear you've become the King's little spy."

"I guess you could call it that," Alex replied with a laugh. "Pretty low-level stuff, though. Crowd reactions, stray comments, jokes, insults, that kind of thing."

"That's called 'intelligence-gathering,' Falcone. And you've been recruited."

"Do you want me to stop?"

Iselin was quiet for a moment before he spoke. "Probably best if you continue. Can't imagine you'll pick up anything interesting that's not already on our radar. Let me know if you do, though. And it's giving us influence with the King."

"Do we have a position on this referendum?" Alex asked. "Do we want a monarchy in Italy?"

Iselin shrugged. "That's a question for the Italians. Personally, I think it's better for the country if the monarchy stays. The Czar gets overthrown in Russia, and we get Lenin, then Stalin. The Kaiser is forced to abdicate in Germany after the Great War, and we get Hitler. I think that's why MacArthur decided to keep the Emperor in Japan. We'll probably avoid trouble down the road. We nuked them, but didn't overthrow their system. Besides, a monarchy seems to keep things pretty stable in England."

"Do you like Umberto?"

A crooked smile came to Iselin's lips. "Not a bad sort for a former fascist. I like what he says about education, but you know it's just talk. Past is prologue to the future. You'll understand that better when you're older."

"He seems sincere," said Alex.

"He probably is. Except he's gonna be the one sitting in a palace, not teaching the little boys and girls. Takes a lot to change the world, and there are a lot of powerful people who like it just the way it is."

"The world just goes around, huh?" Alex asked.

"As long as the world doesn't blow itself up, I've done my job," said Iselin. "Everything after that is just gravy."

* * *

A week before the election, the King was holding a rally in Taormina, Sicily, desperately trying to build up a large lead in Southern Italy to counter his expected loss in the north. By this time, Alex was familiar with the build-up to a speech, and it no longer filled him with anxious anticipation. The King sent for Alex, and he expected to receive the usual instructions before wading out into the crowd. But this time it was different.

"I'd like you to be on the balcony behind me," said the King.

"Why?" Alex asked.

"Indulge me."

"Yes, Your Highness."

The crowd at Taormina was large and early reports were that many from nearby villages were in attendance. The visit of the King of Italy to Sicily was a rare occurrence, and many did not want to miss it, not knowing if they would ever see it again. The speech was to be delivered from the balcony of the City Hall, and Alex jostled with local politicians and businessmen as they struggled to create a space for King Umberto.

Alex watched as the King made his way through the assembled local dignitaries in the large room just adjacent to the balcony. With each person, the King stopped, smiled at them, exchanged a few words, listened intently to their answers, then with a handshake or pat on the shoulder, moved on to the next in line. It was a powerful moment for Alex as he understood for the first time the deep connection that could exist between a leader and his people. The expressions on the faces of those with whom the King spoke were as if they were being recognized and seen for the first time in their lives. There was a gentleness and compassion in the eyes of the King, as if each person he met was a beloved child from whom he'd been long parted but was now joyously reunited.

As the King made his way onto the balcony, he caught Alex's eye and motioned Alex to stand behind him, slightly to his left. Alex nodded and took his position as the King stood in front of the microphone on the balcony, and the crowd cheered his appearance.

Umberto raised a hand in acknowledgment and the crowd cheered even louder. The King smiled in return, but with his hand motioned that they could stop their raucous enthusiasm.

"My dear Sicilian brothers and sisters, I am glad to be among you as your King," he began. From over the King's left shoulder, Alex had almost the same vantage point of the crowd as the King. "I hope you feel the same way about seeing me."

The crowd cheered loudly, and the King smiled, looking back at the relatively few people on the balcony with him, his eyes drifting from Alex to Colonel Iselin. "Sicily has long been a valued part of Italy. She was the first province acquired by the Roman Republic in 241 BC when our glorious armies defeated the barbarians of Carthage, forever obliterating their wicked empire of child sacrifice. The Sicilians and the Italians have traveled many roads together, from the glorious Giuseppe Garibaldi and his Expedition of a Thousand who sailed from Quarto in Italy in 1860 to liberate Sicily from the French, and indeed all Italy, from foreign influence, thus setting the stage for the Unification of Italy under my great grandfather Victor Emmanuel II and his brilliant foreign minister, Camillo Cavour. The Italian and Sicilian people were joined as one, and it was common during those days for our freedom fighters to paint *VERDI!* on the walls of buildings deep in the territory of our enemies, not for the great composer Giuseppe Verdi, but to proclaim *Victor Emmanuel, Rex de Italia!*

"We have also traveled sad roads together, as we lost the flower of a generation during World War I, and later fell under the evil sway of Mussolini and the fascists. I know many of you will blame my father for this result. But I also hope you will remember we turned away early from this barbarism. Our soldiers were brave, and they knew the Americans were not our enemy. How could we be against the Americans?" he asked, raising his hands. "After all, America is an Italian name, after the great mapmaker, Amerigo Vespucci!" The crowd laughed at the King's use of Italian bravado. "But even during the darkest of times, there have been Italian heroes, and nobody knows that better than the people of Taormina." The King glanced back at Alex. "The older people in this crowd may remember the beloved Duke du Taormina, Alessandro de Leone, the Lion of Sicily. He saw the threat posed by Mussolini and rose to fight it, to strangle that serpent in its crib. And he was on his way to Rome, to urge my father to fight against Mussolini, perhaps even to defy the King, when he was gunned down by assassins sent by Mussolini. We remember this great man and his memory, an incorruptible public servant."

The King bowed his head and made the sign of the cross, as did many in the crowd. Alex felt tears streaming down his face. "And in those moments, when we believe God has deserted us, we need to wait for an answer, to allow God's plan to be revealed to us. Many may not know this, but the first American soldier to venture into this town, the home of that great man, was his grandson, Alessandro de Leone Falcone, who was shot and nearly died as he came to liberate you from the Germans. By the grace of God, he survived, pursued vengeance against Mussolini where he gazed upon the dictator's dead body hung up in Milan, and then came to serve on the Allied Control Commission, where he has become my friend. I present to you, citizens of Taormina, the grandson of your beloved hero, Alex Falcone, a returned son of Italy, who joins us in our quest for a better life!" The King stood back and motioned for Alex to appear at the front of the balcony.

Alex's legs felt like jelly, and he struggled to walk the few feet to the front of the balcony. He waved to the crowd, who welcomed him with thunderous applause. He was self-conscious of the fact he was dressed in his military uniform, but it seemed to lend him a legitimacy among this crowd. The Italians might not trust each other, but they loved Americans. Alex looked back at the King, whispered "Thank you," and walked back to his place.

"Alex has returned to his mother country," the King continued, "and we hope he stays with us for many more years. But he is not so very different than many of us, who even though we live in Italy, have turned away from her. We believe things are too corrupt, they cannot change, and what has happened in centuries before is the future that awaits us. But I do not believe that. Perhaps my association with Alex has made me more of an American at heart, hopeful for tomorrow. I ask you to join with me in this peaceful fight for Italy's future. Yes, I am a King, but I do not come before you as somebody who has always done the right thing, at exactly the right time. Like you, I have regrets, as we say when we pray to our Lord, for those 'things I have done and those which I have failed to do.' But from the greatness of our past, from the mistakes from which we have learned, I am asking you all to return to your beloved Italy and let us fight for her together."

The King raised his hands to the crowd, as if a priest at mass, and they cheered him. He smiled and waved, then departed the balcony.

Colonel Iselin came up to Alex, who was pulling himself together. "You okay there, Falcone?"

"Yeah, I think so."

"Got to hand it to Umberto," said Iselin. "He's evolving into a helluva politician. He's got you sobbing like an old woman. I should've put you together with the old king a lot sooner."

* * *

THE REFERENDUM WAS held on June 2, 1946, and just shy of twenty-five million Italians voted. Alex sat with Colonel Iselin and Salvatore in the Commission offices, listening to the radio reporting the results.

"The monarchy looks to be doing well in the south, but not in the north," said Iselin after a raft of numbers was released.

"Doesn't make sense to me," said Alex. "The south was ravaged in the war, the north, not so much."

"The south is more conservative, poor," Iselin observed. "The north wants to be part of the new Europe, without kings and queens."

"But they loved Mussolini. Is it better if they toss out a king and get a dictator?"

"You haven't read your Roman history, Alex. Republics devolve into chaos, and that's when they start looking for the 'strong man' who will fix everything."

"This is true," said Salvatore with a shrug.

"Umberto seems like he'd be great as king," said Alex.

"You just fell for him because he said some nice things about your grandfather," Iselin teased.

"Maybe," Alex answered. "But I like the education effort and the anti-corruption campaign."

"Easiest thing for a politician to be for is education, and the easiest thing for him to oppose is corruption. Question is whether they mean it, and actually do something about it."

They continued listening to election coverage. Turnout was high, with close to ninety percent of the eligible voters casting a ballot. As the numbers continued to come in it seemed as if the south was in favor of the monarchy by about 64 percent, while the north was in favor of the republic by about 66 percent.

"It doesn't look good for Umberto," said Salvatore.

"I don't think we'll get a decision tonight," said Iselin around one in the morning. "But I think we can see how this is all going to turn out."

Over the next few days they kept monitoring the vote, often receiving visits from politicians and journalists, asking for a comment from the Americans, with Iselin giving his standard reply, "It's a question for the Italians."

On June 6, 1946, the election authorities proclaimed the monarchy had lost, although this was still subject to review by the country's highest court, the *Corte di Cassazione*.

Umberto immediately issued a statement, calling the move an "outrageous illegality" and "*a coup d'état*." Umberto was incensed by the exclusion of the Julian March and South Tyrol regions of the country from the vote (which he believed were strongly pro-monarchist) on account of the claim it was not certain whether those areas would remain part of Italy. There were also claims of voting irregularities, such as areas of the north where not a single vote was recorded for the monarchy.

The acting president, Alcide De Gasperi, then issued a counter-statement, which Alex read as an effort to begin to move the King off the stage: "We must strive to understand the tragedy of someone who, after inheriting a military defeat and a disastrous complicity with dictatorship, tried hard in recent months to work with patience and good will toward a better future. But this final act of the thousand-year-old House of Savoy must be seen as part of our national catastrophe; it is an expiation forced upon all of us, even those who have not shared directly in the guilt of the dynasty."

"Gasperi sure knows how to make a statement," said Iselin when he read it.

"Think he's a better choice than Sachretti?" Alex asked.

"He's Minister for Foreign Affairs," Iselin replied. "It's a good post for him. Older guy, stable, he goes down easy overseas. You'll be marrying into one of the great families of Italy. But also a little more low profile, and that's a good thing. You really don't want to be too visible in this life."

The situation deteriorated with the review by the *Corte di Cassazione*, which was supposed to report the final results on June 18 but declared a provisional victory for the Republic on June 10, before all the ballots had been reviewed.

Signor Sachretti came to visit with Iselin and Alex early on the morning of the eleventh to discuss the matter.

"This is very worrisome," said Sachretti. "People are whispering in Umberto's ear that he should proclaim himself King, move his court to Naples where support for him is very strong, and ask the army to protect him."

"Could he do that?" Alex asked.

"Umberto spent his life in the military," said Salvatore. "His support there is very strong. All it would take from him is a word. In weeks, Italy could be aflame, just as bad as during the war."

"What do you want me to do?" Iselin asked.

"I know you have friends around the King," said Sachretti. "Perhaps there could be other people whispering in his ear?"

"The Americans are officially neutral in this dispute," said Iselin. "And besides, how can we be certain that the King is wrong in his claims?"

"You think we Italians have 'rigged the referendum' as the King is claiming?"

"I've seen some irregularities," Iselin replied. "I'm not sure what to make of them."

"And your American elections?" Sachretti asked, "Are they always free of irregularities?"

Alex could sense the tension rising between Sachretti and Iselin and sought to intervene. "I should go," said Alex.

The three men looked at Alex.

"I'd go as 'family' since that's how he seems to think of me. Not in my military uniform. Just my casuals. I'm just going on my own."

"It could work," said Salvatore. "The King does seem to have respect for my young master."

"Yeah, I was his spy," he said with a shrug to Iselin.

"Well, the first time you talked to a King you got him to leave," Iselin replied. "Maybe it's worth a try."

* * *

Salvatore accompanied Alex later that night to the Quirinal Palace, figuring between the two of them they might be able to talk their way in.

Alex wasn't surprised to find that Salvatore knew exactly how to speak to the guards, who then summoned their superior, who then summoned his superior, until finally one of them said, "Let me see if the King will receive you."

After a wait of about fifteen minutes, he returned and said, "The King is in prayer at the Pauline Chapel, but has agreed to receive you."

Alex was led down the long hallways of the Palace to the Pauline Chapel. The guard opened the door to the chapel, lit by hundreds of flickering candles, and made his way toward the lone figure seated in prayer at the front pew. "Your Highness," said Alex as he entered the pew, nodding his head.

"We are in God's house," said Umberto. "He sees no distinction, just his beloved children. Will you pray with me?"

"Yes."

Alex kneeled and prayed in a way he hadn't since his friend Bill Squire had been killed on that night in Taormina.

"I have not prayed enough in my life," said the King after a few minutes, looking over at Alex.

"Me, either," Alex replied.

"I don't know why it's so easy to drift away from God," Umberto said in a soft voice. "As a Catholic, even as a king, one learns you must be submissive to our Lord. And even though we see His picture in so many places, we forget Him. We forget that He loved us, died for our sins, made a vow to never desert us. Perhaps we do not think we are cared for so deeply. Because if we did, we would need to act that same way to the world around us. Love imposes obligations on us to be good to each other."

"Maybe the idea of God is just too immense to wrap our minds around," said Alex.

"Maybe we just feel better thinking we're alone, because if there was something greater, how could it ever look upon us with kindness when we are so flawed?"

The King reached over and placed a hand on Alex's shoulder. "I am glad that you are with me at this moment. You and I, we are reflections of each other. Your grandfather was the first-born son of our great king, but mine was the legal heir. Many thought your grandfather should have taken the throne, but he would not even entertain any thought of it. He said that he was a servant of Italy and the House of Savoy, and nothing more. I have tried to do the same."

"And how will you do that?" Alex asked.

"I am trying to figure that out," said the King, easing himself back into the pew.

Alex did the same.

"Do you mind if I unburden myself to you?" Umberto asked.

"Not at all."

"You know the complaints I have made about the referendum?"

"Yes, I do," said Alex.

The King took a deep breath and exhaled. "There are other things I have been told, but I do not know if they are true, which is what every ruler comes to understand. You are told things by people you have trusted, but you do not know for certain if they are to be trusted. For what does it benefit a liar to be seen as a liar? The best liars are the ones who make you believe things, even when they do not turn out as predicted."

"I think I see what you're saying."

"You understand that your government, the military forces that still remain, in collaboration with my government, have suppressed the political activities of the communists?"

"I've heard that claim," Alex replied. "But Iselin has never talked to me about that."

"Of course he has not," said Umberto. "Because he knows you are young and do not see many things. The communists do not believe in democracy, but they are happy to pretend they do to get power that they will never relinquish. I do not think this is a bad thing we have done. But the communists have not been standing still. They have gone into other groups, using their same networks, agitating against the monarchy, because they believe it will cause more chaos, which would help their plans. I am told this has been done; there is wide agreement on this point when I am behind the scenes with our leaders, but they tell me the vote has been held and I have lost."

"And you believe Italy will fall into chaos if you leave?"

"The French Revolution ushered in an age of terror; thousands executed by the guillotine. The Russian Revolution gave rise to Lenin, then Stalin, a truly terrible regime that denies the existence of God and the human soul. When the Kaiser left in Germany, the Nazis came in. You rightly criticized my father for not standing up to fight Mussolini. And now it is my moment to make a decision. I see this as a fight against Stalin, who sits in Moscow gazing covetously at Rome. I would like to believe it is not so. My life would be so much easier. I would accept the loss and leave quietly. But I am terrified of what may come if I leave."

"What do you think the chaos will be like if you stay?" Alex asked.

"I cannot see that future, either," the King replied. "I am sure that when my father invited Mussolini to form his government, he never imagined how long *Il Duce* would remain in power. Can you tell me what happens in both scenarios with which I am confronted? The future in which I stay and the future in which I leave?"

"I can't."

"You are my honest friend, Alex," said the King. "How much I envy you. Not just your youth, but that you are truly free. I know for the moment you feel trapped by working for the Commission, but it is a temporary position. Your freedom awaits you, and yet no matter what I choose, I will always be a prisoner."

Alex stayed for another hour, and their conversation evolved to smaller things than the fate of nations. Curiously, for the better part of that time the King wanted to hear stories of Alex, of his growing up in San Francisco, the experience of being an American soldier in Italy, what he thought of his native people, and also those things that were simply unique to Alex.

When Alex finished with the King, he felt he should report what happened in the meeting to Colonel Iselin, even though it was late in the evening. Iselin opened the door and peeked out at Alex bleary-eyed.

"He hasn't made up his mind," Alex told Iselin. "But he seems to be leaning toward staying. He's worried about the mayhem Stalin might cause in Italy."

"He's right to worry," said Iselin, rubbing his eyes as he struggled with being awake. "Stalin's not following through on the promises he made in Eastern Europe. The Russian bear seems to like staying in Poland, Hungary, and the Baltics. Greece is going to be a problem as well. But the King needs to go. It's gonna be a black eye for the West if we hold an election and the King doesn't submit. Makes us look as bad as the communists. He might not leave us with any good choices."

"But is he right?" Alex asked. "Was the referendum rigged?"

Iselin was quiet for a moment, gave a small half-smile, and then said, "Thanks for the information, Alex. Now, have a good night."

With that, Iselin closed the door in Alex's face.

* * *

"IT'S NOT YOUR fault," said Dianna as she lay in bed next to Alex. He had had a fitful night of sleep and knew there was a dullness to him, even a numbness. He lay in bed and stared at the white ceiling.

"All I've done is cause problems," said Alex.

"The monarchy probably wouldn't have won anyway," said Dianna. "Victor was not more popular than Umberto. You didn't like the monarchy anyway, even though it could have been you on the throne," she teased.

"What if Umberto doesn't leave?" Alex asked. "Moves with the army down to Naples, proclaims himself King? What happens to Italy?"

Dianna cuddled up to him. "We are so unfamiliar to you, even though you think you know us. We Italians are used to chaos. We thrive on it. Now, let's get dressed and go to the café for breakfast."

Alex smiled at her. "If I don't feed you, I have to put up with angry Dianna?"

"Yes," she said, starting to chew on his arm. "It's been nearly twelve hours since I last ate, and you know how mean that can make me."

"I'll get dressed right now."

When they stepped outside Alex felt the low humidity of the morning, knowing it would get worse as the day progressed. Having been in the city for so long, he understood that during the

summer months the Romans were either up and about early in the
morning, or late at night, when the temperature became comfortable again.

They were approaching one of the large plazas when Alex first
heard the distant, angry voices of the mob chanting their slogans.
As they came to a large boulevard, they saw young men marching
in one direction, shouting about the King, fists raised into the air.
"It's the anti-monarchists," said Dianna, the group who wanted
Italy to be a Republic. Young men tended to make up the bulk
of those in favor of the Republic, and yet Alex couldn't help but
wonder how many of them were secretly communists.

Approaching the vanguard of young men from the opposite
direction was a group of protestors in favor of the monarchy, generally men and women in their thirties and above, workmen, who
carried their own banners and shouted their own slogans.

The vote in Rome had been roughly 54 percent to 46 percent in
favor of the monarchy, although the anti-monarchist forces were
much more vocal than the pro-monarchy side.

Alex and Dianna watched in horror as the vanguard of both
groups raced toward each other, throwing punches, using signs to
batter the other side, kicking, fighting, some retreating, others pur-
suing. Just a few feet away from them a middle-aged man punched
a youth of about twenty, sending him to the ground, after which
the older man started kicking him.

"You want to ruin this country!" Alex heard a large, barrel-
chested man shout at a thin, skinny youth in his grasp.

"The King should've been hung with Mussolini!" the young
man shouted back at him as they continued to grapple.

As the two men fought, bloodying each other as if locked in
mortal combat, Alex couldn't help but see the hatred in their eyes.
This fight wouldn't end until one or the other was dead.

Alex heard a police whistle, saw a group of *Carabinieri* quickly
approaching the scene, wading into the fighting, which seemed to
break up with each group retreating, including the two men he'd

been watching. The appearance of the police seemed to break the temporary madness as the two groups scattered. Within a few minutes the mob had dissipated, with the police helping some of the wounded. Alex saw that many hats and jackets had been ripped off in the heat of the conflict. In some places he even saw fresh blood on the pavement.

"This is going to get out of control," said Alex. "I should get to the Commission offices. Go ahead and get breakfast without me." He gave her a quick kiss on the cheek and walked briskly away from her.

"Be careful, Alex," Dianna said as he left.

He turned and gave her a half-hearted wave, thinking only of those two men who'd briefly been locked together in mutual hatred. How long before the entire country felt that way?

* * *

THE COMMISSION OFFICES were housed in what had once been a private home in Rome, the *Palazzo Marcello alle Colonne*, in a small salon where they had their offices dominated by a fresco of a map of the farthest reaches of the Roman Empire. Beside that was a scene of Roman soldiers at the gates of Rome defending against Hannibal and his horde, the barbarian general atop the last of his battle elephants. Busts of ancient Roman Senators stood along many of the walls. The red carpets and drapes gave a martial quality to the room.

"I just came from a street battle," said Alex to Iselin. "Monarchist and anti-monarchist forces."

"Yeah, it's escalating. Three people have supposedly died in clashes in the north. We're going to need to do something."

"Like what?" Alex asked.

"We have some people around the King," said Iselin. "Voices of moderation. Italian patriots. But there are others, people who've benefitted from the monarchy, who are encouraging him to fight because they'll lose their position and influence."

"And if that doesn't work?"

"All options need to be on the table," Iselin said in a slow, drawn-out voice.

"Like what?"

"You were in North Africa, right?"

"Yeah."

"Do you remember the 'Darlan' affair?"

"No."

"Francois Darlan was the admiral in charge of Vichy forces in North Africa. A real opportunist. Well, shortly after our forces landed in 1942, Darlan realized we'd quickly overwhelm the French soldiers, who weren't really interested in fighting us anyway. Before any real fighting, Darlan ordered his more than a hundred thousand soldiers to surrender to us and the British. Eisenhower appointed him High Commissioner of France in Africa. Basically, the same position he'd had under the puppet Vichy government. Didn't really go over that well in the Western press. After all, we'd promised to fight the Axis powers, and the first thing we did when we landed was make a deal with one of the leading fascists. It became a 'problem.' Two months after the deal, though, on Christmas Eve, Darlan was shot and killed. Problem solved."

"Did they ever catch the guy who did it?" Alex asked.

"Yeah," Iselin answered with a shrug. "Fernand Bonnier de la Chapelle, a twenty-year-old pro-Vichy guy, kind of crazy, who wanted to bring the monarchy back to France. They tried him, convicted him, and the next day they shot him."

"Chapelle didn't do it, did he?" Alex asked, suddenly aware of what Iselin had been hinting.

"No."

"Who did?"

"I did," said Iselin.

Alex felt his blood run cold. So much about Iselin now made sense to Alex.

"And I don't regret it even a little," Iselin added. "The alliance was starting to fracture with the Darlan appointment. Killing Darlan meant it stayed strong. Stalin knew we meant business, that we wouldn't hesitate to get rid of problems. You've been at war, Alex. You know the terrible choices you make all the time. If you have a chance to stop it, and don't, I don't know how you live with yourself. That's what's eventually got to old King Victor. Couldn't pull the trigger, even when the devil was standing right in front of him. I'm not going to get to the end of my life and regret what I should have done."

"We're not at that place yet," Alex protested.

"We're not far from it. What do you think is more important, Falcone, one man or a country in the flames of civil war?"

"Let me keep trying," said Alex. "He trusts me."

"Clock is ticking," replied Iselin.

* * *

ALEX WENT TO the Quirinal Palace several times over the next few days as the crisis continued, but the King did not grant multiple requests to see him. Several times the message came back with Umberto conveying his apologies that he was in important meetings, but reassuring Alex they would speak soon.

The crisis was twelve days old, and Alex was at Dianna's place when a knock at the door came around eleven-thirty at night. Alex threw on his pants and a shirt and opened the door. It was Dominic, one of the King's trusted servants.

"Umberto wants to see you. Get dressed."

Alex quickly complied and within a few minutes had kissed Dianna goodbye and was walking out the door. When they were away from the building, Dominic told Alex to stop.

"This is for you," said Dominic, reaching into his pocket and pulling out a small revolver.

"What's that for?" Alex asked.

"Iselin has given the word. The King is determined to stay. This cannot happen."

"I can convince him."

"And if you can't? Will you let your beloved Italy rip itself apart?"

Alex was quiet.

"More people have died in clashes in the north," said Dominic. "The number is now seven. Some say the civil war has already begun."

Alex closed his eyes and tried to picture the options. Italy in civil war, possibly igniting another European war, this time between the West and Stalin, who had far more troops than the Americans. Or the death of a single man.

"The location has been secured, as well as your escape plans," Dominic continued. "You will leave the country tonight. Iselin said it should be at least two bullets into the King, like you did with Mussolini."

"And somebody else will be blamed?" Alex asked, remembering Iselin's story about Admiral Darlan's assassination, and how Fernand Bonnier de la Chapelle had taken the fall.

"Yes," said Dominic. "In fact, he's already signed his confession."

"Where's the King?" Alex asked.

"He waits for you at the Pantheon," Dominic replied. "He wants to ask you to be his right-hand man in this fight. The two sides of the House of Savoy, united in the fight for Italy."

Alex took the gun and shoved it into his pocket. "Let's go."

* * *

ALEX SAT IN the backseat of the car as Dominic drove him to the Pantheon.

Maybe it was Alex's imagination, but the city, normally bustling with activity at this time of night, seemed deserted, as if people were cowering in their homes, not certain what the winds of fate would bring them.

There were several cars parked in front of the Pantheon, no doubt from the King's security detail. When they arrived, Dominic went to them, talked with the driver, and then Alex saw several of them leave.

"It's just our people now," said Dominic.

Alex nodded and exited the vehicle. As he walked up to the enormous ancient building, he remembered visiting it before with Dianna. She'd told him its history, the construction beginning in 27 BC, its cursed history, until finally more than a century later it was completed under the emperor Hadrian in 126 AD. In front of the building stood the Macuteo Obelisk, likely pillaged from Egypt during the reign of Caesar Augustus, after the defeat of the traitor Mark Anthony and his lover, the Egyptian Queen, Cleopatra. The twenty-foot-tall obelisk, erected during the reign of Ramses II at the temple of the sun god Ra in Heliopolis (modern day Cairo), was made of red granite and decorated with hieroglyphics, celebrating the relationship between the pharaohs of Egypt and the sun god. In Rome, the obelisk had adorned the Temple of Isis, then during the Christian era it had been lost, only being rediscovered near the Church of *Santa Maria sopra Minerva* in the fourteenth century and eventually being placed in front of the Pantheon by Pope Clement XI.

Alex remembered what Dianna had said to him as she explained its history. "Men always seek the favor of the gods, but do so little to earn it by their actions. The Egyptians, the Romans, even we do the same thing. Why should heaven ever answer us when we are always proving ourselves so unworthy?" Alex wondered if he would ever be able to explain to her what he was about to do, or whether she would forever turn away from him.

Alex entered the vestibule of the Pantheon, nodded at the guards who watched the single entry into the main structure and who nodded at him in turn as they opened the doors for him to enter.

As the twenty-five-foot-tall bronze doors closed behind him, Alex felt as if he had traveled back in time to the days of the Roman Empire.

The interior of the Pantheon was lit by candles. Porticoes that once held the statues of Roman gods now held those of Christian saints, testifying to man's eternal need to submit himself to a higher power. Alex stared up at the great dome, over a hundred and forty feet high, creating a vast interior space to mimic the dome of heaven. Even Michelangelo couldn't create a larger interior dome at the Vatican. The pagan world of the Romans may have vanished, but they had left their mark.

At the center of the dome was a large circular opening, which bathed the interior in moon and star light.

"The oculus," said Umberto, standing in the center of the vast space. "It represents the all-seeing eye of God. The Roman emperors always wanted to remind themselves that everything they did was being watched by the gods. Do you believe that, Alex? That everything we do is watched by God above?" Umberto began to walk toward Alex.

"I don't know," Alex replied as the King approached. "I've seen a lot of terrible things. Makes it difficult to believe in God."

"But if we have eternal souls," said the King, stopping just a few feet from Alex. "How can this world ever harm us? Does the mystery of that question not appeal to you even a little?"

"The world seems pretty awful to me at times," Alex answered. "Filled with useless pain and suffering."

The King smiled. "You think like a young man, so certain of the world. I am a King, and there are so many things of which I am uncertain, although everybody around me has such strong opinions about who I am, and what I should do."

"Are you going to fight?" Alex asked.

"Probably," said the King, with a shrug. "Come, I want to show you something," he continued, motioning Alex to a far wall of the Pantheon. As they drew closer, Alex saw a large metallic rectangle in the wall, with the words "Vittorio Emmanuele II, Rex de Italia—1820–1878."

"This is the tomb of our great grandfather," said the King, then pointed to a different section of the wall. "And over there is the tomb of my grandfather, your great uncle, Umberto II. You see, this is supposed to be the final resting place of the kings of Italy. But if I leave Italy, I will never rest in the Pantheon, nor will my father."

"Why?" Alex asked.

"Because the price of losing the referendum is to accept exile. I will never be allowed to return to Italy. I will die and be buried in a foreign land. And for what? Because I tried to do the best for my country? Even Mussolini and Hitler lie in their native soil."

The King turned away from Alex to look again at the tomb of their great-grandfather. "Will you help me fight this future, Alex? I would like you by my side in this struggle. Both sides of the House of Savoy in agreement, as my father and your grandfather should have been."

Alex fingered the pistol in his pocket, drew it out, and pointed it at the back of Umberto's head. "No, I can't."

Alex pictured the spot on the back of the King's head where the bullet would enter, then the area of his chest where the heart was located for the second shot.

He was a second away from pulling the trigger, a second away from ending a life and forever altering his own, when Umberto glanced back, saw the pistol in Alex's hand, gave a half smile, and said, "I knew they would send you."

Alex didn't know how to react, then realized what the expression on the King's face truly meant, "You want to die, don't you?"

The King turned to face him. "Perhaps I have simply chosen to meet my fate, calm and unafraid."

"No, that's not it," said Alex. "You think you want to fight, but even more than that you long for death, for it all to be over. A grand death in the Pantheon, home of the Caesars and the kings of Italy."

"And are you so different?" Umberto asked. "We are all creatures of light and darkness. You're excited at the thought of killing me, and yet at the same time, horrified by it. Am I right?"

"Yes," Alex replied. "I don't want to do this."

The King nodded. "But perhaps before you kill me, and we both enter a darkness from which neither of us will ever return, maybe we should talk honestly for a final time, under the eye of heaven, where no lies are permitted?"

"I said I'd always tell you the truth, so I guess the answer is yes."

The King gave a slight smile. "The Americans have penetrated my palace staff, and this assassination has been planned with their assistance?"

"Yes."

"You were recently brought into this plot and made to believe I will destroy Italy if I fight?"

Alex nodded, keeping the pistol trained on the King. "You will destroy Italy if you choose to fight. Stalin will take it as a pretext to cause more trouble. If you leave, we show that we respect democracy. That's not even counting the Italians who will die fighting each other."

The King didn't respond to this comment but continued to press his argument. "They have promised you safe passage back to America, and another will be blamed for your crime?"

"Yes."

The King laughed. "You know that isn't true. You'll be as dead as I am, probably within an hour of pulling the trigger."

Alex hadn't thought of that possibility. Had Iselin lied to him about Fernand Bonnier de la Chapelle and the Darlan assassination?

"If in bringing you here I am trying to bring about my own death, then you have also made the same choice."

"If that's true, what should we do then?" Alex asked.

"I have always valued your counsel," said the King. "You have no side in this issue, other than the well-being of Italy. I want you to answer my questions honestly."

"Okay."

"Was the vote on the referendum rigged?"

"Probably."

"Was it the Americans, or the communists?"

"I think it was likely both."

The King nodded. "That's what I think, as well."

"But I think you should leave, regardless." Alex lowered the pistol and put it back into his pocket.

"Why?"

"It seemed fair enough," said Alex. "That's all people will remember. There's widespread dissatisfaction with the monarchy. I know it seems like a loss, but it's a single battle, and in the end, I think Italy will be stronger."

"You think I should accept exile?"

"It's better than your own death, or the death of thousands of Italians who will die if you decide to fight. And the war won't likely be contained to Italy."

Umberto closed his eyes, took a few breaths, then said, "The House of Savoy united Italy, and as your King, I cannot divide it. I accept your verdict and will leave." He opened his eyes and looked at Alex. "How do you like it?"

"You will forever be the 'King of Italy' to me, Your Highness."

"Thank you, Alex. For your honesty. For everything."

"You made a different decision than your father. Both sides of the House of Savoy agree with this move."

Alex walked out of the Pantheon and into the vestibule, found Dominic waiting among the guards, and handed him back the pistol. "The King has decided to abdicate. He needs to be taken back to the palace to compose his farewell statement."

Dominic nodded, and to Alex's surprise, seemed to be visibly relieved.

Alex went back into the Pantheon, walked with Umberto back to his car, and rode with him to the Quirinal Palace for the final time.

* * *

COLONEL ISELIN AND Alex stood in the central quad of the Quirinal Palace on the early morning of June 14, 1946, to observe the departure of King Umberto II and his family, who would fly that morning to Portugal where he would become known as the Count of Sarre.

More than two hundred of the palace staff waited to say their goodbyes to their former ruler. Umberto and his family moved slowly through the line, saying a few words to each of the servants, many in tears, several falling to their knees and kissing his hand as if he was a religious leader. And as Alex reflected on it, Umberto had saved the soul of the nation by sacrificing all his future plans.

"Can't believe you pulled it off, Falcone," said Iselin. "A peaceful transition of power in a country that doesn't have much of a history of it."

"And if the King was dead this morning, where would I be?" Alex asked. "On a plane back home or in the grave, as well?"

Iselin just stared at Alex, his dark eyes boring into him, like those of a shark.

"And Chapelle, General Darlan's assassin," Alex continued. "You talked him into killing Darlan, didn't you? That's why you had him shot the next morning. Couldn't take the risk of him telling the real story."

Again, Iselin was silent.

"That's what I thought," said Alex.

"Listen, Alex, the fate of nations is more important than any one man," said Iselin. "You understand that, right?"

"I'm not sure I agree," Alex replied. "Maybe it's how we treat that single person that determines the fate of nations."

"If I was a general and sent you on what I thought was a suicide mission, and you accomplished the mission and made it back alive, nobody would be happier than me to see you pull it off. Or more impressed."

"Can't say that's much comfort, sir."

"You've got a real talent for this sort of work," said Iselin, look-ing away from Alex to the King who was saying his final good-byes. "Things are changing. The war shifts to the communists and Stalin now. They're going to want to cause a lot of chaos in Europe and around the world. Truman knows this. That's why in a few months he's going to announce a new permanent agency. Central Intelligence, they're thinking of calling it. You should join us."

"I'm done fighting," said Alex.

"Suit yourself," said Iselin. "Door's always open."

They watched the King and his family reach the end of the line of servants. "Be well, my beloved people!" said the King, before entering the car with his family, and the long procession of vehicles bearing all their possessions drove slowly away from the palace.

There would never again be a King of Italy.

Chapter Nineteen

VINCENZO STOOD ON THE SAN FRANCISCO dock waiting for Alex's return with the anticipation of a worried father, rather than an uncle. Rosina and Nick crowded on one side of him, with Jacquetta and their sixteen-year-old daughter, Angelina, on the other. Strangely, during the war, Vincenzo hadn't been concerned for Alex's safety, even when word arrived that he'd been wounded in Sicily. In Vincenzo's mind, Alex was on a quest to strike at Mussolini, and Vincenzo considered his nephew to be under some sort of divine protection.

But when Mussolini ended up dead without Alex's help, coupled with the defeat of the dictators in Europe, Vincenzo often found himself paralyzed with fear about what might happen to Alex. There were so many ways in which a young man might die. Being struck by a motor car. A stupid quarrel with another young man. Details had been murky about why Alex had been confined to jail as a deserter at the end of the war, as well as the work he'd been doing in Rome.

In the distance, the gray profile of the liberty ship, the *US Hawthorne*, appeared. As it steamed underneath the Golden Gate Bridge and sounded its horn, Vincenzo felt his gloom lift. Along the railings were hundreds of soldiers, and as the ship slowed near the dock, they could be seen waving to the assembled crowd on the shore.

"I think I see him," said Rosina, pointing to the soldiers near the center of the ship. "He's waving his hat!"

"That's him," said Nick. "I see him."

The rest of the group started shouting Alex's name and caught his attention. Alex gave them a salute and the group started laughing, tears cascading down Rosina and Jacquetta's faces.

The ship maneuvered, came close to the slip a little too fast, the engines engaged into reverse, and then with the slightest of bumps into the dock, the engines shut down. As the gangway swung into place soldiers began exiting the ship. Vincenzo could see Alex waiting in line and could see from a distance his transformation. Before he'd enlisted he'd been a sapling youth, but now, having survived the ravages of war, he was a strong, hardened man.

When it was Alex's time to stride down the gangway, he did so with the same assurance Vincenzo remembered in the Duke's pace, the very embodiment of a young lion, and it sent a chill through him. How could his beloved nephew, the family member he hoped would one day take over his company, be the spitting image of Vincenzo's darkest secret?

Alex reached the bottom of the gangway and stepped onto American soil. About two yards from the group, Alex dropped his duffel bag and, with a big smile, raised his arms.

His mother Rosina reached him first, touching his face, then throwing her arms around him and kissing his face. Alex's father Nick was squeezing his shoulder, tears streaming down his middle-aged face. Vincenzo and Jacquetta circled, looking for an opening. Rosina was talking excitedly about how she'd prayed every night and went to mass each morning to pray for his continued safety.

"I guess you missed me, then?" Alex asked.

"Yes!" she answered. "More than humanly possible."

Alex put his arms around his mother and lifted her off the ground. "Oh, it's so good to see my little mother again! I never realized you were so small and dainty!"

"Put me down!" Rosina said, and everybody laughed.

Nick had his arm draped around his son's shoulders. "Mama's got a great meal waiting for you at home, son."

Vincenzo swallowed, feeling the sadness of a memory flash-back. He'd wanted just such a homecoming as a young man. He'd taken the devil's road to make sure his father was back home with his family, and it had only led to the death of all the people he'd cared about.

Vincenzo felt a powerful hand on his shoulder and saw his nephew's concerned face. "Uncle Vince," said Alex. "Why so sad? Aren't you happy to see me?"

"Yes," he replied, then said in a stuttering voice, "y-you're just such a fine young man. You're a better person than I'll ever be."

"That's not true," Alex answered, a shadow seeming to darken his face. "I saw a lot of dark things over there. Things I couldn't put in my letters home. I don't know if it made me better, or worse."

* * *

AT HOME THAT night, the food and conversation were truly memo-rable, with Alex at center stage. Until he started talking, he wasn't aware of how much he'd kept inside. He spoke about basic training, the landing in North Africa, what it was like in the desert fighting Rommel's Afrika Korps, the landing in Sicily, the dash to Taormina, his walking into an ambush, then waking up at his grandfather's villa. He told them about his convalescence, getting back into the fight after the Allies landed in Italy, the march through Rome, and the stalling of the Allied march in the Apennine mountains of northern Italy. He talked about leaving his post, wanting to per-sonally go after Mussolini, but only arriving in Milan after the dic-tator had been shot and killed. And finally, he talked about how he'd been recruited into the Allied Control Commission.

But he was keenly aware of a few things he left out of his story. The immense guilt he felt over the death of his best friend, Bill Squire, the part Dianna played in his survival, what Salvatore had told him about the killers of his grandfather, pumping two bul-lets into a dead Mussolini, his suspicion that the Allied Control

Commission had probably rigged the referendum on the monarchy, or that he'd been recruited to assassinate the King and had come within a whisper of murdering the man. They wanted to hear stories of Alex the good and America the great, not the more complicated, murky version.

"What about that girl?" his father asked. "Dianna?"

"Decided to stay in Rome," said Alex. "Help her grandfather with the new government."

"I'm sorry to hear that," said Nick. "She sounded very special."

Alex looked at his father and felt a special connection. He saw his father as a man. A man who'd always been good to his mother, had always gone to work, paid the bills, and quietly did all those things his family had needed. He wasn't loud or flashy like his Uncle Dante or the builder of a business like his Uncle Vincenzo. But he was a solid man, a good man, and after all Alex had seen during the war and in Italian politics, he realized that his father was what all of them had claimed to be but rarely were: decent.

"Thanks, Dad," said Alex.

Later that night, his Uncle Vincenzo found him. "I imagine you're going to want to start college, soon," he said.

"Yeah."

"But there are still a few months before you can begin," offered Vincenzo. "I could use a good man to help with one of my crews that needs a foreman."

"I'd like that," Alex replied. He leaned a little closer to his uncle and spoke in a lower voice. "Working on the Control Commission, I got to spend some time with King Umberto. If he had remained in power, he wanted me to stay in Italy. Said he'd help me get set up, but I'd also be something of an informal advisor to him. I told him I wanted to get back to San Francisco and pick up where we'd left off. I said I was a builder, like my uncle. Not a politician."

"I'm glad to hear that," said Vincenzo. "Because I have some big plans and was hoping you would be a part of it."

"Give me a few days to sleep, then I'll be at the office bright and early," said Alex. "After all the work I did for the Commission, it'll feel good to get back to honest work."

* * *

"I'M SORRY YOU ended up in jail for going after Mussolini," said Vincenzo when they were at the construction office a few mornings later.

Alex had already shared with Vincenzo the story of his race from the mountains as the German forces were collapsing and the Italian partisans were rising to kick out the Nazi and fascist forces. "The anger of the people was astonishing," Alex recounted. "Brutal. Savage."

"That is what we are," Vincenzo replied.

"I guess," said Alex.

"You did put two bullets in him, didn't you? Even after he was dead?"

Alex nodded.

"That tells me who you are. And I am proud of you for it. You are a man who does the difficult things."

"There's stuff I haven't told you about the Commission," said Alex, seeming to struggle with his thoughts.

"What is it?"

"I'm not quite sure how to say it," Alex said, "They claimed they wanted free and fair elections, the Italians deciding for themselves. But there were a lot of irregularities. I'm not sure it would have been enough to change things, but I don't think it was clean."

"Yes, I remember reading the papers," said Vincenzo, "and the King did not want to leave."

"And he may have been right about his complaints. But I'm not sure fighting for his throne, refusing to accept the results, would have been a good idea. Because it's likely there would have been a great deal of violence, even civil war."

"The King made a wise decision in leaving," said Vincenzo.

"He didn't want to," Alex said. "He wanted to stay and fight. But my commanding officer said it was up to me to keep Italy from falling apart. And he put a gun in my hand and said I should kill the King."

"But the King is still alive."

"I was ready to do it," said Alex in a voice that seemed much older than his years. "I had the gun pointed at the back of his head and was planning the next shot to the chest when he turned around. I knew then I couldn't do it. It was an evil thing, an unspeakable act I was preparing to commit. Have you ever felt that way, knowing this moment is one that might forever alter your destiny, a sin for which there could never be forgiveness?"

There was a quiet pause between the two men.

"Yes," Vincenzo said finally.

"And what did you do?"

"I tried to stay alive," Vincenzo answered him, surprised at the firmness in his own voice. "I don't know what God wants. Sometimes He is cruel, and sometimes He provides such abundance. But you made the right choice in not killing the King. For the first thing that would have happened after is that your boss would have had you killed. They were making you a pawn in somebody else's game."

"Yeah, I realized that later," said Alex.

"All governments are corrupt," Vincenzo said. "They will always act in their own interest. Not for our benefit. But in dealings with your family, that is something you can trust."

Alex nodded. "I know."

"Good," said Vincenzo. "Now, let's prepare for today's negotiation."

* * *

ALEX STOOD IN front of Mr. Patrio's castle-like home in Pacific Heights with Vincenzo, who clutched a briefcase in one hand and his cane in the other. As a young boy, Alex thought the red-turreted building looked menacing, but in the morning light it reminded him of a fairy tale palace.

The small gate to the property was open, and they walked up the steps to the front door. Vincenzo knocked, and they heard movement in the house, but it was a good two minutes before they heard Mr. Patrio's shuffling feet in the hallway before the door opened.

Alex was surprised to see how Mr. Patrio had aged in the years he'd been away. Alex remembered the older man always having a ramrod straight posture, an iron handshake, and probing, intelligent eyes. Patrio was now stoop shouldered, much of his vitality gone, but his eyes still took in everything.

"You've come to discuss a deal?" said Patrio.

"Yes," Vincenzo answered. Alex couldn't help but notice how nervous his uncle appeared. Alex understood the troubled history between these two men, and even though his uncle had become wealthy, he knew his uncle felt inferior to the older man.

"I told you I wasn't interested," Patrio replied.

"And I asked for the courtesy of being allowed to present the deal to you. And you agreed."

Mr. Patrio shrugged and motioned for them to enter.

"Mr. Patrio," said Alex. "I'm not sure if you remember me. Alex Falcone. Nick and Rosina's son."

Mr. Patrio brightened. "Alex! I didn't recognize you. I am glad to see you are back from the war. Oh, this is a good day now, even though I know I will not take your uncle's deal."

"You should consider it," said Alex. "It's a good one."

"We'll see."

Mr. Patrio led them into his living room, which occupied one of the building's four turrets and looked out onto the Golden Gate Bridge and San Francisco Bay. Alex saw seagulls circling the fishing boats heading out for a day on the ocean, hoping old scraps from the previous day's catch would be thrown over for them. The surface of the bay was blue, but the morning breeze was starting to generate small whitecaps. Around the room were high-backed red couches and dark wood coffee tables. The three of them sat down, Mr. Patrio and Alex on the opposite ends of one couch, with Vincenzo sitting in a nearby chair.

"I know you're in financial trouble," Vincenzo began. "You've overextended yourself. You've given out loans to returning vets, and the slowdown in the economy after the war, as well as your various charitable endeavors, have all affected your cash flow. You're running through your reserves." He opened the briefcase and pulled out a sheet with numbers and passed it to Patrio. "My experts think you've got three months until foreclosures start."

Mr. Patrio looked over the numbers, and then flicked it back toward Vincenzo. "I have friends," said Patrio. "Who will help me get through this difficulty."

"I doubt it," said Vincenzo. "A lot of people are hurting. They'll just be interested in themselves. It's going to get ugly."

"And what do you propose?" Mr. Patrio asked.

Vincenzo reached into his briefcase and pulled out a small envelope. "A check for two million dollars. I get everything. Including your 'book of contacts' as well as your word that whenever I ask, you will call the individual I name and testify to my good character."

Mr. Patrio laughed. "Your good character?"

"Yes," said Vincenzo.

Mr. Patrio pointed at Alex. "I'd sell to him before I'd ever sell to you."

"It is a generous offer. It represents about half of my wealth. And do not underestimate the difficulties I will have in disentangling many of your 'charitable' obligations."

"You and I had a conversation a long time ago, which we never finished," said Mr. Patrio. "I was trying to explain to you that a man who becomes successful has a choice between becoming a shepherd, or a wolf. And you have always chosen the way of the wolf."

"I've chosen the way of the hardworking man," said Vincenzo, angrily.

"Truly? And is that what you did when you fired Pete Goodman, your best friend? When you took advantage of Louis Ricci, after he fell on hard times with the stock market crash? And there is a curious story from a few years back, of a stranger coming to see you, Lorenzo DeBruzzi, who ended up dead in a suspicious fire."

Vincenzo said nothing, but merely narrowed his eyes.

Patrio continued, "And when we first met, I told you of how I'd killed a few Comanche braves, nothing more than teenagers, really, when I was a young man on the Texas frontier. You said that you had killed also, back in Sicily, but you remained quiet. I remember these things. And now you ask for my business, that I have tended like my garden, for more than fifty years. But I do not know you, Vincenzo, any more than that first day we met."

"You killed my grandfather, didn't you?" said Alex suddenly. It all came to him in a rush. Salvatore's story of confronting the assassins in a *pensione* while both were on the run from the fascists. The silent one, the one who'd never shared his name, was Vincenzo. He'd leapt from the balcony, breaking his leg in the fall, and then rushed away into the darkness. Salvatore thought the last assassin must be dead, but Alex realized that wasn't true.

"Alex, how can you believe that?"

Alex shook his head. "It all makes sense. But why did you come here? Why did you marry my aunt? Is this some kind of sick joke?"

"You killed the Duke du Taormina?" Mr. Patrio asked. "The one who would've stopped Mussolini?"

Alex stood from the couch and began walking from the room. Vincenzo got to his feet and chased after him, not reaching him until they were outside on the street. "Alex! Alex! Listen to me."

Alex turned on him. "The truth. Only the truth. I've known you long enough to know when you're lying. You had DeBruzzi killed, didn't you? I remember that man and how you said he wouldn't bother us anymore. I didn't ask how you knew, but I should have."

Vincenzo let out a deep breath. "Yes, I killed DeBruzzi. Paulie and Tommy helped me."

"Why?"

"DeBruzzi threatened to reveal a secret that would destroy me."

"That you killed my grandfather?"

"Yes."

The street was quiet between the two of them. Finally, Alex asked, "Why?"

"I was recruited," said Vincenzo. "Just like you were with the King. Mussolini filled my head with promises of the good life that lay on the other side of that act. Your grandfather had made sure my father was sent to jail for a long time. My mother had to become a prostitute in the streets to feed me and my sister. Mussolini promised to have my father freed so we could be a family again, so that my mother would not have to work the streets and my sister would not have to start. You talked just this morning of understanding that moment when your whole future might be decided. That it was simply luck when you decided not to pull that trigger. If the King had paused for just one more moment, you might have shot him. Well, I didn't have such luck. I pulled that trigger."

"And Mussolini sent his thugs after you?"

"Not only me. He killed my whole family."

"Jesus Christ," said Alex.

"I was at war with your family back in Sicily," said Vincenzo. "But it has not been that way here. I fell in love with your aunt, before I knew she was the daughter of the man I killed. And when I found out who she was, there was another moment when I could have left her. But I could not. I was cursed. First to hate your family, then to love it. All the time knowing if my secret was revealed I would lose everything that was important to me."

"I can't keep this secret," said Alex. "My mom, my aunt, the Italian authorities, they all need to know."

"They can never know," Vincenzo said. "I'm begging you."

"You must tell them."

"I cannot," said Vincenzo.

Alex turned and started walking away from his uncle. "Wait!" Vincenzo yelled, but Alex continued his pace.

* * *

VINCENZO HEARD A streetcar, loaded with early morning commuters on their way to work, looked back, and realized the only path open to him. He had run from his fate for decades, but it had finally caught up with him and he must surrender to it. "Forgive me, Alex!" he cried as he stepped off the curb with the streetcar barreling down on him. He saw his nephew turn in his direction, the look on his face showing genuine horror, and then the streetcar crashed into Vincenzo and he was flying.

When Vincenzo awoke a few minutes later he could feel his body was broken and bleeding, and he could hear the siren of an ambulance. Alex was leaning over him. "Uncle Vince! Uncle Vince!"

"Alex," he croaked.

"The ambulance is on its way. Just hold on."

"There's no escaping this," said Vincenzo.

"Don't say that. You're gonna be okay."

Vincenzo struggled to speak. "Remember what I told you— when you left to fight. A man," Vincenzo took several quick, shallow breaths, "protects his family from the ugliness of the world." He paused again, determined to finish. "It would destroy Jacquetta and Angelina to know the truth about what I did. Protect them. Not me."

"I will," Alex promised.

"You are what I hoped to be," said Vincenzo.

Vincenzo felt his body shutting down, his consciousness leaving him, and in his last moments imagined he heard the voice of the Duke saying, "I will take you now to your family."

* * *

THE FUNERAL FOR Vincenzo Nicosia was a small one, attended by family, some of his workers, and Mr. Patrio. In the days between Vincenzo's death and the funeral, Alex had talked with Mr. Patrio about what his uncle had said on the street. They agreed to keep the information between themselves.

Jacquetta wore black for six months after the funeral, but unlike Dante's death, this time she seemed more resilient. Perhaps it was having a teenage daughter that kept her occupied or taking over the running of the construction company while Alex helped as much as he could with his college course load, but life seemed to move eventually back into a more regular rhythm.

In October of that year, Alex negotiated a loan package to assist Mr. Patrio's business with their financial difficulties. At the time, Patrio expressed the hope Alex would eventually buy him out.

During Christmas break, Alex was working at the office in the late afternoon when he heard the front door open. "Hello?" he called out.

Dianna appeared at the door to his office. "I realized I'm not done with you," she said.

"What are you doing here?" he asked. "You said your life was rebuilding the new Italy, with your grandfather."

"My grandfather kicked me out of the country," she said. "He said a young woman shouldn't be taking care of an old man. Said I needed to live my own life."

He got out of his chair and went to her. "You came for me?"

"Well, you do owe me a life," she said with a shrug, "since I saved yours in Taormina."

"Is that right?" he asked, taking her into his arms.

"And you did offer for me to be the Queen of San Francisco," said Dianna. "After much consideration, I've decided to accept."

"Yes, Your Majesty," he said, and kissed her. "And I'll spend my life as your dedicated servant."

* * *

ALEX AND DIANNA were married in early 1947.

By the time Alex graduated college, Patrio had sold his company to Alex and he began his working life as the owner of the largest construction company in San Francisco, with everybody in the family taking part.

Alex and Dianna had six children, and as the business grew, Alex started taking an interest in politics. He ran for and was elected to a seat on the Board of Supervisors, a position he would hold for forty-five years. Many times he was urged to run for mayor, senator, even governor, but he always turned down such appeals. "I prefer to be a simple public servant," he said to any who questioned his decision.

But behind the scenes he amassed enormous influence, based upon the simple fact he was available to any politician who sought his counsel and usually gave excellent advice. In addition, Alex gave generously to local charitable organizations, usually anonymously. Privately he was proud of the fact that during his honorable career, his advice had been sought from seven mayors of San Francisco, five United States senators, and two presidents.

Alex also remained close to the former King Umberto and even visited several times with the former monarch in Portugal, accompanied by his family when they traveled to Europe. When King Umberto died on March 18, 1983, Alex traveled to the funeral at Hautecombe Abbey in Savoie, France, the ancestral home of the House of Savoy, where he served as one of the pallbearers. Despite appeals throughout the years, the Italian government did not want the former King to return to Italy, even in death.

Dianna died of cancer in 2013, at the age of ninety, holding Alex's hand. Her last words to him were, "I'm not done with you, yet."

"I'm not done with you, either," he had told her.

Remarkably, Alex remained in excellent health into his nineties, no doubt the result of having lived a good life, always trying to walk several miles a day, eat well, exercise, and be engaged in a wide variety of civic activities.

His family thought he was crazy when, at the age of ninety-five, he traveled back to Italy for the ceremony that returned the bones of King Victor Emmanuel III from his burial site in Egypt, as well as those of his wife, Queen Elena, and buried them in the Sanctuary of Vicoforte, near the Piedmont town of Cueno, in northern Italy. Of course, the grandchildren of the former king were arguing his body deserved to lie in the Pantheon. But their appeal fell on deaf ears. During the service for the former king in December 2017, Alex remembered thinking, *I'm sorry I was so unkind to you. I was young and self-righteous. Please forgive me. I know you did your best.*

Alex believed in a life filled with work, service, family, and laughter. At his one hundredth birthday party in 2023, he was happy that most of the world had returned to normal, and was pleased to welcome his six children, twenty-seven grandchildren, and thirteen great-grandchildren. They all had their own lives but were often in touch with him. Most were living fulfilled lives, while a few were troubled, as in any family, and for those members of the family he was usually in daily contact. Alex had arranged his life so he always had something to look forward to during the day.

And on the long walks he takes every day, he usually finds time to walk up the hill to Saint Ignatius Church on the grounds of the University of San Francisco, where he went to college. He enters the church, pauses to dip his hand into the holy water, makes the sign of the cross, sits in a pew, and says a prayer for the soul of Vincenzo Nicosia and all the other troubled souls of this world.

Acknowledgments

I'D FIRST LIKE to thank my wonderful partner in life, Linda, and our two children, Jacqueline and Ben, for their constant love and support. I'd also like to thank my Italian mother, Josephine, and my father, Jack, for their example of compassion and concern for the world. I have the best brother in the world, Jay, and am appreciative of his wife, Andrea, and their three kids, Anna, John, and Laura. I am hopeful that my crazy extended Italian family will love reading this book as much as I loved writing it.

The genesis of this book came from family stories that we were somehow related to the original King of Italy, Victor Emmanuel II. After much research, though, I have reluctantly concluded this is probably not true. However, since I am half-Italian, we never let the truth get in the way of a good story. In my defense, though, the broad outlines I have presented in this novel are in accord with the facts of Italian history.

When Mussolini took over in 1922, there were factions of the government which wanted to confront him. European history would likely have been very different if there had been an actual "Lion of Sicily." There was a direct line from Mussolini in Italy to Hitler in Germany, a point which I feel too few historians acknowledge. Similarly, after World War II there was a referendum on the Italian monarchy, the United States was deeply involved, and King Umberto II lost in a narrow, disputed election. He did not initially accept the results, civil war loomed, but for some reason he finally decided to concede and enter exile from his beloved country. I want to be on record as stating I believe it is a historical injustice that the last two kings of Italy, King Victor Emmanuel III and King Umberto II, have been denied the traditional resting place of Italian kings in the Pantheon, under the eye of heaven, where the climax of this novel takes place.

I've been fortunate to have some of the greatest teachers in the world, Paul Rago, Elizabeth White, Ed Balsdon, Brother Richard Orona, Clinton Bond, Robert Haas, Carol Lashoff, David Alvarez, Giancarlo Trevisan, Bernie Segal, James Frey, Donna Levin, and James Dalessandro.

Thanks to the fantastic friends of my life, John Wible, John Henry, Pete Klenow, Chris Sweeney, Suzanne Golibart, Gina Cioffi Loud, Eric Holm, Susanne Brown, Rick Friedling, Max Swafford, Sherilyn Todd, Rick and Robin Kreutzer, Christie and Joaquim Perreira, and Tricia Mangiapane.

Lastly, I'd like to thank my agent, Johanna Maaghul and her husband, Richard, and at Skyhorse the fabulous Caroline Russomanno and Hector Carosso, and for the faith shown in me over the years by publisher Tony Lyons.